Daisy's Decision

Dixon Brothers book 4

By

HALLEE BRIDGEMAN

Daisy's Decision: Dixon Brothers Series Book 4, by Hallee Bridgeman, Copyright © 2021. All rights reserved. No part of this publication may be reproduced or transmitted in any form or by any means—electronic, mechanical, photocopying, or recording—without express written permission by the author and publisher. The only exception is brief quotations in printed or broadcasted articles and reviews.

Names, characters, places, and incidents are either the product of the author's imagination or intended to be used fictitiously. Any resemblance to actual events, organizations, places, or persons living or dead is purely coincidental and beyond the intention of either the author or the publisher. The characters are products of the authors' imaginations and are used fictitiously.

PUBLISHED BY: Olivia Kimbrell Press™*, P.O. Box 470, Fort Knox, KY 40121-0470. The Olivia Kimbrell Press™ colophon and open book logo are trademarks of Olivia Kimbrell Press™.

*Olivia Kimbrell Press™ is a publisher offering true to life, meaningful fiction from a Christian worldview intended to uplift the heart and engage the mind.

Some scripture quotations courtesy of the King James Version of the Holy Bible.

Some scripture quotations courtesy of the New King James Version of the Holy Bible, Copyright © 1979, 1980, 1982 by Thomas-Nelson, Inc. Used by permission. All rights reserved.

Original Cover Art by Amanda Gail Smith (amandagailstudio.com).

Library Cataloging Data

Names: Bridgeman, Hallee (Bridgeman Hallee) 1972-

Title: Alexandra's Appeal; The Dixon Brothers Series book 3 / Hallee Bridgeman

418 p. 5 in. × 8 in. (12.70 cm × 20.32 cm)

Description: Olivia Kimbrell Press™ digital eBook edition | Olivia Kimbrell Press™ Trade paperback edition | Kentucky: Olivia Kimbrell Press™, 2020.

Summary: Daisy has had a crush on Ken since high school, so going out on just one date with him can't possibly hurt, can it? Even if the man she planned to spend the rest of her life with just been painfully dumped her, and whose unborn baby she carries? Just one little date?

Identifiers: Library of Congress Control Number: 2020952841 | ISBN-13: 978-1-68190-182-4 (ebk.) | 978-1-68190-183-1 (POD) | 978-1-68190-184-8 (trade) | 978-1-68190-185-5 (hardcover)

1. clean romance love story 2. women's inspirational 3. pregnancy 4. messianic Christianity 5. emotional abuse 6. forgiveness redemption 7. secrets and lies

Daisy's Decision

Dixon Brothers book 4

By

HALLEE BRIDGEMAN

Published by

Fort Knox, Kentucky

Table of Contents

Daisy's Decision	I
Copyright Notice	II
Table of Contents	IV
Chapter 1	1
Chapter 2	17
Chapter 3	35
Chapter 4	49
Chapter 5	63
Chapter 6	83
Chapter 7	97
Chapter 8	107
Chapter 9	123
Chapter 10	137
Chapter 11	159
Chapter 12	171
Chapter 13	185
Chapter 14	195
Chapter 15	209

Chapter 16	223
Chapter 17	235
Chapter 18	243
Chapter 19	261
Chapter 20	279
Chapter 21	289
Chapter 22	303
Chapter 23	317
Chapter 24	327
Chapter 25	343
Chapter 26	353
Chapter 27	367
Chapter 28	377
Acknowledgments	387
Excerpt: A Change Of A Dress	389
Reader's Guide	395
Discussion Questions	395
Recipe Menu	399
More Great Books	405
The Dixon Brothers Series	407
About The Author	409
Find Hallee Online	411
Hallee's Happenings	412

Chapter 1

Rare moments in life, we stand at the very top of the mountain. Looking all around in every direction from that lofty height, glorious beauty fills our eyes. The clouds look like a white ocean at our feet. Our hearts race. A light-headed feeling overtakes our senses from the thin air, the chill, the silence. We barely notice our shadows as pure golden sunlight, unfiltered by the clouds below, bathes our bodies like a halo. Even so, our skin turns to gooseflesh. Though exceptionally uncommon, these mountaintop moments do happen and—if we allow them to—overshadow the bulk of the time we exist down in the terrestrial valleys.

Sleeping, waking, showering, sipping our morning cup, eating, taking in the news, cleaning up after ourselves, commuting, working, pondering, planning, teaching, learning; these make up just a few items in the long list of daily mundane tasks we perform while living down on the surface of planet earth. Then, suddenly—and very rarely—utter astonishment coupled with the tiniest sliver of anxious exhilaration completely overtakes us when life suddenly flings us out of our prosaic workaday experience, hurtling us all the way to the mountain's peak in a single rush. Our middles become a flock of butterflies, and our knees turn to water. We barely notice even the most important everyday item from the low valley below as the astounding beauty of that moment cuts to the front of the line of our priorities. Life transports us to the mountaintop in that single heartbeat when we first lay eyes on that one person, that one who God has made especially for us.

For Daisy Ruiz, she first found herself on the mountaintop at the tender age of twelve.

Kenneth Dixon—who went by Ken and never Kenny—and his two brothers joined their youth group. She learned Ken's name just as soon as possible and later learned that his brothers went by Jon and Brad. So-called identical triplets, she had to admit she often had trouble telling Brad from Jon or Jon from Brad. However, she never once had any problem identifying Ken.

Something about the way Ken moved, or how he sounded when he spoke or laughed, or the way he smelled always differentiated Ken from his look-alike brothers. Even at fifteen, his arms and chest rippled with muscles beneath his preferred polo style shirts. As far as identical, at least in Daisy's opinion, Ken looked much more handsome than either of his ordinary-looking brothers.

Her father led the youth group and hosted the high school class each week on Wednesday nights in their home. By the second week, Daisy had enveloped the inside cover of her science notebook with variations of "Daisy Dixon," and she very, very much wanted to feel those muscular arms embracing her while those incredible eyes stared deeply into hers.

The problem, as Daisy saw it, was that Ken Dixon barely noticed her. He was so much older at fifteen, a Sophomore in High School already, and surely just viewed her as a little girl in middle school.

He acted like a perfect gentleman with her parents and mostly stayed quiet in the group. Fairness forced her to admit that Ken handed out this trademark introspective silence pretty equally. He didn't really reserve his reticence for her exclusively. Occasionally, he did have an interesting way of filling in the silences with a baritone word here or there whenever one or the other of his brother's paused while speaking. His brothers would do the same to him, so Daisy rightly assumed this syncopated synchronized speech pattern had something to do with them being triplets.

That first summer, the brothers went on a mission trip to Egypt and spent five whole weeks building a school. Daisy took that time to study. She read a lot and watched a lot of videos trying to get some ideas about how to get Ken to notice her. Brad or Jon—she was never exactly sure which—often included her in their discussions. As a rule, unless she spoke to him first, Ken never even spoke to her after she greeted the brothers at the door. In seven months, Ken never once initiated a conversation with her.

Knowing Ken would return to Bible Study in her home just before school started, Daisy began to pray. She prayed that God would give her some inspiration, like He had Ruth. If not, Daisy prayed that God would at least ease the ache she felt in her heart every single time Ken failed to notice her new hairstyle, or her new dress, or her attempts at makeup.

School kicked off, and Daisy consulted with friends, never naming her crush, always trying to understand exactly how they got boys to notice them. Her mother caught her looking mopey and angsty, and Daisy nearly confessed the name of her heart's desire, but she feared that her parents would keep them apart, so she kept it secret. However, she interrogated her mother about how she knew her father was "the one," how she got him to notice her, and a thousand other questions.

At Christmas that year, though she nearly chickened out a hundred times, Daisy handed Ken a simple Christmas card right after the Cantata at their church. He stared at the card, puzzled, then said, "Oh. Thanks. You guys got the card Mom and Dad sent, right?"

"Yes. Yes, we did." Daisy felt her smile falter just a little bit. His gray eyes had trapped hers, somehow, and she wanted to touch him, hold his hand, something. He just stood there looking down into her eyes, and she took a breath and bravely carried on. "I actually got this card for you. It's from me." After what she instinctively knew was a slightly too long pause, she concluded, "Ken."

Oh, my, how she liked saying his name while he looked into her eyes. She longed for him to say her name, to hear it pronounced with that slight Atlanta southern drawl in that very baritone voice of his.

"Oh." His eyes left hers to look down at the sealed envelope, and suddenly she could breathe again. "Okay, well, Merry Christmas. See you guys after the New Year."

The brothers went on a two-month-long mission trip that summer, once more, leaving Daisy alone with her thoughts and hopes and dreams for the future. By the end of the summer, Daisy had convinced herself that the feelings she had for Ken Dixon amounted to little more than a young girl's crush. Just puppy love.

She convinced herself with the unshakable certainty of every fourteen-year-old girl who has ever lived that the next time she laid eyes on Ken Dixon, her heart rate would stay steady, she would not feel dizzy, she would not feel tongue-tied, and she would have the ability to look away from him at will. He refused to even notice her? She wouldn't even notice him. Ken Dixon was simply not worth her attention.

The first youth group meeting after the Dixon brothers returned from their mission trip, it just so happened that her mother was out of town looking in on a sick cousin. Daisy made sure she had things to do in the kitchen. That way, she didn't even answer the door when they arrived. Her father happily greeted and seated all of their guests. The group had grown and split a time or two to keep the size manageable.

Just before youth group service began, Daisy carried in the last tray of snacks. She nearly dropped it when she saw Ken purposefully walking toward her with an elaborately wrapped gift in his hands.

He had grown at least another few inches. His skin looked evenly tan, making his teeth look whiter and his stubble look darker. She could swear he had more muscles on his shoulders, arms, and chest.

Daisy set the tray down, her heart beating against her ribs like a machine gun as Ken stepped closer. He stood right there in front of her on the mountaintop for a breath or two, smiling, looking her dead in the eye. She wanted that moment to last forever—just the two of them above the clouds with a beam of sunlight spotlighting them and them alone.

"Hey," he greeted.

Her mouth went dry. She swallowed, hoping her voice sounded feminine and mature, not childish and tomboyish. Daisy no longer wore braces, and her teeth looked straight and white now. She remembered to smile before she spoke. "Ola, Ken."

"So, the people in Honduras, they make these really incredible baskets. They make them out of all kinds of things like wicker, palm—heck—even pine needles. Anyway, they are really beautiful. I've never seen anything like them. So, anyway, here." He handed her the elaborately wrapped box with the perfect bow on top.

Daisy's mind, body, and soul froze as she accepted the gift. She dared not hope. She dared not speak. She just spun on the mountaintop like Julie Andrews spinning her way across the Alps, and her mind swayed to glorious music as her skin felt hot and chilled all at once.

"Can you get that to your mom when she gets back?" Ken explained.

Daisy tried her best not to let Ken see her heart explode. He might not have seen it, but she could not understand how he didn't hear the thunderclap sound it made. "Sure." She nodded, exercising incredible poise so as not to make her smile look somewhat creepy. "I'm sure she'll love it, Ken."

Her Freshman year, she finally attended the same school as the Dixon brothers. Ken and his brothers were the most popular seniors at their High School. At seventeen, the triplets had academically surpassed most of their peers and focused a lot of their attention on college-level classes like engineering and CAD. Ken stayed near the top of the honor roll and didn't date very much.

The first time she passed him in the hall, he didn't notice her at all. A few days later, she waved and said, "Hi, Ken."

He turned his gaze toward her, somewhat startled, then knitted his brows as if trying to place her. When recognition dawned, it looked almost comical. "Daisy. Hey. I heard you were coming here this year. Cool."

He nodded, then continued heading to his next class as if the exchange never happened. The next seven times she passed him the hall in the weeks that followed, he didn't seem to notice her.

The fiesta de quince años, also known as a

Quinceañera, is a celebration of a girl's fifteenth birthday in many traditional Hispanic homes. While Daisy's parents didn't consider themselves very traditional in most regards, they wanted her fifteenth birthday party to be very special and chose to honor this tradition.

Hoping Ken would come as well as the rest of the young people in her parent's youth group, Daisy wanted a dress that would devastate even the most oblivious man. Perhaps something low-cut and with sequins, or a gown that dipped in the back. Daisy's mother wanted her garb to look more like an opaque ballerina tutu made of pink cotton candy and hoops.

They compromised with the dress being far more modest than what Daisy had in mind but far less fluffy and childish than what her mother had in mind. Daisy spent the better part of the weeks ahead preparing for her entrance, her segue, and her dances. She practiced walking up and down the stairs in high heels while neither touching the handrail nor looking down at her feet. She walked through rooms with a dictionary balanced atop her crown and spun and spun and spun through the den until her father told her to stop.

Mr. and Mrs. Dixon graciously offered their home for the party. They lived in a 20,000 square foot castle with grounds to match. Mrs. Dixon had told her mom that every fifteen-year-old-girl needed to feel like a princess on her birthday.

Daisy thought that Ken would surely notice her then, in his home, dancing across his floor, looking more elegant and beautiful and grown up than she had ever looked before.

The day arrived. Her parents greeted everyone. Her friends chattered about the castle and their envy over her party. A table draped with linen overflowed with gifts. Her grandparents arrived looking joyful and pleased that this tradition had carried on to her generation. Her father removed the low heels from her feet and replaced them with perfect high heels.

The day could have only been more perfect if her parents had not decided to limit the guests outside of family to young men and women age fifteen and under. Granted, she knew every person in attendance from either school or their church, but the Dixon brothers, and one Dixon brother in particular, would never see her in the flesh on this day. However, Mr. and Mrs. Dixon left an amazing gift before taking the triplets out of the home for the evening.

Her grandfather stole a private moment that afternoon. "My beautiful granddaughter looks far too sad for the occasion. Why are you sad, Cariño?"

Daisy considered an excuse but settled on the truth. Grown women told the truth. "A boy, Papa."

This answer clearly surprised her grandfather. "A boy? Well, boys always disappoint. Bide your time and wait for a *man*. Eh? Is this boy here? I can talk to him about making you sad, you know."

She grinned. "He's not here. That's why I'm sad."

Understanding bloomed. "Ah. I see." He smiled. "You know something, Cariño? I have not danced with you. And tonight, you look exactly as beautiful as your grandmother did the very first time I ever saw her.

That deserves a dance."

They took to the dance floor, and Daisy relished in the smell of her grandfather who always smelled faintly of wool and caramels—and fine cigars he shouldn't smoke but always managed to sneak. At some point in the dance, he spoke to her very quietly. "I trust your judgment, Daisy. You are very wise for your years. I think you are especially wise in matters of the heart. But if I could offer you some advice, I would say this. I think this boy who isn't here? I think he wouldn't want you to be sad on this day on his account. What do you think?"

Daisy thought about it as her grandfather smiled and led her across the dance floor. "What I think is that he doesn't really think about me at all."

After a few seconds, her grandfather said, "Well, everyone here thinks about you and loves you. And I tell you something else. If God has made this boy especially for you and made you especially for him, he doesn't stand a chance. One day, God willing, this boy will think of little else besides you. But it will be in God's good time. Now you just wait and see."

The Dixon brothers turned eighteen and made a big deal about registering for the draft. Christmas came and went, then New Year's, and before anyone could sufficiently brace themselves, Saint Valentine's Day arrived. The National Honor Society began publishing student rankings, and everyone felt confident Leah Wing would take the Valedictorian spot for the graduating class.

In a Georgia high school, the only thing that moves

faster than the track team is the gossip. In no time at all, Daisy heard the news. Naturally, Ken Dixon asked Leah Wing if she would like to go to Prom with him and, just as naturally, Leah accepted.

After that, whenever possible, Daisy closely watched the two of them interact. Or rather, not really interact. They didn't date. They didn't even sit together at lunch most of the time. One day, she watched them pass each other in the hall without even giving one another a glance.

Daisy fantasized about taking Leah's place and going to Prom with Ken. She figured he might not notice anyway, and it would save Leah the expense of buying a formal gown.

In fairness, Ken and his brothers had their sights set on only one thing, and that one thing was Auburn University in southern Alabama. Ken and Brad would let nothing get in the way of that goal. Jon, however, started getting a little bit of a reputation as a bad boy. He started wearing his hair differently, which made it easy for Daisy to tell him from Brad. As usual, she could spot Ken from a mile away just by the cut of his jib.

Meanwhile, her Freshman year, while Daisy mostly warmed the bench in an alternate slot, their Debate Team placed at sectionals and then won at regionals. They ended up in the top twenty-five at nationals held in none-other than Washington DC.

Daisy figured out that she loved debating for several reasons. First of all, she had to think and speak quickly. Secondly, she spent so much time and energy arguing with herself inside her own head, debating gave her a much-needed outlet that helped to still her troubled mind and spirit. Finally, debate grounded her in logic and allowed her to get some perspective about her emotions most of the time.

Most of the time.

At youth group, the Dixon brothers began to discuss their summer mission trip. This summer, they would spend nine weeks in Kenya digging wells and building housing in the slums, helping people get out of the cardboard shacks they lived in now. As soon as Daisy heard about this, she quietly began to petition to go on the mission trip with them. She did all of her research about passports and visas and vaccinations. She read the US State Department travel advisories. She allowed herself to fantasize about stolen moments with Ken while they worked side by side to fulfill God's work.

Gradually, she came to realize that her parents could not afford to send her on the trip. The church could probably assist and offset some of the cost, but right or wrong, that would bring a measure of shame to her father that Daisy would never want handed out. So, she instantly informed her parents she had changed her mind about the entire thing, and everyone breathed a little easier.

Daisy finished the year with honors. At her brother's graduation ceremony, Daisy got a glimpse of Ken wearing his cap and gown. He and his brothers would spend the summer in Kenya and then begin their matriculation efforts at Auburn directly upon their return. Daisy had no idea when, or even if, she would ever see Ken Dixon again.

For the remainder of her high school years, Daisy focused on things like Beta club, Debate and Forensics, History, and English. She went to Homecoming with her cousin, Julian, and went to Prom with the Debate Team's newly minted captain, a Junior named Garcia Perez. Daisy let Garcia kiss her at the end of the night, though Garcia's kiss left her feet firmly planted on the ground. If anything, gravity felt even heavier at that moment.

She ended up ranking sixth in her class. Unlike the majority of her classmates, Daisy knew exactly what career she wanted to take on. Specifically, she wanted to become a litigator. She planned to obtain her Juris Doctorate, pass the bar exam, and become an attorney. God willing, she planned to handle morally relevant cases within her community.

Daisy gratefully accepted a two-year scholarship to Emory just north of Atlanta. She had faith that God would provide some way for her to finish her education beyond the first two years. She made the Dean's list every quarter and finished her first year at the top of her class.

A few days into summer break, her grandfather called her and asked her to join him for a celebratory dinner. He treated her to the Viscolli restaurant on top of the famous hotel. They sat near the windows, and every hour the entire restaurant rotated 360 degrees, giving a perfect view of the Atlanta skyline.

During the entrée, he said, "So, your grandmother and I agreed that if you keep your grades up, we want to pay for the rest of your school."

Overwhelmed, Daisy exclaimed, "Papa! That's amazing! Gracias! Muchas gracias. How can I ever repay you?"

Her grandparents chuckled, and her grandfather said, "Funny you should ask." He folded his hands and met her eyes with a solemn look. "After you pass the bar, promise me you will do something for us."

"What? Anything. I'll do whatever you like."

He nodded. "We would like you to serve as the legal representative and executive director for Gálatas Seis. We hope you can commit to five years. Now, understand Cariño, the position is not charity work on your part. It isn't a lot, but there's a salary."

Her grandparents had built Gálatas Seis from the ground up, using the verses in Galatians 6:1-10 about bearing one another's burdens, doing good, and sowing the Spirit as their mission statement. Daisy had no idea her grandparents ever even had such plans for her. The five-year commitment didn't really concern her. She felt that amount of time was a small price to pay in exchange for a college education and starting out debt-free. She had visited Gálatas Seis a few times in recent years but could not even imagine how she would fit in there. "I don't know anything about running a non-profit."

"That's the idea, Cariño. We teach you everything."

"Why five years?"

"The truth is, life is short. Your grandmother and I, we really want to travel. We want to visit family more. Things like that. For the first few years, you learn everything you can. After that, we hope you can take over a lot of the work there so we can start to move into retirement. Then, for the last few years, train your replacement. The whole time, just relax and rest a little. You will have job security. You'll be doing good work for a community that needs you. Take that time to build your resume and plan for your future."

Daisy sat quietly for a few minutes, pondering the idea. To think that her grandparents had planned this for who knew how long? The idea astonished her. "Have you talked to Dad about this?"

"No. Of course not. I'm talking to you. I trust your judgment, Cariño. If we have a deal, we can talk to your parents together." When she didn't answer again for a few seconds, he prompted, "Do we have a deal?"

Suddenly, Daisy knew the answer, and no amount of additional mulling would change it. "Deal. And thank you again."

She worked hard in school and made the short trip home nearly every weekend. By the first semester of her Junior year at Emory, she even went on a few dates, though her feet still remained firmly on the ground. No mountaintop experiences. Once more, Daisy assumed that her childhood crush had been nothing more than that—merely a youthful infatuation—and that real love felt much more mundane than her childish flights of fancy.

All of these memories, the watershed moments of a lifetime, flashed through her mind. How different might her life have been, Daisy wondered, if only this or that moment had gone differently? Daisy pondered that question and even dared to wonder what the future might hold as she held the pregnancy test and watched the tiny little pink minus sign mercilessly and relentlessly turn into a plus symbol.

Definitely not a mountaintop moment.

Chapter 2

The spacious lobby bustled with activity. A receptionist sat at a circular desk and answered the phone in a constant, cheerful voice, "Hamilton, Hamilton, Bosie, and Taylor. How may I direct your call? Please hold." In the ten minutes she'd sat there, Daisy hadn't noticed a pause in the incoming calls.

Beside the receptionist, a uniformed guard gazed at half a dozen monitors and kept an eye on anyone who walked through the lobby. When she'd arrived, Daisy had asked to see Jason Taylor. She'd handed him her driver's license, which he scanned with a hand scanner then directed her to the waiting area.

She contemplated going to the bathroom, but she worried Jason would come down when she was gone, so she waited. Nerves tingled up her arms and across the back of her neck. What did she have to worry about, though? He loved her.

Didn't he?

The elevator doors opened, and Jason came out. She stood as he walked toward her, a frown covering his face, pulling his dark eyebrows together. He wore a gray suit with a red and yellow striped tie. "Daisy?" He looked around as he approached, scanning the crowd in the lobby. "What are you doing here?"

Her mouth felt like someone had stuffed it with cotton then dried it with a hot air gun. She tried to swallow but thought she'd gag from the effort. "Jason," she said in a breathless whisper. "Thank goodness you're here. I tried to call."

"You know I'm not available on Tuesdays." He put a hand on her elbow and steered her toward the exit. "I'll call you when I'm free."

When she realized he didn't intend to talk to her, she dug her heels in, abruptly stopping them. "No. This is important."

He looked around again, his brown eyes darting around like a cornered cat. "What?"

Confused, she jerked her arm free. "Can we talk in your office or something?"

"Of course not!"

She flinched back as if he'd struck her. "What's wrong with you, Jason?"

As if he suddenly realized how out of character he had just acted, he relaxed. His face smoothed out, his demeanor changed, his mouth moved in a small smile. "Nothing, Daisy. I'm just incredibly busy. I have court in an hour." He straightened his tie, and she gasped out loud when she saw his hand—the one with the wedding band; the wedding band she'd never seen before. He didn't notice. "Is it so important it can't wait until our date on Thursday?"

She narrowed her eyes as she frowned, and she took a full step back away from him. Pieces of a previously unseen puzzle started to fall into place. Answers to questions she didn't even realize she'd asked popped up. "Why Thursday? Does your wife leave town or something?"

He froze, his hand on the knot of his tie, his mouth partially open. Finally, he said, "As a matter of fact, yes. She leaves on Thursday mornings for our practice in Charlotte and comes home Saturday nights. I assumed you knew."

When she realized she stood there gaping, she slowly closed mouth, remembering every word he'd ever spoken to her. She could hear his voice as he talked about their future, how much he loved her, how he longed to be with her forever.

He continued speaking. "Hamilton, Hamilton, Bosie, and Taylor. She's Hamilton. Hamilton-Taylor, actually, but we kept the firm name the same just for simplicity's sake."

"Simplicity's sake?" Was she dreaming? Dare she pinch herself? She exhaled slowly. "You never once said you were married. Never even hinted at it. In fact, what you did was talk about us getting married. Have you conveniently forgotten about that?"

His relaxed facade disappeared, and his eyes started darting around again. "Listen, we cannot talk here."

"Then maybe you should have answered your phone."

"Daisy, I need you to—"

"I'm pregnant, Jason."

He stopped moving again. He just stared at her, immobile, for one heartbeat, then two. At last, he asked, "And?"

With the air escaping her lungs, she repeated his question. "And?"

"And why are you telling me?"

It had to be a dream. She'd wake up tomorrow and wonder what part of her subconscious created this absurd scenario. "You're going to be a daddy, Jason Taylor. Just think. Sometime the last week of February. Isn't that something to get excited about?" She wondered if he'd hear the sarcasm in her voice, if he'd pick up on the subtleties of her fury. "Or are you already a father?"

He glanced over his shoulder then looked back at her. "You need to leave. Please spare yourself the indignity of having security remove you."

Security? With her heart beating furiously in her ears, she stepped closer to him and spoke very low. "Jason, I am pregnant. With your child. Yours. I didn't know you were married. I thought you loved me." Her breath hiccupped, and she paused. He opened his mouth to speak, but she held a hand up to stop him. "I need to know what we're going to do now."

His eyes glinted with irritation. "What we're going to do is take care of that pregnancy. Wipe it away. I'm not going to have you ruin what I've spent a lifetime achieving. If you need a name, I can recommend someone."

Gasping for a clean breath of air that didn't contain his cloying aftershave, she took a step back, then another. "You don't mean—"

"That is exactly what I mean, and exactly where I stop. I can give you some money. End of my part in this."

Her mind whirled with words, accusations. She mentally screamed at him in two languages. Finally, she said, "I'm not going to get an abortion."

He glanced toward the door as it opened and looked at her again. "I guess that's your choice. Isn't that the word bandied about? Choice? Do what you want. I want nothing to do with it."

"Then put it in writing," she snapped.

A confused frown covered his face. "I beg your pardon?"

"Put it in writing. Remove your claim to this child. Legally."

"Fine." He looked at his watch. "I'll have the papers drawn up."

"Great." She gestured toward the chair she'd just vacated. "I'll wait."

"I can't do it here."

Daisy walked over to the chairs and sat down. He took the chair next to her and turned his body toward hers. "I can't prepare the papers. Someone will see them. I'll have to have someone else do them in another practice."

"Great." She smiled, despite the rolling mass of

emotions trying to destroy her from the inside. "I'll wait." He huffed and surged to his feet. As he started to walk away, she added, "If security tries to remove me, I'm happy to ask your wife to draw up the papers."

He cursed at her under his breath, but she heard the word. As soon as she saw the elevator doors close behind him, she pushed a fisted hand against her mouth and closed her eyes, praying for strength to get through the length of time it would take him to come back down with paperwork that would terminate any right he had to her baby.

A tear slid down her cheek, and she furiously swiped at it. She would not cry over him or his lies. She would not mourn something that never actually existed in the first place.

Definitely not a mountaintop moment.

As she sat there, she analyzed every moment ever spent with Jason. What clues had she ignored? Why had she not seen his true character? How had she gotten to this point?

She'd met him at a fundraiser for Gálatas Seis. He'd completely swept her off her feet, dancing with her all night long, attentively listening to her, acting interested in the mission for which she had so much passion. She told him about houses they'd built, homes they'd restored, stories about school supplies, stocking groceries into empty cupboards, supplying new mothers with cribs and diapers. He'd acted interested, insisting on donating money whenever she had an unexplained need arise. He even offered to join the board of directors the next time they had a seat open. Worst of all, he'd talked about their future, a future working together to make Atlanta and the surrounding community a better place for everyone, regardless of economic status.

Basically, he'd lied his way into sleeping with her. He'd tricked her. He'd made her believe him and give herself to him in a way she'd never done before with anyone.

Shame overwhelmed her. Little lights danced in front of her eyes, and no matter how deeply she breathed, it felt like no oxygen reached her lungs. Just when she thought she'd burst to her feet and run screaming from the building, a rail-thin woman with jet black hair and dark-framed glasses approached her carrying a manila envelope.

"Daisy Ruiz?" she inquired.

Daisy stood. "Yes."

She thrust the envelope toward her. "Mr. Hamilton asked me to deliver this to you."

With shaking hands, she took it and opened the flap. She pulled the paper out, and the woman started to walk away. "Wait," she said, "Let me make sure it's what I need."

The woman spun on her spiky heels and crossed her arms, clearly put out by the errand. Daisy scanned the document, making sure he'd hidden no clauses that could harm her in the future. As far as her legal eye could ascertain, everything appeared above-board.

"All set?" the woman asked.

"Yes. This will do." The woman rolled her eyes and spun around, crossing the lobby to the elevators. Daisy turned, clutching the envelope, and walked back out into the Georgia summer.

What could she do now?

Nothing brought Kenneth "Ken" Dixon more happiness than bringing a home up out of the ground. The designing of the plans, working with the engineers, watching the earth breaking under the site work contractor's machinery—it all gave him a sense of anticipation that thrilled him. Brick by brick, stone by stone, plank of wood by plank of wood, the material didn't change the feeling. Twelve hundred square feet or twelve thousand, the size didn't matter. His joy came from watching the house emerge, the details going into the molding, the laying of intricate tile work, the gleaming of new fixtures and appliances.

Today, as he surveyed the faces staring back at him from the conference room table, he acknowledged that as much as he loved the process of building houses, he hated this part of his job. As the residential division manager for Dixon Contracting and Design, he regularly led meetings with project managers, architects, and engineers, even though he would rather just build.

Today, as on every last Monday of the month, the team discussed the status of the three hundred and thirteen residential properties currently planned, in design, or under construction. They had forty-two Dixon designed neighborhoods and five multi-unit apartment complexes under construction in various parts of the southeast. Individual homes with individual contracts took up the remainder.

Ken could remember details, owners' names, budgets, and contractors under each contract with ease. He could get all of these reports in writing, which would aid him in the details. However, his brother Brad, the president of Dixon Contracting and Design, insisted that every department hold monthly status report meetings on set days the last week of every month. Department heads staggered the times of the meetings so that Brad could attend them all.

He looked at Ian Jones, one of the mechanical engineers employed by the company, and said, "I guess we should get the bad news out of the way first. Talk to me about the HVAC issues with the HUD complex in Albany."

Ian nodded and tapped the screen on his tablet, accessing the appropriate file. An email appeared on the screen behind him. "The owner's project manager insists that the HVAC is coming in about fifty percent higher than what he budgeted. All the value engineering I can do will only bring it down about twenty percent. I don't know where he got his numbers or if he just underestimated the size of unit needed. I haven't met with him yet, but I'll be in Albany next Thursday. I want to meet with him in person."

Ken nodded. "Want some company?"

Ian shrugged. "I don't think we need it escalated to the point of having a Dixon present yet, but I can call you on my way back from Albany and let you know how it went."

Ken looked at his agenda and made a checkmark

next to Albany. "Good enough. Let's see what's next."

An hour later, he headed out of the conference room into the sanctuary of his office. His assistant, Toby MacDonald, sat at the desk in front of Ken's office door. "That's done for another month," he said as he walked past Toby's desk.

Toby had attended Ken's family church as a high school student. He'd come to a youth gathering his freshman year with a girlfriend and had fallen in love with the community. Toby approached Ken one night as he prepared for his high school graduation and told him he longed to become a mechanical engineer but had no means for school. He had asked if Dixon contracting had any kind of tuition assistance for employees.

Three years later, Toby had marked the halfway point through school. Ken had never had a more efficient assistant and enjoyed the fact that Toby didn't feel any need to engage in chit-chat. Every blissfully short conversation they shared came with a point. Ken had also never met a more detail-oriented person and knew he would make a phenomenal engineer when he graduated. Toby had signed a five-year contract beginning upon graduation to repay his tuition assistance. He knew the young man would become nothing less than an asset to their engineering division.

"Cool. Don't forget your lunch appointment," Toby said.

"Right. The local charity. What's the name again?"

Toby nodded once, sharply. "Gálatas Seis. I think

this might be a one-on-one with their director, but I don't know for sure. Their director of fundraising reached out to you through a contact at Samaritan's Purse."

As a rule, Ken prioritized charitable work. Toby knew it. "Did you email me the address?"

"Texted. And I gave you an extra hour in your day. Oh, and don't forget I have the first day of the summer semester at three today."

"Right. Have a good first day." Ken turned to enter his office but then paused and turned back to his assistant. "Your mom take a first day of school picture?"

Ken thought that if he didn't have such dark skin, he would've seen the flush that certainly covered Toby's cheeks. "Come on, man." He cleared his throat. "Speaking of mothers, your mom had me clear your morning through early afternoon tomorrow. I backed your first appointment up to two."

Ken nodded and went into his office, letting the door shut behind him. He pulled his phone out of his desk drawer and turned it on. Immediately, a text from his mom appeared. Today, his brother Jon came home from a two-year project he had worked on in Nashville, and she wanted everyone at Ken's lake house tomorrow for family fishing and lunch in lieu of the regular Wednesday night family dinner.

He chuckled, realizing his mother planned for him to host the family tomorrow, whether he'd known about it or not. After sending a reply that he would see them tomorrow, he spent the next hour updating all of his personal reporting with the information he had received in the meeting today. Once he finished compiling his notes, he opened the file on his personal project. For the last two years, he and Brad had completely remodeled and renovated an old apartment complex built in the seventies. They neared the end of the project and had a buyer interested in purchasing it. After running all the final numbers, he realized they would make about thirty percent more than their original investment. Not bad if you didn't count the thousands of hours they put into physical labor in the remodel. Even after supplies and contractors, they still made a hefty profit.

He picked up the phone and dialed his brother's extension. Brad's assistant Sami picked up on the first ring. "Brad Dixon's office."

"Hey, Sami. Ken. Is my brother there?"

"Sure thing."

The hold music barely started when Brad picked up. "Hey."

"Hey. I emailed you an offer we got on the apartments. The owner met our asking price." Brad whistled in his ear. "Yeah. That's about what I said. I'm going to accept it, but it's still a contingent offer since we still have one more unit to finish."

"We can finish that in two weeks."

"Yep." He looked at his watch and stood. "I'm on my way to meet up with that local charity. They're looking for someone to sponsor a build-a-house-in-a-day thing."

"Well, that's a meeting you'll enjoy."

"Can I speak on behalf of us, or just me?"

"Get me the numbers, but I'm confident Dixon Contracting can do it. Jon and I can swing hammers at the very least."

Their parents had raised them to make missions work a priority in their lives. They went on an annual mission trip for several weeks a year, always picking different locations around the world. On a local level, they contributed to their community through their church and other charitable organizations. Ken knew a good portion of that came from his own personal convictions and the way he pressed his brothers to participate. He also knew that they didn't mind. "Hopefully, I'll come out of this meeting with all the details."

"Great."

On his way out, he stopped at Toby's desk. "Forward my office extension to my cell and pass any need-be items straight to me. You enjoy that first day of school. See you in the morning."

"Thanks. See you," Toby said, picking up the ringing phone. "Ken Dixon's office," he said. Ken didn't stick around.

The directions took him to a strip mall anchored to a chain grocery store. He checked the suite number and found the sign for Gálatas Seis centered between a family dentist and a take-out Chinese restaurant.

When he walked in the door, a young woman in her twenties with mousy brown hair and big blue eyes greeted him. As he came through the door, she paused typing on her keyboard and turned her chair to face him completely. "How may I help you?"

"Ken Dixon with Dixon Contracting. I have an appointment with someone here today."

She raised both eyebrows and asked, "Do you know with whom?"

He shook his head. "Sorry. No. Didn't make the appointment. Your fundraising department contacted us through another ministry."

Just then, a woman came around a partition. She had rich black hair, dark brown eyes, and skin the color of warm caramel. She wore a bright red sleeveless top and white Capri pants. "Bev, Irene just sent me a message that she set up a..."

She stopped in her tracks and stared up at him. "Ken? Ken Dixon?"

Hearing his name threw him. She could have recognized him from any number of events that would put her ministry in his path, but no one could tell him apart from his brothers except their mother and Brad's wife. Maybe she saw his name on an appointment calendar. That would make sense. "Yep. Ken Dixon."

He extended his hand, and she hesitated only slightly before placing hers in his. "Wow. Ken! Oh, my goodness. Ken Dixon. I haven't seen you since high school."

Keeping her hand in his, he stared into her brown eyes and tried to place her. Something about her felt very familiar; something about her voice, the shape of her chin, and the name of this place. Finally, a spark went off in his mind. "Daisy? Daisy Ruiz?"

He grinned. She had practically grown up with him. He spent many, many hours in her basement with her older brother Diego and their father. "I can't believe I didn't recognize the name. Gálatas Seis. This was, what? Your grandparents'? Didn't your grandfather start this?"

When she pulled her hand from his, he realized he'd still held it. She nodded and smiled a smile that filled the room with light. "Yes! Twenty years ago. I've taken over the position of Executive Director for the last year now."

A slow smile covered his face. "That is amazing. It's so good to see you." He gestured at the woman she had called Bev. "I was just telling Bev, here, I had a meeting today but didn't know who with."

She held up her phone. "That's so funny. I had a message that Irene had set up a meeting, but I didn't know who with." She laughed. "Well, follow me."

She took him around the partition. He could make out three different workspaces, all partitioned off. She gestured to the door, and he followed her into a break room with a small table and three chairs.

"How did you get into doing this?"

She opened a cupboard and grabbed a folder. "My grandparents agreed to pay for my law school with the understanding that I would take over the charity for five years once I passed the bar. So, here I am."

"Passed the bar?"

"Oh, yeah. I'm a real-life lawyer."

"Wow." Ken could not stop smiling. "How many people do you have working for you here?"

"Well, lots. But many are volunteers. Bev out there is part-time. Irene and I are the only full-time employees. She handles fundraising. I take care of the legalities of everything we're doing and set up all of our projects. We have an executive board that meets monthly and chooses our projects."

She set the folder in front of him, pulled the chair out, and sat down across from him. He glanced at the press kit but didn't study it. "My message was that this was to help you with a build a house-in-a-day project."

"Oh. The message I had wasn't detailed. We are looking for sponsors who can help with the materials and equipment needed to build a house on Labor Day weekend. We have a family of six that are in deplorable conditions and had a major contributor pull the funding kind of at the last minute."

He watched her facial expression and saw the discomfort around her mouth and eyes. He was tempted to dig into the reasons why this particular sponsor made her so uncomfortable but thought he should probably stay on task.

She smelled very good.

He tried to drag his brain back to the topic of conversation. "What are the project specifics?"

"We're scrambling to get sponsors. But this is so last minute. We're just a couple months away." She pulled out her phone and swiped at the screen, then read off the numbers for equipment and supplies.

The numbers sounded very low to Ken. "Are you getting special deals through the suppliers and equipment rental places?"

She nodded. "We work hard to minimize cost. We use a lot of recovered materials from demolition sites.

Like, a *lot*. Most places sell us new materials at a fraction above cost. This is a charitable donation for them. We worked with several of these places for years."

Ken crossed his arms over his chest and sat back in his chair. He liked the way she let everything she felt show on her face. He found that incredibly refreshing. He didn't want this meeting to end. He wanted to keep talking to this woman. Before he could talk himself out of it, he said, "Have dinner with me tomorrow night."

She gasped. Her eyes widened, and she sat back almost as if pushed by force. "I, uhh…"

Disappointment crept along the back of his neck. "Sorry. You're seeing someone."

"Uh…" Daisy opened and closed her mouth as if she didn't know what to say.

"Course you are. Look at you. You're the most beautiful woman I've ever seen."

She tucked her hair behind her ear, and half chuckled. "No."

"'No,' you're not beautiful? Don't start a fight with me, here, Daisy." He could hardly stop looking at her lips.

"No. I mean, I'm not seeing anyone."

Ken felt every molecule of air that filled his lungs. "Good. Dinner it is."

"Ken, I just don't think…"

"Good. Thinking gets in the way of good things sometimes. Have dinner with me, Daisy. I can tell you want to."

He was teasing, of course. He could tell she didn't

want to. But he wanted to for the first time in his life. Finally, she said, "Okay. Sure. I'll have dinner with you tomorrow night."

"That's great. Can't wait." He grinned and tapped the folder. "As for your project, consider your cost met. Dixon Contracting and Design will fully fund this project."

She sucked in a breath and asked, "Fully?"

He nodded, enjoying the look on her face. He felt like he could sit and talk to her all day long. But he really, desperately wanted to escape so he could analyze these strange feelings he had from the moment she came out from behind the partition. He stood and asked, "Pick you up at seven?"

She nodded. "Yeah, sure. Seven is great." She stood as well. "I suppose you need my address."

Chapter 3

For what seemed like the millionth time, Daisy stared at herself in the mirror and asked out loud, "What are you doing?"

In answer, the reflection of herself wearing the little black dress with the red embroidered roses along the hem and the clunky red beaded necklace looked down at her from the mountaintop and answered, "Going to dinner with the man of my dreams."

As she turned away from the mirror, she picked up her black beaded clutch purse and slipped her cell phone and a tube of red lipstick inside it. "And, we know we're pregnant. Yes. That has been established for a solid week now. But come on. It's Ken Dixon. What will it hurt to go on one little date?"

Before she could answer herself and explain to her reflection exactly all the ways it could hurt—again—the doorbell rang. It pulled her out of the conversation and brought her back into a place of reality. Not only did the doorbell ring, but Ken Dixon stood on her front porch waiting to take her on a date. Giddy excited butterflies had sprung loose in her stomach. She could not even contain herself over the idea of this dream come true.

She soared over the peak of the mountain and opened the door. He stood there with his wavy brown hair, gray eyes that cut right through her, wearing a blue button-down shirt open at the collar, and a pair of gray slacks. "Hi," she said on a breath. "Did you have any problem finding the place?"

She stepped back and gestured for him to come inside. He slipped his hands into his pockets and stepped across the threshold. "No. Actually think I used to own this building."

Confused, she asked, "What?"

He looked at the ceiling and the hall closet door and nodded. "Pretty sure I built it and all these townhouses on the street. Don't remember if we sold them or if we're renting them out." He narrowed his eyes at her. "Do you rent, or do you own?"

She tilted her head to study his face. "I rent it."

He pursed his lips and nodded. "Do you pay Mason-Dixon?"

"Mason-Dixon?"

"Mason-Dixon Realty management. That's our branch of property leasing. My brothers and I build a lot of properties as investments. We either sell them immediately or hand them over to the rental division. I just can't remember what we did with this building."

"I don't pay Mason-Dixon Realty." This line of conversation confused her and threw her off her game. "Can I get you something to drink? Water? Soda?"

"No, thanks." He glanced around her living room. She had wood floors stained black and accented them with a black rug covered in red, yellow, and turquoise flowers. Her television sat on a low bright pink table that ran the length of one wall. It matched her pink coffee table and brought out the pink flowers on the black throw pillows on her yellow couch. Through the doorway, he could see the turquoise wall of her dining room. "Good colors. Makes the room feel bigger. Brighter."

It shouldn't have pleased her so much to get his approval of her style. "Thank you. It's a gradual work-in-progress. I tend to do most of my shopping at flea markets."

He looked at his watch. "We have reservations at seven-thirty if you're ready to go."

She grabbed the red shawl she had tossed onto the back of her chair and said, "I'm ready."

He led the way out of her house. She paused to lock the door, then followed him to his pickup truck. As he opened the door, he stopped her. "Sorry. I get a little too far inside my head sometimes. That wasn't the best start of a date."

This close to him, she could smell his aftershave, the spicy fragrance that brought images of cowboys and the wild west to her mind. It suited him. "I don't think you should apologize. It's kind of neat that I live in a house you built."

His smile came quick and made her heart kick it up a notch. "Appreciate that." He gestured to the interior of the truck. "Your carriage awaits."

Using the step on the side of the truck, she climbed into the spotless cab. She could smell leather cleaner mixed with glass cleaner and felt a warm rush of emotion at the thought that he'd cleaned his truck before coming to get her.

As they drove into downtown Atlanta, they chatted about her brother. "Diego has his own church now down in Panama City."

Ken nodded. "I know. When we went down to Florida after the hurricane a couple of years ago, we partnered with his church."

"Oh, wow. I didn't know that. He had so much going on at that time."

"He fed about two hundred people a day. The storm leveled most of the city." At a stoplight, he glanced over at her. "We stayed at his house. His wife was pregnant at the time."

"Yeah. Little DJ. The light of our lives." Instantly, she thought about her baby. Right now, the only other person on earth who knew about it had signed away his rights to it. What would her parents say? She remembered the elaborate announcement of Diego's baby. The memory of the celebrations her family enjoyed filled her with sadness. What was she going to do? "How about your brothers? Any nieces or nephews?"

"Not yet. My parents are more than ready, though. Apparently, thirty-two is the age the parents quit being coy and start dropping actual hints."

He pulled into the valet area of a building. She recognized the Viscolli hotel, the same place her grandparents had taken her when they offered her the job. After he stopped the truck, he sat for a moment, then turned to face her. "Out of curiosity, did you know I was coming to your office yesterday?"

"No." She thought of the message she'd gotten about the meeting. "I just had a message that someone was coming to talk to me about the project. No specifics."

His eyes darkened with intensity. He ignored the valet attendant who came to his door. "How did you recognize me?"

With a frown, she asked, "What? What do you mean?"

"When you saw me, you said, 'Ken.' You didn't pause and wait for me to identify myself."

Suddenly nervous, she licked her lips. "I've always been able to recognize you. You don't remember that?"

He searched her face as if examining her, then finally relaxed and smiled. "I do now. I'm surprised you still could after all these years." He opened his door and got out of the truck, handing the key fob to the attendant. Seconds later, he opened her door and held a hand out. His hand felt warm, the skin rough. "You know no one else can, right?"

Surprised, she asked, "Why?"

"Because, Daisy, we're identical, my brothers and me. Only my parents and Brad's wife can pick one from the other. Even Valerie stumbles over Jon and me."

She shook her head. "I can tell Brad from Jon, but it takes one of them speaking. You, I could always pick you out."

They walked into the hotel. Daisy looked all around, taking in the green marble floors, the elegant furniture, the giant vase of flowers in the middle of the lobby. Ken led the way to the bank of elevators and hit the call button for the top floor. "Best steak in Georgia," he announced.

When the doors opened, they walked into the waiting area of the restaurant. The maître de greeted them with a smile. "Welcome to the Viscolli Grand. May I get the name on the reservation?"

"Dixon," Ken said.

"Absolutely, Mr. Dixon. We are delighted you are here with us. Mrs. Westcott has instructed us to spoil you."

Impressed, Daisy followed him to the table next to the window. The dim lighting and hushed tones, leather chairs, and candlelight all accentuated the establishment's elegant feel. They looked out at the skyline of Atlanta. "Thank you," she said as he handed her a menu.

"Will you be interested in our wine menu this evening?"

Ken glanced at her, and subtly, silently shook his head. Relieved, Daisy also shook her head. Ken said, "No, thank you."

"No problem. Your server, Phil, will be with you momentarily."

Daisy skimmed the entrees. She didn't even know

where to begin ordering. "So? Who's Mrs. Westcott?"

Ken didn't look up from his menu. "Madeline Viscolli Westcott. This is one of her hotels."

"You know the owner?" She set aside the menu and sat back in the comfortable chair. "And why is she spoiling you?"

He shrugged. "I think it's a standing order for our family. We built this place. Anyway, she and Brad became friends. I doubt anyone called her and told her I had a reservation or anything." He turned his attention to the arriving waiter.

"Good evening. I have a list of recommendations from the chef, Mr. Dixon. He'd like permission to serve you, personally."

Ken glanced her way. "That okay with you?"

She chuckled. "I was going to ask you to recommend something because the menu is so extravagant I don't even know where to begin."

Ken looked at Phil. "I want a steak. Medium rare. For everything else, please tell the chef to feel free to express himself."

"Absolutely. May I ask how you like your steak?"

They discussed specifics on the menu, Ken ordered them both water to drink, and then when the waiter left, he sat back in his chair. "I've been trying to put you in the place of the Daisy I remember, but it's just not working. I remember you in a pink hoodie, with glasses and braces."

"Oh, goodness," she exclaimed, putting her hands on her cheeks. "You had to go back to my awkward fourteen-year-old phase?"

"That's where my mind stops. I mean, we were in your home weekly for years. But even last year when we were in Florida, Diego was talking about you and in my mind's eye... pink hoodie."

Why should she feel embarrassed about tween Daisy? But she did. "If you'd come to my Quinceañera, you'd have seen the whole blossoming into womanhood ceremony."

"Quinceañera?" He raised his eyebrows.

"It's where you become a woman. There's even a ceremony where the dad removes the shoes of a little girl and replaces them with a woman's shoes. I practiced how to walk in those high heels for weeks."

His quick smile made her heart flutter. "I bet that's a fun ceremony."

"It was. Your mom let us have it in your house. It was such a beautiful setting. I was disappointed that you..." she hesitated and added, "... you all couldn't stay. My parents limited it to kids my age. Most of Diego's friends were seniors that year."

"Well, it was for you and not Diego, right?"

She obviously couldn't tell him she would have wanted him to attend as her guest, not Diego's. Instead, she shrugged and said, "That's right."

The waiter arrived with two ceramic spoons on a tray. He set one in front of each one of them. "Chef Armand would like you to start with an amuse-bouche of fresh salmon and avocado with a hint of chili and lime."

He disappeared as quickly as he had arrived. Daisy didn't know what to do with the spoon in front of her until Ken picked it up and took a bite of the whole thing. She followed his lead. The flavors exploded on her tongue, and she closed her eyes as she relished the fresh taste and the kick of heat.

"Oh, my word. That is amazing."

When she opened her eyes, he stared at her with such an intense look that she thought she had done something wrong. Then a slow smile spread across his face that warmed her from the inside out. "I like a woman who enjoys flavor."

Suddenly self-conscious, she licked her lips and smiled, then took a sip of her water.

Intense morning sickness had not hit Daisy. She hoped it wouldn't happen as she got further along in her pregnancy. But she did feel moderately queasy the moment she woke up and normally had to lay still in bed and let it pass.

This morning, she languished in the memories of last night. Every single part of the meal she shared with Ken tasted amazing. Beyond that, his presence, his personality, everything about him exceeded anything she could have imagined. That silly little schoolgirl crush she had on him as a teenager had matured into a full-blown grown woman attraction to the ninth degree.

Now she faced a brand-new problem. They had made plans to go out on Friday night. He would arrive at six to pick her up and had instructed her to dress casually. Daisy had no idea what that meant, but she knew one thing with absolute certainty.

Daisy Ruiz could never go out with Ken Dixon again.

She wanted to, of course. Dating Ken fulfilled all of her dreams. When he walked her to her door last night, the wild and crazy side of her wished he would kiss her good night—kiss her in a way she had dreamed of since her twelfth year on this earth.

Of course, he had simply brushed his lips over her cheek. She pressed her palm against said cheek as if she could still feel his lips. Oh, she'd definitely made a mistake in going on that date.

Even as her stomach settled, she didn't immediately get up. Instead, she went back through every single word they had spoken, every flicker of his eyes in the candlelight from the table. In her memory, she listened to his voice, watched his mouth move, watched his hands as they helped him tell stories.

She was seriously in trouble here.

"Yep. I like you a lot, Ken. A lot a lot. A *lot*. There's just this issue of another man's child. You don't mind, do you?"

Rolling her eyes at herself, she got out of bed and headed straight for the shower.

By the time she grabbed a banana and a bottle of water, she was five minutes behind schedule to get to her church. She led a Bible study on Thursday mornings and had the key to unlock the classroom door. Maybe everyone else would arrive late, and she wouldn't find them waiting on her. Although she doubted it.

As she walked down the hall of the church, she saw three women standing in the hallway. "Hola, sisters. I am so sorry I'm late."

Daisy's Decision

Mrs. Yancey stepped to the side as she pulled her key out of her pocket. "We just got here."

Daisy's father had worked as a youth pastor at churches throughout Atlanta her entire life. When she started college, he encouraged her to find a church connected to her college Christian fellowship group so she could grow her relationships inside the Christian world separate from his ministry. As a college student, she had aged out of his youth group. She had contemplated her grandparents' church, but the drive would take her over an hour.

On her second Sunday of college, Daisy found this church, and when she walked through the doors, she felt like she had completely come home. She'd attended with two girls from her college group and discovered that many of the church's leadership had worked with her father in various aspects over the years.

In her household, attending church meant volunteering at church. Before the end of her first semester of college, she taught a Sunday School class. Throughout her undergraduate years, she taught every Sunday, and by the time she started law school, she'd added the Thursday morning Bible study. Her job as executive director of the ministry gave her the freedom to continue to teach in the middle of a Thursday morning, providing a much-needed position in the church. When she first started teaching, older, retired women comprised most of the class. Over the years, a younger crowd had joined, giving a great dynamic to the group. One homeschool mom came every week, and her teenage daughter minded the younger children in the nursery. Daisy helped pitch in to pay her.

As the fluorescent lights flickered to life, she thought again of the candlelight last night. She should never have gone on that date. The idea that she would have to cancel a second date made her stomach hurt.

While they rearranged the tables and chairs to accommodate their class, she thought about how she would have to tell the women here about the baby. She had no idea how or when she would do that. What would they think about her then? How would they react?

Fifteen minutes later, thirteen women sat around the table with their Bibles and study guides open. "So, last week, we left off with session three. Who can tell me what words in verse six resonated with your heart and mind this week?"

As always, the discussion flowed well. She loved this group of women. She loved the range of ages and experiences, and she loved the way they wanted to dig deeper into God's word the same way that she did. She never walked out of this class without something very profound coming clear to her. It amazed her because she had prepared the lessons every week herself instead of relying on publications.

After Bible study, she drove the three blocks to her office. Bev didn't work today, and Irene worked from home on Thursdays, so she would have the place to herself. Which was good. Right now, she needed quiet so she could think.

When her grandfather set up the mission, he did it with the intent to provide groceries for families, pay medical bills, and provide rent assistance. In the last five years, a lot of his time and energy had gone into refurbishing homes to improve living conditions, then building new houses for families. He had arranged with a local bank to finance land at a low-interest rate, with the house serving as collateral. The bank set the condition that the family getting the loan didn't have to have good credit, but they couldn't be behind in any payments or have any old debt at collection agencies.

That generated a whole different level of help needed as they worked with potential families to remove debt in a culture where debt was normal. She established a relationship with a Christian organization that helped families with financial planning and signed up all of her potential families for that class. She made it a requirement before they could get a house.

The family receiving the house Labor Day weekend had worked for two years to meet all the qualifications. When Irene started the fundraising process, Jason had stepped forward and promised his firm's commitment to supplying the bulk of the funding necessary. When she saw him last week, she had not thought about this project. Then a clerk in the accounting office of his firm emailed revoking the promise to pay. Irene went into a frenzy to come up with tens of thousands of dollars needed to build a home for a family of six.

Ken Dixon had come in and saved the day. Maybe she should have learned from her lesson and not put all of her eggs in one basket, but sitting out a little over two months from the day they broke ground with no funding made her rather desperate for help and thankful for his offer.

She walked through the office, past the cubicle areas where the volunteers worked, and into the very back office. Thinking of Jason pulling the funding made her think of the baby. It always sat right there at the forefront of her mind, springing forward without warning. She set her purse and keys on top of her desk and collapsed into her chair. With her hands pressed against her eyes, she said out loud, "Just stop thinking about it. Just work. You have to work."

Chapter 4

Ken dunked his tea bag in hot water until it sufficiently steeped, then tossed it in the garbage can. He carried it over to the table where he'd set his plate of scrambled eggs and toast. Once he settled into his seat, he bowed his head, thanked God for the food, then picked up his fork.

As he chewed his eggs, he looked around the living space. He and Brad had spent two years refurbishing the units, and Ken had lived there from the beginning. For a while, Brad had lived with him in the old apartment offices, but once he and Valerie got married, they moved onto his parents' property and lived in the guest house.

The apartments would change hands on the sixteenth of August. He pulled a notebook out of his shirt pocket and picked up the little pencil he kept in the rings. As he ate, he made notes about the final phase of the project, including removing everything that made this a living area and converting it back to an empty space for cubicles and desks. He'd work around himself for a while but then would have to make other living arrangements. He'd either need to find a house, move to his parents' castle, or move into one of the empty apartments.

In the middle of a thought about tile and carpet, Daisy's brown eyes wafted in front of his vision. He felt a tug in his heart that he had never felt before. What was it about her?

He'd never really dated much, just here and there to appease his brothers. Even so, he'd never felt fully comfortable having to sit across from a woman and make conversation. Not so last night. Everything about Daisy made him feel right and centered. He had plans to take her to the jazz festival happening downtown tonight. He didn't know if she liked jazz, but he did.

Before he could talk himself out of it, he picked up his phone and sent her a text.

Good morning. Looking forward to tonight.

Succeeding in applying enough attention to Daisy Ruiz so he could focus again on his work, he went back to his list. He estimated two more weeks to finish the last unit and then another week and a half to finish this area. He had six weeks before closing, which gave him time for unexpected scheduling conflicts and supply issues.

Once he figured everything out, he emailed Brad all the final specifics. It didn't surprise him that his brother replied almost immediately, even though it was only six in the morning.

He washed dishes then got ready to leave for work. He loved Wednesdays. Wednesdays usually meant job site visits and breathing fresh air out in the sun instead of conditioned air under fluorescent lights. Today he had to walk through a thirteen-thousand-square-foot mansion on an old plantation right outside of town before he had to go back to work for a post-lunch meeting.

Expecting the nightmare of Atlanta traffic, he left about twenty minutes earlier than he needed to. While on the drive there, his phone sounded the text signal. He used the car's system to read the text message back to him.

I'm going to have to cancel tonight. Sorry.

After crossing two lanes of traffic to pull over on the side of the road, Ken picked up his phone and called Daisy. She answered on the fifth ring. "Hello?"

"Hey Daisy, this is Ken. I got your text. I'm sorry you can't make it."

"Yeah, I have an unexpected conflict."

Ken felt his brow furrow. Something was wrong with her voice. "Everything okay?"

"Everything's fine. I'm really sorry."

He didn't like her distant, unengaged tone. "That's okay. We can reschedule. What are you doing on Saturday? My family's throwing a big Fourth of July party at my lake house, and I'll be setting off the fireworks. I'd love the company."

After several long heartbeats, Daisy replied, "I have plans for Saturday, but I can check my calendar to see when I'm free again and get back with you. Sorry to cancel last minute. Goodbye."

When she hung up, he took the phone off of his ear and stared at it for a minute. Had he done something wrong?

He thought about the conversation about her house. What had prompted him to have such a ridiculous conversation with her? It didn't fall into the purview of his business to know to whom she made out her rent checks. And he had acted all uppity, saying he didn't know if he owned that property or not, as if he owned so many properties he couldn't keep them all straight. Which was true. The number of builds had exceeded his personal ability to track without an assistant and a computer years earlier. He could give minute details about current jobs, but he mentally set aside past projects to make room for new work. Even so, he had come off to Daisy like a braggart, which was well out of character.

He closed his eyes and rested his head against the back of his seat, and sighed. Had he done something so terrible that it had no hope of getting fixed? Should he call her back?

Feeling decidedly drained of energy, he started back on the road toward the job site. Despite looking forward to this, he finished with the job as quickly as possible. The house looked fantastic, and the interior craftsmanship rivaled anything he had ever supervised before. He sent himself a note to talk to Brad about giving the men on that project a bonus for their hard work and finishing ahead of schedule, then headed back to his office.

When he got there, he bypassed his office on the eighth floor where the residential division lived and headed straight for the tenth floor and the commercial project managers' offices. A clerk hopped in the elevator before the door shut and said, "Good morning, Mr. Dixon."

Most people at their offices couldn't tell the Dixon brothers apart. By the end of the day, they stood separate by their clothes. Most of the time, Ken enjoyed that anonymity. Despite that, the fact that Daisy had always been able to tell him apart from his brothers pleased him on some fundamental level that he couldn't name, generating a feeling for which he had no words to explain.

He went straight to Jon's office and walked in without knocking. His brother smiled as he set his phone down. "Yo, bro."

Like Ken, Jon wore his wavy brown hair short. Today he wore a blue collared shirt with a gray striped tie that he'd loosened at the neck.

The project managers did not have huge offices. The intent of the room was to provide quiet and privacy. He had room for a plans table, a couple of bookshelves, and two chairs in front of his desk. If he wanted a meeting with more than two people, he'd have to go to a conference room.

Ken's office was much bigger because he ran an entire department. He briefly wondered if Jon knew Brad planned to promote him soon.

"Yo, yourself." Ken threw himself into the chair

across from Jon's desk. He decided to just go straight to the issue at hand. "So, here's some news. Daisy Ruiz canceled our second date tonight."

"She figured out what a big fat nerd you are already, huh? Smart girl. Did you wear your ComicCon shirt on the first date or something?"

Ken felt his heart twist in his chest. Could that explain things? Had she classified him as a huge nerd? Jon's face fell as if he realized his teasing hurt him. "Why?"

"No idea. She suddenly had other plans."

Jon waited. Finally, he asked, "Did you agree on a different night?"

"Tried. Got a 'we'll see'." He rubbed at his eyes, exhaustion draining him. "I'm trying to nail down where I went wrong. We had a great time the other day. Been going over it in my mind. Did I say something or do something…?"

Jon leaned forward. "You've never really done a lot of dating, I know. It's hard to figure women out, brother. Really kind of impossible." Ken felt a little knee-jerk objection to the words but then realized that Jon spoke the truth. Brad had pined for his love, Valerie, and never wanted to date. Jon had dated and played and had fun, and never wanted to settle down. Ken wanted a woman who appreciated him and understood the way he thought but never really pursued any kind of relationship. He told himself he found contentment inside his own skin, in the quiet of his own mind, and had no need to make space for anyone else. His family could fill any other kind of need he had. But, spending time with Daisy the other night really opened a well in his heart that he didn't know existed, and he suddenly realized how very alone he was all the time. Jon continued. "Why don't you go see her in person? Let her look you in the eye and tell you what day works for her? It's easy to hide behind a text message."

Ken stared at him, processing the idea. Finally, he stood and slapped the top of Jon's desk. "I think I'll do that." He glanced at his watch. "I'd go right now, but I have a one o'clock."

Jon stood and quickly dashed out a text before slipping his phone into his pocket. "Eat yet? Want to grab something?"

"Yeah. Sounds good." Ken gestured at the job binder on Jon's desk. "That job in Marietta will keep you local for a couple of years."

"I know. It's time. I'm trying to convince the girl I had in Nashville to move here and keep working as my assistant."

Jon had mentioned his Nashville assistant before. Ken had met her on the two occasions he'd gone to the job site. He knew she had a lot of natural talent for administrative organization. "What's stopping her?"

Jon shrugged and opened his office door. "Youth. Fear of the unknown. She's only twenty."

They walked along the corridor, passing the project managers' offices on one side and the sea of cubicles of assistants and junior project managers on the other. He couldn't imagine turning down such a good job without having a good reason. "Great opportunity."

Once in the elevator, Ken crossed his arms over his chest and leaned against the wall. He had something else he wanted to talk to Jon about. "We're selling this apartment building next month. Closing on the sixteenth."

"Wow. You've been there for a couple of years."

"A lot of work. Probably would have been easier to knock it down and start fresh."

"I know. I helped here and there, but just seeing the difference is awesome."

The elevator stopped, and they stepped out into the busy lobby. Ken gestured toward the cafe, and Jon nodded. Ken thought about the news given on Wednesday. Brad and Valerie were going to have a baby. The thought filled him with all sorts of excitement and love. He couldn't believe a baby Brad would soon enter the world. "Brad won't be up for another big project. I'm trying to decide what I want to do next. Would you be interested in going in on an apartment with me?"

He stared at the menu. The eggplant sandwich looked good. While Jon processed what he asked, he went ahead and ordered. After they both paid and stepped back to wait on their food, Jon finally said, "I don't know. I might want to build a house."

With relief, Ken slapped him on the shoulder and nodded. "I'm swinging toward a house, too. But I didn't want to have you expecting an apartment."

"Nah, man. I think I just want to slowly build, take my time. Maybe by the time I finish, I'll have someone to share it with."

Ken pondered those words as they waited for their orders. "I know what you mean," Ken admitted. "Thirty-two years old. Mom and dad were married twelve years already by our age."

"Can't rush God's timing."

His heart twisted painfully in his chest. "True. But, honestly, I'm ready whenever He is."

Jon smiled and nodded. "Amen, brother."

Ken stared at Jon for a second. "Man, I really like Daisy. Can't get her out of my mind since our date. What's going on with her?"

Jon shrugged. "Go find out."

Wondering if he should eat quickly then cancel his one o'clock meeting, he nodded. He would go find out.

Tomorrow would start her seventh week of pregnancy. Daisy skimmed through the website about the baby's development. It had a head and face. Tears filled her eyes at the idea that someone with a good enough microphone could detect the baby's heartbeat. She glanced through the symptoms that she should feel right now and felt like she could just use the list as a checkbox for everything she had experienced. Only morning sickness wouldn't get a check, and she figured she ought to feel thankful for mild nausea.

She needed to find a doctor, but she just didn't know where to start. If she asked someone for a recommendation, that would begin the notification of her pregnancy. Could she handle that yet?

Maybe she could find a doctor based on online

reviews.

She sighed and said out loud to herself, "You need to put your shoulders back and just talk to someone. Find a young mom in church and deal with the stigma."

Would they allow her to continue to teach at the church? Years ago, in one of her father's older churches, a woman had made a public confession of a sin, and a leader in the church subsequently asked her to sit out of the praise team for a time. She remembered her parents having long conversations regarding that decision.

She shut the lid of her laptop and closed her eyes as a tear slid down her cheek. "God, I did not behave in the manner that I know is right. I didn't act in the way in which I was taught. It's worse that I let myself be manipulated. But regardless of his actions and his sin, I was wrong with him from the beginning. Please, forgive me."

Since it was Friday, she had the entire day off of work. Intentionally setting the laptop aside, she rummaged through a drawer until she found a notepad and pencil.

Upstairs and into the spare bedroom, she looked at the never used desk. Originally, she'd run the charity out of this room. But when she moved into the strip mall, the desk in here gradually became the catch-all for the fringes of her life that had no place to go. Bags of Christmas gifts she didn't know what to do with, books she'd ordered but not read yet, winter clothes that never made it into boxes—all piled on top of each other. With a heavy sigh, she contemplated the amount of work she needed to put into this room to make it a nursery and the amount of energy she just didn't have right now.

Using the pencil, she opened the lid of the notebook and started writing things down:

Crib

Dresser

Changing table

Diapers

Suddenly overwhelmed, she thought maybe she'd tackle it another day. As she pulled the door shut, the doorbell rang. Coming down the stairs, she saw Ken through the door's window. Her heart started skipping. She'd canceled their date tonight and successfully put him off from setting another one. Why was he here?

Since her car sat in the driveway, she didn't think she could get away with not answering the door, so she took a deep breath, steeled herself, and opened the door. He wore a golf shirt with the Dixon Contracting logo on the left chest and khaki pants. He looked fresh and crisp compared to her yoga pants, purple tank top, and messy bun.

"Ken, hi. What are you doing here?"

He smiled a half-smile that made her pulse skitter and asked, "May I come in?"

She stepped back and opened the door wider. "Of course."

He didn't speak again as he came into the house.

She shut the door behind him and followed him into the living room. He sat down on the couch and looked at the coffee table in front of him.

"Would you like something to drink? I have some lemonade." He shook his head and tapped his knee with his thumb. She took the chair across from the couch. "Is everything okay?"

His hand paused, and he looked at her with serious eyes. Finally, he asked, "Did you have a good time the other night?"

She thought about the elegance of the meal and the conversation that flowed and the way he looked and smelled and... "Definitely. It was one of the best nights of my life," she answered with sincerity.

"I did, too. I thought we hit it off really well. To be honest, I didn't want the night to end."

With a wistful smile, she looked down at her hands and realized how tightly she gripped them. She intentionally relaxed. "Me, either."

"But you don't want to go out again?"

Her heart begged for her to move across the room and sit next to him so she could feel his body heat, smell his aftershave, see the little green specks in his gray eyes. "I definitely want to go out again. I just can't."

His eyebrows drew together in a sharp frown. "Why not?"

Because I'm pregnant. "I don't want to talk about it." Giving in to the compulsion, she went around the coffee table and sat next to him, angling her body toward him. "I have always wanted to go out with you." As she spoke, he shifted his body to face her. She took advantage of the opportunity to reach out and take his hand. "I used to intentionally put myself in a position for you to notice me. Silly schoolgirl dreams." His eyes widened as if he couldn't believe what she said. "Wednesday night was an actual—no-kidding—dream come true for me."

"Then—"

"But I am nowhere near a place in my personal life to consider dating anyone new for a while."

He turned his hand so that her palm rested against his. She could feel the hard callouses on his skin. "I don't understand. What's stopping you?"

Maybe she could give him enough information, but not all the information. "I was in a serious relationship until very recently. He wooed me with words of love and our future. Then a few days ago, I found out he's married. Happily married."

"Happily married?" Ken raised an eyebrow. "Clearly not."

She shrugged. "Well, whether he is or isn't doesn't matter to me anymore. But I'm just not in a good place right now. It's too soon. I'm sorry."

His hand closed over hers and completely engulfed it. She wondered if she should feel threatened instead of suddenly very safe. "Look, Daisy, I'm not married. In fact, I've never even come close. Heck, I've never even had a serious relationship. Truth is, I only casually dated when my brothers insisted it had been too long since I had." He stared into her eyes, and she found herself mesmerized by the shift from gray to green and back again. "What I'm saying is I'm not the same as this idiot you were with. And I would very much like to take you out tonight and treat you like you deserve to be treated."

She closed her eyes for a moment, if only to stop the hypnotism. After taking a deep breath in through her mouth and very slowly releasing it out through her nose, she opened her eyes and said, "Okay. Let's go out tonight. Casual?"

The smile transformed his face, and his eyes lit up as if a light shone behind them. "Casual. I'll be here at six."

She walked him to the door and shut it behind him, leaning against it with her arms crossed over her chest. "And just what was that, Daisy?" she asked herself. "Just agreed to go out with Ken Dixon? Oh, sure. Keep it casual, Ken? Oh, man."

Chapter 5

Daisy carried the cupcakes through the back door and set them on the kitchen counter, making sure the red and blue frosting she'd piped on each one hadn't gotten damaged too badly during transport. "Mamá? Papi?"

"In here!"

She found her parents in the hallway. Her father, Marcus, wielded a mop. He was tall and thin with salt and pepper hair. He wore red pajamas and a dark blue robe. Her mother, Rita, wore a pink house dress and fluffy green slippers. She still had thick, black hair that fell in waves to her shoulders. She glanced at her over her shoulder. "The bathroom sink had a moment earlier. Thankfully, your uncle knew exactly how to fix it and talked Papi through it."

Daisy grinned. "I guess all those years with a plumber for a brother paid off."

"Happy Fourth of July." Her mom gestured with her hand, and they walked back into the kitchen. "Thank you for the cupcakes. Are you staying?"

In a couple of hours, her parents' home would fill with teenagers for a backyard pool party celebrating the holiday. In every church he'd served as a youth pastor, he'd had this annual Fourth of July party. Daisy had never missed one. "Actually, I have a date."

Her mom raised an eyebrow. "Jason?"

Trying not to shudder at the sound of his name, Daisy said, "No. We broke up last week. This is with Ken Dixon. Remember him?"

"Ken Dixon? Of course! Although I'm not sure which one was Ken. I do remember the Dixon brothers, though. I even remember one time they switched their names just to mess with your dad. It was rather funny." She cupped her mouth and said in a conspiring whisper, "Your Papi didn't think so."

Daisy chuckled. "Well, apparently, his family is having a big thing at Ken's cabin on Lake Oconee. So, I'm going out there. I think he'll even do a big firework show from the water."

Her mom grabbed two coffee cups and headed for the carafe. Daisy did not tell her mother she didn't want coffee because she didn't want to explain why she didn't want it. "So, how did you end up on a date with Ken Dixon?"

"His company's donating the materials and equipment to build the house we're raising on Labor Day. Our paths just kinda crossed."

Her mom handed her a coffee cup then toasted her

with her own and said, "I love it when God does stuff like that. Don't you?"

Thinking of the way she'd likely disappointed God and how she deserved no special arrangements filled Daisy with embarrassment and shame. Her cheeks heated, and a bitter taste filled her mouth. "I do. Especially when you can look back and see it." She set the untouched coffee cup in the sink and said, "I have to run. I have barbacoa in the Crock-Pot, and I need to make some tortillas to go with it. I was telling Ken about it last night, and he insisted that I make some for him. I'm going to surprise him with it today."

Her mom grinned. "Cooking for him already?"

"Mamá!" She kissed her cheek and breathed in the familiar smell of cinnamon. "I'll see you soon."

"Have fun with Ken Dixon. You have to tell me everything. Can't wait to hear about it."

"Tell Papi bye for me. Have a good party!" Making a mental list of everything that she had to get done between now and the time she needed to head to the lake, Daisy went back out the back door and headed to the grocery store. She knew it would take an hour to drive there, and possibly more depending on traffic. Ken had assured her she could use the oven there to warm up her dish.

At home, she spent the next hour making a couple dozen corn tortillas, then packed everything into her car and followed the directions to Ken's lake house. On the drive, she had a talk with herself.

"You know, of course, that this will only end in heartbreak. You need to *tell* him not cook for him."

She grimaced and met her eyes in the rear-view mirror. "But, he's so nice and so, you know, Ken Dixon. I can enjoy today, right?"

Focusing back on the road, she gritted her teeth and said, "No, but apparently, you're going to, anyway."

She arrived to find cars and trucks filling the dirt and pine straw covered yard. She'd pictured a wooden cabin, like one would find near a snow-capped mountain, not the square gray-stone structure with the red tin roof. When she went inside, though, the beautiful tile floors and fully furnished kitchen surprised her. The kitchen opened up onto the main room that contained tables bowing under with food. She set the stone crock in the oven she'd asked Ken to preheat. It would need more than a few minutes to get back up to temperature. She found the spot reserved for her dish and set the basket of tortillas next to the empty Crock-Pot shell. She looked up as the door opened, and one of Ken's brothers came in.

"Well, if it isn't Daisy Ruiz, as I live and breathe," he said.

She smiled because she liked both of Ken's brothers. She used to have the ability to tell them apart when they spoke, but apparently, that skill had declined over the years. "And you are...?"

He laughed and said, "Jon."

"It's good to see you, Jon. It's been a long time."

"It has. How's your brother? It's been a couple years since I've seen him."

"He's doing very well. Still at a church in Panama

City. DJ is a joy and has just started saying auntie."

He walked into the kitchen and opened up a door revealing a large walk-in pantry with an ice maker. He grabbed a cooler from a shelf and filled it with ice. When he lifted the cooler, his muscles rippled beneath his T-shirt sleeves. "Ken's out there. I can take you if you want."

"Thanks. I'm just about done." She found a dish towel and used it as an oven mitt to take the crock out of the oven and carried it over to its shell. She plugged it into the extension cord someone had run to the table, then put the glass lid on it and turned to Jon. "All done."

He wiggled his eyebrows and said, "That smells amazing. I remember your mom's barbacoa. I know where I'm headed first thing."

Jon led her out the door he'd come through and gestured with his chin toward the dock. Then he carried the cooler of ice in one direction, and she walked down to the dock in the other. A large tent covered about twenty tables and chairs. Red, white, and blue flags hung from banners all around the edges of the tent. A couple played volleyball at a net, and another group swung from a rope swing and fell into the lake. Country music piped from somewhere to the speakers set up all around the perimeter. As she walked into the crowd, she realized that she didn't really recognize anybody. Finally, she found Ken.

He wore a pair of red shorts and a dark blue tank top. Sunglasses hung loose on a strap around his neck. He had a red cap with the black Dixon Contracting logo.

"Hey, Ken."

As soon as he heard her voice, he turned in her direction with a smile covering his face. "Daisy!"

When she approached him, he put his hand on the small of her back and gestured at the woman standing in front of him. She had blue hair pulled up into pigtails with red and white pompoms fastening them. She'd secured a sparkly blue star on the side of her face. "This is Brad's assistant, Sami. Sami, this is Daisy Ruiz."

Daisy looked down at her simple outfit of cutoff denim shorts and a sleeveless white shirt and felt a little less patriotic. "I love your style," Daisy said. "I would never have the guts to pull it off."

"I often get a double-take at work after people see me at a party." She laughed. "Most of the extreme hair color is temporary."

Ken grinned. "Think this is something? You should see her at Christmas."

Sami excused herself, and Ken gestured to the raft next to the dock. "Hope you're up to going out on the water with me tonight. There's nothing like fireworks when you're surrounded by water."

"I'm looking forward to it."

He had taken her to a jazz festival yesterday. They'd had the best time walking around, listening to different jazz performers, eating food on sticks, and drinking frosty fresh lemonade. They'd stayed until well past sundown. When he drove her home, he insisted that she come today. Even though she promised herself she would say no to the next invitation, she found herself agreeing to come and then looking forward to it all morning.

The music stopped, and a sharp whistle sounded over the speakers. She turned and saw Ken's dad, Philip, standing near the big white tent with a microphone in his hand. Like his sons, he stood about six-six and had a brown and gray goatee. She remembered being so afraid of him when she was younger. One day, she'd fallen in the church parking lot. He'd helped her to a bench where he tended to her bloody knee in such a gentle way that she'd never felt intimidated by him again. In a deep voice, he said, "We're going to ask God to bless this food! Bow your heads, please."

Silence descended upon the crowd. Philip prayed a prayer of thanksgiving over the nation's birthday and then asked God's blessing on the food. As soon as he said amen, the music started back up, and people headed into the building to get their dinners.

While milling around, waiting for the line to die down, Ken introduced her to Brad's wife, Valerie. Valerie had beautiful skin the color of rich milk chocolate. She wore an orange sundress that perfectly complemented the caramel color of her eyes. "It's nice to meet you. Ken talks about you often."

It felt weird to say that because she had only spent a little bit of time with Ken. But in several conversations, he exuded his love for his family.

Valerie smiled and cut her eyes toward Ken. "I wish I could say the same thing. You have Auntie Rosie and me just dying of curiosity. Ken never dates, and Auntie

Rosie remembers you from church. Somehow, I don't remember you, but I do remember your parents."

Daisy really appreciated her directness, even if it made her laugh a little nervously. "Since Papi led the youth boys, they spent a lot of time at our house during my formative years." She put a hand on Ken's arm. "I would love to know some stories from when he was younger. I understand you have all the scoop on that."

Valerie threw her head back and laughed. "I have so much scoop. You can come to me and get it all."

Ken said, "Hey now. Let's save the dirt for a little more time to go by, can we?"

Valerie shrugged, and her eyes gleamed with amusement. "We'll see how it goes."

For the rest of the evening, Ken stayed by her side. He introduced her to friends and family and coworkers and made her feel like the most important person there. As the sun went down, he helped her onto the flat wooden raft. She fastened her life preserver and helped him untwist a strap on his. "You're going to want these," he said, holding out a pair of headphones.

It surprised her how much noise just went away once she slipped them on. She could even hear herself breathing. She slipped them back off and let them hang around her neck. The din of the crowd and the sound of the music immediately returned.

"Those are for the shooting range. But they work great here."

Once he secured the raft, he showed her his sequence of order for lighting the fuses. Jon manned the music they had choreographed for the fireworks. He pulled out his phone and accessed the stopwatch.

"What can I do?" she asked.

"Just have a seat. They're already set up in order. I just have to light them. So, the hard work's over. Time to enjoy the fruits of our labor."

She sat down, feeling surprisingly steady on the flat craft. During their short journey, the sky had gradually darkened. "Here we go," he said, then hit a button on his phone. Seconds later, he said, "Thirty seconds." He hung up without saying anything else and started the stopwatch.

Thirty seconds later, she slipped the headphones back on while he lit the first in the line of rockets. Seconds later, fireworks lit up the night sky with glorious white and red colors. All around her, the water reflected the explosion, and it felt like she bathed in the light.

A grin covered her face as the show encompassed her. The fireworks exploded overhead, filling the night with color and flashes of pure light. For fifteen minutes, Ken lit fireworks in sequence to his stopwatch. He focused entirely on his job, allowing her to watch him as much as she could in the flashing, dancing, reflecting light.

As soon as the last rocket flew up into the air, he sat down next to her so close that his arm brushed against hers. "Grand finale," he said loud enough for her to understand him through the headphones. She smiled at him and leaned against him. Soon his arm came around her. Nothing had ever felt more perfect than the weight of Ken's arm. She leaned into his chest as the last of the embers dissipated into the sky that suddenly seemed so very, very high.

Daisy slipped the headphones off and let them rest around her neck. She and Ken sat like that for several moments before he pulled her close and hugged her. She felt as if she soared higher than any of the rockets that had just raced high overhead. The air felt crisper, and the world vanished except for the feel of Ken Dixon's arms around her.

"You did a great job," she said.

He waved a hand dismissively toward the spent explosives. "I do this every year. Once you plan it out, it's not so hard." As they slowly maneuvered their way back to the dock, Ken said, "I really enjoyed the dish you brought. What meat did you use?"

"My family's tradition is goat, but I couldn't find any, so I used lamb. Similar flavors."

He nodded. After a moment, he said, "I think I'd like to try the goat."

Pleased, she smiled. "I think I'd like to make you some."

When they approached the dock, Brad and Ken both helped secure the raft, then Brad held his hand out to help her up onto the dock. She stepped back as Ken hopped off the raft.

"We'll leave them on the raft for now," Ken said. "That way, they completely cool before we throw them away."

She looked at her watch. It was already well after ten. "I'm going to start heading back." She lifted her hand at his brothers and said, "It was so good to see you guys again."

After they said their goodbyes, Ken held out his hand. "I'll walk you to your car." It felt natural to slip her hand in his. It took several minutes to work their way through the crowd of people wanting to thank Ken for the fireworks. Eventually, they made it into the house, and she grabbed her empty dish that someone had already washed. She found the basket and slipped it into the dish, then set the lid on it.

"Looks like it was a hit," Ken said, taking the empty slow cooker from her.

"It always is with my family." By the time they made it out to the yard, more than half of the vehicles had gone. She looked at a pup tent in a nearby clearing.

"A lot of folks will just camp out here tonight." He set her slow cooker into the trunk of her car. "I couldn't convince you to, could I?"

She didn't think he meant that in an underhanded way, but she still giggled a little nervously. "No, I'm afraid I have to go. But I bet it's fun to camp out here."

He used his head to gesture toward the house. "I have a bed there. It's built into the wall. That lets me use that main room as living, dining, or bedroom without having my bed out in the open."

She would enjoy seeing the way that worked. "Roughing it, I see."

He chuckled. "There'll be a lot of tents out here tonight, but I'll be in the bed. I won't be the one complaining."

She opened up her door and turned to face him. "Thank you again for inviting me."

Ken stepped forward and surprised her by cupping her cheek with his hand. She could feel his rough palm against her skin. "I had a selfish reason."

"Selfish?"

He nodded, his eyes never letting hers go. "I've wanted to kiss you since last night."

She gasped, imagining it as she had hundreds of times. In an unusually bold way, she asked, "What's stopping you?"

Even in the darkness, she could see the flare in his eyes. Seconds later, his mouth covered hers. The feeling of his lips against hers stunned her, sucked the breath right out of her body. She put a hand on his chest and just left it there, unable to move, just feeling his heart pound against her palm. He ran his hand down her neck, and she felt his touch all the way through her chest and down her body to her toes. She relished the feel of his lips, the smell of him, the taste of him.

When he lifted his head, she realized she clutched his shirt in her hands. He looked down at her face and gently brushed the side of her cheek. "Can I see you tomorrow?"

"Yes." *Yes? Yes? What do you mean yes? Are you crazy?* "Yes. I hope so. I should be free by late afternoon."

She knew she shouldn't see him ever again. But somehow, standing up here on the very peak of the mountain, her heart once again overrode her brain. Then he gave her one more hard kiss that stole her breath and every thought. He stepped back and said, "Please let me know when you get home."

As she drove away, she brushed her lips with her fingertips, trying to remember how it felt to have Ken Dixon kiss her. As many times as she had imagined it, nothing compared to the real thing. Nothing. She could lose herself in kisses like that.

She looked at her reflection in the rearview mirror. "You are absolutely insane, Daisy. You cannot keep doing this."

She looked back at the road, shaking her head. Her mouth tingled with the taste of Ken Dixon's lips.

The clock on the coffee maker read four-thirty. Ken hit the button, and the sound of beans grinding filled the little kitchen. While the coffee brewed, he slid his Bible across the table and found the spot where he'd left off yesterday.

As he stared at the paragraph he'd just read three times, he couldn't remember what it said because kissing Daisy good night on Saturday night overwhelmed his thoughts. Nothing had ever felt so good and right as that kiss, as if he'd waited his entire life for that single moment in time.

He lived life as a cautious, careful man. Ken was the brother who didn't jump his bike over homemade ramps and break a leg or impulsively talk back to adults. He made sure to make every move careful, methodical, concise. He made plans, wrote lists, and systematically managed every minute of his life, content and at peace.

Ever since Daisy came around that corner of the cubicle, chaos suddenly interrupted his perfect order.

His thoughts weren't clear. He had a hard time staying on task. He just wanted to call her and listen to her voice.

And kiss her.

He could feel her hesitation to date him, and he could sort of understand. The idea that some other man had used her so deviously filled him with anger. Even though he wanted to know more about it, he didn't want to pry or press. He hoped she would eventually trust him with the story on her own. If he had the responsibility of a woman's heart, if she loved him, he would do everything in his power to protect her and everything he could to prevent harm from ever coming to her. He would never use her and discard her.

He also couldn't help but think about the wife of that man. What would it be like to have a spouse who could treat other people that way? Personally, he held his integrity to very high standards, and he just naturally expected all men to do so as well.

Maybe the problem lay in his expectations.

Either way, he needed to figure out how to break through the barrier that Daisy had put up because of that other man's actions. He wanted to make sure she knew she could trust him and that he would never do anything to hurt her. It certainly had become a matter for centered prayer for him.

He closed his eyes and tried to focus on this time he had set aside to spend with God, not to get distracted by chaotic or judgmental thoughts about another human being. He needed this time to center his day and set his focus. Feeling more in control of his mind, he went back to the spot he left on in the book of James and continued reading.

An hour later, as he raised his head from his prayer, his phone rang. Only one of his parents or brothers would call this early, and they often did. "Hey," he said to Jon.

"Hey. The Nashville tornadoes destroyed the home of an employee last night. Can you put her into one of your apartments since you haven't closed yet?"

He thought about the empty units in building three. "Yeah, sure. If she signs a lease, we can make her part of the closing agreement. We've had people moving in as each building gets finished. I have eight apartments ready to go right now."

"Thanks. She's a good kid. She just needs a break right now."

"Being a Dixon Company employee just became that break," Ken snorted. "We can throw in furniture and put her up rent-free for the first sixty days."

"You're way ahead of me. Thanks, Ken."

His mind started clicking into gear. He opened the key box and grabbed the key for apartment 311. On his way out the door, he poured a cup of coffee. As he crossed the parking lot, he looked over at the cars parked under the streetlights in front of the first two buildings. It always felt good to know people lived in a building he built. This one, he and Brad had spent two years ripping apart and putting back together. He knew it would have required less work to knock everything down and start fresh, but he personally gained so much satisfaction with every swing of the sledgehammer, every installation of a kitchen counter or cupboard. He hadn't asked, but he guessed the woman Jon had called about was his assistant in Nashville. Knowing her tiered salary, he chose a first-floor apartment in building three.

He let himself into the freshly painted apartment. The door opened onto a foyer with the door to the laundry room immediately on his left, and the hall closet on his right. He could go right and head to the master bedroom or the doorway to the kitchen. Instead, he walked straight into the living room. They'd stocked it with very simple furniture that lacked any true style or color, giving the resident plenty of room for expression. A gray couch and matching chair sat on the teak hardwood around a coffee table.

He thought he'd have a television installed since she'd lost everything in a tornado. He knew one bedroom held a double bed, and the other was empty. Maybe he'd ask his mom to set up the kitchen for her.

He wouldn't normally go to this much trouble for a new tenant, but Jon really respected his assistant's skills and work ethic. As an employee, he considered her a member of the family. The Dixons took care of family.

He took a couple of pictures to send to his mom. On his way out of the apartment, he called her.

"Good morning, son," she greeted.

"Hi, Mama. Jon's assistant lost everything in a tornado last night. She's coming to work for him here, and I have a furnished apartment for her. Can you maybe stock the kitchen and do sheets and stuff? She's coming with nothing."

"Of course, I can. I have the whole morning free. Can you get me a key?"

He thought about how much time it would take to get to his parents' house and then make it to work on a Monday morning through the horrendous Atlanta traffic. Instead, he said, "Brad has a key to my apartment. If he's still there, you can get it from him. Otherwise, I can leave my door unlocked, and you can get the key off of my counter."

"Let me check. I'll let you know."

"Thanks, Mama. Apartment 311."

Once he settled that business, he kicked his shoes off and went into the small yard outside the area he used as his apartment. As the sun rose, he got into the starting stance and then performed a series of taekwondo forms. Keeping his mind focused on his body, how his muscles moved, and the perfection of his stance and kicks, he went from the white belt form and progressed up to the third-degree black belt form. It took him just under thirty minutes to go through them all. When he finished, he went back into the beginning stance and started on the judo forms.

Martial arts gave Ken a deep sense of calm and allowed him to stay centered throughout his day. He focused better the mornings he gave his complete attention to the workouts.

He and his brothers had all taken Taekwondo all through middle school and high school. As soon as they achieved black belts, Jon and Brad had just coasted, but he wanted to discover other martial arts. He went on to Judo, got his black belt, and currently had a high Aikido belt as well. His brothers jokingly called him an overachiever, but he knew they respected his skills.

As he finished the last kick, he brought his body back to the starting form and relaxed. His muscles felt loose, and sweat trickled down his back. He rolled his head on his neck and headed into the apartment to take a quick shower.

Ken occasionally still went to his old dojos whenever his instructors needed an extra hand with the younger kids. He enjoyed working with them and seeing them progress through the ranks. His mind wandered to Brad and Valerie and the baby. A warm, loving feeling flowed from his heart, imagining a child that would be a blend of Brad and Valerie. He wondered if he would ever be a father, and unbidden, his mind went back to Daisy.

They had enjoyed an early dinner yesterday before she had to go back to her church. They'd grabbed a bucket of chicken, then went to a park and watched the ducks swim in a pond while they chatted and ate. Ken had kissed her goodbye and promised to call her this morning. He wondered if six-thirty was too early and realized he should have asked.

Ken found dating rituals uncomfortable. He found making small talk more like some kind of torture. He could count on one hand the number of women he had dated. Instead, he found his social contentment with his family, people who understood his stretches of silence and didn't require chit-chat when unnecessary. Even more than his family, he enjoyed the times he spent alone, no conversation necessary, no one to pull him out of his own head and force unwanted discourse or bothersome social rituals.

But with Daisy, he felt like a whole person. He found that very odd because he had never considered himself incomplete until he shook her hand that day.

With his hair still wet from the shower and his cheeks tingling from aftershave, he sat down with his notebook and made a list of things he needed to accomplish this morning. Using his phone, he wrote a quick email to a friend who worked as a loan officer at a bank and asked him to keep an eye out for a construction foreclosure. His friend had hooked him up a couple of times with houses that construction companies never finished building. With an original investment of way less than the house's worth, he would finish building it and sell it with a nice profit. Since he could perform most of the work himself, he considered it an easy moneymaking venture. Banks usually just wanted to get back the money they had invested.

If he didn't hear back from him within a week, he would go ahead and plan to move into one of the empty apartments. He had plenty of options.

After he showered and ate some breakfast, he checked the time again. It was seven-ten. He could probably get away with texting. Ken found that rather ironic because he personally hated texting. He just didn't want to disturb her with an actual call too early.

> Good morning. Thinking of you. Wasn't sure if it was too early to call, but I wanted to say hello.

After he grabbed his coffee cup and keys, he headed out the door. His mom had texted and had Brad's key, so he locked the door behind him. With a full day ahead of him, he had a feeling that the paperwork portion would take much longer because of this sudden inability to focus currently happening to his mind. Before he got out of the parking lot, he got a text back.

> Good morning. I'm an early riser. I've been up for hours.

A grin covered his face, and he actually laughed out loud. If he sat down and wrote out the perfect woman's exact qualifications for him, someone who ran a charity that helped people, loved Jesus, and an early riser would pretty much top his list. He looked up at the roof of his truck and said, "Thank You, God. I love seeing You work."

Chapter 6

Trying to ignore the overwhelming smell of flowers, Daisy leaned against the counter of her cousin Camila's flower shop. While Camila put together a dozen pink roses with baby's breath into a glass vase, she closed her eyes and took a deep floral-scented breath. Drawing from some inner courage, she announced, "I'm pregnant."

Camila stopped moving. She looked at Daisy with wide brown eyes, her mouth partially open, and then finally asked, "I beg your pardon?"

Daisy nodded. "Pregnant. According to the Internet, I'm due February twenty-sixth." Suddenly, sharp tears filled her eyes. "Oh Lord, what have I done?"

Camila rushed around the counter and pulled Daisy into her arms. "Oh, Daisy, I'm so sorry. What can I do?" She patted her on the back and then asked, "Is it

Jason's?"

With a snarl, Daisy replied, "According to him, it is if I let him pay for an abortion. Otherwise, he's already signed the necessary forms to revoke all of his parental rights." She wiped her eyes, wishing she could simply refuse to shed any more tears about this. "It is not his. It is mine. He's married."

"Married?" Camila gasped. "Are you kidding?" Daisy shook her head, and her cousin said, "Oh, I have a few choice words that would describe him. But I don't think God would approve, so I will keep them to myself."

Despite the conversation, Daisy chuckled. "You're the only one who knows."

"My cousin, your secret is safe with me. I have your back. If you need anything, you let me know."

After taking a series of deep, cleansing breaths, Daisy said, "I honestly feel a lot better now. I think I just wanted someone else to know."

"Is this why I haven't seen you at church?"

Guilt burned heat into her cheeks, and her stomach knotted. "I've been there. I've just been filling in with the kids. I had nursery last week and the two-year-olds the week before."

"Mmm hmm." Clearly, her cousin knew she had intentionally avoided the music and sermons. Camila went back to putting the bouquet together. "I have to finish this because Xavier will be here to deliver it in just a few minutes."

"I know. It's okay." She leaned against the counter again and drew her finger along the edge of an index card that Camila had taped to the glass. "I've also been dating Ken Dixon."

Camila stopped working again and stared at her. "Wait. The Ken Dixon?"

With heat flooding her cheeks, Daisy nodded. She knew that Camila knew about her crush on Ken from the moment it happened. Camila's brother Xavier attended youth group with Ken and his brothers. So, Daisy and Camila would often hang out while waiting for her older brother to get out of youth group. "How did you manage to get a date with none other than the Ken Dixon?"

She shrugged. "His construction company is funding a house project next month. He just showed up at my office. Neither one of us knew who we were meeting that day. Irene had set up the meeting without names." She met her cousin's eyes. "I tell myself after every date that I won't see him anymore. Then it's so perfect to be with him. But it's wrong. I'm not being fair to him." She made a small noise of frustration and looked back down at her thumbnail as it played with the edge of the tape.

"Daisy, you are not going to be a size two for very much longer. You're going to have to say something."

With a snort, she replied, "Yeah, I know. I've been practicing. How about this? Ken, I really like you, but I'm pregnant by this married guy. Hope you don't mind."

Camila nodded. "I see you've been working on what to say." She pursed her lips. "I don't envy you."

"Yeah." She straightened as she heard the bell ring,

announcing the opening of the door. "Me either."

She turned her head toward the door as her cousin Xavier strolled into the building. "Daisy! Good to see you." He looked at his sister. "So, delivery boy wrecked your van?"

Camila snarled. "Don't text and drive." She shook her head. "He's the third driver I've had this year. If I can't get flowers delivered, then I'm going to have to close down. And now my insurance is going to go way up. Again."

Xavier went around the counter and put his arm over her shoulder. "I got you, Camila. I work remotely. I can code all night and deliver for you all day. We'll get you through this."

Daisy watched them interact and realized how much she missed having her brother around. Maybe she would call him tonight.

"Guess who Daisy's dating." Camila wiggled her black eyebrows at her cousin. Daisy gasped, then put her hands to her cheeks.

Xavier finished going through the orders that had automatically printed as they came into the online portal, then looked her up and down. "Ken Dixon."

She gasped. "How in the world?" She looked from Xavier to Camila. "If I hadn't been right here with her this entire time, I'd swear she called you."

"No psychic powers between siblings." He held up a piece of paper. "He just ordered you a bouquet of daisies and yellow roses." Camila plucked the paper out of his hand, and he teased by asking, "Would you like to wait for them, or shall I deliver them?"

Before Camila could read the greeting Ken had sent, Daisy snatched the paper from her. She scanned the order and found the message block.

Thinking of you. Thought I would give you a reason to think of me. —Ken

"I guess it's good I said something before you saw this order, then," Daisy said. She fanned her face with the piece of paper. "Yes, I think I will wait for them. Thank you, Xavier. You are very kind."

She pulled out her phone and started to text Ken but decided to call him instead. She stepped far enough away from the counter that they would have a hard time hearing her. Over in the far corner of the flower shop, she examined the sunflower wreath hanging next to a sign that said, "Order your wreaths for August today."

Ken answered before the second ring finished. "Hi."

She smiled and turned her back on her cousins. "I don't know if you knew this, but my cousin Camila owns a flower shop. And, so, I was just hanging out here talking about my love life, and this order comes over the printer."

Ken chuckled and said, "Oh, yeah?"

"Thank you. I honestly didn't need any help thinking about you, but it'll be nice to have a visual."

"You've been talking about your love life, huh?"

She should feel nervous about flirting with him over the phone, but, somehow, she didn't. "I was. I really enjoyed watching the ducks with you yesterday."

"Me, too."

"Are you free tonight?" *What are you doing, Daisy?*

"As a matter of fact, I am."

This flirty banter is fun, but you have to tell him. You need to tell him. It isn't fair to grow this relationship any further without total honesty. "Can I cook you dinner tonight?"

"I couldn't imagine a more perfect evening. What time?"

Daisy silently pounded the flat of her hand against her forehead twice. "Six?" *You have to tell him!*

"I'll see you at six."

Say something. Say anything. Why did you call him in the first place? The flowers! Right! "Thank you for the flowers, Ken."

"Oh, you're welcome, Daisy. Glad they bought me a home-cooked meal." She chuckled as he said goodbye.

When she went back to the counter, she watched Camila put the finishing touches on her bouquet. "This is beautiful. Thank you."

As Camila pushed the vase toward her, she said, "You need to tell him. Quit putting it off."

"I know." Nerves danced in her stomach, and she picked up the vase. Her cousin kept staring at her skeptically. "I said I know." Daisy angrily jerked her head toward Xavier, and Camila relented.

"Fine. As soon as you get home, put water in the vase. There's already a solution in it to keep them fresh longer."

As Daisy walked out the door, Xavier made kissing noises and said, "Say hi to Ken from me."

Daisy chuckled and shook her head.

In the background, the hum of the dishwasher broke the occasional silence. Daisy sat cross-legged on her couch with her back to the arm and faced Ken. She held a glass of water and rolled it between her palms, hoping the cool feel of the glass might anchor her to her current reality and keep her grounded somewhere near sea level.

She'd grilled chicken and served it with Mediterranean flavored couscous and veggies. The baklava she'd found at the store had inspired the meal and provided the perfect ending to it.

Now, Ken sat in the center of the couch with his arm across the back and his body turned toward her. "Your cousin did a nice job with the flowers."

"I hope she refunded you your delivery fee." She smiled and turned her head to look at the beautiful bouquet sitting on her dining room table. The yellow flowers perfectly matched the turquoise and yellow decor of that room. "And yes, she did a good job with the flowers."

"I remember Xavier, but I don't remember Camila."

Her mind went to the days of youth group at that church. Camila would ride the bus home with her on Wednesdays. Xavier and Diego would walk home together from high school. Her aunt or uncle would pick up the cousins in the evening. "The nights she came over, she usually stayed in my room. They would come home from school with us on Wednesdays, so she was usually holed away before you guys got there."

He nodded. "Makes sense." He set his drink on a coaster on the coffee table. "I have my Wednesday family dinner tomorrow. Want to join me?"

She bit her lip and shook her head, wishing she had the freedom to join him for family dinner. "I have to go to a fundraiser tomorrow."

"For Gálatas Seis? What kind of fundraiser?"

"A local women's club is having a silent auction dinner. I have to go with Irene. She sets everything up. I just talk when it's my turn."

"Do that kind of thing a lot?"

She shrugged. "A few times a month. We have twenty people on our Board of Directors. All of them work with Irene to create fundraisers inside their spheres of influence."

He stared at her for several seconds before he said, "Love to go with you one time."

"Sure." She grabbed her phone off of the table and scrolled through her calendar. "There's one the last Tuesday of this month. It isn't a particular group. The restaurant contacted us about hosting it. The owner is contributing the food and staff. I'm really excited about that one. It's a Haitian restaurant."

Ken raised both eyebrows. "*Bon Manje*?"

Surprised, she asked, "How did you know that?"

He shrugged. "Friend of mine is the owner. She's an amazing chef. You should have a big turnout."

"I hope so. The money raised at this fundraiser is going to go to furnishing the house we're building in September."

"I'll be there. So will my family." His eyes lit up in excitement. "What about Thursday?"

She shook her head. "The second Thursday of every

month is a board meeting. My grandfather always brings food in."

The time had come for her to come clean. Her heart started pounding, and her mouth went completely dry. "Ken, I need to tell you something." Just then, her phone rang. She pressed her lips together and picked it up to see the caller ID. "Papi?" she asked as a greeting.

"Daisy, I'm at the hospital. It's your mother."

She stood. Panic grayed out her peripheral vision. Sweat beaded her upper lip. She needed her purse. And keys. "What happened?"

Ken stood with her and put a hand on her shoulder. Immediately, she felt steadier and calmer. Her father said, "Her blood pressure went very high. They're admitting her and giving her medicine through an IV."

That didn't sound too terrible, provided the medicine did its job. "Which hospital?"

"Atlanta community. She's in room 603."

She hung the phone up and looked at Ken with wide eyes. He put both hands on her shoulders and squeezed and rubbed. "Tell me where to drive you."

Thankfully, Ken drove because she didn't think she would have the focus to remember how to operate a car, much less how to get to the hospital. Ken asked her to buckle up, then he didn't say another word. He didn't ask any questions or try to make small talk. Even in his silence, she felt his presence, his strength. He silently soothed the turmoil in her mind. He drove safely and with precision. Within twenty minutes, they stood in the elevator.

Ken spoke for the first time since asking her to

buckle her seat belt. "Has your mom ever had issues with blood pressure before?"

Daisy shook her head. "No. Nothing that I knew about."

He nodded. "It's one of those things you don't know is bad until it gets really bad."

She leaned forward and rested her forehead against his shoulder. He ran a hand up and down her back. "I don't think I'm thinking very well right now. Thank you for driving."

He used his finger to lift her chin, so she met his eyes. "If you ever need anything, I'm here for you. Even if it's just giving you a ride to the hospital."

Did I truly only reconnect with this man less than a week ago? How can I feel like he had always had a presence by my side? How can I feel like he has always stepped up to help me? Maybe because he's never left my mind?

The elevator doors opened, and the sign on the wall told them the direction to her mother's room number. There they found her dad helping to shift the pillow behind her mother's head. He looked up as they came into the room. "Ola," he greeted. He glanced at Ken and grinned with recognition. "Which one are you?"

Ken smiled and lifted his hand in a slight wave. "Ken. Good to see you, Marcus."

"And you. It's been a long time. Maybe eight years?" He looked down at his wife. "Better?"

"Yes."

Daisy nervously stepped closer. "What happened, Mamá?"

Her mother replied in Spanish. "I just had such a bad headache. In the back, you know. And then I started seeing spots in front of my eyes, and I felt so nauseated. I tried to talk your dad out of taking me, but he insisted."

"*Beuna*," Daisy said. Good. Then she turned to Ken. "I'm sorry. I just realized that was all in Spanish."

He shook his head. "¿Era que?" he asked. Was it? With a grin at Daisy's surprised look, he included her father in the conversation and asked, "Get you a coffee or tea? Anyone?"

Marcus nodded. "Coffee, please. And, if you can, find some food? Neither of us have eaten. We've been here for hours."

Ken checked his watch and said, "It's nearly eight. I'll see if the cafeteria is still open. If not, I'll work something out."

Daisy walked to the door with him. He put a hand on her cheek, and she raised her lips for a kiss just as naturally as if she'd done it a thousand times before. "Thank you. You're my hero."

With a wink, he left. When she turned back to the room, both of her parents watched her with interest.

"Something to tell us?" her mom asked.

Blushing, she said, "You knew I was seeing him."

"No. I knew you went to a party at his house on the Fourth. I did not know you were kissing him in front of your father."

The laugh choked out of her. "I'm sorry, Papi."

He waved a hand in her direction. "I think you're old enough." He rubbed her mom's shoulder. "The doctor said it was good that I brought her when I did. She had a very dangerous blood pressure, and it wasn't coming down, so they admitted her."

"I'm so sorry, Mamá." She grabbed one of the chairs and brought it closer to the bed. "Is your head better now?"

"I don't know. They gave me something." She put a shaking hand on the top of her head. "I have medicine head, and I think the headache is still there, just masked by the painkillers."

"Well, tell me what I can do for you. Do you want me to call Diego?"

"Your father called." She held out her hand, and Daisy took it. "It's not anything you need to worry about. They said they'll do the IV drugs, and once it comes down, they'll get me a prescription that will keep it down."

"And we need to change our diet," her dad said. He pulled a pamphlet out of his shirt pocket. "I have a list."

Daisy took it and glanced through it. "This isn't too bad. No pork. We don't eat a lot of pork, anyway. You like papaya and guava, so that will be a treat."

"I'm considering a radical diet change until everything is fully under control."

She handed him back the pamphlet. "What do you mean?"

"Nothing but plant-based foods until we get everything regulated."

Daisy smiled, thinking of her parents' preference for beans and rice over meat and cheese. "With your diet, that would hardly be a change."

"But some change. Here and there." He rubbed her shoulder. "It will be okay."

Daisy could see the distress in his eyes. Clearly, her mom had given him a scare today. She stood and walked around the bed. "Papi," she said, putting an arm over his shoulders, "You did a good job getting her here, even if she didn't want to come. Let me know how I can help you with the new diet. I'm here for you." He leaned into her, and she squeezed him. "Now, have you taken time to pray?"

They called her brother, and while they had him on the phone, the three of them held hands. Daisy bowed her head and said, "God, we love you. And we know Mamá loves you. Please guide the doctors, give them wisdom and understanding, and help Mamá and Papi process everything to understand what's happening. Bring Mamá's blood pressure down to a perfect level and let her healing be a testimony to everyone who has anything to do with her for Your healing power. Give them both the strength to make lifestyle choices that will help her. We love You. Amen."

After each member of the family prayed, they let go of hands, and she took a step back, using her shirt sleeve to wipe at the tears in her eyes. When she looked up, she spotted Ken in the doorway. He held up some aluminum containers. "I just ran over to *Bon Manje*. Hope that's okay."

Daisy asked, "How did you get back so fast?"

Ken shrugged. "My friend Calla met me at the door with some beans and rice and a plantain dish."

"That's perfect," her dad said, taking the containers from him. "What do I owe you?"

"As many times as you fed me when I was a kid? Not a thing, Marcus." He looked at Daisy. She felt overwhelmed with emotion for him that she didn't quite know how to label. "You good for a ride? Want me to stay?"

Before she could answer, her dad squeezed the back of her neck. "Can you take Daisy home?" Daisy tensed. Her father met her gaze. "I'll call you if we need you."

With a frown, she asked, "Are you sure?"

"Positive. Let Ken take you home. We're in good hands here." He held up the square aluminum dish. "And now, thanks to Ken, we won't starve."

Back in the elevator, Ken pulled her close. He kissed the side of her temple and said, "I love that your family prays together. That was a beautiful thing to see."

It didn't require a response. She slipped her arms around his waist and squeezed him close.

Chapter 7

In the waiting room of the obstetrician named Doctor Reynolds, Daisy tried to casually look around at the women waiting with her. Most of them had someone else with them. She sat alone.

While pretending to read a magazine, she kept glancing over the top at the couple across from her. The woman looked quite advanced in her pregnancy and kept showing the man beside her pictures in a catalog. He wore a business suit but had loosened his tie and unbuttoned the top button. He kept looking at his watch and rubbing the back of his neck. She found him curious. Did he hum with nerves about the upcoming birth, about sitting in this room instead of in his office, or something else entirely? What was the source of his apprehension?

Forcing her eyes off the couple and back down to the open article on how to choose the right baby carrier, Daisy silently started lecturing herself on how she just categorized that man as someone who had something to hide simply because of her experiences with Jason. She immediately prayed that this specific brand of prejudice would not take root in her heart as if it pertained to all men.

Daisy knew good men. Her father, her brother, and her grandfather all came to mind. She had more experience with good men than bad and had no reason to assume all men hid some dark secret.

"Ruiz? Daisy Ruiz?"

She looked up and saw a nurse at the doorway holding an electronic tablet. She stood, grabbing her purse to take with her.

Sitting in the church nursery, she listened to two mothers nursing their babies while they chatted about their births. Both of them had Dr. Reynolds as their obstetrician, and both of them had nothing bad to say about her. That Monday morning, Daisy called the office the second they opened and requested an appointment. They'd scheduled one for a few weeks from now but called her this morning after a cancellation.

After examining her and taking some blood and urine samples for testing, Doctor Reynolds said, "Most everything looks great. Your due date is February twenty-sixth. We are sending a prescription for prenatal vitamins to your pharmacy on record." She sat on her stool and propped the tablet up against her thigh. She had short silver hair, violet eyes, and a ready smile. "Do you have any questions?"

Uncomfortable and nervous, clutching an ultrasound photo of what looked like a little kidney bean, Daisy said, "I probably have a thousand questions, but I honestly just can't think of anything right now."

The doctor slipped her glasses off and put them in the pocket of her lab coat. "There's something that my husband jokingly calls 'pregnant brain.' I want you to know that it's a real thing. Start keeping notes. If you think of a question to ask me, write it on something you'll have with you when you come to your next appointment. You're going to lose track of details and forget things. That's all perfectly normal. It's all part of the fun journey of bearing children." She smiled. "And I have staff on call at all times if you have any other questions you feel can't wait until your next appointment."

"Thank you, Dr. Reynolds."

When she got in her car, Daisy closed her eyes and rested her forehead on the steering wheel. Loneliness crept through her, tightening the muscles in her neck and leaving a gaping hole inside her chest. The ringing of her phone startled her. Ken's number flashed across her screen.

You have to tell him.

She stared at herself in the rearview mirror and said, "Not over the phone. I'll tell him in person."

She closed her eyes again, took a deep breath, released it, then answered the phone. "Hi, Ken."

"Hi. I scored four Braves tickets for tonight's game. Want to come?"

Thinking she just might need an energetic and fun

baseball game, she said, "Definitely."

"Great. My brothers can't make it. Jon's out of town for the weekend, and Brad's working on his house. Know anyone who can use the other two?"

She thought of Camila. "Maybe. Can I call you back?"

"Sure. Game starts at six."

"Give me ten minutes."

Instead of calling, Daisy drove straight to Camila's shop. She walked in and found her cousin carefully placing long-stemmed red roses into a silver box.

"Those are beautiful."

"Twenty-fifth wedding anniversary. Isn't that nice?"

She thought back to her parents' party for their twenty-fifth. "That's quite an accomplishment these days, isn't it?" She leaned against the counter. "Want to go to a Braves game tonight?"

"I always want to see the Braves. Unfortunately, increased insurance rates and fiscal responsibility." She put the lid on the box and slipped a silver ribbon around it. "Why?"

Daisy shrugged. "Ken is taking me. He has two extra tickets. Would you like to come? Bring Homer?" She thought of Camila's long-time boyfriend and how much he loved Atlanta baseball.

Camila raised an eyebrow and stared at her. Finally, she asked, "Did you tell him yet?"

Daisy sighed and said, "No. I was about to tell him, and Papi called about Mamá in the hospital. Like at that exact moment. So, no. Not yet."

Camila cocked her head and said, "And that was

three days ago. So, there's a reason you haven't said something in the last three days?"

"Being with him, it's like a dream. It's what I always wanted." Daisy frowned. She knew exactly why. Maybe being honest with Camila would help her be more honest with herself. "I just know once I say something, this dream will end. I'm just clinging onto it as long as possible."

Shaking her head, Camila said, "Daisy, it will only be worse..."

"I know. I know I know." Unexpected tears sprang to her eyes. "I just have always wanted this. You know that."

Her cousin leaned forward and said very softly, "It's not right. If you really want this, you'll do what's right."

Impatience had her snapping out. "Look, do you want the tickets or not?"

Camila pressed her lips together and said, "I will take them and bring Homer, but on the condition that you tell him by tomorrow."

She set her jaw. "You say I need to do what's right? I'll tell him when it's right for me." She turned and started to walk out, then turned back. "Game starts at six. Come to my house at four, and we'll eat first. Or don't. Whatever."

When she had her hand on the handle of the door, Camila called out, "I love you. I'm just worried about you."

Daisy knew that, of course. She and Camila had a relationship like close sisters. She wouldn't hurt her intentionally or try to steer her in the wrong direction because she did love her. However, Daisy felt like this thing with Ken had nothing to do with Camila, and she needed to keep out of it. She would not allow her cousin to pressure her into doing something she'd regret later. She already had enough regret to deal with for this lifetime.

Daisy set the platter of hot dogs on the table next to the buns. She'd chopped onions, diced pickles, and set out of a bowl of potato chips and a platter of sliced cantaloupe as well. Just as she finished examining her handiwork, the doorbell rang. She rushed to open it and grinned when she saw Ken on the other side of the door. "Just in time!"

She held the door wider, and he stepped into the house. When he put a hand on her waist and pulled her close, she readily lifted her face for a kiss.

For heartbeats that passed like hours, they kissed. Tension she hadn't realized even existed simply evaporated from the small of her back and her shoulders. She wanted to keep kissing him, but he pulled back with a grin and a chuckle. *Tell him. You have to tell him.* She opened her eyes and said, "I made hotdogs. I thought we could eat before we go to the stadium. My cousin Camila is coming with her boyfriend."

"I'm glad." He wore a pair of blue shorts and an Atlanta Braves T-shirt and ball cap. He had turned the cap around backward. As they separated from the kiss, he flipped the cap back around forward. "My parents have had these tickets my whole life. When my brothers and I got older, we all thought about getting our own tickets, but it's so rare for all of us to be free on the same game night, so we all just kinda share them."

"I'm always ready for a Braves game."

"You," Ken reached out slowly and touched the collar of her shirt. "You look fantastic."

She blushed and grinned. She'd selected a red skirt and a white Braves T-shirt. Copying Sami's look from the Fourth of July party, she put her hair in pigtails and had used some face paint her mom had to put the red A logo on her left cheek.

She'd felt silly when she looked at herself in the mirror, but Ken's compliment lit her up from the inside, and she was glad she'd gone to such an extreme. Especially when Camila and Homer arrived and her cousin asked her to paint her face as well.

Homer met Camila when he started going to her church. They both played instruments for the praise team. He stood tall and thin with shaggy brown hair and black-framed glasses.

He'd asked her out two Christmases ago, and the entire family waited with bated breath for the coming moment when he would surely ask her to marry him. Daisy and Camila had decided together that he probably wanted to wait for graduation before he popped the question. He had one semester of seminary to go.

Ken and Homer filled plates with hot dogs and fixings while Daisy painted the red A on Camila's cheek. She wore a blue T-shirt and white shorts. "I'm going to do pigtails, too," she exclaimed, then ran upstairs to the bathroom. Minutes later, she came back down, and Homer insisted on taking their picture. "You ladies look terrific."

Excitement for this double date made it so that Daisy could barely eat. She managed a few bites of melon and half a hot dog before they had to leave. "Let's just take my truck," Ken said. "I have a parking pass."

During the drive to the stadium, Daisy and Camila easily chatted, often bringing Homer into the conversation. As usual, Ken remained mostly quiet, but when he did speak, he interjected some quick wit and often had a smile on his face. Daisy knew he didn't enjoy chitchat and rarely spoke unless he had something to say. His relaxed demeanor and easy smile made her less worried about drawing him into the conversation.

They settled into their seats, right behind home plate. "I like night games," Ken said. "Never too hot, and the sun never gets in my eyes."

The hum of excitement in the air was almost visible. The smile on Daisy's face didn't go away the entire night. They sat in the incredible seats and cheered, sang, booed, and completely embraced the spirit of the game. When the Braves won with a double play in the ninth inning, Daisy honestly felt like she'd just watched the best game she'd ever seen.

At the end of the night, they waited in their seats for the bulk of the crowd to dissipate. Homer moved, so he stood in the row below them, facing them. "Dude, any time you have extra tickets, I am your man."

Ken grinned. "I'll keep you in mind." He put a hand on the back of Daisy's neck and squeezed. She thought she might give him about an hour to stop that. It felt so good. "Glad you came tonight."

"Me, too," Daisy said. "I don't think I've ever enjoyed a game more."

"These seats were unbelievable." Camila stood and slipped her purse over her head, letting it cross over her body. "I love the Braves, but it is so late, and I have an early flower delivery tomorrow. Do you think the crowds have thinned?"

Ken looked around. "Probably. Let's go."

Even though they had already waited for a while, Ken still had to battle a lot of stadium traffic to leave. It took nearly forty-five minutes to get from the exit of the parking lot to Daisy's driveway.

"I'll talk to you tomorrow," Camila said, hugging Daisy. "Thanks, Ken!"

Ken just waved and nodded. Camila and Homer got into Homer's car, and Ken walked Daisy to her door. He paused with one foot on the step and leaned against the brick wall. "I'm going to say good night here. My alarm goes off at four whether I like it or not."

She raised both eyebrows. "No break for a late night?"

He shrugged. "Nah. I have a system. I get my Bible study and workout in before I head to work."

Standing on the step put her at eye-level with him. She slipped her arms around his neck and leaned forward. "I guess we'll say good night here, then."

Passion flared in his eyes as she leaned into his kiss. As his arms came around her, it occurred to Daisy that she'd never initiated a kiss with him before. She loved the feel of the muscles moving under his T-shirt, the way he smelled like outdoors, and the popcorn they'd eaten. She thought she could just sink into him and kiss him forever. But, way sooner than she'd like, he put his hands on her hips and set her back away from him.

"Good night," he insisted, his voice gruff and low.

She pressed her lips together, still savoring the feel of the kiss, then took a step back. "Good night, Ken," she answered softly. "I'll talk to you later."

Chapter 8

The fishing pole jerked hard in her hand. Daisy squealed and stood, making the boat rock. Immediately, Ken had one hand on her pole and the other on her hip, guiding her back down to a sitting position. "You got this," he said. "Just set the hook and slowly reel it in."

Following his instructions, she gradually reeled in the fish. It jerked to the left and right, but she held firm. Ken kept his hand ready to grab the pole in case she lost control. Soon, he leaned over the side of the boat and scooped the large bass into the net. It jerked, splashing him in the eye.

"Nice one," he said, looking over his shoulder at her and grinning as he used his multi-tool to pull the hook out of its mouth. "Now, we have dinner."

He opened the cooler and dropped it in with a splash. The two bass Ken had caught earlier sat still in the water, their gills moving in and out. As soon as the other fish joined them, they all swam in aggressive circles, jockeying for position in the confined space.

"Do we have to cook it? Could we just let it go?"

Confused, he thought for a moment, then frowned and shrugged. "What's the point of catching it, then?"

"Well, we have yours, right?" She pointed down into the cooler. "The first one you caught is bigger, anyway."

The ruthless sunshine pelted down on them. To combat it, Daisy had put on a white, wide-brimmed canvas hat. She wore a red T-shirt and denim shorts. Over her shirt, she wore an orange life preserver. He didn't think he'd ever felt more attraction for her.

"You're right," he said. "We have mine." He reached into the cooler and scooped her fish back out. It wiggled its tail furiously. "You really want to toss yours back?"

"Yes, please."

"Alright. Hold out your hand, and you can toss him back."

She held a hand up in a halting motion. "No, no. You do it."

The fish plopped as it went back into the lake water. He silently stared at her long enough that she started to feel nervous. "What?"

"Just wondering what you're going to eat, now."

After a few seconds, Daisy realized he was teasing her and could not stop herself from laughing. Ken grinned. He set the net down and turned back to her. "You want to keep fishing?"

The expressions crossing her face made it clear that she did not want to stay out here, but she sat there obviously trying to decide how to word that thought so they could stay and keep fishing if he wanted to. The female brain fascinated him. He decided to end her misery. "I'm hot. Could use some of that air conditioning up at the cabin. Plus, I need to cook my fish while you figure out what you're doing for dinner."

Her face lit up in a way that made his mouth go dry. "Okay, sure. Let's head back."

Soon they had the boat under cover at the boathouse, and Ken carried the cooler around to the sink he'd installed over the water. A pump brought lake water through the sink, and the drain sent it back. On the side of the sink, he'd built in a thick wooden cutting board from oak and cedar. Daisy leaned against the wall of the boathouse as he set up to clean the fish. She slipped the hat off her head and fanned her face.

"Do you like it out here?"

He glanced at her. The red flush on her skin worried him slightly. He decided to watch her more closely. "Usually." He slipped his fillet knife out of its sheath. "At night, the bugs get a little loud. There's a family of hoot owls that lives up in those trees." He pointed in the direction of a copse of pines with the fillet knife. "But after the first night, I barely hear them until the next time I come back."

Daisy watched him quickly kill and begin to clean the smaller fish. "You like quiet, don't you?"

Naturally, Ken didn't bother to respond, making the answer to her question even more self-evident. His silence agreed with her and answered her at once. "Do you stay here a lot?"

"I buy bank foreclosures, refurbish them myself, and flip them. I do the work in the evenings and early mornings in-between my day job." He looked up from the fish and took a long, hard look at the property. He went back to scaling the fish. "I stay here when I need to stop work all the way. Biblically, that means at least once a week. There are occasions I'm here more often, but that's rare lately."

She looked around, and he tried to see the place through her eyes. She took in the little cabin with the foldout bed, the boathouse twice the cabin's size, the dock that stretched out far into the lake, the rope swing they used during summer parties. He considered this place his sanctuary from the world. For some reason, it felt terribly important that she see its beauty the way he did.

"Have you ever thought about living out here full time? Making this your home?"

How did he verbalize the depths of pondering he had dedicated to that concept? The emotions and the prayers? He thought about his desire to build a home on the adjacent acre where he would move when he retired, where his children and grandchildren and great-grandchildren could escape from the city's noise and lights and find peace beneath a blanket of stars. He'd build big enough to always have room for his brothers and their families. Did he give her the full rundown or keep it simple?

"Maybe someday. Not right now. It's an hour or

more into the city on a good traffic day." He slit the belly of the bass in one smooth stroke. "But, one day." He glanced at her as he pulled the innards out of the fish and tossed them into the lake. She wrinkled her nose, and he chuckled. "Ever clean a fish before?"

"No."

He held out the knife. "I'll teach you."

With some hesitation, she stepped forward and took the knife from him. He stepped aside and positioned her in front of the wooden cutting board. He stood slightly behind her and to her side so he could guide her hand with the knife. As he leaned in, he could smell the sun in her hair and feel the warmth of her skin. He took a deep breath through his nose and let it out before he spoke.

"Put the blade here. Yes. Right there. Now, run the knife around the head. Careful. That knife is really sharp. Ease up. Not so much elbow grease. Just let the knife do the work. Yes, like that." He put a hand over hers. The slight tremble in her hand made him curious. "Now press along until you feel the backbone. And go down. You hear that? You want that clicking sound as the knife touches the backbone."

"I'm sorry." Daisy dropped the knife and stepped to the side. "I think I got too much sun, but this is making my stomach upset."

The color fled her face as if someone had pulled the drain. He pumped water with the pedal at his foot and rinsed his hands. "Hang tight."

He rushed into the boathouse and onto his boat and grabbed a bottle of water out of the cooler. On his way back outside, he poured some water onto a clean towel. He found her leaning against the boathouse with her hands on her knees, and her head bowed. "This is gonna be cold," he said as he draped the towel over the back of her neck.

She raised her head and looked at him. "How bad is it for our future that cleaning a fish made me sick?"

He held out the bottle of water and crouched until he was eye level with her. "Every relationship has its challenges."

Something flashed in her eyes he didn't understand, then she accepted the water from him and took a small sip. "They make counselors for things like this, right?"

With a grin, he kissed her temple and straightened. "Feeling better?" She nodded, took the towel from around her neck, and wiped her face with it. "Good. Why don't you get on up to the cabin? Get the air conditioning going. I'll finish the fish. Just a minute or two."

Ken watched Daisy as she walked slowly up the hill toward the cabin. Once she crested the hill, and he couldn't see her anymore, he turned back to the fish. It took him three minutes to finish filleting them and discarding the carcasses. He set the fish into the container he had left out, then scrubbed the cutting board and knife, cleaned out the sink, and rinsed out the cooler. He stored the cooler back in the boathouse and carried everything else up to the cabin. He found Daisy curled up into the corner of the couch with the towel over the back of her neck again. "You still feeling puny?"

"I'm feeling a lot better." She looked up and smiled.

"The cool wet just felt better."

He held the container of fish up. "You gonna be able to eat this?"

"Are you kidding? I love bass. And this fresh? It's going to be amazing." She took a sip of her water. "But I am terribly embarrassed. I don't normally get queasy over things like that."

"No need to be embarrassed. It's really hot out there." He set the container in the refrigerator. "I shouldn't have kept us out so long."

"Gotta love Georgia in July." She looked around the room. "Why do you have a kitchen that's bigger than the living area? Hardly a single guy's sanctuary."

He examined the space. The kitchen had long counters, a double refrigerator, a big gas stove, and an oven built into the wall. The wide and deep double sink could accommodate restaurant-sized pots. By contrast, a couch and a chair crowded the small living space. Before he pulled the bed out of the wall, he had to move the chair into the kitchen.

"Easier to host parties when the kitchen can accommodate it. After the first big thing we had here, I redid the kitchen. Made it as big as I could and still have room to bring out the bed."

He moved to sit on the other side of the couch and turned to face her. Much to Ken's amusement, Daisy stretched out like a kitten. She spread her arms out and said, "I think if I had this, I would have a hard time going back to the city." She smiled. "Have you thought about putting in a screened-in porch to overlook the water?"

He had. He just hadn't taken the time to do it yet.

"It's on the list." He smiled. "You up to a walk? Cooled off? I can show you the whole property."

He wanted to show her everything. He wanted to take her to the acre next door and explain his dream house. He wanted to hike up the back trail that went around an inlet of the lake, let her see all the boundaries of his eight acres. She smiled, and her eyes lit up. "I would love to walk with you."

She stood and pulled a hair tie out of her pocket, then grabbed her hair and twisted and turned until she formed a messy bun on the back of her head. "Do I need the hat again?"

Mouth dry, heart pounding, he stood and shook his head. "It's mostly woods."

As she turned away, he put a hand on her shoulder, and she stopped moving. She turned to look at him, and he cupped her cheek with his hand. Without a word, he kissed her, wanting to convey what he thought and felt without having to formulate the words. Why did he always have to talk? He felt like he had talked all day, and it made him feel tired. Finally, he said, "Daisy, I'm really glad you're here."

He could see the emotions in her eyes when she said, "Me, too."

Daisy fielded a call from the bank that worked with her clients. The bank president sat on her Board of Directors. They had a deal that the bank would underwrite the loan for the land for the houses they would build regardless of the potential homeowners' credit scores, provided the homeowners had no current outstanding debts.

"Good morning, Nigel. How are you?"

"Great. We have a problem with the upcoming closing."

She frowned as she opened her desk drawer and pulled out the thick file for the Osborne family. "Oh? What's the problem?"

"Credit report shows an outstanding debt to Atlanta Memorial. It's small, but it needs to be resolved before we can finalize everything."

She grabbed the sticky note and wrote Atlanta Memorial on it. "How much?"

"Ninety-eight dollars. It is three years in arrears and is currently in collections."

"Okay. We'll take care of it."

She hung up the phone and looked up the number for Natalie Osborne. She answered on the second ring. "Hi, Natalie. Daisy Ruiz, here."

After a brief pause, Natalie said, "Ms. Ruiz. Hi."

"I got a call from the bank."

"Oh no, we're not to get the house, are we?"

The panic in the woman's voice was the kind fueled by the desperation of living a life where nothing ever turned out the way it ought to. She had worked with this family several times. The place where they lived had two bedrooms, and they had four children. Her husband worked as a laborer for a construction company and barely made a living wage. Natalie worked as a server in a diner but had to juggle shifts with available childcare. Their oldest son had special needs.

"The bank can't do the mortgage for the land if you have any outstanding debt."

Natalie paused and said, "We paid everything. Remember? It took us two years."

"Except for ninety-eight dollars to Atlanta Memorial."

She heard Natalie's intake of breath before she said, with a forceful voice that Daisy had never heard from her before, "No. We're not paying that bill."

"Natalie, you understand that if you don't pay this bill, you don't have land, so we can't build a house? You get that, right?"

"We contested that bill. We shouldn't have to pay it. It's wrong."

"What is a ninety-eight-dollar bill from the hospital for three years ago? That seems like a small amount."

"That was the last of the bill, from when Sissy was born. We were paying regular like we said we would, and then someone told us to get a list. What do they call it? With all the charges on it?"

"Itemization?"

"Yes! We requested an itemized bill and found out they charged us for circumcision."

It took a moment for Daisy to understand what Natalie said. "Circumcision on your daughter?"

"Yes! We wrote the hospital a note and said we wasn't paying anymore. And they told us we shoulda contested it sooner and that we had to pay it. So, we just quit paying."

Daisy nodded as if Natalie could see her. "Okay. I'll take care of it."

She hung up the phone and made some notes on the sticky note. Then she called Atlanta General and maneuvered her way through the automated phone system until she received a human being in accounting.

"Hi, I'm calling about a past due balance owed by Natalie Osborne."

"Is this Natalie Osborne?"

"No. I'm calling on her behalf."

She argued with the woman who answered the phone and finally managed to work her way up to a supervisor, her goal all along. As he answered the phone, she took a deep calming breath then explained the situation.

"I cannot discuss patient records with you."

"I'm not asking for the records. I'm explaining to you that you charged a young mother for the circumcision of her daughter. That debt needs to be removed from the account, and if they paid any portion of it, it needs to be refunded to them."

She heard the clicking and clacking of a computer keyboard, then the man's gruff voice returned. "This bill was turned over to collections more than two years ago. You'll need to settle the debt with the collection agency."

Struggling not to sound impatient, Daisy said, "I'm aware. I am explaining that Atlanta General turned an incorrect charge that was billed in error over to collections. I'm calling you so you can correct the error and remove the debt."

"I'm afraid that I cannot discuss this with you. Please have Natalie Osborne contact us." The line went dead.

Daisy stared at the receiver of the phone, unable to believe that he had hung up on her. She turned to her computer and typed out an angry letter with all the legalese that she could muster. She copied the hospital accounting department, the hospital director, the head of the maternity ward of the hospital, and the member from her Board of Directors who also sat on the hospital board. She had plenty of experience with hospital bills holding up her families from getting their land financed.

Once she hit send on the email, she printed the letter, signed it, and set it aside for Beverly to mail out to all the parties.

She imagined she would start getting replies to her email by tomorrow morning, no later than nine. She rolled her eyes at the ridiculousness of going through this over something that common sense should have taken care of the first time the family contacted the hospital. The helplessness of people without resources facing bureaucratic red-tape made her so angry.

"It shouldn't take this. It just shouldn't," she muttered.

She thought she might need to get up and go walk off some steam, but the phone rang. With Bev still running to the bank, she went ahead and answered it. "Gálatas Seis. How may I help you?"

"My name is Sasha. My cousin told me you helped him one time. My kids and I are about to get evicted from our apartment. Can you help me?"

Her anger toward the hospital accounting department dissipated immediately, and she pulled open the appropriate file on her computer. "Hi, Sasha, my name is Daisy. Let me get some information from you."

An hour later, she got off the phone with the apartment manager. She checked her bank account and decided to get Sasha and her children some groceries. On a whim, she called Ken. "Are you free? I have some extra money, and I was going to go pick up some groceries for a family in need. Do you want to go shopping with me?"

When she pulled into the grocery store parking lot, she found Ken waiting for her. Out of the norm, he wore a pair of gray slacks and a white shirt and red tie. She smiled at him as she got out of the car. She hadn't seen him since their fishing excursion on Sunday. "Wow, you're sure dressing up for construction work these days. Where were you?"

He gestured with his thumb over his shoulder. "'Bout a mile that way. New project breaking ground. Had a big hoopla with the press and City councilmen. It's Brad's job to smile pretty, but he had a conflict. Jon said he would cover it, but he had to go to New York for some reason, so he asked me to fill in."

She raised her eyebrows. "Fill in as in pretend to be Jon pretending to be Brad?"

He frowned. "No. We don't do that anymore."

"I never could figure out how you got away with it anyway. You're very different from Brad or Jon." Ken gave her a one-sided grin but otherwise remained still. She gestured at the grocery store. "Ready?"

"Definitely. Thanks for the invite. I like stuff like this."

She paused inside the grocery store and looked at the produce section. "I'm shopping for a single mom with three kids. I have no idea what their storage space is like, or even if they have electricity. Since Gálatas Seis just paid three months' rent to keep them from being evicted, I almost want to say there's likely no electricity. I think we need to be careful with what we buy."

"What's the address?" Ken pulled his phone out of his pocket. Daisy handed him the note pad that she had written the address on. She listened to him call the power company while she loaded the cart with apples, oranges, and bananas. He handed the pad back to her as he hung up his phone.

"What did they say?" Daisy asked.

He nodded. "You were right. No power. I paid the arrears and padded a few months and got it turned back on."

She shook her head. "You didn't have to do that. I would've gone through the proper process once I evaluated the entire situation."

"No doubt. Just saving time is all." He put a watermelon into the bottom of the cart. "Since the power was cut, we should probably assume they have no perishables at all."

She nodded. "Good assumption."

They bought canned meats, canned veggies, various kinds of boxed pasta, fresh meats, cheese, eggs, and milk. She saw yogurt with fun cartoons on the packages and bought a couple of packs of that. By the time they got up to the cash register, she had a full cart.

Ken followed her to the address. She recognized the neighborhood and the rundown apartment building. Only people with an income below a certain low threshold could live here. Ken grabbed two bags of groceries while she led the way to the apartment door. A little boy with a runny nose wearing a torn T-shirt answered her knock.

"Hi. Is your mom here?"

"Who is it?" The voice came from somewhere beyond the door.

She recognized Sasha's voice and said, "Sasha, it's Daisy Ruiz from Gálatas Seis."

Immediately the door opened, and a young woman in a fast-food uniform answered. "Daisy, thank you. You saved us. And the electricity, I didn't even ask for that."

Daisy gestured toward Ken. "We have some groceries, too. Do you mind if we bring them in?"

Tears filled Sasha's eyes and streamed down her face. "I don't know how to repay you."

She took the offered bags of groceries from Ken. He left to get more, and she stepped inside. "Sasha, I don't do this to be repaid. Help someone one day when you can."

The children danced around the groceries, exclaiming every time one of them pulled something exciting out of a bag. She wondered how many children in middle-class America got excited over groceries. Every child had bitten into a piece of fruit before Ken even finished bringing all the groceries in.

"Sasha, it's not a requirement to receive help from us. But, if you would like to attend, I do a monthly budgeting class. We can look at your total income and what you need for output and help you determine how you can keep up with everything." She put her card on the worn kitchen table. "Like I said, no pressure."

"Ain't no one ever wanted to help us before. Seems like I have to scratch and beg for everything." As she and Ken started to make their way out of the apartment, Sasha said, "Thank you."

"You're very welcome." Daisy watched the power and beauty of the storm of emotions raging behind Ken's eyes. She knew he wanted to whisk Sasha and her kids away and put them in a bigger, nicer home. She didn't need to tell him that Atlanta had thousands of Sashas, and they could only help as much as they could.

On the way down the stairs to the parking lot, he stopped her. "Thanks for calling me," he said gruffly.

She didn't understand why God had allowed someone as incredible as him into her fractured life. She stepped into his kiss and hugged him tightly to her. His body felt hot and strong, like warm metal. But his lips, oh, his lips, and his kiss made her entire body hum and vibrate. She thought if she could just keep kissing him, she might not even need to sleep, or eat, or breathe. All she needed was his kiss.

Chapter 9

Ken lifted the box springs and carried it from the building and out onto the trailer, setting it up against the side. The heat inside the trailer closed over him. As he walked back out, he took a deep breath of the fresh air and spied Jon as he got out of his truck. "Thought you were in New York."

Jon clicked the lock on his truck key fob and followed Ken into the apartment. Brad stood on a step ladder, unplugging the cords for the television.

"Got back about thirty minutes ago."

Ken nodded. "Good trip?"

Jon opened his mouth and then closed it again. "Surprisingly so." He turned his attention to Brad. "Need a hand?"

Ken left them attending to the television and went into the bedroom and grabbed his mattress. His buddy at the bank had come through with a brand-new home project that had closed down when the contractor failed funding. He didn't know anything about it, but that didn't bother him. He bought it as soon as he saw pictures of the foundation and standing framed out structure. Whatever the status, he could finish construction.

He carried the mattress out to the trailer and set it up against the box springs, then secured them both with nylon rope. Sweat poured down his face, and he used his shoulder to swipe at it. On his way out of the trailer, he grabbed the hand truck. Back in the room he'd used as a bedroom, he secured his dresser to the hand truck using bungee cords.

Soon, they had everything out of the building. They filled holes in the walls, painted the wall where the television had hung, and pulled up the old carpet.

"When's the floor guy coming?" Brad asked.

Ken picked up one end of the carpet, and Brad picked up the other. "Tomorrow. Eight."

They tossed the roll of carpet into the dumpster and went back into the building. Jon had removed the sink countertop that held the stovetop and worked at pulling out the cabinet. Brad grabbed a chisel and started pulling up the linoleum.

Ken looked all around. Any evidence that he'd used this area as a living space for the last two years had completely disappeared. He'd refurbished the bathroom yesterday, removing the shower and upgrading the sinks and toilets. Now, the big empty room stood ready for desks and partitions for an apartment building office.

"I think that's it."

"We did good work here," Brad said. "Now it's time to get us moved."

Ken crossed his arms and leaned against the door frame, thinking of moving Brad and Valerie out of the guest house on their parents' property and into their new home. "Tuesday, right?"

"Yeah, but we hired movers. I won't need help with the move. I need help with painting and landscaping."

"You're not hiring painters?" Jon asked.

"No. You see, my wife is an interior designer. There's something with colors and fabric and whatever that makes her happy."

Ken chuckled because Brad sounded very long-suffering. However, Ken knew Brad would lasso the moon if Valerie ever asked. "Yeah, you got it rough." He straightened. "I'm hungry."

Ken rode with Brad so he wouldn't have to haul the trailer to the restaurant. They all agreed on Chinese. Soon, they sat around the table sipping hot tea and munching deep-fried noodles while waiting on their entrees.

"So, the weekend in New York?" Brad asked Jon. "Did you see Alex?"

Fiddling with the rolled-up silverware, Jon said, "Not sure if I'm really ready to talk about that yet. However, I need to go back there again Thursday morning. I'll fly back that same night."

"Day trip?" Brad asked.

"Yeah," Jon confirmed.

That surprised Ken. Jon had spent so much time

away from home the last few years and for the last month had talked only of coming home and staying home. The thought that a woman could interfere with that plan really piqued his curiosity. "You've lost it for this girl."

Jon made eye contact and nodded. "There's more, but I'm not ready to share."

Ken respected that. He had to process things for a long time before he ever wanted to discuss anything. He rarely wanted to talk at all, even with family.

Brad moved his teacup as the waitress placed an appetizer platter in the center of the table. "We're here when you're ready, bro." He looked at Ken. "Where is the house?"

Ken pulled a crumpled receipt out of his pocket. He had scribbled the address in pencil on the back. "Ivey Lane? Ivey with an *e*, which is weird."

Jon frowned. "Don't know it. Where is it at?"

Brad's eyes widened. "That's on the way into my neighborhood. I wonder how close your house is to mine."

Ken thought about the maps he'd looked at. "It's too new of an address. Doesn't show up anywhere. I have basic directions."

Jon chuckled. "I can't believe you bought it without even inspecting the site."

"I saw pictures." Ken slipped the paper back into his pocket. "Besides, what does it matter? It's the shell of a house. There's nothing they've started I can't fix. And I have nothing but time."

They bowed their heads and asked God to bless

their food and fellowship, then they filled their little appetizer plates with miniature spring rolls and barbecued chicken wings.

"I've been home for two weeks, and I'm already missing the barbecue brisket in Nashville."

Ken's mouth watered at the thought of the restaurant Jon had discovered. Well, he overstated the place by calling it a restaurant. In reality, it was a shack with a smokehouse attached that only took takeout orders. However, he'd never tasted better barbecue in his life. "Be worth taking a job in Nashville for two years to eat that every night."

Jon shook his head. "You can have it, brother. I'm home."

Ken looked at Brad. "How is Valerie feeling?"

Immediately, his brother's face softened then transformed into a grin. Ken felt a tug in his heart, a desire to have a wife who brought that same look to his own face. "She's very tired. I'm trying to get her to go part-time at work so she can get more rest, but a lot of her projects are at critical stages. I think she wants to get everything into a good stopping place before she has the baby."

"I think that's marvelous," Jon said.

Brad had loved Valerie from the moment his hormones started flowing. When he and Valerie got married, Ken watched contentment come over his brother he had never seen before, much less experienced for himself.

"February seems so far away. I mean, it's July."

Brad shrugged. "It's kinda rushing at me, bro.

Ken laughed. "I bet."

Brad's eyes turned serious, contemplative. "And you and Daisy Ruiz?"

Immediately, Ken's pulse skittered. He thought of the sunlight shining on her hair and the way her brown eyes glowed when she smiled. "We went shopping yesterday. Groceries for a family she saved from eviction."

Brad sat back in his chair. "Honestly, if I was going to find the perfect woman for you, Ken, she would do things like shop for groceries for a family she had saved from eviction."

With a chuckle, Ken said, "Exactly."

Jon slathered hot mustard onto a spring roll. "Do they need anything else?"

Ken shook his head. "There's always someone else to help. Daisy says we got her back on her feet. The rest is up to her now. Tomorrow thirty more people will need help."

Jon chewed and swallowed. "I can't imagine the day-to-day drain on emotions that job takes. That is certainly a calling from God."

Ken agreed. He wanted to take that family today and put them in one of his luxury apartments with marble countertops, sunken carpet, and a swimming pool in the back of the complex. He wanted to spoil those kids and buy each one a bicycle and set up a college fund for them all. However, that wasn't Gálatas Seis's mission, and it wasn't up to him to do that. God had clearly equipped Daisy for what she did, and he couldn't imagine doing it himself.

Daisy's Decision

Like Daisy told him, several thousand more people in Atlanta needed the minimal help they had given Sasha today. No matter how fast she helped people, she said, more people took their places.

They sat silent for a few moments. Brad asked, "Can you see a future with Daisy?"

Ken didn't know how to word all the thoughts and emotions flowing through his mind. Did he see a future with Daisy? Absolutely. Did she see one with him? How could he expect her to know after just a couple weeks?

"That's my prayer."

Their entrées arrived just as Ken finished off the last of a chicken wing. As the waitress set the plate of General Tso's chicken in front of him and the steam wafted up and teased his nose. His stomach growled audibly, and his mouth watered. He thought about Daisy and wished she sat next to him and enjoyed this meal with him. He needed to find a way to quit having every thought that occurred to him get taken over by thoughts of Daisy Ruiz.

As Brad picked up his chopsticks, Ken asked, "So, what are we hoping for? Boy? Girl? One of each? Three of each?"

Brad smiled a sheepish smile. "Wouldn't that be fun? To have her have triplets? Mom and dad could have three to spoil at once. It would make up for us taking so long to give them grandchildren."

Jon shook his head. "Nothing will make up for that. Mom will make us suffer for that until our dying days."

All three of them knew that he spoke the truth.

Jon rubbed his chopsticks together. "Guys, I need to talk about something with you."

The seriousness of his tone gave Ken pause. He noticed Brad give his full attention, too. "What's up?"

"I can't do a mission trip this year." He expertly speared a bamboo shoot. "I know we were planning Guatemala in a few weeks, but I have something personal going on, and I need to stick to U.S. soil." He chewed and swallowed. "Besides, Brad has Val right now, and Ken is just getting things going with Daisy. Maybe we need to take this summer off."

Ken actually agreed. He didn't want to go out of the country for two weeks this summer—not without Daisy, anyway.

Brad said. "I think that's fair."

Ken nodded.

Jon relaxed. "I appreciate it."

"Anything we can help with?" Ken asked.

Jon shrugged. "Nah. I'm still processing. But, when I'm done, I'll be ready to spill it."

"Whatever you need, bro," Brad repeated, dishing rice onto his plate.

After opening her Bible to the place where she left off, Daisy pulled out a pink notebook and a purple pen and prepared to do some in-depth digging for her Bible study class next week. They'd completed their book this morning, and Daisy had offered to take the rest of the summer off, but the ladies in the class all agreed that they wanted to keep meeting. Consequently, now she needed to build a curriculum for the next six weeks.

After looking at all of her possible options, she had settled on redemption. But she didn't want to gloss anything over and just touch on the surface of redemption. She wanted to dig in to what it meant and what led up to Christ's role on the cross.

"God, I can't write something like this without You, but I feel like You and I need to have a talk." She stood and walked over to the stove, turning the heat on under the kettle. "I just don't know how to bridge this gap I feel. Obviously, I'm the one in the way." She grabbed a mug covered in three dimensional white and yellow daisies and tossed a tea bag into it. "I guess what I'm asking is that You place someone in my path who will help me reconcile whatever it is going on in my heart and mind that's keeping me away from You. Because I know that You have not set me aside. Your word tells me that that wouldn't happen. So, I know it's all this guilt and angst that I feel over my current situation. But that's hardly Your fault, is it?"

Steam wafted up out of the cup as she poured the boiling water over the bag. Daisy wished her stress and anxiety would waft off her and just dissipate into the air above her life.

Daisy took a deep breath and resolved to try to work even though she still felt this gap. She set the tea on the table. Just as she started to sit down, the doorbell rang.

She glanced up at the ceiling. "I assume this is somehow an answer to my prayer."

Finding Ken on her front porch did not surprise

her. She grinned. "Hi." She opened the door wider and stepped back. "Come in."

He slipped his keys into his pocket and stepped through the threshold. "Just left my brothers. We had dinner down the road."

"Hey, do people stare at you when you guys are in public together?"

He shook his head. "People stare. They always have, so we're used to it. Once in a while, I realize it, and it bugs me. But most the time, it just is what it is."

She rolled her eyes at herself. "I'm sorry. That was probably rude, but I'm just very curious. I bet it's when you're just with one of them, too, isn't it? Tall, handsome twins?"

He shrugged. "Usually." He gestured at the table. "I disturbed you."

"Actually, I was just getting set up. I hadn't actually started anything, so no disturbing." She led him into the kitchen so she could grab her cup of tea. "Would you like one?"

He gestured over his shoulder. "I can go. I don't want to interrupt your Bible time."

She waved her hand in the direction of her Bible and made a pfft sound. "I had Bible study this morning, and we finished our unit. I was going to outline a new study, but I hadn't fully fleshed out my idea yet. So, I'm letting it marinate a little bit longer."

She carried her tea into the living room and sat on the couch, nestling the corner against her back. "Did you get moved out?"

He nodded. "I was going to the new place, but I've

never been there before. Since it's already dark, I figured I'd wait until daylight."

She raised both eyebrows. "Where are you staying?"

"At my parents'. Could have stayed in an empty apartment, but my parents' is easier, and they already have coffee made in the morning."

With a grin, she said, "So, here is Ken Dixon with no work to do tonight. I don't think I've ever seen that Ken Dixon before."

He gave her a one-sided toothless grin. It looked like the left side of his mouth twitched. "Want to watch a movie or something?"

With a shrug, she grabbed the television remote and turned it on. She accessed a streaming network and clicked her way through to available movies. Once she had access to that menu, she handed him the remote. "You pick the movie. I'll go make popcorn."

In the kitchen, she tossed a bag of popcorn into the microwave, leaned against the counter, and then watched the bag rotate around and around through the filtered door. "I'm guessing You want me to talk to Ken," she muttered to God. "I hear You."

She huffed out a breath and dug through her cupboards to find a bowl big enough to accommodate the snack. As the buttery smell of popped kernels filled her kitchen, she put two glasses of ice on a tray, sliced some lemons, and pulled two bottles of sparkling water out of the cupboard. Once she poured the popcorn into the bowl, she balanced that on top of the two glasses and carried it all back into the living room.

Ken had chosen a dramatic biography of Neil

Armstrong. "Oh, I've wanted to see that," she said, setting the tray on the coffee table and moving the bowl off of it. "Good reviews."

"I remember," Ken said.

"You remember?"

Ken studied her, and his half-grin slowly transformed into a full grin. "You mentioned it once."

He took the offered glass from her, and she tried to remember mentioning the movie. That's right, over dinner on their first date, she tried to describe the type of movie she liked but couldn't narrow it down. She'd mentioned it then.

As he poured the water into his glass, she watched his profile. Honestly, he was the perfect man, especially for her. Attentive, attractive, giving. Without thinking about it, she reached out and put a hand on his shoulder. He turned and glanced at her, a pleasant expression on his face.

"I'm really glad you're here," she said.

"Yeah?"

She nodded. "Yeah."

He leaned forward and gave her a quick kiss that spread through her chest and all the way down to her toes. "Me, too," he admitted with a smile.

An hour later, Daisy sat next to Ken on the couch, curled up against his side. She had her legs crossed and the popcorn bowl nestled in between them. She tried very hard to pay attention to the movie playing but could only think about the baby in her womb and how Ken had gradually become the most important person in the world to her.

You have to tell him, Daisy. You can't wait another minute.

Without realizing it, she shook her head and replied to the voice inside her head that only she could hear.

We're just having a nice, quiet evening; just the two of us! Why wreck it right now?

She couldn't keep this secret much longer. Soon, nothing would hide it. Maybe she could take a job somewhere for the next six months and...

No. You have to tell him. Daisy Ruiz, you have to tell this man the truth.

She paused the movie and then shifted her body to face him. He looked at her with a raised eyebrow. "Everything all right?"

Suddenly she lost confidence. Actually, she really lost her nerve. She held up the empty popcorn bowl. "Do you want a refill?"

You're pathetic. Put down that bowl and tell him. Tell him right now.

He shook his head. "No, thanks. Still full from dinner."

Her shoulders slumped. She could not keep going on this way. "Ken, I find myself in a situation. And it's because I made a bad decision. No, that's not right. I made the wrong decision. And, yes, I had someone who helped that decision along, but ultimately, it was me. My choice."

She stared at her hands and waited. Nothing came from him. Finally, she looked up. He stared at her, his face mild, his half-grin charmingly in place, his eyes calm. Why hadn't he reacted?

"You need some kind of help?" He must have misunderstood her.

"No. Clearly, I'm not explaining myself well." She closed her eyes and let out a deep sigh while the voices in her head argued.

Say the words. Say "I'm pregnant." Just say it.

Her eyebrows knotted. *I need better words. I should rehearse exactly what I'm going to say.*

Finally, she opened her eyes and said, "You know what, it's okay. I'll tell you about it another time." She pressed play on the remote then settled back against him.

You are gutless. Spineless! Since when did you ever give in to fear? This is not just unfair to him. You're being unfair to yourself!

Feelings of cowardice and failure rippled through her. She knew the second the words came out of her mouth, Ken would pack up and leave. She would never see him again, and he felt so good beside her, so much better than the couch. He felt warm. He felt strong. He smelled like Christmas morning.

You aren't giving him a chance. If you tell him now, you might have a chance of keeping him. Keep putting it off, and it will seem like intentional deceit. Are you trying to lose him forever?

So what if she wanted just another nice evening with him? What could it hurt? The next time she saw him, she would tell him no matter what.

Chapter 10

As Ken backed the trailer into the spot next to what would eventually become a detached garage, he pondered the conversation with Daisy last night. What kind of trouble was she in? What kind of mistake had she made? Money? Legalities with her nonprofit? Something else?

He wished she would let him help her. For the last week, he could feel something off about her attitude. She was jumpy, almost a little manic sometimes. He would do anything in his power to help; she just needed to tell him how he could. He couldn't imagine an issue she had that he couldn't help solve. But, until he knew the issue, he had no power.

He reviewed every second they had spent together since they first shook hands that day. Had he done or said anything that might lead her to believe she couldn't trust him? Had he acted as if he didn't care about her? Ken knew that he had a tendency toward stoicism. Had his reticence misled her as somehow uninterested? It didn't feel like that when they touched or kissed. It didn't feel like that when they just spent time together doing anything at all, from shopping for groceries to fishing or munching popcorn.

He paused his thoughts about Daisy and looked at his surroundings. Most of the lot contained pine woods, but the contractor had cleared the area around the house, and the exposed red Georgia soil could handle sod. In his mind, he removed more of the pine and made a more expansive back yard, one with a pool or perhaps a fish pond. He had three acres here, with plenty of room to expand on the house.

The house had a pseudo-Tudor style, with cream and gray bricks, arched windows, and dark brown trim. It looked like it had a solid foundation. The packet he got from the bank said the contractor had reached the stage to consider it dried-in, which meant they had completed the roof and the exterior brickwork.

He'd read the completed scope of work. He knew the plumbers and electricians had completed at least the foundation of their work. Brad's new house was less than a mile away, so he could make do for a week or more if the need arose.

He walked up the wide front steps and surveyed the porch. Just a concrete slab right now, he could picture a decorative railing, furniture, hanging ferns, and a stained-glass wind chime. He walked around the porch, discovering that it wrapped the house completely and ended at the back where it looked like contractors had already poured the foundations for a deck. Ken liked wraparound porches. He liked porch swings, hanging ferns, and little tables with plants on them.

Back in the front of the house, he opened the front door and stepped inside. Plywood sheets lay where a floor should go. No drywall hung from the bare studs. He didn't see bare walls, though. In his mind's eye, he saw an entryway that led to a formal living room with a fireplace that dominated the exterior wall. Through another set of wall studs, he envisioned a large formal dining room with plenty of room for built-in cabinetry. In the area where plumbing pipes came up for kitchen appliances, he saw a room for the table over by that big picture window and the island that would divide the breakfast nook from the kitchen. He'd move this stud frame and that and create a kitchen large enough to handle a table filled with children. Around another corner, he stepped down into a den that led to that future back deck.

Imagining mahogany railing, he carefully walked up the frame of stairs to the second floor, watching where he placed his feet. He found the master suite that took up almost half the layout of the house. Down a hall, he found two bedrooms that shared a large bathroom and one more bedroom with an in-suite bath. Cautiously maneuvering back down the stairs, he looked up and saw the opening for a balcony railing.

Standing in the middle of the front room, he relaxed his mind and saw the studs, empty walls, exposed wiring, pipes, and open floor.

He went outside and stared at the detached garage,

making plans for a workshop addition and an apartment over the garage. He would have to get an electrician back out here right away to run at least forty amps into that building. Yes, this would do nicely.

In his truck, he pulled out a brand-new leather-bound notebook and opened it up to the first page. Taking the pencil out of its holder, he started scribbling notes. Two hours later, he had filled the notebook with sketches and plans, reminders, and ideas. He would open bids for subcontractors tomorrow.

He mentally pictured the work he needed to do and where he needed to start so he wouldn't box himself in. It was a big house, but not a giant house. He looked over his notes and sketches one last time. As he surveyed the details, Ken felt a sudden surge of joy.

This was not just a house. He had finally found a *home*. He had found a home where he could bring Daisy—and raise a family.

As he unlocked the trailer door, he heard the crunching of gravel beneath tires and turned his head to see Brad pull into the yard. He swung the trailer door open, and Brad said, "This was a find! Well done."

Ken nodded. "I wasn't sure what I'd find. It has good bones."

Brad walked up to the trailer and asked, "What goes first?"

Ken gestured at the fiberglass stall. "Need to install a shower and one of the bathroom sinks. Can you help me unload, then run to the store and get me a toilet while I'm installing?"

"Sounds like a plan."

They started unloading the trailer and carrying Ken's supplies inside his future home.

Irene shifted the large basket of baseball paraphernalia over and stepped back, examining the table filled with items for the silent auction. Tonight, she wore a maroon dress that flared at the knee and sparkly black earrings that dangled from her ears. Her outfit perfectly accented her wavy strawberry blonde hair and pale skin. She moved in her three-inch heels like she didn't even have them on her feet.

Irene had served as the fundraising coordinator for Gálatas Seis since Daisy's grandfather had gotten to the point of needing one. Daisy inherited her when she started running the charity.

Daisy knew invitations had gone out to hundreds of potential donors in the community to come and participate in the dinner and silent auction. Irene examined the table, tilting her head to the left and right, then said, "I think we're ready."

The restaurant owner, Calla Jones, had personally created a menu especially for the party. Calla had grown in popularity as one of Atlanta's most sought after chefs in the last few years, and her contribution to the fundraiser helped attract a lot of the ticket holders. Calla had donated the time of the kitchen staff and wait staff. She billed Gálatas Seis for direct cost reimbursement of the food, and nothing else. Knowing how much money Calla could have charged them to put on an event of this caliber humbled Daisy. She and Calla had talked a little bit one day last week about missions and priorities, and relationships with Christ. She knew in her heart that she had discovered a sister.

Finding out that Ken knew her brought another level of serendipity to her relationship with him. Apparently, Calla's husband worked for Ken, and she had once worked for Dixon Contracting as well.

To set up tonight, Calla had asked Valerie Dixon to come help. Daisy hadn't had a chance to see her since the Fourth of July party. She had spent the afternoon helping arrange tables and decorations.

"She's an interior decorator," Calla said as Valerie stood on a step ladder and tacked a nail into the wall to hold a string of lights. "I've never had a knack for visual things. I always have to rely on my friends. Valerie and my friend Sami helped design the interior of this restaurant for me."

"Sami?" Daisy asked. "I think I met her at the Fourth of July party."

Calla grinned and pushed her glasses up on her face. "If you're remembering red, white, and blue hair, then, yes, you did."

Valerie finished with the lights and climbed down the ladder. She brushed her hands on her yellow yoga pants then walked down the silent auction table. "What an incredible amount of donated items for your auction. I can't get over some of the things people are giving away."

"Irene does good work with the community. She always comes up with the best stuff." Daisy walked from basket to basket. She had signed baseballs with VIP tickets and weekend getaways. One painting company had donated an exterior house painting. "This woman can convince anyone to donate something. I always get nervous asking, but she just doesn't. Obviously, she's doing what God designed her to do."

Valerie crossed her arms over her chest and looked around. "I agree. I've been to a lot of fundraisers, and this is beautiful."

Irene shrugged. "I truly enjoy it. It gives me great energy."

Daisy stood in the middle of the nearly empty restaurant and looked around, appreciating the lighting and the ambiance that set the backdrop for all the auction items. She had really enjoyed working with Valerie and Calla today. Obviously close friends, they worked really well together. It made all the setup and moving things around inside the restaurant go smoothly. She looked over at her. "Thank you for your help."

"It was my pleasure." Then Valerie chuckled. "Plus, my husband and his brothers are busy painting my house for me. So, I have taken the easy route to do this today."

Daisy grinned. "Oh, yes. I heard about that."

Valerie slipped her arm into Daisy's and said, "It's so good to see Ken so happy."

"You think so?" Daisy asked.

"I've known him nearly all my life. He seldom says anything. So quiet. But lately, all he talks about is someone named Daisy." Valerie gave her a questioning look.

Ken's face swam through her mind. Her heartbeat

accelerated slightly. A soft smile came unbidden to her lips. "Ken is a wonderful man. He makes me happy."

They hugged, and Valerie stepped back. "I am going to go clean up and see how the painting went today. I will see you ladies in a couple of hours."

As Valerie walked away, Daisy noticed a slight limp, and it puzzled her. She suspected that would be an entirely different conversation one day. Daisy turned to Irene. "I think we're ready. You did an amazing job with this one, Irene."

She dismissively waved her hand. "Actually, Calla did most of the work. It gave me more time to really focus on getting good donations."

Calla came back out of the kitchen. She'd changed out of the T-shirt and shorts she'd worn earlier and now wore a black chef shirt and striped gray pants. She had her hair pulled up behind her head and tucked into a black engineer's cap. "You all set for tonight?"

Daisy looked at her and said, "I should be asking you that."

The chef waved her hand in dismissal. "Are you kidding me? This will be nothing compared to a full house and my full menu. Three entrée choices will be a walk in the park."

Daisy grinned. "I can't imagine the organization that goes into your kitchen."

"It is certainly not something everyone can do." She looked at her watch. "I am going to let my staff go and get ready for tonight. What time will you be back?"

Irene interjected. "I live in Marietta, so I am here." Daisy had offered to let her come home with her and relax before the event, but Irene had set up a portable workstation at one of the restaurant tables and planned to work for the afternoon.

"I should be back by five-thirty." Daisy checked her watch. That gave her about an hour and a half to get ready. "Thank you again for tonight."

"It's my pleasure. My husband and I chose to continue to live in the States so we can raise money for missions. Otherwise, we would be out in the field full-time."

Daisy left them and walked out into the hot Georgia sunshine. She raised her face to the sun and soaked in the heat of the rays while she stood on the sidewalk. She loved late July weather. Hot sunlight dried the red clay. Afternoon storms rushed in with fury and left the earth washed clean. Then the hot sun steam cleaned the streets again. She loved the humidity and the way the pine trees smelled in the summer sun.

At home, she changed into a pale pink skirt and a white blouse covered in red and pink flowers. She shifted back and forth in front of the mirror, trying to decide if she could detect the thickening of her center. When she untucked the shirt, it looked sloppy and wrong. When she tucked it in, she could see the slightest baby bump.

Maybe you should change into a different outfit. Or you could tell Ken the truth like you promised you would the next time you saw him.

Just then, a text came from Ken.

Looking forward to seeing you tonight.

A scared empty feeling formed a hole in her stomach. She ran her hand over her belly and decided to quit acting so paranoid. No one could tell anything yet. Especially if they didn't know.

Likewise. I've missed you the last couple of days.

After pulling her hair up and twisting it into a simple knot on the back of her head, she freshened her makeup and applied pink lip gloss that matched the accents in the flowers in her shirt. She grabbed her nude-colored heels and her tablet that contained all the big donor names and information.

She stopped at her kitchen table and set everything on it, then sat on a chair and bowed her head. "God, thank You for the way You have blessed Gálatas Seis. I know You've taken my grandfather's vision and added to it in ways that I can't even see yet. I know You brought Ken into my life right now for a reason. God? Can You please start preparing his heart for my news?"

She felt like a burden lifted immediately from her shoulder blades. Maybe instead of panicking about it for the last month, she ought to have just prayed in the first place.

She slipped the shoes onto her feet, gathered everything she needed, and then headed back to the restaurant. By the time she got back there, the two valets she had hired had set up their stand in front of the drive. A uniformed valet opened her door and handed her up out of her car. She reached into the back seat and retrieved her tablet and purse. "Good evening. I will be here until way past the very end, so you can plant my car way in the back."

"Yes, ma'am."

Delicious, tempting smells assailed her when she entered the restaurant. She stopped for a moment, closed her eyes, and just thought about all the people who would walk through those doors with this very smell to greet them. When she stepped all the way inside, she spotted Calla and Irene at the drink table. She headed in their direction.

"Hello, ladies." She looked around but didn't see anything different from how she left it a couple of hours earlier. "Anything needing to be done?"

Calla turned toward her, and she could see anger flashing in the edges of her eyes. "Did we ever discuss specific drinks?"

"I am positive that we did," said Irene. "I can't imagine that I did not."

Daisy thought back to email exchanges and telephone calls and shook her head. "I don't remember specific drinks. I remember no bar tonight. Is there a problem?"

"Right. I told you no bar tonight. And I remember talking about it as I showed Irene the space. The wine she brought tonight is going to have to go away."

Irene shook her head. "The people who are coming tonight are going to expect wine."

"Not if they're coming here." Calla crossed her arms over her chest. "Period."

Daisy quickly put her hand on Irene's arm as a way to signal her to back off. She couldn't believe Irene had intentionally brought wine into an establishment that didn't want it. However, she contained her anger over it. "That is completely fine. You have done so much for us, Calla, and we wouldn't want to risk your restaurant by breaking any rules. We'll have the wine removed and put it in my car. Did you brand a drink for dinner tonight?"

Calla jutted her chin out, and Daisy could see that she hadn't completely appeased her yet. "I did—a sangria style drink made from sparkling grape juice. I have someone who will serve it here as part of the dinner. We'll have water and tea, too."

"That sounds perfect." Daisy looked around and spotted Irene's son Nate and waved him over. Nate often worked the events for Gálatas Seis as a way to earn some extra money. "Nate, do you mind carrying the boxes of wine out to my car?"

He exuded a pout only capable of a seventeen-year-old boy. "I just carried them in."

"I know. That's what your mom said. I appreciate that. We aren't going to need them after all." She opened her purse and pulled out her spare key fob. "They should fit just fine into my trunk."

Calla headed back to the kitchen, and Daisy turned and faced Irene. "Irene, you and I both know she didn't want any kind of alcohol here."

"You and I both know we needed to serve wine tonight." Irene jutted out her jaw. "We have the president of the Atlanta wine Society attending. How can we have him here without wine to serve to him?"

Daisy held up both hands and shrugged her shoulders. "Irene, it was talked about ahead of time. You knew. If you didn't want to have him here without wine, you should've invited him to the next event where wine would be served. She said she didn't want to have a bar. And just because you thought you could bring in a table of wine is really out of line." She rubbed her forehead. "Why would you want to damage this new relationship?"

Irene set her jaw. "I thought she just didn't have the staff to handle it. I was going to staff and handle it."

Daisy shook her head. "No, I think you thought you could just get away with it by bringing it in anyway and thinking that no one would dare say anything. I appreciate your enthusiasm and desire to cater to our guests, and I have always admired your tenacity. However, this crosses a bit of a line."

Irene had pressured an event host to accommodate what she wanted twice before. She had a passion for fundraising and got tunnel vision at times in the quest for that check written by a donor. Daisy considered relationships with hosts like Calla just as important as donors.

"Daisy, I'm not going to argue with you about this. You've already embarrassed me in front of Calla and in front of my own son."

She clenched her teeth together and withheld the retort that she didn't do anything embarrassing. "You're right. We have guests arriving in thirty minutes. We don't need to argue about this now. This can be talked about later."

Daisy spun around and stormed to the restaurant's entrance, where they'd placed a sign-in table in place of the hostess stand. She glanced up as the door opened, and the two college girls she had hired for the night came in. "Good timing," she said. "I was just about to call you and find out where you were."

"Two-ninety-five was more of a mess than usual. I think we're lucky we arrived at all." Brittany set her book bag on top of the table. "So, just like last time?"

Daisy nodded. She unlocked the tablet. "It's all been prepaid, and we sold out. If they're not on this list, one of you text me, and I'll come and personally handle it. When guests arrive, just hit the little button next to their name."

She slipped her phone into her pocket and hid her purse under the skirt of the table. Brittany and Tina took their seats. "Our friends are so jealous we get to eat here tonight."

"I know! I can't believe I get to eat here, either!"

They had worked for her for several events, so Daisy left the greeting of her guests in good hands and went back into the restaurant.

She could not find Irene anywhere. A part of her hoped she had left, but only a small part. Irene had a bad temper, but after she reacted, she usually cooled off pretty quickly. Daisy saw no need to make lifelong decisions in the heat of the moment tonight. This fundraiser meant a lot to Gálatas Seis. Specifically, it meant furniture for the Osborne family. She saw Irene come out of the bathroom. Relief coursed through her. "There you are. Tina and Brittany are here. I got them set up."

With a hard mouth and an edge in her eyes, Irene clearly decided to play pleasant. "Terrific. They've done this enough times to know what to do."

"I agree. They were a great find."

"Thank you."

A voice came from behind her. "Place looks great."

Heart in her chest, she spun and watched Ken saunter into the dining room. He wore a pair of navy-blue dress pants and a light-yellow shirt with a blue and yellow striped tie. "Well, don't you look nice?"

He approached her and gave her a soft kiss on the lips. "Can't even begin to compare. You look amazing."

She stepped back and gestured. "Irene outdid herself. Have you met her yet?" She beckoned Irene closer and said, "Irene, this is Ken Dixon. Ken, my brilliant fundraiser, Irene Clark."

Daisy watched as Irene's features softened, and a smile came to her eyes. "So nice to meet you, Mr. Dixon. I have met your brother, Brad. When you came in, I wasn't sure if that was you."

"Common problem." He shook her hand. "This really looks great. I've eaten here several times. I can see the work you've put into it."

With a smile, Irene said, "Thank you." She looked at Daisy. "I'm going to make a quick phone call. I'll see you later."

As she walked away, Daisy faced Ken. "I'm excited you're here. I'll show you around."

They walked the length of the silent auction tables and talked about the different items. While they talked, Calla supervised the setup of the buffet line and the drink table. Daisy excused herself from Ken and approached Calla.

"I'm sorry about earlier."

Calla shifted her glasses on her face and smiled. "Don't worry about it. I could tell you weren't part of it. I just tend to react to people who try to manipulate situations. I'm sorry. I had someone handling me for a few years, and it makes me kind of defensive."

She pressed her lips together and thought about how to word what she wanted to say so as not to gossip but rather to affirm. "Irene bends over backward to facilitate potential donors. Sometimes, that means those of us in the mix get stepped on, but it's not necessarily malicious. I think for a moment she forgot how much you're giving by doing everything you're doing."

She waved her hand. "I don't want or need recognition for that. I just expect my facility and my people to be respected. So long as we agree on that, you and I are good."

"Thank you."

Calla smiled over her shoulder. "Hello, Dixon Brother."

Ken chuckled. "Ken."

"Sorry. At work, I could almost always tell by the way you guys dress. In this situation, though, there's no way."

"Good to see you, Calla. Really looking forward to tonight. Valerie brought some of your food over with her today."

"I'm so glad she shared. She told me you guys were painting her kitchen while she played with tablecloths and lights." She looked at her watch and tapped it.

"Sorry. I need to go see a sous chef about a sauce. You two have fun tonight."

Ken put a hand on the small of Daisy's back, and she leaned into him and looked up at him. "Does that ever get old?"

"What? Calla's food? No way." She could tell by his expression that he teased her.

"You know what I mean."

He shrugged. "No. It's normal. People have mixed us up since birth. That is if I'm actually Ken. What if some maternity nurse put me in the wrong bed."

Daisy rolled her eyes and smirked. "I'm sure that's what those little identity bracelets were for."

He tapped the side of his temple. "Yep. My parents left those on us for weeks. Every picture during infancy, we had hospital bracelets on. Eventually, our personalities came through, and they could tell us apart at a glance."

"What do you think about the fact that I can tell who you are?"

"I think if either of my brothers ever tried to kiss you, we might have words." She studied his face. His little half-grin didn't hide the fact that he sincerely felt protective of her.

He ran a hand from her shoulder to her elbow. His skin felt warm, but his fingers felt rough. "Valerie can pick Brad out of the crowd. I think when God knows something is meant to be, He makes a way."

The idea that God might have made her especially for Ken flooded her with warmth. It also made the decision she'd made in the past harder to bear.

"I like that." She placed her hand on his cheek and stood on her toes to kiss him. "You worded that well."

She started to say something else, but the phone in her pocket vibrated. She glanced at the screen. An unregistered guest had come to the door. "They need me up front. There's an issue with someone's reservation."

"Do what you do. I'm good."

Hours later, Daisy sat at an empty table and munched on a piece of ice from her glass. Guests had long gone, many carrying the baskets they won in the auction. The auction tally had exceeded Daisy's projections by seventeen percent. Calla's food had completely blown her away. She didn't think she'd ever eaten anything so good in her life as that meal.

Ken sat next to her, leaned back in his chair with his tie loosened. Jon sat to his right, and Calla sat at the table's head, making notes in a notebook. Next to her sat Valerie, then Brad, and their mother, Rosaline Dixon.

"If your fundraisers look like this every time, count me in." Ken smiled a tired smile.

She chuckled. "They're not all this nice. Some have rubber chicken and a bad sound system. Having it here was a gem."

Calla paused in her writing and glanced up. "That's very kind. You're welcome to use my restaurant any time."

Knowing how Irene had offended Calla made her statement all the more humbling. "Well, I appreciate it. That means a lot." She covered her mouth with her hand and yawned. "I am going to go home. It's been a really long day."

As she stood, she looked at Rosaline. "It was so good to see you again. I can't believe you haven't changed in fifteen years."

Rosaline put a hand to her hair. She wore it shoulder-length. Subtle blonde highlights wove through the mahogany tresses. She had big gray eyes, a thin face, and a ready smile. "I think you're being very kind."

Daisy smiled. "You know my mom still has that basket you got her in Honduras. She uses it as her fruit basket. Every time I look at it, I think of you."

"Your mother is a beautiful woman. I can see she raised a beautiful daughter. Please give her my best."

"I will for sure." She addressed everyone at the table. "Thank you for coming and supporting me tonight. It meant a lot."

Brad rubbed his wife's shoulder. She looked as worn-out as Daisy felt. "Missions are important to us. And you are important to Ken. That makes us being here kind of a given."

Tears sprang to her eyes. She blinked them back but worried they'd fall. "Thank you."

Ken stood with her. "I'll walk you out."

"We'll be here at eight tomorrow morning to tear down, Calla. I teach a Bible study at ten on Thursdays, so we'll get done quickly."

"See you then."

She and Ken walked through the empty restaurant and out the front door. The valets had brought everyone's car to the front before they collected their pay and left for the night. She pulled her key fob out of her pocket. "What did you think?"

"It was a good event. What will you do with the money?"

She shrugged. "It's earmarked for furniture for the Osborne's house we're building on Labor Day. We raised enough to get appliances and furnish the entire place."

He put his hand between her shoulders and slowly rubbed while they walked. "My brothers and I did mission trips every summer all our lives. Mom and dad used to take us, but we went on our own once we got to high school. They wanted us to see the world without their filter."

They reached her car, but she didn't unlock it. Ken never had a lot of words to string together at one time, so she didn't want to interrupt the story. "We've gone all over the world. We've seen a lot of need. It always made me look for it more here at home. Taking care of my community is the burden God placed on my shoulders. I believe bringing you into my life was just His way of affirming that."

"Where will you go this year?"

"Actually, we decided a week ago not to go anywhere this year. Jon has something personal going on in New York. Valerie's due, so Brad's out."

Daisy gasped. "Oh! How fun! When is she due?"

"Sometime in February."

February? She wondered how close their due dates were. The parking lot light lit up his face. She could see the tenderness in his eyes. "Did you know that you came to my office one month ago today?"

He brushed a hair off her forehead and tucked it behind her ear. "Is that all? Seems longer."

"Is that a good thing?" she asked.

He shrugged. "I know I lived a life before that day, but I can't remember anything about it." He stared into her eyes. She could tell he searched for words. "I don't really remember living life without you in it."

Tell him. If you want to keep living life with him in it, you have to tell him.

She clicked the button to unlock her car. "It feels like yesterday, and it feels like five years ago. I don't really understand the way time is moving right now."

She reached for her door handle, but he got it before she could. She took a deep breath, but before she could speak, he asked, "Daisy, would you like to go to dinner on Saturday night?"

"Oh. Sorry. I can't. My brother is coming in town to see my mom. He's worried about her after her blood pressure spiked." She started to get in her car but paused and said, "Would you like to come by and see him? I know Diego would love to catch up."

He nodded. "I'd like to catch up. I'd like that a lot." He cupped her cheek and gave her a soft kiss that made the pulse rush in her ears. "Get some rest. I'll be here at eight to help."

She knew she couldn't talk them out of helping. And she didn't want to. Instead, she smiled brilliantly at him and said, "You are wonderful, and I will see you tomorrow."

Chapter 11

Ken tossed some cash onto the table for the tip and followed Jon out of the restaurant. They stepped out into the hot August sun, and he immediately felt sweat break out on his forehead. He'd originally thought he might drive to some job sites and inspect them today, but since the heat index currently pushed close to a hundred and fifteen degrees, maybe he'd spend the day in the air conditioning finishing up paperwork instead.

"Good night! Why didn't we eat at the office?" Jon asked, looking up at the sun.

Ken smirked but, as usual, didn't reply. He'd suggested the sandwich shop in the lobby of their building, but Jon had wanted barbecue. He slipped his hands into his pockets and considered the rest of his day. He hadn't seen Daisy this past weekend because her family had come to town, worried about her mother's recent hospital stay. Instead, he'd spent the weekend working on his new house: getting air conditioning running in the main room, assisting with an electrician buddy on upgrades, and making sure all the installed electrical was up to date on the specifications he'd found filed at the county building offices.

They'd had regular contact, though, texting and calling. But he hadn't actually seen her face for a solid week and realized that he had just about reached his limit. He might pin her down to pick a night this week for dinner. Tonight, he had the regular weekly family meal, but maybe tomorrow they could do something.

He walked into the lobby of their building and stopped short. A woman sat in a chair in the waiting area. She had blonde hair, a tear-streaked face, and a suitcase at her feet. She bent her head and pressed her fingertips to her eyes as if to contain more tears. As he started toward her, concerned about a crying woman, Jon spoke from behind him. "Alex?"

She whipped her head up and met Ken's eyes. For a moment, a confused look crossed her face, then looked over his shoulder at his brother. "Jon," she said, licking her lips and standing. "I'm sorry to drop in. I—" Her breath hitched, and she froze, putting a hand over her chest.

"Hey!" Jon said, stepping around Ken and putting his arms around her. "It's okay." He met Ken's eyes over her head. "Clear an elevator, please."

Ken dashed across the lobby and caught an elevator door as it slid shut. Putting his boot in the door's path, he jerked his head toward the lobby. "Out," he said to the six people in the car. "Please catch the next one."

No one said a word of challenge to him. With rapt curiosity, they just got out and watched Jon guide Alexandra, with her tear-stained face, into the elevator.

As soon as she got into the elevator, she shored her shoulders and shifted slightly away from Jon. "I'm sorry. I'm a little overwhelmed right now." She looked up at Ken. "Hi. I'm Alex."

Even if Jon hadn't said her name, he'd have guessed as much. Jon had dated someone named Alex while in Nashville. When he and Brad visited him last month, he'd left them one afternoon to go have a lunch date with her. He knew Jon's trips to New York had something to do with her. "Ken. Youngest son." He gestured at his brother with his chin. "He's the oldest."

A look of understanding crossed her face. "I thought you must be his brother. You two look very much alike."

Surprised, Ken raised an eyebrow. "Like identical alike?"

Alex looked between them again, first at Ken, then Jon, then back to Ken again. "Well, not really."

A grin crossed Jon's face. "I cannot tell you how happy I am that you said that."

"So," Ken prodded, "I'm better looking is what you're saying."

Jon barked a chuckle. "You're very pretty, Ken."

Alex just looked between the two of them with

curiosity. The elevator stopped on the tenth floor, and Ken followed them down the corridor with offices on one side and the sea of cubicles on the other. When they reached Jon's door, Ken kept walking. Suddenly, as if he remembered the social graces at the last minute, he paused and turned. "Very nice to meet you, Alex. Hope to see you again soon."

After running interference, he headed back to the elevator and went to his floor. He went to his office and shut the door behind him. He wanted to go back to Jon's office and find out everything he could about Alex's tears and suitcase. And, more importantly, how he could help her. But, he didn't. Jon tended to keep to himself about his personal life, and Ken tended to not pry.

Jon had worked on a job in Egypt a couple of years ago. While there, he had gone back to the village where the three of them had helped build a girls' school during their first solo mission trip before their sophomore year in high school. The day Jon got there, religious extremists had burned down the school with all the children locked inside. Jon had witnessed it, and it had broken him. When he came home from that trip, Ken barely recognized him. He sulked, drank, argued, and completely shut himself off from everyone, including their parents.

After a few months, he asked Brad to send him away from home so he could re-commune with God without the pressure of the family around him. Brad had assigned him to a two-year project building a shopping mall in Nashville.

After meeting Alex in Nashville, he found out she had been in that very same village on the same day. A picture she had taken during the tragedy had earned her a Pulitzer nomination. That news had thrown Jon off-center. The three brothers had spent hours talking about serendipity and God's ultimate authority and plan and His perfect timing.

Ken had grown closer to his brothers and closer to God himself during that conversation. He hadn't realized until that time how much of a rut he had fallen into in his relationship with the Almighty. His deep and abiding faith had become mere habit. Everything he said to Jon and Brad that night in the form of counseling his brother to help him come to grips with this memory that caused him so much pain had resonated with his own soul and in his own daily life. It made him pay more attention to Whom he worshiped and why he worshiped Him.

Not even a month later, he had walked into Daisy's office. As he sat here today contemplating the time with Jon in Nashville and then the timing of Daisy coming back into his life, it occurred to him how God had prepared his heart for Daisy through that time of fellowship in Nashville.

He picked up the phone and called her. She answered on the second ring. "Hi, there."

"I miss your face."

He heard her sharp intake of breath, and then she said, "You always seem to know exactly what to say, and yet you actually say so little over the course of the day."

He didn't even know what that meant. "You free to share a meal anytime the next few days?"

"My brother leaves tomorrow. He'd love to see you. Can you come to my parents for dinner tonight?"

"Love to, but I have family dinner." He contemplated his schedule. "How about breakfast tomorrow?"

She paused momentarily, then said, "Breakfast would be great. Would you like to come to my place?"

"Seven okay?"

"Hmm, let me check with my brother. He's still on central time. But I know they are planning to be on the road by two. I have to be at church by ten for the Bible study, so earlier is better."

"Let me know. I have a nine o'clock at my office, so I need to leave your house by eight-thirty."

"I will get up with you later this afternoon." She paused. "Ken? You make me happy."

He felt the corner of his mouth twitch. "Likewise. Bye."

He tried to focus on the pile of work on his desk, even though he had no desire to track expenses, log hours, write memos, or approve accounting requests. All of that just got in the way of him wearing a tool belt around his waist and holding a hammer in his hand.

When the time had come for his father to contemplate retirement, he knew he needed to appoint one of the three of them as his replacement as the CEO of Dixon Contracting and Design. He pulled all three of them into his office and said that he would leave it up to God by having them draw straws.

If they didn't know him as well as they did, they

would have thought he was joking. Instead, they gathered around him as he held three straws in his hand, and they each drew one. The relief Ken felt at Brad pulling that short straw had nearly brought tears to his eyes. The thought that a single decision of which straw to pick stood between him and a lifetime with a tie around his neck in an office day after day, hour after hour, would have driven him completely insane.

He believed sincerely, as did his father and brothers, that God had directed that exchange. Everyone knew Brad was the fit for CEO, but their dad wanted to make sure none of them thought he had played favorites.

Even though he wouldn't have chosen it for himself, Brad had embraced his role and new responsibilities with perfection. In the time since Valerie had come home and come back to him, he had only gotten better at his job.

As the director of residential building, Ken loved building communities. He loved planning shopping and transportation, dining, and entertainment. They had bought several hundred acres outside of Columbus, Georgia, where they built a community of one-bedroom townhomes to three-bedroom houses, with a Main Street that had little shops and restaurants all along it. They'd sold every unit halfway through construction.

The final house closed three months ago, and the last time Ken drove through there, the Main Street bustled with activity looking much like the architect's concept drawings. He looked forward to taking part in more communities like that.

But he also enjoyed the mansions. He loved the intricate detail that went into the woodwork and the quality of the expensive materials that went into the construction.

Ken knew Brad planned to put Jon in charge of the commercial side of the corporation. Jon would build schools and malls and civic centers and airports and parking decks. He wondered if Jon knew about that yet.

Deciding the paperwork wouldn't go away unless he did something about it, he woke up his computer and grabbed the first stack out of his in-box. Twenty minutes later, while he read an interoffice memo from an in-house architect, Toby tapped on his door. He called out, "Enter."

"I'm back from lunch. Do you have anything specific you need me to do before I get back to what I was doing before lunch?" Toby asked.

He gestured at his out-box. "There's some sensitive accounting stuff in there. Can you get that over to them?"

"You got it." He left the office, and Ken looked at the clock, then at his in-box, and performed a mental calculation. He had another good hour of work left to do before he could escape to a jobsite. Maybe by then, it would have cooled off a bit outside. Sitting here thinking about it wouldn't get the work done. He refocused his attention on the memo and grabbed his tablet to make some notations.

Ken pulled into the circular drive at his parents' urban castle, the shadows of the turrets darkening the cab of his truck. He remembered classmates had teased him all through middle and high school for living in the castle his father had built for his mother. Their jealously had never bothered Ken in the least. His father built it in a show of love for his mother, fulfilling a promise he'd made to her in high school. Nothing embarrassed him about that.

He had arrived last. Brad's truck and Jon's truck had already claimed the prime parking spots.

His parents had Wednesday meals with the family most weeks. He hadn't seen Jon since he left him and Alex at Jon's office door after lunch today. He hoped he had a moment to speak to Jon privately and find out what happened with Alex, and if he could personally do anything do to help her.

Ken walked into the dining room and found both of his brothers already there. Brad and Jon both gave him mildly curious looks. "Mom said dinner. Not something I'm willing to turn down."

"It's great you're here," Jon said. "It's your turn to do the dishes."

Ken snorted. "You wish." He pulled his phone out of his pocket. "I actually keep a list." He didn't keep a list, but he may have to start now that Jon was home.

Brad laughed. "You would."

"Yeah, because I always get stuck doing them. Now I can prove when it's not my turn." He glanced at his phone. "It's Jon's turn."

Brad looked skeptical. "You sure?"

Ken nodded. "Wouldn't have said it if the topic were up for debate. It's Jon's turn for the next two years or so. That's how long he was in Nashville. Got to catch up."

Brad laughed, and Ken grinned.

"That's fine," Jon said. "I'll remember, too. Maybe I'll make a list."

Alex walked in from the kitchen, carrying a large salad bowl in one hand and two dressing containers in another. She hesitated at the table, then set the salad bowl down. She looked less stressed-out than she had this morning but still had circles under her eyes. "Alex, meet my other brother, Brad. Brad, Alex Fisher. And you met Ken this morning. Alex will be staying with us for a while."

Alex looked Brad up and down, then looked at Jon. "He actually looks like you."

Jon slipped an arm over her shoulder and hugged her to his side. "Just a little."

It fascinated Ken that she could tell them apart. He wanted to dissect that and examine it. Valerie could, but she had grown up alongside them, so that made sense to him. Was there a significance?

The kitchen door opened again, letting his mom, dad, and Valerie into the room. His mom set a bowl of baked beans next to the corn, and his dad walked to the head of the table.

Once everyone sat at the table, their father said a prayer over the meal, asking God to bless them and bless the food. As soon as he said, "Amen," platters and bowls started circulating.

Ken chatted with Valerie about her ideas for painting the baby's room when his mother spoke to him from her end of the table. "Ken, how's the house coming?"

"I got drywall up in two of the rooms last week. It was a busy week at work, so I didn't get as much done as I wanted." He didn't bore her with the electrical work or any other mundane tasks he had accomplished. He knew her interest lay more in the layout and final design than anything else.

Brad gestured at him with his fork. "You going to keep the trees in the yard?"

"I've been thinking about it. I think I'm going to create a perimeter and cut down those trees, get good landscaping in, but keep the wooded line on the edge."

"That's probably a good idea."

It never occurred to Ken that he spoke more with his family than at any other time or to any other people. "I think I want a pool. Maybe even a garden. Would want sunlight to have a chance."

As he finished speaking, he heard the end of Alex's conversation with his mother. "I'm looking forward to that part of the pregnancy being over."

A hush settled over the table, and everyone looked at Jon and Alex. Ken processed what he'd just heard. Jon's girlfriend was pregnant? What?

Alex's eyes widened, and she looked from his mom to his dad. "I'm sorry. I assumed you all knew."

From the head of the table, his dad said, "It wasn't our news to share. But, let me take this moment to officially and formally congratulate you, Alex—and

Jon as well. I'd also like to reiterate what Rosaline told you earlier, that you are welcome here, and whatever you need, just ask."

Valerie grinned and clapped. "When are you due?"

"March fifth."

"So close to us!"

Jon leaned toward Alex and murmured to her. Ken looked from Jon to Brad. Both of his brothers had babies coming. His heart constricted in his chest almost painfully. Would he ever get that opportunity to announce such exciting news to his family? He tried to imagine what family dinners would look like a year from now and could hardly picture it.

Ken met Jon's eyes and lifted his water glass in a mock toast. He felt a little envy, yes, but he also felt sincere in his excitement for his brother and wished him and Alex all the best.

Chapter 12

Ken crossed his arms and leaned against Daisy's sink. She hulled washed strawberries, then sliced them in half and tossed them into a bowl of blueberries.

"Remember that girl Jon was seeing in New York?" Daisy nodded. "Name's Alex. Alexandra. She showed up at our office yesterday with a suitcase. Jon took her home. She moved into the castle. Good thing Brad and Valerie moved out."

"What happened?" Daisy paused in her work and looked at Ken. "Is she okay?"

"No idea. She's pregnant." He paused while Daisy's eyes widened, then said, "Baby's due March fifth."

The knife dropped out of Daisy's hand. "That's about the same time...." She turned all the way to face him with very wide eyes. She fumbled behind her and turned the water off. Ken wondered what her thoughts might be as he watched her expression. She looked as if she waged an internal war. Finally, she said, "That's about the same time Brad's wife is due, isn't it? Valerie?"

He shrugged. "She's due in February sometime. Don't know what day."

"Ken." Daisy grabbed a towel and dried her hands. She cleared her throat and straightened her spine. "Ken, I need to talk to you about something."

"That so?" He nodded and raised an eyebrow, grinning a half-grin. "Are you actually going to tell me this time? Or are you going to find another excuse not to?"

She gasped and asked, "What do you mean?"

"You keep saying you want to talk to me, then you put it off. Now enough is enough." He put his hands on her shoulders. Tension vibrated off of her in waves. He gave her a little shake, and she looked up into his eyes. "Tell me what's wrong. Tell me how I can help."

Her brown eyes swam with tears, and her lower lip trembled. Finally, she said, "I'm pregnant."

He had anticipated about a dozen other things that she kept losing the courage to tell him. He had even planned how he would respond to any one of them. Money problems, legal problems, personnel problems, any of that he could have whipped out a little prepared script and handled it gracefully. Out of all the scenarios in his mind, pregnancy never once entered it. His heart pounded, and blood roared in his ears. Without a grin in sight, he whispered, "How can you be pregnant?"

As soon as the words came out of his mouth, he felt foolish asking. Of course he knew *how*. He just didn't understand when, or who, or why she hadn't said anything before.

"Remember when I told you then that I had been in a serious relationship and found out he was married?" She pulled away from him and turned her back to him, putting her hand against her forehead. When she spun back around, she crossed her arms over her chest. "I don't know how he managed to seduce me. I don't know why I believed his lies and let him. But the morning I found out I was pregnant, I thought, he'd fix it."

Her hand fell to her side. "I thought, 'I'll go see him and tell him, and we'll get married, and no one will know just how out of order my life has gotten.' Except he was really angry because I had come on an off day. Come to find out, his wife also worked in that office. He spent the whole time I was there worried she would see me there. I was humiliated and pregnant, and suddenly all alone."

His mind whirled. Pregnant. By the married man. So, pregnant this whole entire time? He couldn't focus on one thought. "Daisy…"

She held up a hand. "No. The problem, Ken, is that this has nothing to do with you. And I have been in love with you since I was thirteen. You came into my office all these years later, and I discover that none of those feelings I'd had for you had paled over time. You were still Ken Dixon. You're the man of my dreams. Even more, now, with everything you do and everything I do. And then you asked me out. Me. How many times had I wanted you to ask me out? Hundreds? Thousands? Wrong as it was, I couldn't help myself."

She sniffed and gasped, and speaking very quickly, she said, "I tried to tell myself I didn't really love you like I did all those years ago. Maybe it would have worked, but then you kissed me, and I knew I loved you. But I know you can't love me. I know you can't. This has nothing to do with you."

He suddenly realized she was ending their relationship on the heels of admitting she was in love with him. Panicked, he stepped forward and grabbed her arms. He wanted to shake and beg and scream to make her just listen, but he just gently rubbed his hands up and down and said, "This has everything to do with me. *You* have everything to do with me."

Tears poured out of her eyes. He pulled her close and soon could feel the wet tears soaking his shirt, hear the gasping of her breathing. "How?" The sound came out as a wail.

How did he put into words the emotions churning inside his heart? He squeezed her tight and pressed his lips against her hair. "Because I love you, too. What else matters?"

She hiccupped, then shifted back so she could look up at him. He put his hands on her wet cheeks and brushed her tears away with his thumbs. "How can you say that? When I..."

He pressed his lips to hers, swallowing her protest. Her salty tears and trembling lips made him long for the power to take her fear and pain away. As he kissed her, the chaos in his mind and heart stilled, and he knew with certainty that God was with them and had a hand in bringing them together in His perfect timing.

He raised his head and looked down at her. She wouldn't meet his eyes. He brushed the hair off her forehead and lifted her chin until he could gaze into her eyes. "I love everything about you. Including that baby you're carrying. The baby is a part of you."

"Will you still love it after it's born?"

He didn't try to resent the question, but he felt a knee-jerk response and pulled back the retort that sprang to his mind. Instead, he simply said, "Yes. Of course."

She took a deep, shaky breath and slowly let it out. "The baby's father signed away all his legal rights. I made him do it that day. I think he was relieved."

The thought of how completely alone Daisy must have felt for the last six weeks made him see red at the periphery of his vision. "All the better."

She pulled away from him. His hands suddenly felt very empty. "You can't possibly mean that. You can't mean you're okay with the fact that I'm carrying my married lover's child. I don't believe you."

Ken slipped his hands into his pockets to hide his clenched fists. "What will it take? I don't know how to word what I'm thinking."

Ken wanted to tell her it didn't change how he felt about her even though this happened. He wanted to tell her he trusted God and how God had worked this situation out with the timing. He wanted to explain to her the depth of love he felt that encompassed the baby, too. Ken wanted to say all those things, but he didn't know how.

"Okay. Here." She pressed her fingertips to her

temples. "I want you to go home. I need to take the day off work, and I want you to go to the house you're building. I want you to sit on that huge front porch, and I want you to think about me, and this baby, and us. And if you spend the day doing that and come back tomorrow still feeling this way, then I will believe you. But if you come to any other conclusion, I want you to just be honest with me."

Time alone to process? Time to pray and ponder by himself while he used his hands to build? The fact that Daisy had given him exactly what he would need if he actually had to work through this problem affirmed her place in his life even more. But he didn't say that now because she didn't need to hear that now. He'd tell her tomorrow morning. "Deal." He closed the distance between them and cupped her chin with his hand. "See you tomorrow."

He pressed a soft kiss to her lips. He tasted her salty tears as he pulled away. Then he turned around without another word and walked out.

The scent of flowers no longer overwhelmed her. She much preferred this phase of pregnancy. She sat in Camila's shop on a chair behind the counter and cupped a mug of blueberry tea in her hands. Camila thanked her customer and handed over the bouquet of sunflowers tied with an orange ribbon. A second later, the bell jingled on the door announcing the customer's departure. She spun around and faced Daisy.

"So?"

Daisy gave a faint shrug and took a sip of her tea.

"So, I guess I'll know tomorrow."

Her cousin pursed her lips and leaned her hip against the glass counter. "Yeah, but what do you think? How do you think that he's going to take it? I mean, he told you he loved you, right?"

Shaking her head, Daisy laughed an ironic laugh. "You know, I would stand in my bedroom and make-believe Ken Dixon was holding me in his arms and telling me how much he loved me. I was fourteen. Fourteen years later, he did it. He said the words. While holding me in his arms."

Camila snapped her fingers. "Exactly! You told him the last thing any man wants to hear, and his reaction is to pull you in his arms and tell you he loves you. That means something. You and I both know it." She straightened and picked up her own mug of tea from the counter and leaned against the wall. "I think we both know what that means."

"I think it means that he needs to process the information. Because he clearly hadn't had time to do it."

"I don't know why you're being so down on him. Give him more credit than that. I see good things here."

She snorted. "You're not the one who's pregnant by some married guy."

Camila pulled the paper off the printer that just came in. "Hey, out of curiosity, are you going to tell the wife?"

Her eyes widened almost painfully. "I beg your pardon?"

"The wife. Are you going to tell her that her husband is a dog who schedules his lovers around her travel schedule?"

She tilted her head and studied Camila's face, trying to decide if she joked or not. Finally, she said, "No."

She didn't elaborate. She didn't want to tell the wife because she didn't want to risk Jason punishing her by ripping up that document he'd signed and coming after her baby. As much satisfaction as she'd get watching him squirm and embarrassing him the way he'd embarrassed her, she wouldn't risk it. She stood and set the tea on the counter. "I appreciate it. I do. I appreciate your optimism. I'll see you later."

She had her hand on the door when Camila said her name. "Daisy!"

Daisy turned and looked at her. "I'll call you tomorrow."

"One more thing. You need to let God speak to your heart. Quit hiding out in the nursery. Go to church."

Fear rippled through her at the thought. What did God have to say to her? Did she even want to listen?

She didn't reply. Instead, she waved and walked to her car. Before she started it, she met her eyes in the rearview mirror. "You're a coward, you know that?" One perfectly manicured eyebrow rose. "Oh, yes, I'm talking to you. So, you go into a relationship with that man and let him seduce you, and you weren't afraid to face God then, were you? Nope. You wait until you're pregnant when the evidence of your relationship will soon become apparent to anyone paying attention. Kind of like that scarlet letter, but instead of an A, you get a big, bright P. 'Look, world. She preaches 'love Jesus' and sleeps with married men.'"

No longer able to look herself in the eye, she rested her forehead on the stirring wheel. "You're not just a coward. You're also a hypocrite." She let out a long sigh and stared at her reflection again. "You need to be looking God in the eye and having this conversation with Him."

Trying to shake off the dark mood, she drove to the shopping mall and parked outside of a big baby store. When she walked in, a smile crossed her face. A giant stuffed monkey swung from one of the rafters above. She could barely see the other side of the store. Who knew so many baby items even existed in the world?

While she stood there and tried to get her bearings in the gigantic store, an employee in a bright turquoise vest approached. "Hi there. Can I help you?"

"Um, actually, I would like to create a baby registry, and I would kind of like to peruse newborn furniture and such."

The older woman smiled. "Absolutely. Come with me."

She took her to a kiosk with a baby registry sign above it. After getting some information from Daisy, she handed her a scanner. "If you see something you like, just scan it, and the computer will record it in your registry. No limits. Have fun."

Daisy slipped her purse over her head so that it slung across her body and slowly made her way to the furniture section. She ran her fingers over the smooth cherry wood of a crib that cost as much as a week's pay for her. Suddenly, she thought of everything she needed to purchase. Her heart started pounding, and sweat beaded her upper lip. How could she afford to have this baby? She made the smallest salary possible to keep the nonprofit running.

Then she remembered the size of her family. She didn't doubt that once the shock of her unwed pregnancy raced through the family grapevine, they would all meet her basic needs. Instead of looking at furniture, she decided to look at the fun things like decorations, lamps, and little green baby booties.

For two hours, Daisy indulged in a wish list. When she walked out of the store, she felt lighter than she had since that plus sign appeared on the pregnancy test. No longer burdened with the secrets she kept from Ken, she practically floated on air back to her car.

Of course, she needed to tell her parents. She probably should have done that during her brother's visit, but she didn't want to add more stress to his time here while everyone focused on her mother's health. Daisy decided to wait till next week to talk to her mom and dad. She had time.

Ken flitted through her thoughts, and she wondered about his state of mind right now. She wanted desperately to drive to his new house and sit with him on his porch, but she didn't want to interfere with his processing. She wanted him not to regret any decisions and to know that he had thoroughly considered all of his options.

Of course, she knew what he would choose. He couldn't stay with her. How could he? How could he want to?

Ken sat back in his chair with his feet propped up on the porch railing. Honestly, he just bided his time until he could go to Daisy's in the morning. When he heard the crunch of tires on the gravel, he opened his eyes and watched his mom park next to his truck.

She crossed the yard toward him, carrying a thermos. He knew without being told that the thermos contained homemade chicken soup. "Your father told me you called in sick to work today."

He nodded. "Yes, ma'am."

"Well, I have soup here for you. But you don't look very sick to me."

"No, ma'am."

"And I called you, but you did not answer. Since you've never taken even one sick day in your entire career, in full disclosure, I really came out to see if you were still alive."

"I'm alive." He chuckled and lowered his feet to the ground. "I promised Daisy I'd take the day and think about something she told me. So, I'm keeping my word."

His mom nodded and sat on the chair next to him. She wore a pair of pink Capri pants and a white blouse with pink flowers on it. She'd pulled her hair up into a ponytail. He thought she did not look old enough to have thirty-two-year-old triplet sons. "I see. Is there anything I can do?"

He didn't know what to say. How did words come out that would make sense? "Daisy's pregnant."

"Ken!" Her mouth fell open. "I'm sorry. I just had this conversation with your brother. I don't..."

She looked elated and disappointed at the same

time. He imagined only a mother's face could make that particular combination of looks. "It's not mine, Mama."

Suddenly everything about her changed. She grabbed his hand with both of hers and said, "Oh, honey. What news to hear!"

He looked at the sky and slowly shook his head. "Doesn't feel bad. It feels like God is ready to do work here."

She waited, but he didn't say anything else. Finally, she said, "Do you know…?"

He knew what she meant. Could he name the baby's father? He shrugged one shoulder. "I don't know his name, and I don't care. She broke it off with him before me."

"What are you saying, Ken?"

Words filled his mind. But the right sequence eluded him. He sighed and bowed his head. "I love her, Mama."

She sat back in her chair. "You're dating for a month. You find out she's pregnant by another man. And all you want to say to me is that you love her?"

He looked around the yard and said, "You know, when I bought this property and this shell of a house, my plan all along was to complete this home, then marry Daisy and carry her over this threshold."

"Oh, Ken."

"Ask Jon. I told him about it a couple of weeks ago. I knew then that I loved her, that God had made me for her and her for me. But I'm a patient man, and I planned to give everyone the time that people seem to think people need. I was going to wait. Six months, maybe a year. Doesn't matter to me. Ultimately what would happen was she would be in this house with me as my bride. And this is where we would raise our family."

After a moment of silence, she said, "I see." She took a deep breath and let it out in a slow sigh. "And so she's coming with a ready-made family."

"Seriously, Mama? Condemnation?" He focused his attention on her. "Okay. If I had met her, and she already had a child of any age out of wedlock, would that have presented a problem for you?"

She shook her head. "There is no problem. No condemnation. I am simply providing you with the words people are going to say to you. And to her. Are you prepared to hear them?" She reached out and took his hand. "I love you, and I trust you. I am not here to judge your feelings. Because I love you and I trust you, that will be transferred to Daisy as well." She sat back and picked at an imaginary piece of lint on her leg. "I think you need to talk to your father about this."

"Why?"

"Because his advice would be much better than mine. He's a man. You're a man. I doubt he'd play devil's advocate like I just did."

"See, the thing is, Mama, I did not ask you for advice in the first place."

"I know. You think I was being nosy." She stood and bent, kissing him on the top of his head. "You're my son. I'm your mama. That's my prerogative." She walked away but then turned back and looked at him. "Go talk to your dad."

Chapter 13

As Ken walked out of his house, his dad's truck pulled up in the driveway. Brilliant orange and yellow dawn had just cracked in the sky, and the birds danced through the trees, singing loudly for all to hear.

Ken walked out from under the trees to a patch of grass on the side of the house and set down his water bottle and towel. As he kicked his shoes off, his dad approached. He wore the pants from a Korean taekwondo uniform and a black T-shirt.

"Morning."

"Morning, Daddy. You're out early."

"Yep." He kicked the sliders off his feet. "Thought I'd work out with you."

They warmed up by going through taekwondo forms. His father had earned his first black belt about a year after his sons had. After about half an hour of forms, they turned and faced each other and began sparring in choreographed movements.

As Ken landed on the hard ground, his feet swept out from under him and his chest aching from the clap of his dad's forearm, he looked up at him and said, "I didn't ask for advice."

He took the offered hand and raised himself up. Philip replied, "I didn't give you any."

Ken held the bottle of water out and his father took it. He slipped his shoes back onto his feet and headed back toward the house. "How about an opinion?"

With a chuckle, his dad said, "Son, there's a saying about opinions. But I won't darken this beautiful morning with coarse talk. In my opinion, I have your back. Whatever you need."

They walked into the dim interior. Philip looked around as Ken went to the makeshift kitchen area and pulled another bottle of water out of the dorm fridge plugged into the corner. After downing half of it, he rinsed two mugs out in the portable sink and splashed coffee into each of them.

"Drywall's looking good."

"The original plan was weird. I rerouted some of the rooms." He showed his father the evidence of the old framing and explained how he'd expanded the kitchen and recovered some wasted space.

Ken gestured toward the kitchen space. "A lot of these modern homes have kitchens that are too small to handle the families that would live in houses this size. I've never understood that."

"Can't wait to see it when you finish." His dad accepted the coffee mug from him, and they headed

Daisy's Decision

back outside. Soon they sat in the very same chairs he'd shared with his mom yesterday.

His father had not asked him a single question, nor had he intruded on his thoughts. The birds sang loudly in the trees. Ken listened to the silence between him and his dad and decided to continue to contribute to it. He wondered what the older man didn't say in the midst of the quiet.

He had maybe one sip of coffee remaining in his cup when he realized his father didn't plan to initiate any kind of conversation with him. Ken decided to go ahead and cut to the chase. "If Daisy lets me stay in her life, her baby becomes mine. Boy or girl. White, black, brown, or purple. Don't care."

Philip took a sip of the coffee and slowly nodded. "Exactly."

Ken understood that to mean that his mom and dad would also see that baby as his. He knew his brothers would, too. He just needed Daisy to see it that way. "She asked me to think and pray for a day, so I did. I'm going over there this morning."

"Think she'll have you?"

Did he? Could he contemplate the alternative? "I think it's God's plan. My faith needs to be in Him. If I believe her faith is in Him as well, then I shouldn't have anything to worry about."

His father downed his coffee then stared off in the direction of the rising sun. "You've always been the quiet one, Ken."

Unsurprisingly, Ken didn't make a response. His father continued, "You love her. Maybe that surprises you. Maybe not. But the way you look right now is the way I looked the second I first saw your mother. I was not a man worthy of her at that time. I was just a shadow."

Ken turned to look at his father, trying to imagine him as a young man, a man unworthy of the love of Rosaline. His father continued, "But she loved me, son. Rosie realized that if all I showed the world was a shadow, something had to have cast that shadow. She looked beyond that darkness and found the man who cast the shadow. She loved me, and it brought me back to the man I once was. I'd like to think I'm a better man because of her than I ever would have been alone."

Ken nodded, though he didn't really understand. His father recognized it and explained, "You've always been the quiet one, son. It may be time for you to speak up. Get her to look past the present shadow and see what heights you might reach together."

To any outside observer, Ken may as well have been a statue. He neither moved nor reacted. After perhaps five seconds, he nodded just once and quietly said, "Thanks, Dad."

Philip reached over and slapped Ken's shoulder with his big hand. He squeezed and shook him affectionately. "Keep us updated."

Ken sat in silence until he finished his coffee, and his dad stood. "We're having a cookout after the game Saturday. Reckon you'll be working here for most of the day, but if you come over around five, you can help me on the grill."

Ken nodded. "We'll see what the day brings."

His father didn't say goodbye. He handed Ken his

empty mug and headed to his truck. Seconds later, Ken heard the truck door slam and the crunch of tires on the gravel drive.

Daisy sat at her table and stared at the steam dancing above her cup of tea. She tried not to obsess too much about the morning's lateness and the fact that Ken hadn't come by this morning. Honestly, she hadn't believed he would. As every second ticked by, though, she realized how much she had hoped to be wrong.

Just as she got up to rinse her breakfast dishes, she heard the slam of his truck door in her driveway. She had the front door open before he could even ring the bell.

"I didn't think you'd come."

He stepped inside as she stepped to the side. "I had no reason not to come back. I'm not the one who suggested I leave in the first place."

He smelled like fresh spicy soap and aftershave. She wanted to step closer to him and let him wrap his strong arms around her, but he slipped his hands into his pockets and stood next to her couch.

"Would you like some tea?"

"No, thanks. Listen, I did exactly what you asked me to do. My opinion and thoughts about the subject haven't changed."

Her heart leaped at his words. "You seriously don't have a problem with the fact that I'm pregnant by another man?"

She watched the emotions danced across his eyes, but his expression stayed very mild. "I have a problem with the fact that a man hurt you. That he lied to you and used you, then discarded you. What if I met you and you already had a kid from another man? Is that supposed to change the way that I feel about you? Because I don't think it would."

She clasped her hands together so that he couldn't see how much they shook. "I don't know what the next few months are going to do to my body." Her breath hitched. "I'm going to get fat..."

His eyes flashed, and he grimaced. "So now you're adding shallow to my list of attributes?"

She gasped. "No! I think if I was having your baby, the things my body was going to go through would be things we would anticipate and celebrate. But that isn't the case. What if you start resenting the baby? What if..."

Ken scrubbed his face with his hands, and his voice impatiently snapped. "Daisy! Why would I resent an innocent child?" When Daisy jumped in startlement at his near shout, he lowered his voice. "Why would I have a problem with your body changing while you nurture a living human being? I don't even understand what you're saying."

She felt foolish. Heat flooded her face, and she wiped angrily at the tears on her cheeks. "Me either. I don't think I'm handling this well."

He stepped closer and cupped her wet cheeks with his hands. "Daisy, listen to me. I am in. This is me saying I'm in."

She slipped her arms around his waist and rested her cheek against his chest. "People are going to think it's your baby."

She felt his chuckle almost more than she heard it. "Daisy? I never once cared what people think."

Finally, he put his arms around her, and they stood like that for several moments. The stress and anxiety she'd carried since the moment he asked her to dinner the first time slowly seeped out of her. She didn't even realize how much she'd clung to it until it faded away. "I guess we both have to go to work now."

"I reckon so." He pressed a kiss to the top of her head and stepped back. "How about we have dinner tonight or tomorrow?"

"I can't. I'm going with my parents overnight to my cousin's Quinceañera down in Columbus, remember?" She wanted to see him this weekend, though. She swallowed the invitation to have him go with her and instead said, "How about Sunday?"

"Sure. Want to go to church with me Sunday? I'm on the agenda to speak about the Labor Day house. Thought you'd like to be there."

"Uh, yeah. I can do that." She tried to think if anything required her presence at her church on Sunday, but nothing came to mind. "What time?"

"Ten. Pick you up at nine-thirty?" He looked at his watch. "Better get going. I have to cross town, and traffic was already bad getting here." He cupped her cheek and pressed a soft kiss to her lips. "Have a good trip and enjoy your family. I'll see you later."

After he left, she went up to her room and looked in the full-length mirror behind her door. She lifted her shirt and turned sideways. She had just passed eleven weeks, more than one-fourth of the way through her pregnancy, and still could only see subtle changes in her body. Her waist had thickened, her breasts had gotten fuller, but her clothes still fit.

She grabbed her overnight bag and headed back downstairs. She'd go to her parents' house and tell them now. Putting it off any longer would only make it worse. It might ruin their trip this weekend, but the stress of not telling them would as well.

It didn't take long to drive to their house. She knew her dad stayed home from work today because they wanted to leave right after lunch. She walked into the back door and found them both at the table, coffee cups steaming. The kitchen smelled like toasted bread and oatmeal.

"Daisy! We didn't expect you so early," her mom said, smiling as she stood and walked toward her. "What a pleasant surprise. Have you eaten?"

"I have Mamá." She hugged her, then went to her dad, bending and kissing his cheek. "Hi, Papi."

"Niña." He set his paper down and slipped his glasses off his face. "How are you?"

"Good. I'm…" Her mom picked up her cup and took a careful sip. Daisy looked from her father to her mother and blurted out, "I'm pregnant."

For a moment, no one moved. The cup stayed suspended halfway between her mom's mouth and the table. Her father stared at her, his hand resting on top of the folded paper. Finally, he spoke. "I see." He sat back in his chair and rubbed his chin with his finger. "I'm a little disappointed. Ken has always struck me as a most responsible man. A man of character. I didn't think there was any cause for concern."

Daisy's mouth dropped open. He talked like they were teenagers. "Papi, Ken is not the father."

Her mom frowned. "I don't understand."

She had to swallow past the humiliation that stuck the words in her throat. "The father knows and isn't interested. He's signed over all parental rights to me."

"No. That's not right." Her dad shook his head. "A man—"

"A man who is already married isn't going to leave his highly successful and beautiful wife for the pregnant woman he had on the side, Papi." The shattered silence brought to light how callously she handled this conversation. "Obviously, I didn't know he was married," she murmured. A tear slipped down her cheek, and she impatiently swiped it away. "I told Ken yesterday. He said he loves me and still wants to be with me. Ken is everything you thought he was."

"I am not surprised."

"But will he marry you?" her mom demanded.

Daisy shrugged. "How should I know? Now isn't really the best time to be talking about something like that."

Her mom raised an eyebrow. "I think now is the perfect time to be talking about it."

She frowned and shook her head. "Why should he rush into a decision to cover someone else's mistakes? Even if he offered—and he didn't—I think I'd turn him down."

Her father rubbed his forehead in slow, weary

movements. "Daisy, I'm not sure that's the right decision."

With a heavy sigh, Daisy said, "Well, Papi, I respect that. But whether you think so or not, it's my decision. I know in my heart that I love Ken Dixon and want to be with him for the rest of my life. Let's see how he feels after the baby."

"When are you due?" her mom asked, tears in her eyes.

"February twenty-sixth. I'm about a quarter of the way there."

They sat silent for several moments. Tension hung in the air like a cloud. Finally, her mom reached out and took her hand. "How about we pray together? I think that's just what we need."

Her dad slowly raised his head. She searched his eyes, seeking any indication as to what he felt right now. She got disappointment, but not condemnation nor anger. "I'm really sorry," Daisy said in a wobbly voice.

"Daisy, all of us have failed God in some way. I would not even begin to piously judge you. I can only love you and support you and tell you that if you need anything, we are here." He held a hand out, and she placed hers in his. He sandwiched her hand with both of his. "I've never been unmarried and pregnant, so I can't give you empathy, but I can give you my shoulder, and I'm ready with advice whenever you ask."

She bowed her head and rested her forehead on the back of his hand. "Thank you, Papi," she whispered.

Chapter 14

On Saturday, Ken worked from about four in the morning until two, when his body finally decided he'd done enough manual labor for the day. He headed over to his parents' house to watch the baseball game but could barely concentrate on the action. He could only think about Daisy's news. He wanted to pull her close, hold her inside the shelter of his arms, and protect her from gossip and condemnation.

But, at this point, nothing could change what had happened. She had to face it. At least she didn't have to face it alone.

Buddy, Valerie's uncle and his dad's best friend, arrived in the middle of the fourth inning with a platter of hand-formed hamburgers and some deer sausages to put on the grill. At the top of the seventh inning, Brad and Valerie arrived carrying bowls of potato salad and coleslaw.

When the game ended, Ken's mom went to the store to get buns and pickles, and he helped haul food down to the pool house. He and Brad carried the grill to the poolside patio.

As Ken lit the grill, Brad asked, "Did you hear from Wade this week?"

Back in college, they'd become friends with Wade Snyder, a basketball player on scholarship to Auburn University. He'd joined their Bible study group the first week of school. Even though Wade had started school older than most Freshmen at twenty-one, they'd easily become friends.

For four years, Ken and his brothers prayed with him, studied scripture with him, and went together on several mission trips. He'd entered politics young and became the first black United States Senator from Alabama. Now, he was running for President.

Ken said, "I heard from Evan." Evan Strickland, another college buddy, ran Wade's campaign. "They're the favorites, according to Evan. He asked for financial support."

Brad grinned. "Yeah. I've been following the campaign. Wade might actually do this." He shook his head. "We told him that, remember? How good he was with people and politics."

"So, it's our fault?" Ken asked.

"Right." Brad grinned. "They're planning a fundraising dinner thing here in October. I wanted to make sure he'd reached out to you."

"I told him I'd come. He reminded me to bring my checkbook."

"Sounds like Evan." Brad laughed then asked, "How are you doing?"

He pondered telling Brad the news but decided not to. He still had some processing to do. "Honestly? Couldn't be better. How are you? How's Valerie feeling?"

Brad glanced at the pool house door. Valerie had gone inside to make sure they had enough plates and cups down there. "She's mostly okay. Some mornings are worse than others, and she is super tired in the afternoons. I've come home twice to find her sleeping."

Ken nodded. "She worked really hard up to the moment you found out she was pregnant. Between work and your new house, she might need a break."

As she came back outside, Brad chuckled. "Yeah? Tell her that."

Valerie walked up, and Brad slipped an arm over her shoulders, hugging her to his side. "Tell her what?"

Ken said, "That you might need to take a break now that your house is done."

"Oh, really?" She raised both eyebrows. "I see. And are you going to start calling me the little woman, too?"

He grinned. "I might. I might and then say Brad said I should."

Soon, Alex and Jon arrived. They walked down the path to the pool house, hand in hand. Ken studied Jon's face when they got closer. He looked relaxed, happy, content.

While Ken manned the grill, they all stood around it and discussed the game. Ken watched Alex closely, mostly out of curiosity. He observed her interaction with Valerie, her reserved manner, the way she sought out Jon. He worried about the red shade of her cheeks when they had arrived. Maybe she needed to go into the pool house. But Jon always paid attention, and Ken knew his brother would insist if it came down to it.

As they all finished eating, Jon stood and said, "Alex and I have an announcement." A hush settled over the crowd, and he continued, "We decided to get married. We want to make it official as soon as possible, so I'm looking at two weeks from today. If that date is bad for any of you, please let me know right now so we can come up with another date."

After congratulations ran through the family, Jon disappeared into the pool house with his father. Ken sat, stunned. Jon and Alex were getting married.

His heart pounded, and he felt cold sweat on his brow. They were getting married, and here he sat, trying to work out his place in the life of the woman he loved. He wanted to marry her and bring her home to the house he was building for her. But they'd only had a few weeks together, hardly enough time. What could he consider the right thing to do, the right time to act?

He glanced over at his future sister-in-law and observed her trembling hands and bright red cheeks as she drank half of a bottle of water. He frowned. "You might want to get out of the heat."

She fanned her face with her hand. "It was so hot today. And I'm usually so sick in the morning. I think I started this adventure off a little dehydrated."

He gestured with his head toward the pool house.

"That building is air-conditioned. There's a couch in there you can go lie on."

She stood and put her hand on the back of the chair as if to steady herself. "I feel like their conversation is too important to interrupt. I think I'll just go back up to the main house."

He stood. "I'll walk with you."

She held up a hand. "Ken, I'm okay. I'm just overheated."

He shrugged. "Yeah, me too. Besides, I want to get a drink out of the main house fridge. This is a good excuse." He walked next to her down the brick path. "You settling in okay?"

Glancing at him under her lashes, she said, "I don't have the words to express my feelings for your family. You have been more welcoming to me in the three days I've been here than my family was to me for my whole life."

Ken pondered just what kind of family Alexandra had for her to say such a thing. Even so, they didn't speak again. When they reached the back of the house, he opened the door for her, and she preceded him inside.

They went through the mudroom and into the kitchen, where he headed straight for the refrigerator. "See you later, Alex."

She turned as she reached the kitchen door. "Thanks for gallantly rescuing me, Ken. The cool air feels so good in here. I probably should have come in an hour ago."

"Just don't pass out on me. Jon might have something

to say about that." She waved goodbye and left the room. He grabbed a soda out of the fridge then walked through the house. Once he made sure Alex felt better and rested comfortably on the couch in his mother's den, he went back out to the pool house to help clean up from dinner.

While he cleaned the grill, his mind wandered back to Jon's upcoming nuptials. Oh, how he longed to make Daisy his. When would that timing be right?

Daisy sat in the hard pew next to Ken. He had his arm around her shoulders, and the smell of his aftershave tickled her senses. She had managed to volunteer with the children's program of her church every Sunday since getting her positive pregnancy test. Today marked the first time she'd sat and listened to a sermon. As the pastor read from the book of John, recounting about Jesus writing in the dirt and the woman actively caught in sin had been dragged in front of him, her mind started spinning.

Why did all of these examples of confronting Jesus with sexual sin have to do with women? She thought of the woman at the well who lived with a man who was not her husband; this woman caught in the act of adultery with a man then dragged through the streets; and then the prostitute who wept at Jesus's feet, washing his feet with her tears. Why all women and no men?

Where could she find the story of the man who preyed on an innocent woman, told her lies, and seduced her, getting her pregnant then rejecting her and the unborn baby? Where was that story in God's word?

She closed her eyes and willed herself not to start crying. Jason did not carry all the blame here. She went into everything with both eyes wide open. They didn't do anything she didn't want to do.

Perhaps that's why she felt so guilty. Because she willfully did something she knew opposed her moral standards and her faith. Then, instead of it just staying hidden like some dark secret, soon everyone would know, and her hypocrisy would come fully into the light.

Yet, God already knew, and she'd spent the last several weeks avoiding Him as if she could hide. She hadn't stopped to pray for the baby, its future, its life. Why? Dare she search her heart and find out the truth?

A tear slipped down her cheek, followed by another and another. Soon, she had to dig through her purse and find the package of tissues. Her fingers trembled as she tried to open the little plastic flap. Finally, she just ripped the whole thing, and it fell open into her lap. She picked up two tissues and pressed them to her eyes. So much for her carefully constructed makeup.

Ken rubbed her back between her shoulder blades. He couldn't possibly know why she suddenly felt so upset, but he didn't ask or question, just supported. When she thought she could raise her head without wailing, she slowly looked at the pastor. He talked about Christ's love and wisdom, how the crowd dispersed without stoning the woman to death because of Christ's challenge of he who is without sin cast the first stone. Left alone with the woman, He asked her, "Has no one condemned you?"

When she admitted no one had, Christ said, "Neither do I condemn you. Go and sin no more."

"Beloved," the pastor said, "let's take a moment and look at that. What does it mean to condemn? It is the Greek word *katakrinō,* which means basically to judge worthy of punishment. Now, her accusers say that the law of Moses required her to be stoned to death. However, that's *not* what the law says. This kind of wordplay reminds me of the serpent as he addressed the first woman and asked, 'Did God really say...?'"

He held up his Bible. "What the law of Moses says is that if a man and woman commit adultery, then they should both be put to death. But that's not what they were doing here. They only brought half of the sinful couple, and in doing so, they were trying to trick Jesus. Because, after all, who was He to go against the law of Moses?"

The congregation murmured in amusement. He continued. "So, stoning her to death was not following the law, and Christ knew that. But, beyond that, what He said to the woman is most encouraging! 'Neither do I condemn you. Go and sin no more.' Which is to say, 'Neither do I judge you worthy of punishment.' Now, how is that possible? She was sinning! Whether they brought her partner with her for judgment or not didn't take her sin out of the equation. Did Jesus really not judge her?"

He slammed his hand down on the pulpit and pointed at the congregation. "I do not for one second believe that Jesus condoned her sin. What I believe is that He knew her heart and could see her desire for repentance. So, what did He do? He forgave her and told her to go and sin no more. He didn't say, 'Girl, you're good. Those are old laws. They don't apply anymore.'" He paused as everyone chuckled. "He simply said, 'Go and sin no more.'

"Now, one sidebar worth mentioning here. He didn't say, 'Go back to your sinful ways. It's cool.' He said she shouldn't sin anymore. He knew she felt repentant.

"How often do we find ourselves sinning, then asking for forgiveness, then kind of hanging out and waiting, making sure it really happened? We ask ourselves, 'Am I really forgiven? Like, really truly forgiven? I just can't believe it!' And you know what? That's true. We really don't believe it. Instead, we focus on our pasts, our mistakes, our sins. They drag us down with the weight of guilt and regret until we can barely walk forward.

"But Christ has given us the out. He is here to share our burdens, lighten the load, and pay the cost for our sins so we can claim that we are redeemed! He didn't tell her to go and think about what she'd done! No! He said, 'Go and sin no more.'"

He paced to the front of the platform, his Bible in one hand and his other hand casually in his pocket. "Now, I don't know about you, but that encourages me. It frees me. It removes the burden of sin off of my shoulders and lays it at the feet of my Savior so I can go out, sinless, guiltless, blameless, and work for Him and

His kingdom. It would be impossible to serve Him while struggling under the weight of my past. He doesn't want that. He wants me out here, working, doing, being the light and the hands and feet! And that's what He wants for you, too."

As he spoke, his wife, who led the worship team, stepped onto the stage, followed by the musicians. Daisy felt such a weight lifted from her heart as she listened to the chords of a song softly filling the room.

The weight of her decision to involve herself in a physical relationship with Jason had overwhelmed her, dragged her down, weighted her with guilt and shame. Even though she'd admitted her sin to God and asked His forgiveness, she really had just kind of been hanging out, worried He was mad at her, thinking He could never possibly forgive her for embarrassing Him this way.

But He wasn't that kind of God. He loved her and wanted her to give Jesus her burdens, let Him take up the yoke so she could continue in the ministry where He'd placed her. He wanted her to go and sin no more. Not sit here and make sure the forgiveness really stuck.

Daisy wanted to stand up and applaud. What perfect timing for a sermon of this caliber! She glanced at Ken. He must have sensed her gaze because he turned his head. She could read the concern in his eyes and smiled at him to help alleviate his worry.

With her legs crossed, Daisy leaned her head back and looked up at the ceiling of the gazebo. Ken lay across the bench with his head in her lap, and she casually ran her fingers through his hair. They had just finished eating lunch with most of his family. At first, she worried about how his parents would treat her because she had broken down so openly in church. But they never asked any questions, just treated her with welcome kindness.

"I'm glad you came today," Ken said.

"Me, too. I had no idea that you were taking up an offering for Gálatas Seis. I just thought you were going to talk about it."

His church had handed her a check for more than a thousand dollars from an offering they had taken after Ken spoke about the charity.

"Nothing special. We do that monthly. The charity on the books for the last year got folded up into a larger company that we don't typically support. My dad sits on the committee and asked if we could highlight you instead."

"I really appreciate it. Every little bit helps."

They sat in comfortable silence for several minutes. The sound of tweeting birds and buzzing insects filled the air. Daisy found her eyes resting on the surface of the pond. The coy breached the surface like an orca out in the ocean. She jumped and then giggled. "I didn't know they did that."

Ken apparently knew what she referred to because he didn't even turn his head to look. "When we first got them, lots of them did that all the time. Apparently, that's normal when they come to a new place. That one is just crazy, I think. Never did settle in."

"How do you know which one it was?"

He smiled, and she stared down at his face. "We've had the same fish for fifteen years. I know which one it was. It's not my first day."

She looked around at the gardens and the edge of the castle she could see. "I can't imagine growing up here."

"Yeah, we had it rough." His chest shook with a silent chuckle. "Actually, it was just my brothers and me and Valerie. This entire property was our playground. We played, too. Can't imagine a better place to raise triplet boys."

"That's right. Your mom raised Valerie."

His head moved back and forth on her lap as he shook it. "No, her uncle Buddy raised her. Mama had her during the day with us. She and Buddy lived in the cottage down that path there." He pointed then closed his eyes as if completely relaxed. "She moved out right before your dad came to our church."

Daisy thought of the close relationship Brad and Valerie obviously shared. She wondered if spending so many of their formative years together contributed to that.

"The sermon today really resonated with me. As I sat next to you on that pew, it occurred to me that this was the first sermon I've heard since I found out I was pregnant. I think I've had a bit of a Jonah experience as I have volunteered to work with the children or nursery service at my church for the last six or seven weeks."

Ken opened his eyes and looked up at her. His eyes had shifted to a shade of blue-gray in the afternoon sunlight. "Why?"

She pursed her lips and thought about it. "I think because I hadn't quite accepted that I was really forgiven because I had a physical manifestation of my sin. And I don't mean that against the baby at all. I just mean it's not something I'll be able to hide. It's not something I was able to identify that I had done, come to God in private and seek forgiveness and repent, and then be forgiven and walk away like it was some secret, private dealing in a back room. No matter how forgiven I am, in a few short months, it will all come out."

With graceful movements, Ken sat up and shifted his body to turn and face her. He slipped his arm across the back of the bench so he could put a hand on her shoulder. "And?"

"And facing judgment is nothing I've ever been good at." She didn't feel emotional, and it occurred to her that she truly heard the sermon's point today. "But I can take it and get through it. It's not like they'll actually take me outside and stone me these days. That's what the cross was for, right?"

He stared at her for several moments, his eyes serious, his expression focused. Finally, he asked, "You're okay?"

She smiled. "I am okay."

He tilted his head, studied her face, and finally said, "Good. I'm glad."

He lay back down, and she continued to run her fingers through his hair. Finally, he said, "Jon and Alex are getting married."

Daisy's heart gave a jealous little tug at the news. "Really? When?"

"Two weeks. A week from Saturday."

"I look forward to meeting her."

"You will today, I hope." He reached up and wound a strand of her hair with his finger. "How was the Quinceañera?"

He butchered the pronunciation, so she corrected him, and he said it again, this time properly. "It was a beautiful party," she said. "My parents were slightly emotional and acting a little weird, but if anyone picked up on it, they didn't ask me about it."

"Do you think it will end up being okay with them?"

"I really do." She rested her hand on his chest, feeling his steady heartbeat under her hand. "They just need to sort it out. We called my brother on the way down to Columbus. He was less overwhelmed at the beginning of the conversation than my parents were."

"Well, he's our age. Different perspective."

"True."

He picked up her hand and brought it to his lips, pressing a kiss to her wrist. The feeling of the touch raced through her arm and sent her pulse rate skittering. She watched the koi jump in the pond again and thought that if she could just sit like this for the rest of her life, she'd die in perfect contentment.

Chapter 15

As he stirred the tomato sauce into the aromatics on the stove, Ken looked over at Daisy. She propped her chin in her hand and watched him cook with confidence. "I've never seen anchovies as the base of a sauce before," she remarked.

He winked at her. "Trust me. Briny, salty, garlicky." He kissed his fingertips. "They build the best sauces." He slid the bass fillets into the pan and put a lid on the skillet. Daisy resumed chopping the cucumber for the salad as he stirred couscous into boiling water.

The ease with which they made this meal in her kitchen filled her with a sense of security. She'd told him, and he was still here. What did that mean? Dare she hope for a future with him?

Everything her little fifteen-year-old heart had longed for had started coming true. Except for one thing.

Ken put the lid on the couscous and walked over to her. She sat across the bar from him, perched on a stool. Ken had hooked up his phone to her Bluetooth speakers, and a popular song from the eighties played quietly in the background. He slid the salad bowl into the center of the bar and filled it with the contents of a bag of rinsed lettuce.

"How's the house coming along?" she asked.

He rolled the top of the bag closed and put it in the fridge. "Steady. Drywall's up in the first floor. Working on the second floor. Lot's to do." He grinned a sheepish grin. "I'd get more done if I didn't enjoy being with you so much."

"So, it's my fault," she chuckled. "Good to know."

She slid cucumbers and tomatoes onto the lettuce, then carried the bowl to the table. A few minutes later, Ken carried plates with the fish and the aromatic sauce sitting on a bed of couscous to their spots at the table. Her mouth watered as she took his hand and bowed her head, listening to his voice as he asked God's blessing over their meal.

At the first bite, the salty, rich flavor filled her mouth in a beautiful way. She closed her eyes and just enjoyed it, then opened them to watch Ken staring at her with a very stoic expression on his face. "It's so good," she said, gesturing at the fork halfway to his mouth. "Taste it."

He smiled and nodded. "I plan to."

Heat flushed her face, but she didn't reply. She just kept enjoying her dinner.

An hour later, with the kitchen clean and the sun

setting around them, Daisy sat nestled against Ken on the swing on her front porch.

"I really enjoyed going to church with you yesterday." She sighed and closed her eyes. "It was nice to sit next to you."

He kissed the top of her head. "Think you can sit through a sermon again this Sunday?"

She chuckled. "I could be persuaded to if you were sitting next to me."

"Hmm." His arm squeezed her close. "Your place or mine?"

"Either or both. I'm good." Despite not wanting to, she shifted away from him. "It's getting late."

"Yeah." He moved slowly as if fighting against a force trying to keep him down. She stood with him so she could kiss him goodbye. He cupped her face with his hand, giving her the slowest, sweetest kiss. "Good night, Daisy."

Nestling her head under his chin, she said, "Good night, Ken."

After squeezing her shoulders, he set her away from him and walked to the stairs. Before descending, he paused and turned back to her. "You free tomorrow night?"

She thought about it. Nothing came to mind, and the idea of spending more time with Ken definitely appealed. "I'm free. Why?"

"We're getting together tomorrow at Brad's to plan Jon's wedding. I hoped you'd want to come."

"Me?" She slipped her hands into the pockets of her shorts and leaned against the porch railing. She'd met Alex briefly yesterday. She and Jon had come home from New York as Ken walked her out. "What does that have to do with me?"

"Because we're together." He tapped his chest above his heart. "Also, thought you might want to recommend Camila for the flowers. I checked with Jon today. They hadn't looked at florists yet."

Ken's thoughtfulness astonished her. It shouldn't have at this point, but he continued to surprise her. Camila would flip for the chance to do the flowers for a Dixon wedding. Ken was so quiet, but a lot was going on beneath that calm exterior. He was so thoughtful and observant. She realized she hadn't answered him. "Sure. Of course. What time?"

"After work. I'll pick you up."

"I'll meet you. That way I don't have to leave my car at work." She pulled out her phone. "What's the address?"

Anticipation made jitters run up and down Ken's spine. He and his brothers shared a bond born of the special circumstances of being identical triplets that most siblings would never understand. They knew how the others thought, reacted, felt.

Brad had married the girl he fell in love with as a young man. Right before their freshman year of high school, Valerie and her uncle moved out of the guest house on his parents' estate and into their own home, causing Valerie to change schools. It ripped her away from them, and they went from seeing her daily to seeing her on holidays. The day before they moved, they all wrote their secret wishes down, placed them in sealed envelopes, and hid them in the gazebo.

At Brad's wedding, he pulled out the box that contained the wishes and read his. "To marry Valerie..."

Ken saw Jon the day after he met Alex. He could see the change in his countenance, in the look of his face, in the tone of his voice. When he spoke of Alex, everything softened, and the pain that Jon carried with him from his time in Egypt just fell away as if removing a cloak. Knowing his brother, knowing how he felt and what he thought, he knew that Alex was the woman for him, the person who would complete him and make him whole.

Ken knew that Daisy was to him as Valerie and Alex were to his brothers. At this moment, his heart's desire was that the women would all become friends in a way that would eventually bind them all as sisters. If he had his way, Alex and Valerie would be aunts to Daisy's baby, and Daisy would be an aunt to his brothers' children. He prayed all last night and throughout his day today. Would Daisy like them? Would she want to spend the rest of her life with them and be a close part of it?

As they entered Brad and Valerie's kitchen, he immediately smelled coffee and cinnamon. Everyone sat around the table, slices of cake and steaming cups at their elbows. Valerie came forward and hugged Daisy. "I'm so happy you came with Ken!"

"Thank you for inviting me."

Alex stood and walked over to them. "It's good to see you again."

"It's good to see you again. I'm excited about y'all's wedding."

"Me, too. But as we're planning, I realize we might should have pushed it back a week. Back home, I could throw together a do in a week. Here, I started with two weeks, but one is half up already, and I don't know the local caterers or florists."

Valerie slipped her arm over Daisy's shoulders. Ken felt the stress start to subside at Daisy's smile. "We do. Trust us."

"My cousin is a florist. Have you already contacted one?"

"No! Oh, please call her!" Alex leaned closer. "Do you think she also knows a caterer?"

"Oh, no, Honey. That's covered. I've already called Calla," Valerie said with a confident wave. "She's my friend with the restaurant. She already knows what to do, how many to do, and gave me a list of bakers who could have a cake for you by next Saturday."

The women started talking over each other, and Brad and Jon stood and maneuvered their way toward the sliding door that led out to the back yard. Ken inched around the girls and joined his brothers.

Brad gestured with his thumb. "Uh, we are just going to be outside if you need us."

Valerie and Alex both waved them away as Daisy pulled a notebook out of her purse. They moved to the table, and Valerie handed Daisy a coffee cup. "I'm sorry to say it's decaf," she said. "I finally gave in just for the taste of coffee."

Daisy smiled and took it from her, then looked at

Alex. "What flowers do you want?" she asked as she poured coffee into her cup.

Outside, Ken sank into a lawn chair. "Well, I reckon I was worried about nothing."

Brad raised both eyebrows. "Worried about what?"

He shrugged and pulled the ring box out of his pocket. "Asking Daisy to marry me. I was worried she might not get along with Val or Alex."

Jon looked over his shoulder through the glass door. "They seem like fast friends."

"An answer to prayer," Ken said.

Jon gestured with his chin. "So you're getting married, too. So soon?"

"Haven't asked yet." He couldn't betray Daisy's confidence. He'd tell his brothers about the baby when the time was right. "I'm keeping this with me so the perfect moment doesn't catch me unprepared."

Brad chuckled. "If it was anyone but you, I'd advise caution. But you've been cautious with your heart your entire life. Clearly, Daisy is right for you."

"I have no doubt."

"What does she say?" Jon asked.

"She says she was in love with me from afar back in high school."

Brad snorted. "I know what that's like."

With a smile, Ken said, "That's right. You do."

Jon asked, "And now?"

Ken shrugged. "I guess we'll find out soon." He sounded more confident than he felt. He squeezed the ring box and slipped it back into his pocket. "Hey. Y'all want to come hang the last of my drywall so we don't get roped into going back in there?"

Jon looked at the door and back at him. "I don't know. I think we should—"

"Stay out of their way," Brad said. He stood and pulled his truck keys out of his pocket. "Come on. It's less than a mile away. If they need us, we can get back in five minutes."

"Don't tell them we're leaving until we're there," Ken said, standing with his brother. "In case they say no."

Jon chuckled. "Fine. But I want it on record that I dissented."

"Course you do."

Once they hashed out the wedding's details, the women moved into the living room and sat around in couches and chairs. Alex took a sip of the decaffeinated coffee and closed her eyes. "I know I shouldn't enjoy this so much, but I do."

Valerie toasted her with her cup. "Auntie Rose figured out I was pregnant because I wasn't drinking coffee." She laughed. "That's one astute woman there."

"Where did the guys go?"

Valerie looked at Alex. "Probably to Ken's house. It's just down the road, and him sitting around staring at his brother's faces when he probably has a thousand details to handle tells me that they're over there working."

Alex chuckled. "Do they ever stop?"

Valerie shook her head. "No." She looked at Daisy. "How are the plans going for building that house?"

She realized they meant the Labor Day weekend house project. "Everything's all set up. We've done this many times before, so the biggest part of it at this point is the organization during the actual weekend, and I have that nailed. Since it's Labor Day weekend, we get an extra day. I have some extra donations going toward that house, so I have painters coming in Sunday night that I'm actually paying instead of volunteers. They will get the house ready for all the final trim and everything Monday. Adding that extra twelve hours on Monday makes me think I should always do them on holiday weekends."

Valerie propped her elbow on the armrest and rested her temple against her fisted hand. "I can design a house. That was part of getting my architect's degree, obviously. I don't. I preferred the interior design aspects. But I don't think I could organize a crew to build a house in three days."

Alex shook her head. "I can't fathom the kind of organization it takes to do that. My skill set lies in taking pictures and throwing high-class parties for Connecticut's elite." She laughed and took a sip of her coffee. "I sit here among great women."

Daisy watched Valerie and Alex as they interacted with each other and with her. She thought of their interaction with Brad and Jon and realized that she liked these women. A lot. The thought of being in their circle gave her a warm glow.

"I wouldn't know how to throw a party for the elite of Connecticut." Daisy smiled. "I hire someone to do those kinds of things. My fundraising organizer is brilliant, and I'm thankful for her. Because there's no way I could do what she does."

Valerie nodded. "I think it comes down to the same thing that building a house and designing a house does, and that's organization. Lists."

Alex lifted her hand. "Lists! Yes!"

"My list will be permanently affixed to my hand the entire weekend we're building that house." Daisy chuckled. "With all different colors of markers."

Alex turned to Valerie. "You have been wonderful. Thank you for being so welcoming to me. I think that knowing I have a friend is making this transition easier."

Valerie shifted her body and rubbed her hip. "It used to just be those boys and me. Everywhere we went, all the time, people called us Valerie and those boys. I love those brothers. Since I came back to Atlanta, it's been my prayer that they find amazing women who can love them the way I love Brad. I think it's incredible that Jon found you and recognized you. That's all God. I hope you know that." She looked at Daisy. "And I'm not afraid to be frank and tell you I have never once known Ken to date. He's thirty-two years old, and you're the first woman he's ever actually introduced me to. I like you. I hope you keep him."

Daisy didn't know how to respond to that. "I fell in love with Ken when I was fourteen."

Alex said, "Aww. I love that."

Daisy shrugged. "He didn't even know I existed. I was just his friend's little sister. I remember him coming back from some mission trip, and he had this present in his hands, and he was handing it to me, and the whole time I thought, 'Oh, it's for me. He's finally going to admit these feelings for me that I know for sure he has.' I then went to this whole dialog in my head about how I would accept the offer of his heart, and we'd be together forever. But as he was talking, it occurred to me he was asking me to give it to my mother. It's a basket she uses as her fruit bowl."

Daisy and Valerie put their heads back and laughed. Valerie said, "I knew him at that age. He's not the same man he was then, either."

Daisy smiled. "It still would've been nice to grow together, wouldn't it?"

Valerie's face grew serious. "Yes. I left after high school and came back a different person. Sometimes I wonder what life would be like if I had recognized Brad's feelings for me and stayed."

Alex interjected. "It's interesting how God maneuvers us, isn't it? It's something I've been thinking about for the last few weeks. I haven't grown up in a godly state of mind. To my family, who are Jewish, it's all about culture and tradition and not about a relationship. But I was in a terrible situation in Egypt and took a picture. It was published, and I was nominated for an award. The crazy thing is that Jon was in that picture."

Daisy gasped and asked, "Did you meet him that day?"

Alex shook her head. "No. But when I met him, I felt like I had seen him before. It wasn't until he showed me the picture that I realized why he looked so familiar to me."

Valerie said, "I've seen the picture. Even though he's not the subject of it, you can still see him very clearly. It's incredible the serendipity that brought you two together."

Daisy set her empty coffee cup on the table in front of her and brought the conversation back to something Alex said. "So, you recognize that God wants a relationship more than tradition and culture?"

Alex looked above Daisy's head as if forming her thoughts. "I think I'm becoming more aware of the fact that He is way less detached from my day-to-day than I would have thought. Six months ago, I think you could've told me God didn't actually exist, and I could have been convinced. Now I think I would stand and fight to the bitter end because I know for a fact that He does exist. Does that make sense?"

Valerie cocked her head. "I think that makes a lot of sense. It also makes me very happy. Jon has struggled, and it comes from his experiences in Egypt, stemming from his observations of the poverty and desperation he has witnessed all over the world. To know your faith is growing and firming up, and his faith is strengthening, tells me you two will be completely fine together. And that God's got you both."

The front door opened, and the sound of the brothers' voices floated toward them. She turned her head as they came into the room. Drywall dust sprinkled on their boots gave evidence of where they'd gone. Valerie had called that one.

"So! Wedding all planned?" Jon asked. He walked over to the chair where Alex sat and perched on the arm of it.

Alex grinned up at him. "All planned. Thanks for all your input and assistance."

He grinned. "I'll be wherever you want me to be whenever you want me there."

Daisy looked up at Ken, who had come to stand next to the couch. "Did you get the last of the drywall hung?"

"Yep. Many hands make light work."

She chuckled. "That is one of my mantras."

Jon and Alex stood. "We are going to head back. See you all for family dinner tomorrow?"

"Wouldn't miss it." Valerie stood and stretched her leg. "What about you, Daisy? Are you coming to family dinner?"

"I, uh, don't know." She glanced over at Ken. "Am I?"

The smile that covered his face lit him up like a light bulb. It made her heart twist almost painfully in reaction. "If you want to come to family dinner, that would make me very happy. Besides, it's Jon's turn to do dishes, so we'd have it easy."

Jon laughed. "I think you need to consult that list of yours one more time."

Daisy stood. "I guess I'll see y'all tomorrow. Thank you, Valerie, for your hospitality. I really enjoyed it."

Valerie walked up to her and hugged her. "It was great to spend time with you."

Daisy looked at Alex. "Your wedding is going to be amazing. I can't wait to see it."

Daisy hugged Alex, and then Ken put a hand on her lower back. "I'll walk you to your car."

As she walked out of the house, Daisy realized that she hadn't once thought of her pregnancy tonight. She actually felt drawn into that community of the family and felt like she had a place there.

At the car, Ken leaned his hip against the back door. She opened the driver's door and tossed her purse inside, then turned toward him. "Thanks for asking me to come tonight."

He slipped his hands into his jeans' pockets. "I'm happy you got along with them."

She smiled. "We got along great. It probably helps that you guys abandoned us to our planning."

She was teasing him, and he knew it. He brushed a piece of hair off of her cheek. "Hanging drywall was better than picking out flowers."

His arms came around her easily. But even as she raised her face for his kiss, she wondered how much longer she could keep this up. Once his family knew, they wouldn't accept her the same way he did.

Chapter 16

Daisy stared up at the big stone structure. What was she doing with him? People who grew up in castles like princes and kings did not allow their heirs to date women who got pregnant with another man's child. Then, Ken opened the door, a grin covering his face. "There you are!"

The welcome from him helped center her and gave her legs the strength to walk toward him and climb the steps. When she got to the top step, he kissed her and said, "I'm glad you texted about that wreck. I would've been worried you changed your mind."

"You can always depend on Atlanta traffic to be undependable."

They walked into the massive foyer. The hand-laid tile formed a sapphire blue and gold compass rose in the center of the foyer. A table with a large bouquet of sunflowers sat in the center of the compass. She looked above to the ornate ceiling twenty feet high and all around at the doorways with twelve-foot-tall doors.

Her heels clicked on the tile floor, echoing around them as they walked to a door on the far right. He opened it, and she stepped into a dining room with a table long enough to hold twenty. The room had a glass wall that faced a rose garden. An ivory linen tablecloth covered half of the table, and ceramic bowls and plates in varying colors of autumn graced the tabletop, giving it a very festive feel. A smaller vase than the one in the foyer held a similar arrangement of sunflowers and sat on the unset end of the table as if set aside. From outside, Valerie walked up to the glass door and slid it open, coming into the room. "Daisy," she said with a smile. "I'm so happy you joined us tonight."

One of the brothers came through a doorway carrying a soup tureen. Valerie walked toward him and kissed him, so Daisy identified him as Brad. He set the ceramic dish near the head of the table and said, "I heard about the wreck on two ninety-five. I wondered if you would make it in time for dinner."

She raised an eyebrow and patted him on the cheek. "Auntie Rose would've waited for me." She grinned over her shoulder at Daisy. "She'd have waited on Daisy, too."

The kitchen door opened again. Jon came through with a breadbasket covered in a russet napkin. He looked at Valerie and Daisy and said, "Hello, ladies."

"Where's Alex?"

He gestured with his chin in no particular direction.

"Upstairs. She's on her way down."

Philip Dixon entered the room through a door opposite the kitchen. As he crossed the room, he clapped his hands and rubbed them together. "I heard it's chili night."

Ken looked down at Daisy. "Our mom makes the best chili. She has a recipe handed down from generations of Louisiana Bayou women."

Daisy's stomach rumbled. "I love chili."

Soon, Alex arrived, and Rosaline came out of the kitchen carrying a salad bowl and some glass containers of dressing. They all sat around the table and held hands while Philip asked God's blessing over the food and his family. Daisy sat with Ken on her right and Jon on her left. He sat across from Alex, who sat next to Brad with Valerie on his left. She sat next to Rosaline.

While the dishes got passed around and everyone loaded up on chili and salad, Rosaline asked Alex questions about the upcoming wedding. "We have a meeting with the Rabbi tomorrow."

Jon added, "We also found a house. Same neighborhood as Brad and Ken's."

Philip nodded. "Good area. Will you close before the wedding?"

Jon smiled and shrugged. "Unknown. I'm going to wave the inspection and try to fast track everything. We'll see."

Daisy watched the family dynamics as they scooped soup, buttered rolls, and chatted with each other. They made certain to include her at every opportunity in the conversation. Alex gushed over Camila's flower samples. Rosaline talked about working with the charity years ago with Daisy's grandfather. Ken talked about re-structuring the house he bought as he planned the rooms. Valerie talked about painting the baby's room. Through it all, conversations about Daisy's parents and brother and herself flowed through the conversation. She had never felt so included in a family not her own before.

At the end of the dinner, she went with the women into Rosaline's study. Ken's mom wheeled in a tray with herbal teas and cookies. "Philip and the boys tend to resort to business talk after our Wednesday night dinners." She looked at Daisy. "I don't mind listening to it, but since this is your first dinner with us. I'd rather not subject you to it."

She smiled and took the cup of herbal tea. "It's part of who they are as father and sons. Besides, Valerie works there, too." She looked over at Brad's wife. "Would you rather be in there with them?"

Valerie shook her head. "And miss a chance for some girl talk?" She grinned over at Alex. "I heard you found a dress."

Alex accepted the cup of tea from Rosaline and said, "Off the rack! I walked into a store this afternoon, and there was. I tried it on, and it needed absolutely no alteration. I can't believe it. If I was getting married in New York, I would've had three designers fighting over the chance to specially design my dress. And here I am walking into a store and thirty minutes later, walking out with the garment bag." She chuckled. "I feel like that was God saying, 'You got this.'"

Valerie clapped her hands. "Girl, I told you."

Alex grinned. "You did."

They talked more about the wedding and the plans, and Daisy grew more and more comfortable chatting with these women. Rosaline treated her with such kindness. By the end of the evening, Daisy felt like she had gained another friend.

An hour later, Ken walked her to her car. She leaned against the driver's door and looked up at him in the moonlight. Around them, she could hear the sounds of crickets and, far off in the distance, an owl. He smiled down at her. "Sorry to abandon you to the women after dinner. A rather archaic tradition."

She grinned. "I liked it. We talked about wedding stuff. Last night when we did that, you and your brothers escaped, so I figure you probably would rather not have been with me anyway."

"We had some work details to discuss. The conversation devolved into talks of overhead and profit margins." He tucked a strand of hair behind her ear, leaned down, and kissed her softly. He raised his head and stared at her for several heartbeats before he said, "Be safe going home."

After she got into the car, he tapped the roof, and she drove away. As she came to the end of the drive, his truck lights appeared in her rearview mirror. She found herself grinning almost the entire way home.

Mrs. Yancey followed the rest of the class out of the room but paused at the doorway and looked back at

Daisy. "I'd stay and help with the room, but I have an appointment."

Daisy shook her head. "It's not a problem. I'll see you Sunday."

She planned on breaking the news of her pregnancy with the women in her class today, but she just completely lost all courage as they went through prayer requests. Instead, they continued to study the Gospel of John, and she prayed again for God to endow her with the courage to admit her mistakes.

As she stood, she cried out, and a sharp cramp forced her to sit back down again. She put a hand over her lower abdomen and tried to breathe around the pain. Moving with very precise and cautious movements, she slowly stood up again. She didn't need to look to confirm that she was bleeding.

"Okay, Daisy, think straight. Don't panic." She talked to herself the entire walk down the long church hall and into the parking lot.

She drove straight to the hospital, and gingerly walked into the emergency room. The woman at the front desk looked up at her and asked, "May I help you?"

Daisy nodded and tried to speak around her dry mouth. "I am fourteen weeks pregnant and cramping and bleeding."

The woman immediately stood and gestured toward triage. "Go on in there, hon. I'll meet you."

It didn't take long to get her triaged and registered. Soon, she lay in a bed and stared blankly at the tech who wheeled in an ultrasound machine. She plugged it in, opened a drawer, and pulled out a pink sheet that she used to cover Daisy's lap. Then she lifted up the bottom of her gown, exposing her abdomen. She held up a squeeze tube of gel. "Don't worry. I keep mine warm."

The sensation of the warm gel hitting her flesh felt weird. Daisy wondered in the back of her mind if cold gel might have been better. The tech moved the wand across her belly, tapping on the keyboard. Daisy could see the screen and the images that appeared. A shiver started in her belly, a reaction to the gel cooling in the air.

She gasped as the baby came into the picture.

The first ultrasound she'd received, the baby looked like a little kidney bean. Today, it looked like a full-fledged baby. She could make out the head, the body, even the little nose.

"Here we are, mama." The tech tapped and zoomed and clicked on the keyboard, then hit a button, and the room filled with the noise of a beating heart. It sounded like it came from under water.

"Is that me?"

She smiled and shook her head. "Nope. That is that little person right there."

Daisy stared at the image and realized that a part of her had hoped the cramping and bleeding meant the worse. The tech left, and she lay there, cold and shivering under the thin blanket they left her. She analyzed her feelings, digging through, and finding the root of the disappointment.

Shame.

Despite everything, she still felt ashamed by what she'd done. How could she get past that?

Before she could start a conversation with herself, the doctor came into the little room. "Ms. Ruiz, how are you feeling?"

What a loaded question. She bit back the sarcasm that sprang to her tongue and said, "I'm still cramping."

"I'm sorry. You can take something from an approved list."

Out of nowhere, a sob escaped. The doctor sat on a stool and slid closer to the head of the bed. "Is the pain that intense?"

She put a shaking hand over her eyes. "No. I—" She gasped and cried and struggled to find the words again. "I just found myself hoping that this was over. That somehow, God had intervened on my behalf."

How could she feel this way? This little child inside of her with that beating heart belonged to her and her alone. Despair overwhelmed her heart until a bitter taste filled her mouth.

The doctor slipped a pamphlet out of her jacket pocket. "Is the father with you?"

Daisy fisted her hand and hit the bed. "No. I imagine he's with his wife somewhere."

After a long pause, she said, "I see."

"It doesn't matter." The storm had passed. Embarrassment clawed at the back of her head from her emotional display. Shame filled her heart from the thoughts she'd had.

"Your blood work is good. Your HCG levels are on point. The baby looks great. That little heart is beating perfectly. There doesn't appear to be any distress. The ultrasound showed a small subchronic hematoma. That's when the placenta has slightly detached from the wall of your womb. It's not uncommon, and I don't see evidence of a serious risk factor. What you should do is go home and rest. You need to stay hydrated. Call Doctor," she paused and looked on the paper, "Reynolds in the morning. She'll have access to our reports and imaging and will be able to monitor it. If the hematoma doesn't get bigger, you have nothing to worry about." The doctor set the brochure on the tray next to the bed. "I'd like to add that if you're not ready for a baby, you have other alternatives."

As soon as she realized what she meant, Daisy's eyes widened, and she gasped. "No! No! I couldn't possibly."

"It's not a recommendation. But, sometimes, your emotional state is worth protecting, and sometimes termination is the best way to do that." She stood. "Do you have any questions?"

Daisy's mind whirled with questions, but she didn't want to talk to this particular doctor anymore. "No. I'll talk to my doctor tomorrow."

"I understand." She walked to the edge of the curtain. "I'll send the nurse in here to discharge you."

Daisy lay on the bed, staring at the still ceiling fan above her. She noticed a cobweb that reflected the light and realized she should probably dust. Letting out a deep sigh, she rolled over onto her stomach.

She hadn't left her bed for anything other than

necessities since Thursday evening. She lay there, blankly staring at the television as she binge-watched some ridiculous television drama, and over and over again thought about how she felt as she went into that emergency room thinking she might lose the baby.

All evening Thursday, all day Friday, all night last night, the thoughts overwhelmed her until her mind swirled. She answered texts from Ken with generic platitudes but didn't engage him. Camila came by, but she didn't get out of bed, and she left after making sure she was "okay."

"Okay." What did that mean, anyway? No, she was not okay, and she didn't know how she would ever be okay again.

Now, like a whisper in her ear, she thought of how much easier it would be if she had just silently lost the baby. Most people she regularly dealt with would never even know she'd ever been pregnant. She wouldn't have to face her grandparents, experience their disappointment. Ken wouldn't have to pretend to connect with another man's baby.

The sob tore through her, surprising her. She curled into a ball, as tightly as she could, pressing her knees to her eyes. The idea of what she wished had happened actually physically hurt her heart. Did it point to a lack of trust in God?

A horrible sound filled the room, something that would come from a wounded animal. She gripped the covers and pulled them over her head. Even though she knew she should pray, she couldn't find the right words. How did one pray in a situation like this? For what should she appeal to God to do?

Make the "subchronic hematoma" bigger and, in doing so, place that perfect baby she'd seen on the screen in mortal danger? Is that what she actually hoped for?

Or did despair and shame flood her with the impossible desire to go back and reset her decisions so that the day Ken walked into her office, she could face him pure and unblemished?

"What is wrong with you?" she demanded of herself.

Her doctor had suggested taking a long weekend of bed rest. Today, though, Jon and Alex would get married. She needed to get up and face the day, face Ken and his family, and actually look herself in the mirror.

It took hours before she garnered the energy to get up. The cramping had eased considerably, the bleeding much less. The gray and dark skies fit her mood perfectly.

Lightheaded, she headed downstairs. Her body said to eat, but her soul rejected the idea of using energy to digest food. She settled on a bowl of plain yogurt. She curled into the corner of her couch and slowly ate it, not really tasting it, staring blankly at the dark television screen.

After the last bite, she carried the bowl into the kitchen and rinsed it out. As she went to put it in the dishwasher, it fell out of her hands. For several moments, she stared at the broken pieces on the floor. Then she left them where they fell, shutting the light off behind her.

Chapter 17

Ken arrived at two sharp. He wore a dark blue suit with a starched white shirt and a yellow and blue striped tie. Her heart pounded when she looked at him. By the time he got there, she had managed to find the energy to pretend to be happy to see him and excited about the wedding.

"You look really nice," she said.

He glanced at her purple lace dress and purple and blue butterfly necklace. "I could say the same," he said.

He took her to Camila's shop. When they walked in, the overwhelming scent of flowers made her gag. Her hand flew to her mouth, and she pinched her nose.

"I'm sorry," she said to Ken. "The smell this morning."

He put a hand on her elbow, concern etched in every feature. "I can take care of this."

Camila came out of the back room carrying a box. "Hi, you two. Here you go."

Daisy lifted her hand as she backed out of the door. She heard Ken say to Camila, "The flower smell got to her this morning."

Clutching the corner of the building, she lost her yogurt. Long after she had nothing left in her stomach, she stood there, resting her face against the cool brick, listening to the rain hit the awning above her. Cold sweat broke out on her body, and she wondered if she should have brought her makeup bag. Annoyed at the thought of her appearance instead of the physical state of her body, she slapped her hand against the wall and straightened just as Ken pushed the door open.

He walked straight to her. "You okay?"

She pressed a shaking hand to her mouth. "I'll be fine," she snapped. Then she closed her eyes and took a deep breath through her nose. "I'm sorry. I'm just not feeling well today."

"You don't need to apologize." He set the box in the back of the truck. "Do you want me to take you home?"

"No." The shop door opened again, and Camila came out with a bottle of water.

"You need to sit?"

"No. I'll be fine. Ken's parents' house isn't far from here." She took a small sip of the cool water.

"Oh, yeah. The castle," Camila said.

With her eyes, Daisy begged Camila not to say anything about Thursday. "Yeah. Thanks. I'll talk to you later."

Her cousin stared at her with concern, as if she could see the dilemma in her soul. Instead of enduring the inspection, she walked to the truck and ripped open the passenger's door. Before she could shut it, Ken was there, blocking it.

"What can I do for you?"

"I'll be fine. Just don't hover." She wouldn't meet his eyes. Finally, he gently shut the door.

After a few minutes, they arrived at his parents' house. While he pulled into the drive, she checked her face in the visor mirror. She still looked a little pale, but at least she felt like she could function again. Ken came around the front of the truck and opened the door as a valet approached them with an umbrella. "Good afternoon, Mr. Dixon," he said.

"Afternoon, Charles. Thanks for doing this."

"Beats picking up trash on a jobsite today. Plus, your guests always tip us well."

Daisy looked up at the massive castle. "I always think it looks like something out of a fairy tale."

Ken smiled a sheepish smile. "Helps bring that handsome prince charming point home."

Despite the heaviness of her heart, she chuckled. He grabbed the box of flowers out of the back of the truck and led the way into the house. As soon as she stepped under the overhang, Charles shook off the umbrella and turned back to the valet stand.

They crossed the massive foyer and went to the kitchen. She could smell coffee and her mouth watered at the thought of having a cup. Shaking her head, she opened the box Ken set on the wooden table. She did a quick inventory as the door on the far side of the room opened, and one of Ken's brothers came in.

"Hey guys," he said. "Mom's down in the pool house."

"Hi, Brad." Ken gestured at the box. "Guess we'll leave this here for now."

"Guess so." Brad looked at Daisy. "It's really good to see you, Daisy. How are you?"

Even as she smiled, it felt overly bright. "I'm great, Brad. It's really good to see you, too."

"Where's the groom?" Ken asked.

"Upstairs." Brad rooted through the box and removed a white rose boutonniere, which he fastened to his lapel. "Did Ken tell you what Jon and Alex are doing?"

Daisy focused on the conversation. "Yeah, um, they're getting baptized before the ceremony, right?"

"They are. Never thought I would ever see Jon so settled. It's nice." He extended a boutonniere to Ken, who frowned. "You gotta do it, bro. I don't make the rules."

Ken took the flower and stared at it. Daisy stepped forward. "Let me help."

By the time she finished pinning the flower to his lapel, she felt more like herself.

Valerie strolled into the kitchen with a barely noticeable limp. She wore a royal blue dress that flowed around her. A bright pink belt secured the waist. "Well, hi there, Daisy!" she said. "How are you?"

Before she could answer, Alex entered the room. She wore a pair of shorts and a white T-shirt. Daisy smiled at her and said, "I don't think I've ever seen a bride less ready so close to the ceremony." She chuckled. "I guess makeup and hair are moot when you're going to be dunked under the water."

Alex put a hand up to her hair, which she had pulled back in a ponytail. "It's crazy how fast I'm going to have to get ready."

"Don't worry about making us wait," Ken said. "We will have Calla food. You'll have a captive audience."

"True." She gestured at the box. "Can I see the flowers?"

Camila had designed a simple but stunning bouquet of white roses with shoots of green leaves coming out, making the bouquet look like it had movement of its own. "This is perfect." She touched the bundle of baby's breath. "I'm going to do something with this in my hair. I'm going to do a braided bun, and I think I'm gonna put these throughout the braid."

Valerie and Daisy nodded. Valerie said, "That will be simple but lovely."

A couple of hours later, Jon and Alex got baptized while their friends and family watched. Their rabbi explained the history of baptism in the Jewish culture. His words filled Daisy with such wonder at how God provided such a visual representation of putting off the old, dying to oneself to become new creatures in Christ again. Beside the pool, Daisy stood in the circle of Ken's arms and thought about the perfection of starting married life together as new creatures in Christ.

As soon as Alex went into the pool house, she looked up at Ken. "That was beautiful. It was worth getting dressed up and witnessing. I wish all baptisms were such lavish affairs."

Ken smiled. "Just as important as the wedding,

don't you think?"

"I'm glad you understood what I was saying. I didn't think I'd worded it well."

He gave her a soft kiss. "I understood."

Valerie met her eyes, and she slipped away from him. "Ready to go help Alex? She's probably out of the shower by now."

"Yep." She smiled up at Ken. "I'll be out later."

"I'm going to go find one of those platters of hors d'oeuvres that the waiters are carrying around."

About thirty minutes later, Daisy pinned baby's breath throughout Alex's blonde braid. The simple braided bun fit Alex's style perfectly and looked great with her dress. She couldn't believe how quickly Alex had showered, dried her hair, and put on her makeup.

"Perfect?" Daisy asked, stepping back.

Alex held the mirror up and looked at the back of her head. "Yes. Perfect. Thank you."

She held her hands over her eyes as Daisy sprayed hair spray, then she slipped on her ivory-colored sheath style dress. Valerie helped her zip it.

"It's a little tighter around the middle than it was just a few days ago," she remarked, running her hands over her still mostly flat stomach. "I'm glad it still zips."

"Oh, you still have a little bit of room," Valarie said. While Valerie helped fasten the necklace that Rosaline had loaned Alex, and which Valerie had also worn in her own wedding, Daisy used Alex's professional camera to take pictures. She thought about how recently Alex had come into this family's lives, and how so quickly they made her welcome. She realized that they'd done the same for her.

Of course, they didn't know she was pregnant with another man's child. That would make a big difference in what they thought of her.

"I appreciate both of you. I appreciate your help so much," Alex said. She slipped her feet into the gold sandals adorned with crystal flowers along the top strap. Daisy bent to help her fasten them. "I know the guests are probably tired of waiting."

"You've only been in here for forty-five minutes. That's probably some kind of record for a bride getting ready."

Alex sent a text to let everyone know she was ready, then walked to the door and hugged first Valerie then Daisy. "See you out there," Valerie said, handing Alex her bouquet then slipping out the door. Daisy followed as the minister called the guests to order.

Daisy stared up toward the front, toward Ken, who sat on the front row next to his mother, an empty seat beside him. She knew he had saved it for her.

You don't belong up there with him. You don't even belong here at all.

She started walking in that direction but fumbled. If they knew the way her thoughts had gone for the last thirty-six hours, they'd never want her anywhere near their family again.

As Alex and her uncle took their places in the back of the crowd, Daisy quietly made her way back into the pool house and back to the bedroom where she had just spent precious time with Alex and Valerie.

Makeup containers in varying sizes and styles were strewn in a chaotic jumble on a small table. A hairdryer hung over the back of a chair, and a container of hairpins sat on the seat. A garment bag and hangar lay discarded on the bed.

With shaking hands, Daisy hung the hangar and garment bag for the dress in the small closet and then lay on top of the bed, pressing the heels of her hands into her eyes.

Chapter 18

Ken watched Valerie take her seat next to Brad as Alex and her uncle moved to the back of the crowd. He looked around and spotted the edge of Daisy's dress as she went back into the pool house. By the time he realized she wasn't coming back out, the ceremony had begun. As much as he wanted to get up and investigate, he sat still and waited through the exchanging of vows, rings, and finally the first kiss as husband and wife. As soon as Mr. Jonathan and Mrs. Alexandra Dixon walked down the aisle together, holding hands, he slipped out from the crowd and went into the pool house.

The smell of cooking filled his senses as he stepped into the small building. He threw Calla a quick wave of greeting and kept walking through the house toward the bedroom in the back.

Daisy had missed the entire ceremony. Something

was wrong, something important enough for her to remain in here throughout the entire wedding. She had looked okay during the baptism. He searched his mind for any possible explanation and didn't like any of the conclusions he reached. His anxiety grew with every step. Finally, he tapped on the little door twice, then opened it to find Daisy curled up in a ball on top of the bed.

His middle felt suddenly empty and hot all at once. He had been right. Something was wrong. He rushed forward. "Daisy? You okay?"

When he touched her shoulder, she jerked away from him. "Leave me alone," she said on a sob.

He knelt next to the bed and asked, "What's wrong. Did something happen?"

Choking on tears, she spit, "You don't want to know."

He brushed a damp tendril of hair away from her face. "Course I want to know. Talk to me."

The bed shifted as she pushed herself into a sitting position. She wiped at her face, and he snatched some tissues out of the holder on the nightstand. She wouldn't meet his eyes as she took them from him. "I was at the emergency room Thursday afternoon."

His heart started pounding, and sweat beaded his upper lip. A thousand possibilities raced through his imagination, and he pushed them back, needing more information. He carefully sat next to her but made no move to touch her... yet. Softly, he asked, "Are you okay?"

She bowed her head and pressed the tissues against

her eyes. He felt helpless and hopeless and wanted to fix whatever was wrong for her, but he didn't know what he needed to fix. "The ER doctor said I have a subchronic hematoma."

He wracked his brain and couldn't even begin to guess what that meant. "Did he give you a prognosis?"

"She."

"She?"

Daisy nodded. "The doctor was a woman."

Ken grit his teeth. He could not care less about the sex of the physician right this second. He took a slow breath and intentionally relaxed his jaw before he spoke. "Cool. Did she give you a prognosis?"

Daisy stared at her hands in her lap as they clutched the soaked tissues. She started ripping little pieces of the tissue and spindling them between her finger and thumb. "It's something that could be major if it gets worse, but it probably isn't going to. My symptoms made me think I was having a miscarriage."

Anxious, he put a hand over hers. "But you didn't? The baby's okay?"

"No. I didn't." Her shoulders shook, but no sound came from her. Finally, she said, "But, Ken, a part of me wanted to miscarry."

The breath escaped his body. *What? Why?* His hands turned cold. "Explain."

She finally looked at him with watery, red eyes. "When the ultrasound tech told me the baby was there and let me listen to the heartbeat, I felt just a moment of disappointment. Then the doctor came in, and she was really understanding, and she gave me this flier about terminating the baby, and I almost took it home with me."

Something was very, very wrong. This could not be the Daisy he knew. This was not the Daisy he loved. The way she spoke, no longer through tears but weirdly calm, made his skin tingle with involuntary gooseflesh. Could this be her training as a lawyer? She spoke so matter-of-factly.

Miscarriage. Terminating the baby. Killing the unborn child with intent and forethought. Abortion.

Completely horrified and at a loss for words, he whispered, "You didn't..."

"No. No, of course not." She stood and crossed the room, wrapping her arms around her stomach as she turned and faced him. "I couldn't. For the last two days, I just laid in my bed and tried to understand what I was feeling and why. I realized that I am ashamed of myself."

She balled up the tissue in her fist and closed her eyes. "Everything would be so much easier for me if I just wasn't pregnant anymore. I wouldn't have to face anyone. No one would know what I had done. The proof of my sin would just vanish."

Words filled his mind; words of condemnation, understanding, rejection, love, acceptance, disgust, wisdom. He didn't even know where to begin. Finally, he said, "God would know."

"You think I don't know that?" she snapped.

He stared at her as her quick anger evaporated as if it had never existed. He processed every word of the conversation so far before he spoke. "Quite frankly, I don't know what you think right now. The idea that you would even think about bringing harm to an innocent life to cover your mistake, your sin, makes me think I don't know anything about you." Bitterness filled his mouth like bile. "But I want to understand. Explain it so I understand."

"Understand? I didn't do anything to this baby. I got up this morning and even took my vitamins like I ought to do. I'm trying to tell you something that happened to me and give you the honesty of my thoughts and feelings because you claim to love me and care about me. I'm really struggling here, and I don't know what to do to make it better." She walked back toward the bed. "How do I stop thoughts like that?"

Ken suddenly realized that he might never understand. The secular world has this philosophical notion that if it were somehow possible to strip away everything physical and cultural from, say, a man, that you would arrive at just a pure "core" identity of a sexless person. The secular belief then purports that if it were somehow possible to replace everything that was first stripped away with, say, female physicality and female cultural mores, then that once man's "core" self could equally and effortlessly shift to "identifying" as female. The belief concludes that the converse is equally true, and so a female could just as equally and effortlessly act as a male.

Ken had analyzed this philosophical notion about gender and come to an undeniable conclusion. As a result, he knew something the secular world didn't realize. Without any sliver of a doubt, Ken knew that this entire notion was utter and complete nonsense built on untestable fictions. He knew that the Creator of the universe determined a person's gender before He even knitted that person in a mother's womb.

Ken Dixon had spent uncountable hours of his life to date pondering mysteries and analyzing evidence, puzzles, and challenges that life presented. He had identified the mysteries that loomed larger than his intellect. He also knew what he knew with unshakable certainty. One thing he knew for certain: God had made him male. All he wanted to be was the best man he could be.

Setting any religious knowledge or philosophical hypotheticals aside, Ken knew he would make a horrible female. Thankfully, he never had been, and never would be, a woman. However, that also meant that Ken would never have to carry a child inside his body.

Therefore, Ken could never fully understand Daisy's feelings, but logic and reason had served him well his entire life. So he silently reasoned through this puzzle just as he always had. He analyzed. He considered what advice he could offer. His mind took in all the facts and all of the social constructs and came to just one sound logical conclusion. It followed almost like a symphony, like the most elegant syllogism he had ever pondered. Why had Daisy not reached that same conclusion already as well?

He knew that the decisions she'd made so far formed the foundation of this deep anger with herself. He decided to start there. "What would lessen your shame?"

"I beg your pardon?"

He no longer wanted to quibble. He needed facts. He shrugged his shoulders and shook his head to try to express impatience and frustration. "It's a simple question, Daisy."

She stared at him and opened and closed her mouth as if she didn't quite know where to start. Finally, she said, "I imagine that if no one knew what I had done, I would have no shame."

Ken had already calculated every possibility before he ever framed the question. Trying not to sound impatient, he said, "Not a realistic option. Everyone will know pretty soon. Right? Wind the clock forward three or four months. You're obviously pregnant, and everyone knows it because there's no hiding it. Realistically, what would lessen your shame?"

She pressed her lips together tightly. She tilted her head as if trying to see him more clearly. "Being married, I guess."

"Exactly right." He nodded. "So, let's get married."

"What?" She held up both hands. "No!"

"No?"

"No! No way!"

"No way?" Every muscle in his body tensed. "You do realize I am proposing to you, Daisy." It wasn't a question.

She shook her head. "You're not going to ask me to marry you out of pity. So you can fix my problem? If you ask me to marry you, it will be because you love me and you want to marry me."

He released his breath and shot to his feet. He slowly cocked his head to the right then the left, feeling his neck bones pop and crack like knuckles with the forced release of tension. He righted his head and stared down at her, his face perfectly composed. "Daisy, I imagine your emotions are chaotic right now. It's a stressful situation coupled with flooding hormones. Thoughts born out of desperation are going to happen."

Slowly, without ever losing eye contact, he lowered himself down onto one knee before her. Locking her gaze with his, he pulled the ring box out of his pocket and opened it. The princess cut diamond glittered in the sunlight streaming through the window, making it look as big and bright as a full moon. "The fact is, I've just been waiting for enough time to go by, waiting for the right time and place. If that's here and now, so be it."

She gaped at him and wagged a finger in his face. "That has to be the most unromantic proposal ever in the history of ever." She snatched up her purse. "I have to go home."

He snapped the ring box closed. "I'll drive you."

She spun and said, "You will not drive me. I'll get myself home."

As she ripped open the bedroom door, he said, "Daisy, Peter tells us to cast our cares on Him because He cares for us. If you can find the way to do that, truly do it, that will lessen your shame. He will bear that burden with you and for you."

Without leaving, she slammed the door closed and

turned and looked at him. "You know what, Ken? I was reared up by a youth pastor. I'm a PK, a preacher's kid. If I wanted platitudes, I would have gone to my father."

She ripped the door open again and left the bedroom. He forced himself not to follow her. He wanted to make sure she got to the main house okay and then got into a cab okay, but he didn't. Instead, he waited.

About twenty minutes later, he heard music. He took a deep breath and let it out, then made his way back out to the wedding reception.

Daisy's phone rang three days later, and she glanced at it. Seeing Valerie's number, she steeled herself and answered it.

"Hi!" Valerie greeted before Daisy could even speak. "I'm outside your door with two cups of tea. Open up."

Realizing Valerie had bypassed trying to make plans which Daisy would just decline, she chuckled and made her way through the office to unlock the front door.

Valerie stood outside the glass door wearing a pink skirt and matching jacket. She had on pink heels and a white blouse. Daisy looked down at her comfortable jeans and felt decidedly underdressed. She unlocked the door and smiled as Valerie breezed inside.

"You look incredible. I wish I looked like that at four in the afternoon."

Valerie held out a paper cup of herbal tea and waved her hand in a dismissive gesture. "It's just the color. It hides a whole lot of tired."

As they walked through the office to the kitchenette, Valerie looked around. "Good use of space."

Daisy smiled at her as she turned on the kitchenette light. "When all the volunteers are working at one time, there's enough space for everyone. That's rare, but it used to be in my dining room, so I like having this as an option."

They settled in at the small table, and Daisy opened a tin of butter cookies that someone had left for them. Valerie took a sip of her tea and said, "We missed you at the reception. Is everything okay?"

Actually, no. Everything was not okay. Everything was very, very wrong. "Ken and I had a pretty serious disagreement. I couldn't face him. I had to leave. I'm sorry I missed the reception."

Valerie shook her head. "You don't need to apologize to me. I'm just here to see if you need anything."

She smirked. "What I needed was for Ken to give me some support and sympathy. What I got was a lecture and a sermon."

"You said, 'lecture and a sermon'?" With her hand over her chest, Valerie chuckled. "I'm sorry. I'm sure this is no laughing matter to you. But, honestly, that's what you get from Ken. Well, when he says anything at all, that is."

Daisy had some personal theories, but she suddenly wanted a third party's insight. "Why do you think he's so quiet?"

Valerie shrugged and smiled a self-deprecating

smile. "When I was younger, I thought it was so he could make himself sound somehow more important whenever he actually did condescend to speak with us mere mortals. You know, like handing down words of wisdom."

"You don't think that anymore," Daisy prompted with a hopeful grin.

Valerie shook her head. "No. I think Ken Dixon grew up way too soon. I think he was deeply insecure as a child, thinking he could never measure up to his brothers or his father."

"Really?" Daisy asked, seeing the truth of it even at the instant Valerie said the words.

"Really." Valerie nodded. "And I believe he is very, very smart, and thinks about absolutely everything from every possible angle, hoping to live a life that's true and pure."

Daisy nodded. "I completely agree."

Valerie grinned, enjoying Daisy's obvious interest in this particular subject. "Ever notice something? He's always thrown himself into physical activity that doesn't require a lot of talk or explanation. I believe that's because he's terribly shy, and conversation drains him. But peace and quiet restores his soul."

Daisy thought about how Ken silently threw his body into things like martial arts or framing out a house. He just as silently cast a hook or manned a grill. "That makes so much sense."

Valerie sat back and said, "So it isn't really surprising that you felt like he gave you a little sermon. Whenever it's not some quick witticism, it's always some profound thing or other. But you know as well as I do that he doesn't mean anything by it."

Daisy knew that. She'd had an emotional, knee-jerk reaction to his words—or lack of them. Now, she didn't know if she could possibly build a bridge back to who they were before she walked out on him. She didn't know if she had the emotional wherewithal to try.

She sighed. "I know. But, tell that to the emotional, hormonal woman three days ago when she might scratch your eyes out for looking at her sideways."

"Gotta love the hormones." She reached over and took a cookie out of the tin. "I hope you guys get back together. You two are perfect for each other." She lifted her teacup. "But, regardless, I hope we can stay friends."

Daisy smiled and took a sip of the tea. "Thank you. I really appreciate that."

Sitting at her desk, Daisy hung up the phone and made a notation in the file. Then she opened the email that had just arrived from Toby at Dixon Contracting and Design. Just the thought of Dixon Contracting made her heart beat a little faster. She opened the email.

Dear Ms. Ruiz:

Ken Dixon asked me to contact you to confirm arrival at the job site for the Osborne Family house at 7:00 a.m. this coming Friday, 4 Sept. We have 8 carpenters and 15 laborers

> scheduled to work that job through 6 p.m. on Monday, 7 Sept.
>
> If these details have changed, please contact my office right away. Find my direct line below my signature.
>
> Signed,
>
> Toby MacDonald, Assistant

She had received two other communications from Toby in the last couple of weeks, which kept her from worrying that Dixon Contracting would withdraw their support for the coming house. But she couldn't help but wonder if Ken or his brothers also personally planned to work on this house. She shot a quick email back confirming the information and thanked the company for their support.

Daisy hadn't seen or heard from Ken since the wedding. She hadn't reached out to him, either. She completely understood his perspective, but she didn't appreciate the way he went into logic mode immediately while she lay there crying. She needed him to put his arms around her, and instead, he preached at her.

In hindsight, though, it occurred to her she should have told him what she needed. With his arms around her, wrapping her up, she would know everything would be okay. In the end, nothing was okay. Everything was wrong. She didn't know how to bring it back to right.

She imagined she couldn't do anything about it at this point. Ken had made it clear what he thought of her emotional reactions.

He'd also had a glittering diamond ring on him. Why had he had a ring in his pocket?

She stood and rubbed her belly. She had started to swell slightly. In the mirror, she could easily see her baby bump, but clothes still hid it well enough. She had received a summons from her grandfather last night and knew that her mother must have told him. She did not look forward to going to see him today. Knowing she'd disappointed him was almost more than she could bear.

After she gathered her purse and turned off her computer, she walked to the front. Beverly returned from lunch just as she made it to the lobby. "Hey. I'm headed to my grandparents'. I don't know for certain if I'll be back today."

Beverly glanced at her watch. "Sure. Do I need to do anything for Friday?"

"Nope." She pushed open the door. "See you tomorrow."

"See you."

On the drive, Daisy tried to decide what to say to him and how to say it. She prayed for God to give her words, but she didn't receive any kind of divine guidance. She pulled into the drive behind their sedan and took a few deep breaths before she walked up to the door.

Her grandmother answered, smiling ear-to-ear. She didn't even stand five feet tall and had short, curly, salt-and-pepper hair and bright brown eyes. "Daisy! I'm so happy to see you!"

"Of course, I won't miss a chance to have lunch with you, Abuela."

Daisy bent and hugged her, then let her grandmother lead her into the house. She could smell the spicy tang of meat grilling. Her grandfather stood by the sliding glass door that led from the dining room to the back porch.

"Daisy. Glad you could make it."

"Abuelo, I was happy to get the invitation."

"Is that so?" He gestured at the table. "Your grandmother has some things to finish in the kitchen, but we can sit."

He acted very cool, not his normal loving, warm self. She mentally shored up her courage, reinforcing it in anticipation.

"I'm guessing Mamá told you about my situation."

"Si, si." Daisy marked his emotional state by his reflexive reversion to Spanish. Her grandfather rarely spoke anything other than English. His eyes stayed hard. "She did not share the details, only the circumstance. She said if I needed more information that you would explain yourself."

"I see."

He tightened his mouth and prompted her with, "This is your opportunity to explain yourself."

She clasped her hands tightly in her lap. "I am pregnant and due in February."

He gave one sharp nod of his head. "And? The father?"

Maintaining eye contact, she said, "Has nothing to do with this."

"One might think the father has everything to do with this."

"Yes, one might think." Daisy lifted her chin. "Nevertheless."

He raised his eyebrows and gestured in her direction. "You dare to speak so flippantly to me?" She wondered if he realized he had switched from English back to Spanish again. "So disrespectful?"

She gently shook her head. In Spanish, she said, "Abuelo, I have absolutely no disrespect for you at all. I love you, and I'm sorry that you're upset with me."

"No." He tapped the top of the table with his finger. "We are not going to discuss your emotional state right now. We're going to discuss actions and reactions. So, explain to me why you would become pregnant by a man who now will have nothing to do with the child."

She licked her lips and tried to formulate words that would properly explain the situation. "Unfortunately, I didn't know he was married. He wooed me with promises and plans that he didn't mean, but I believed. Maybe I just wanted to believe. Maybe I ignored the clues. When I first discovered I was pregnant, I went to talk to him, and that's when I found out for certain."

She'd had two solid weeks since her emergency room visit and had time to think about exactly how she felt about this baby. She knew she spoke the complete truth with the next words out of her mouth. "I spent weeks scared and sad and angry. I even, to my shame, contemplated how easy everything would be if I just wasn't pregnant anymore. But I have been on my knees for the last two weeks giving everything over to God, and I can tell you that I love this baby, and I am thankful that the father wants nothing to do with the child or with me. He is not a good man."

Unexpectedly, tears filled her grandfather's eyes. "I wish you had made a different decision."

She pulled a verse from Romans eight out of her mind. "All things work together for good, though, don't they? God can use this. I'm not proud of myself, but I'm very much looking forward to meeting my baby."

"Granddaughter, when I gave you the mission that I had spent my whole life building, I trusted you to maintain a certain character and hold yourself to a certain moral standard. This tells me I was wrong in trusting you."

Her breath hitched. "Abuelo, do you think I have a loose moral code? I made a single mistake one time and was seduced by a very skilled liar. I love God, and I serve Him. Everything I do day after day is to serve Him. The Bible says that all have sinned and come short of the glory of God. I'm sorry my sin is something that's manifesting physically. But the fact is, no man is good. No, not even one."

She just quoted three different Bible verses in one conversation. If he didn't accept her words, then he had thrown a veil over his own eyes that prevented him from grasping it. And if it meant that he revoked her position as Executive Director of his ministry and handed her a bill for law school, then so be it.

He held his hand out, palm up. She looked at the wrinkled skin the color of soft leather for several moments before she put her hand in his. He squeezed tightly as tears fell from his eyes. "I am proud of your courage today."

When he let her go, her grandmother came into the room with a meat platter next to a pile of corn tortillas. "Time to eat, yes?" she said with a grin. "I made you lingua."

"Thank you, Abuela, it smells amazing." Her grandmother knew how much she loved beef tongue. As she set out her roasted pepper sauce and a pitcher of water, Daisy noticed that her grandmother never mentioned her grandfather's obvious emotional state or the tense air around them. It made her wonder how much she knew and how much she'd heard.

By the end of the meal, they didn't treat her any differently than they always had. When she left, they both hugged her goodbye.

Chapter 19

Ignoring the other women in the waiting room, Daisy turned the page in her book and continued reading the details about what to expect during the sixteenth week of pregnancy. From the picture in the book, she should already show a little more. She ran her hand over the slight swell of her stomach and wondered if it was normal to still be so small. She'd have to ask Dr. Reynolds.

"Daisy?" She glanced up and spotted Valerie.

Her heart immediately started racing, and her mouth went dry. "Uh, hi, Valerie." She glanced around but did not see Brad. "What are you doing here?"

Valerie gestured at her much larger stomach swell. "I'm here for my monthly appointment." She raised an eyebrow and looked at the book, then pointedly at Daisy's stomach. "What are you doing here?"

Her face flooded with heat and sweat beaded her

upper lip. Even her scalp heated up. She hadn't seen Valerie since having coffee with her two weeks ago.

"Same." She cleared her throat. She had not prepared herself for this conversation. "I, uh, see Dr. Reynolds."

Valerie carefully sat in the empty chair next to her and turned her body toward her. "Because?"

Unexpected tears burned her eyes. "Because I'm pregnant. Sixteen weeks tomorrow."

Valerie gasped. "I'm seventeen weeks tomorrow. Are we seriously only a week apart?"

"Yeah, uh, looks that way."

With a grin, Valerie grabbed her hands with both of hers. "How exciting is that? Does Ken know? What did he say?"

"Daisy Ruiz?"

Silently thanking God for the reprieve, she pulled her hands free and grabbed her book as she stood. "That's me. I'll see you later."

She went through the appointment with edgy nerves fluttering through her stomach and down her arms into her hands. Her fingertips felt ice cold. She could barely answer the doctor's questions. Her mind focused on Valerie and how she could possibly explain everything.

The doctor checked the placenta on an ultrasound and made sure everything still looked good. The baby's heartbeat filled her ears, sounding very fast and very loud.

"I don't think the subchronic hematoma is going to give us any more problems." She smiled and wiped the ultrasound gel off Daisy's stomach. "If you start bleeding again, just go straight to the ER. But call here first."

Daisy got dressed, then went to the appointment desk and made next month's appointment. Once she fully checked out, she headed back out into the waiting room to leave. When she saw Valerie sitting in a chair by the door, she stopped short.

When Valerie saw her, she smiled and stood. "Hey, there. I thought we could have lunch. Are you free?"

With a heavy sigh, Daisy said, "I am free."

Valerie raised a perfectly manicured eyebrow. "But you don't want to be?"

Steeling herself for a conversation that needed to happen, she shook her head. "It's okay. Let's go."

Soon, they sat across from each other in a little cafe. It was early still, only 11:15, so they had this corner of the dining room to themselves. Valerie squeezed lemon into her water and stirred it with the striped paper straw. Daisy tried to think of a way to start the conversation.

Valarie leaned toward her very slightly and, in a low voice, asked, "Does Ken know you're pregnant?"

She guessed that she could start there as well as anywhere. "Yes."

"Oh. He does." Valerie sat back and laced her fingers together, placing them in her lap. She looked puzzled and thoughtful for a few seconds, then said, "I have a hard time reconciling the Ken I know with this situation. The Ken I know doesn't abandon his girlfriend when she's pregnant, no matter what kind of fight they had."

She thought of a dozen things she could say. Most of them she'd practiced in the car on the way here. All of them sounded wrong. Finally, she said, "It's not Ken's baby."

"Oh!" As Valerie assimilated that fact, all the puzzle pieces clicked into place then immediately tumbled into disorder again. She gasped and slapped her hand to her chest. "Oh, Daisy."

She'd expected revulsion, not sympathy. Unbidden, tears sprang to her eyes. "I've loved Ken forever. I really think I've loved him since the very first second I ever saw him. All through college, I thought about him. I've compared every man I have ever known to him. And then I started dating this guy I met at one of my fundraisers. He swept me off my feet, completely pulled the rug right out from under me."

Valerie pulled a packet of tissues out of her purse and handed her one. She dabbed at the tears streaming down her face. "But?"

She took a long sip of ice water and finally blurted out, "But he was married. And when he found out I was pregnant, he made it clear how he felt about it."

Her friend reached across the table and took her hand in both of hers. Her skin felt cool, smooth compared to her own hot and sweaty palms. "Listen, Daisy, I understand."

She shook her head. "How can you understand?"

With intense, focused eyes, Valarie said, "Because when I lived in Savannah, I dated a married man. I even moved in with him." Valerie pressed her lips together. "Let's just say it ended badly."

Daisy gasped. "Is he the one who—?

With a nod, Valerie said, "Who beat me for a year then threw me off a balcony? Yes. He was married, too."

Suddenly, it occurred to her that Valerie would not condemn or judge. Valerie would listen and be her friend. "I don't know how to get Ken back. I said something, and he reacted, and now we're here."

"What happened? What did you say?"

"It's not important. I was emotional and stupid."

Valarie grinned. "It's hard to imagine you being stupid. I can see emotional, but stupid is a stretch."

Daisy shook her head. "What happened was stupid. I wish I could go back in time and change everything that happened."

Releasing her hands, Valerie sat back and said, "If it helps, he's completely miserable."

"At least we have that in common."

Valerie licked her lips. "Did you guys break up because he found out you're pregnant?"

More tears. "No. He said he loves me and loves my baby."

A waitress served their soup and salad. Daisy tried to regain her composure while she went through the ritual of presenting dishes and offering pepper. When she left, she said, "I don't quite know how it happened. But knowing he's miserable gives me hope that it can be rectified."

"You'll see him tomorrow, right?"

She sighed. "Yeah. All weekend."

"Then I guess that's your chance."

Ken ran his hand down the stair handrail, feeling for any rough spots he might have missed. It felt smooth all the way down, so he walked over to the makeshift table he'd created out of two sawhorses and a sheet of plywood and picked up the wood stain. He'd give it a good mahogany stain, then finish it with a high gloss varnish.

For two weeks, he'd worked non-stop on the house. Every room upstairs had drywall and trim, and most rooms had flooring. Painters spent the day upstairs painting bedrooms and bathrooms.

He'd started on the downstairs in the formal dining room on Tuesday. He built cabinetry and shelving, staining everything rich mahogany and then treating the wood varnish so it gleamed. Last night he finished the last of the trim in that room, and today he planned to start on the front room. Before he could begin, though, he had to put up the stair rail because he'd stored it on the fireplace hearth while he decided on wood stains and lighting.

Ken mentally replayed the conversation with Daisy over and over again while he worked. He hadn't handled things well, but neither had she. Two weeks later, the silence between them screamed back at him. He missed her with every molecule of his body. Should he reach out or continue to wait for her to come to her senses?

Tomorrow, he would see her, build a house with her. He wondered if she'd even actively have a part in the construction or if she just set everything up and wouldn't show. He didn't think he'd ever wished tomorrow would come harder than now.

As he climbed the ladder to measure the wall above the front door, he saw headlights turn into his yard. He climbed back down the ladder and moved it out of the way so he could open the door just as Jon walked up onto the porch.

"Evening," he greeted, opening the door wider.

"Yeah."

His brother had looked better. He had dark circles under his eyes and lines around his mouth. "What's wrong?"

"I messed up with Alex."

"That was fast." He led the way to the back of the house to the room beyond the kitchen. Here, he'd set up a small living area. He gestured at one of the folding chairs and took the other. "Spill."

Jon rubbed the back of his neck and leaned forward, his elbows on his knees. "Alex comes from a different world. Estates, helicopters, power, a house full of servants. When she got pregnant, her father stripped everything from her, evicted her, even applied influence at the bank to withdraw her trust. Her friends were told to shun her, and they did so that they didn't suffer the same treatment from their families."

Ken had a hard time understanding what kind of a father would do that to a child. "Why?"

"Because he was trying to pressure her to have an abortion."

It took a moment for his words to sink in. "That's horrible."

"I know. It's very hard to take a passive approach

with her family when I want to just charge up to Connecticut and introduce myself."

Ken shook his head. "I'd be your wingman."

"I have no doubt. Anyway, when she first arrived, Dad offered to connect her with someone to get her a job. She declined and later told me that her father had opened every door for her, and because of that, he had the power to shut them. She wanted to make it on her own. I respected that. So, when she said Wade's campaign called her, I assumed you or Brad had contacted him on her behalf, not knowing about her situation. Instead of just admitting we were friends, I congratulated her on the call."

Ken tried to process the situation. "When did you tell her?"

He rubbed the back of his neck. "I didn't. She found out while researching Wade's past."

"Dude," Ken said.

"Yeah," Jon agreed.

"That's messed up," Ken observed.

"Yeah," Jon agreed.

"So, you lied by omission." Ken pursed his lips.

"Pretty much. So, when she left here to work with Wade, she was just hurt and felt betrayed and, honestly, was a little bit angry."

Knowing his brother's propensity to hit the bottle when life overwhelmed him, Ken decided to do a quick status check. "How's the drinking?"

Jon shook his head. "I'm not doing that right now."

That impressed Ken. Jon had discovered alcohol at a high school party. Actually, all three of them had at the same party. Brad had accepted a beer and sipped on it for hours. Ken and Jon drank like their lives depended on it. Jon had done fine. He laughed too much, talked a lot, made friends with everyone at the party, and woke up the next morning without an issue.

Ken had fallen deep into his own psyche. He'd examined every moment of his life and saw everywhere he came up short. He couldn't walk, couldn't speak, everything spun and appeared to fall apart then come back together. The next morning, he thought he'd died and gone straight to hell. Then he wished he could die. He never took another drink in his life and didn't plan to ever again.

He studied his brother. For maybe the first time, Ken realized that Jon was actually committed to his sobriety this time. "That's good, Jon. Welcome to coping with your emotions without a buffer."

"You're so pretty."

"Yeah, that's what mama says." Ken brought them back to the serious matter at hand. "Are you two speaking?"

"We are. I made her promise to call me at least once a day. So far, she's been terse, but she laughed this morning, so I have that going for me." He sighed and rested his elbows on his knees. "I can't lose her, man. She is everything to me."

"Yeah." He cleared his throat. "I know what you mean."

Jon stared at him. "Still no Daisy?" He frowned. "What happened there, anyway?"

Ken scoffed. "She's pregnant."

"What?" With wide eyes, Jon sat up straighter. "What are you doing here? Go get that girl!"

"It's not mine." Jon quit speaking and waited. Finally, Ken spoke very succinctly. "She dated a guy before me. Married guy. It's his."

"Dude," Jon said.

"Yeah," Ken agreed.

"That's messed up," Jon observed.

"Yeah," Ken agreed.

"So she lied by omission," Jon said.

"Pretty much." Ken shifted the ball cap on his head. "I love her, Jon." He pursed his lips and uncharacteristically elaborated. "I need her." He met Jon's eyes. "I never needed anybody. But I need her. And I love that baby as if it were mine."

"Can you, though?"

Ken just stared at him.

Jon said, "Look, I know how I felt when Alex told me she was pregnant. First, I was afraid. Then I was ridiculously happy. But, the baby's mine. The fear faded pretty quickly and left nothing but joy."

Ken kicked his legs out in front of him and crossed them at the ankles. "I don't know how to explain it. I just know her baby has filled my heart the same way she did. I never think about the fact that my DNA isn't there. It truly doesn't matter to me."

"What will the biological father say?"

"He already said it. Told her to kill it. Then signed over his parental rights so his wife wouldn't find out. All legal and documented. Daisy's protected."

"She tell you who he is?"

"Nope." Ken shook his head. "Don't care, and it doesn't matter."

Jon nodded. "So, what's the problem?"

Ken had started to feel tired from all the talking a few minutes earlier. He nearly froze at the thought of revealing such a personal matter with his brother, but he really did need to talk about this. "The week of your wedding, she had a miscarriage scare. She said she wished she really had miscarried."

Jon tilted his head back and stared at the ceiling for a moment, then said, "I can understand that. She's in ministry with specific expectations and moral standards. She teaches at her church. She runs the risk of losing all of that as soon as people know she's pregnant out of wedlock from an adulterous affair."

Ken stared at his ceiling and didn't meet Jon's eyes. "She talked about abortion, too."

"What? Daisy Ruiz?"

Ken shrugged. "Said the ER doc tried to push an abortion flyer on her, and she thought about taking it."

They sat in silence for about half a minute that stretched out like a long, cold night. Finally, Jon said, "She must have really been hurting to even feel that temptation."

The words twisted Ken's heart. He harshly cleared his throat. "I have analyzed that to death. I know I didn't react well when she told me. But the idea that a mother could wish that..."

"Easy for you to say. You're not the one in her position. Men never are the ones in that position. We can sit back and issue judgment and condemnation, but in the end, we can walk away, and no one looking at us would ever know. Women get pregnant, carry babies, have children. There are no secrets there."

Ken glared at his brother. "Good men don't walk away."

Jon sat back and gestured at his surroundings. "So, what are you doing here?"

Ken pressed a fist to the bridge of his nose. What was he doing here? Building a house for a woman who would never be his? "I asked her to marry me."

Jon's bark of laughter had more to do with shock than amusement. "Imagine that went over well. You're dating for a month, and suddenly you're asking her to marry you."

"Jon? I would have asked her to marry me the day after we went on our first date. I know who she is to me. I'm building this house for her. I've had a ring in my pocket for weeks now."

Jon nodded. "I knew you loved her the first time I heard you talk about her. But she doesn't know that. Right? She doesn't understand that you've never dated, and you intentionally waited until you knew someone was right for you before you even asked her out."

Ken shifted uncomfortably. Jon continued, "She doesn't know how you think just *all the time*, and just how carefully you speak, and how much is constantly churning under the surface of that pretty face."

Ken turned to give him a disgusted look. Jon shrugged, "We all know just how pretty you are."

Ken could not believe that his brother would tease

him at this moment, and it broke through the steel gates of his thoughts. He half-grinned, and Jon smiled in return, then gripped his shoulder and said, "What she knows is there's this man who obviously adores her and was willing to marry her out of pity just to rescue her from social embarrassment."

Ken chuckled. "Exactly when did you become the wise one?"

Jon smirked, "Same day you became the pretty one."

Ken sat back and, with a perfectly deadpan delivery, said, "I'm much prettier than you are wise."

Jon grinned. "I feel very wise. I think it's the lack of alcohol. It's like all of these repressed senses suddenly came fully to life. Who knows what I could have accomplished if I'd stayed out of the bottom of a bottle all this time?"

Ken nodded. "Exactly." He pointed at his brother. "But you came to talk about you. How can I help you, oh, wise one?"

"I want to build a pool house. Nothing as extravagant as mom and dad's, but something simple just to have a kitchenette and a bathroom right there. If I get it started, can you help with some of the heavy lifting?"

Ken imagined Jon's property, envisioning the structure in his mind. "Your yard's layout is perfect for it. You want it complete before Alex gets back home?"

"Actually, I want it complete for when she stops back in October. Wade has that fundraiser dinner here on a Thursday. She'll be here for two days so she can work in a doctor's appointment."

"Guess you better get some building permits going."

Jon chuckled. "Already have that in the works. I just wanted to make sure I didn't need to hire some labor."

Ken shook his head. "You don't need to hire labor. You have all the labor right here."

"Yeah. Brad said the same."

Ken took a deep breath and slowly let it out. "Alex was betrayed by the person who should always have protected her. Because of that, she doesn't know how to trust you yet."

Jon nodded, "I didn't do myself any favors."

"She'll come around."

"That is my prayer." Jon stood, and Ken stood with him. They shook hands. "I'll let you know when I need the exterior walls raised." He gestured around. "This place is looking decent. You need anything?"

Ken shrugged and shook his head. "Thanks." He walked his brother to the door. "I'm half a mile away. Keep not drinking. Sober suits you."

Jon slapped him on the shoulder and went outside, shutting the door behind him. Ken took the opportunity of the break to down a glass of water and then reset the ladder so he could climb up and measure the wall above the door.

At seven a.m. on Friday morning, Daisy looked up at the morning sky and thanked God for clear blue skies and sixty-degree weather. She knew the afternoon high would climb to eighty-five, but they could get a lot of work done before the afternoon heat.

Beverly approached with Thomas Osborne. Daisy

walked forward and held her hand out to him. "Good morning, Mr. Osborne. How are you?"

"Thomas, please," he corrected, shaking her hand. He wore a pair of worn jeans, a dark green T-shirt, work boots, and a tool belt slung low on his hips. "I can't tell you how much this means to us."

Daisy smiled her professional smile. "Having the ability to do it means the world to me. We have a lot of support."

She heard the rumble of vehicles and turned to see four black pickups pull up. Beverly whistled under her breath. "Look at that workforce headed our way."

Daisy watched as the trucks pulled into the parking area. Her eyes scanned each person who exited a truck, desperately hoping to see Ken but also hoping that he had decided not to come. She recognized Phillip Dixon as he walked toward them. Like his sons, he stood tall and had a wide chest. Unlike his sons, he had a shaved head.

He wore dark blue jeans, a black T-shirt with the Dixon Contracting logo over the pocket, and a red hardhat. His biceps bulged out from under the sleeves of the shirt. "Daisy Ruiz," he said in a deep voice, "it's good to see you again."

If she worried that Ken had told his father about their falling out and he'd treat her differently, his warm greeting alleviated those fears.

"You, too, Mr. Dixon." She gestured at Thomas. "This is Thomas Osborne. We're building the house today for his family."

Phillip held out his hand. "Pleasure." He gestured

at Thomas' belt. "That looks like it's been used, son. Where do you work?"

Thomas shook Phillip's hand as his cheeks brightened. "Yesterday, I finished a house for Culpepper. They didn't have anything new, so I'm looking again first thing Tuesday morning."

Phillip narrowed his eyes, looking from the younger man's worn boots to the white hardhat on his head. "I'll see you in my office Tuesday morning. Seven a.m." He lifted his chin. "Do you know where to come?"

"Uh, yes. Yes, sir."

Phillip turned to Daisy. "Plans?"

She smiled and led the way to the table where she'd rolled out the house plans. "It's a four-bedroom. They have four kids, so I think they're planning to give the two older kids their own rooms, and the two little kids will share." She gestured at the lumber pile. "My project manager confirmed the inventory last night. Plumbers finished up at four yesterday, and electricians laid their groundwork. They're coming back tomorrow afternoon." She tapped a clipboard. "Here's the proposed schedule."

"Who's your project manager?"

"He's a retired PM from the school board. He used to oversee their construction projects and now sits on our board of directors. Harvey Madison."

"Harvey?" Mr. Dixon's face lit up. "I've worked with Harvey many times. Will he be here?"

She nodded. "He'll be by around lunch. He sets everything up, and I initiate on the day of."

She held up the clipboard, and he glanced at the

top page. "How many of these have you done?"

She pursed her lips. "Uh, two a year from the time I was twelve. And I've done six since moving into the executive director position. This makes seven."

Over his shoulder, Daisy saw Ken approaching. Her mouth suddenly went dry, and her heart started pounding. She tucked an imaginary hair behind her ear. "Uh, hi, Ken."

His smile didn't make it to his eyes. "Daisy."

Phillip looked between the two of them. "Excuse me, Daisy. How did you know this is Ken?"

She shrugged. "I always know." She gestured with her thumb behind her. "Can I talk to you for a minute?"

"Sure." Ken slapped his dad on the back. "Morning, Daddy."

"Son."

As Ken followed Daisy away from the crew gathering around the coffee urn she'd put at the end of the table, she tried to think about what to say. She should already know. She'd had fifteen conversations with herself in the mirror between last night and this morning.

"I didn't expect you to come." Daisy tentatively met his gaze, steeling herself for anything.

"I made a commitment to come." He raised both eyebrows. "I keep my word, Daisy. Especially to you."

"No, you made a commitment to support us with Dixon Contracting. It had nothing to do with you personally."

A muscle ticked in his jaw. The look on his face silently informed her he inferred she would prefer he had not come. He glared at her, his eyes angry and hard. "I made a commitment to come," he repeated. "I did that before I knew you. It has nothing to do with you personally. I'm here to work."

Daisy realized that she didn't feel the same. It felt very personal to her. "But you don't have to be here."

Ken stared at her. For a few seconds, she thought he would just remain silent as usual, but he surprised her. He leaned in close enough so that only she could hear him and whispered, "Good talk."

He spun on his heel and walked back to the table. As she watched, he unrolled a set of plans and took a small notebook out of his breast pocket and a pencil out from behind his ear. His dad leaned in toward him and ran a finger over something on the plans. Ken nodded and made a notation.

Finally, she realized she had stood there alone for nearly a full minute, just watching him, and she walked back to the crew. She picked up a clipboard off of the table and whistled sharply. "If I can have your attention, please."

Chapter 20

Ken walked down the line of people at the ready. Some worked for him. Others had volunteered. "Ready!" he yelled, and they all bent, securing their section of the framed-out wall with leather-gloved hands. "On one. Three, two, one!"

As a unit, they bent and lifted the wall. Brad stood on one end and Jon on the other. As soon as they could, they grabbed the wall and helped square it off.

Ken showed a volunteer how to use the nail gun and explained the distance between nails. Once he made sure she had it under control, he climbed the ladder and walked across the beam to start nailing from the top.

As he worked, he glanced down at the flurry of activity below. Workers hammered interior walls, trained carpenters secured trusses that the cranes had set, and his team worked on the outer walls.

If he was honest with himself, he'd admit to going up top so he could scour the crowd and pinpoint Daisy's location. He'd kept an eye on her all day, noting the times he saw her drinking water, taking a break, getting up from a break too soon.

What he hadn't done was approach her. Oh, but he wanted to. He wanted to talk to her, joke with her, touch her, make her smile, listen to her laugh. His heart physically ached with the need to be next to her.

If that was going to happen, one of them would need to bridge that gap. He'd thought she intended to this morning but had walked away from that conversation with a lasting sense of disappointment.

He looked up at the setting sun. They would have to put up the exterior wall plywood sheets tomorrow.

When the final nail secured the last outer wall, his team assembled in the drive. "Seven tomorrow morning," he said, "I'll have those donuts you wanted, Maddie," he said, tapping the hardhat of a high school JROTC cadet.

After they left, he walked the site, checking to ensure no cords remained plugged-in and all equipment had been secured. He met up with his family at the plans table. Daisy sat in a folding metal chair and made notes in her notebook. Jon filled his cup with water. His dad conferred with Harvey Madison over something on the plans.

"Got dinner plans?" he asked Daisy.

She looked up from the notebook and stared at him as if she had to translate what he asked from some difficult foreign language, like Klingon. Finally, she said, "I'm going to eat the sandwich I made myself this morning. This is not my first rodeo. I knew if I didn't have something ready for me at home, I'd cave and do fast food."

That effectively shut him out of offering to buy her dinner. He smiled a tight-lipped smile and said, "Enjoy."

He spun on his heel and started to march away, but she rushed after him. "Ken!"

He walked a few more steps toward the parking area before turning in her direction. "What?"

She huffed out a breath and looked down at her notebook, then back up at him. "I want to say that I'm really glad you're here this weekend. You've been a tremendous help."

He waited. Perhaps she intended to add that she had missed him as much as he'd missed her, but she didn't say anything else. Finally, he said, "Not my first rodeo, either. That's why I brought so many of our own crew. If you partner every volunteer with a pro, you'll be in tall cotton."

He stopped and waited. She licked her lips and said, "Well, thanks." She turned and started walking. About twenty feet away, she spun and said, "I've missed you. I was really happy to see you."

He lifted his chin in acknowledgment and waited another ten seconds or so before he turned away again and headed for his truck.

Daisy stood on the top step of the ladder and held a long piece of trim with one hand and a nail gun with the other. As she pulled the trigger, a dizzy spell washed over her, flooding the back of her throat with bile. She started to topple but put both hands on the wall to steady herself, effectively dropping the nail gun. It crashed to the concrete slab below.

Immediately, Ken appeared at the base of the ladder. "What happened?" he demanded.

She closed her eyes and pulled the safety glasses off her face. "Dizzy," she whispered.

Before she even realized it, he had another ladder next to hers and climbed up beside her. He put a hand on her waist. Even though she immediately felt steadier, she slapped at his hand. "Leave me alone," she whispered.

Keeping one hand on the wall, she put another on the top of the step ladder. With quaking knees, she slowly descended. As soon as her booted foot touched the concrete, she collapsed to a sitting position.

Ken knelt next to her, but she didn't look at him. Instead, she kept her eyes closed, concentrating on breathing and not throwing up.

"What do you need?" he asked.

Pull me into your arms again and tell me how everything is going to be okay. "Nothing." She felt better. The cool concrete floor and the steadiness of solid ground helped. She finally had the strength to look him in the eye. "I'm okay now."

A frown covered his face. He started to reach out his hand but withdrew it.

"Really, Ken, I'm good. I get vertigo with heights. I guess vertigo combined with my condition isn't the best combination."

He looked up at the ladder and back at her. "How about we let a volunteer knock out the moulding? Maybe someone who isn't..." he paused and looked at her stomach then back at her face, "... prone to vertigo?"

Despite the annoyance she felt, she chuckled. "Probably wise. Thank you for coming to my rescue."

"I always will," he said softly, then smoothly rose to his feet and walked out of the room.

She put a hand on her heart and leaned against the drywall. Emotions surged through her veins as if coming to life. How did she fix this with him? How did she make the first move? She's the one who walked out, so she needed to be the one to initiate. But how? What happens if she tries and he laughs her away?

God, please, help me.

She pushed herself up and picked up the nail gun, inspecting it, thankful that she didn't break anything on it. Then she found one of the Dixon Contracting carpenters and asked him to take over the moulding installation. She put on a pair of kneepads so she could install the baseboards.

On Monday afternoon, as he finished installing the last baseboard into the fourth bedroom, he turned from his knees and sat against the wall. A crew had come in and painted last night, giving them a chance to go behind them and get all the trim installed today. He sat on new carpet and looked up at a new light fixture and ceiling fan. The smell of fresh-cut wood combined with the scent of fresh paint and new carpet.

He knew the kids who came into this house would remember that smell for the rest of their lives.

Ken worked alongside his brothers as they helped finish the house. He remained impressed at the organization of supplies and labor that went into this project. Many things happened behind the scenes. The house certainly didn't actually get entirely built in four days. But the structure and all the interior finishes did.

The brief interactions with Daisy of the last few days dug deep into his heart, breaking it more thoroughly. He could clearly see the swell of her stomach now and wondered how many people noticed. He wanted to put his hands on either side of her belly, and talk to the baby, tell it how much he loved it already and how he prayed for it all the time.

What had he hoped to accomplish here? Did he think to impress her with his mad skills enough so she'd fall at his feet, begging him to take her back? Or had he hoped for a way to go back two weeks and handle the conversation at the wedding better?

One thing he knew, he didn't want it to stay like this. He wanted to find a way to reach her. But how? She had walked out. She needed to be the one to come forward.

Didn't she?

His dad walked into the room. "Sitting down on the job, eh?"

Ken smiled. "Just thinking about how impressed I am with this project."

Philip nodded. "I've done them before, of course, but this one went rather smoothly." He gestured with his thumb toward the outside window. "I hired the husband. He starts with us tomorrow."

Ken wondered how many Dixon's had offered Thomas Osborne a job this weekend. "I know. I told him to come see me tomorrow, and he said he already had an appointment with you."

"I watched him work all weekend. He definitely knows what he's doing."

"I think that he could get a job higher than a laborer. I don't think he asserts himself like he could."

His dad nodded. "I'm contemplating giving him to Buddy as an apprentice. What do you think?"

Ken remembered working under Buddy. The years working with him had taught him what exhaustion really meant, but he learned more under him than he could have from anyone else. "I think Osborne just caught the break he needed." Ken pushed himself to his feet and pulled the handkerchief off of his head. "I'm going to do a walk-through and make sure that we didn't miss anything."

As he started out of the room, his dad asked, "Did you fix things with Daisy?"

Ken paused in the doorway and turned and looked at his father. "No."

He thought about more he could say, but as usual, didn't find it necessary to elaborate. He moved down the hall to the farthest room, inspecting lights and paint, confirming the volunteers had laid the floor properly and that the closets had shelves. He examined doors and made sure they shut flush against the frames. He ran water in the bathrooms and flushed toilets. He checked the stair rail's sturdiness as he walked down to the first floor, then went into the kitchen, affirming that the appliances all had power and water where needed.

Finally, he stepped out onto the front porch. Daisy sat in a canvas chair, holding a bottle of water against the back of her neck. "Ninety-seven degrees. I may need to move to Alaska. I have a friend there who posted pictures of this year's first snowfall already."

His heart pounded at her conversational tone. He walked over to the faucet and turned it on, holding his handkerchief under the water. He rinsed it out really thoroughly then soaked it. When he went back onto the porch, he laid it across the back of her neck.

Her eyes widened. "That feels really good."

He nodded and remembered doing that for her at the lake. He leaned against the corner of the freshly built porch. Someone would need to stain the bare wood, but he didn't think the work scope for this weekend included it. He had so many things he wanted to say, to include making sure she understood that he knew he had overreacted badly and how sorry he felt about it, but he didn't want that conversation to happen here. She didn't need distractions from him right now.

"I heard your dad hired Thomas Osborne."

"Dad has an eye for people." He watched a landscape crew lay sod over freshly raked dirt. "He'll help anyone who's willing to work." He turned his head and assessed her. The handkerchief clearly cooled her off. Her face had lightened to a much less dangerous shade of red. "You did an incredible job with this project."

Her gaze flew to his then she looked down at the porch. "Thank you. I like all aspects of this ministry, but weekends like this really feed my soul." She looked at her watch without making eye contact with him again. "The Osborne's went to get their children. I'm expecting the furniture any moment."

Just as she said that the furniture truck pulled up in front of the house. He watched her hesitate before she got to her feet. "You sit. I can handle furniture," he said.

"I'm fine," she snapped. She raised her hands above her head and stretched, then bent and picked up the clipboard at her feet. As she started down the steps, she turned and finally looked at him. "Do you have people here still? A lot of the stuff is going to need to be assembled."

He nodded. "We let the laborers go. Brad and Jon are still here. My dad's inside. The four of us can handle it."

With a nod, she simply said, "Thanks," then walked down to meet the truck. Using her inventory sheet, Daisy directed the furniture delivery men to the rooms where each box went; beds, bookshelves, and dressers to bedrooms, a table and chairs to the dining room, couches and bookshelves into the living room.

Ken knew the furniture company had donated half of this order, giving Daisy a chance to fill the house with more furniture than she normally would. A picnic table and gas grill went onto the back porch. Ken followed it out and found Brad and Jon in the backyard, finishing a swing set fort the construction supply company had donated.

He walked over to them. "We have some furniture to assemble."

"Yup." Jon seated the slide and ducked under it to secure the bolts. "Dad just called out the window."

Brad slipped his cap off of his head and swiped his sweaty forehead with his sweaty forearm. "Shouldn't take us long to knock that out."

The three of them walked into the house together.

Chapter 21

Ken sat in front of Marcus's desk and studied the room. He couldn't believe how little had changed in the last fifteen or so years. Different church, different room, but the desk and decorations remained the same. Framed photographs of youth groups with the brass year plaques covered one wall. While Ken sat there, he counted twenty-three photos. He knew four of them contained his brothers and him.

His body ached. They'd worked hard all weekend building the house. On his way home tonight, he'd impulsively called Marcus. He had an appointment with a group of young men from his youth group that night, so he could meet Ken at the church at seven-thirty. Ken had immediately taken the next exit and headed straight for the church.

He got there about seven-thirty-five. He'd found the side door unlocked as Marcus had instructed and followed the directions to his office.

Within five minutes of sitting down, Marcus rushed into the room clutching a worn Bible and three books. He set them on the corner of his desk and shook Ken's hand. "Sorry, I'm late. It's good to see you."

Nerves suddenly flooded Ken's chest. He smiled, anyway. "No problem. I have sat on the receiving end of your counsel. I know how it can go."

"That's right. You have."

When Marcus counseled one of the students in his youth group, he took no phone into the room with him, and the room had no clocks. He intentionally made it an area of no interference. Ken had gone to him the day after he had gotten drunk at that party. He had been hungover, embarrassed, and concerned at the way his psyche had processed the alcohol. Marcus had prayed with him and talked to him, and helped him through the strange emotional time.

"Thank you for seeing me tonight."

"My door is always open to you." He gestured toward him. "You look like you worked hard today."

Ken looked down at the dusty jeans and T-shirt. "I helped build the house for Daisy's mission."

"Oh, right. That was this weekend. We had a big state youth counsel that interfered, so we couldn't get out there this time. Labor Day weekend is always tricky." He moved around and sat in his chair. "How can I help you?"

Ken cleared his throat. "Well, sir, I plan to ask Daisy to marry me. I came to ask for your blessing."

Marcus raised both eyebrows, then leaned back in

his chair. He rested his elbows on the arms and tapped his fingers together. "I see. She told me you know about her situation."

"Situation?" Ken repeated softly. Pushing down the knee-jerk anger, he calmly clarified his statement. "You mean the baby?"

"Yes, Ken. Of course, I mean the baby."

"Then, yes. She told me."

He waited. Marcus stared for several long moments, then asked, "How do you feel about it?"

"The baby? Or the situation?" He didn't air quote the word situation, but he thought about it.

Marcus glared at him. "Are you asking her to marry you because she's pregnant?"

Ken sat back, and his eyelids lowered. "Honestly, I expected better from you, Marcus."

Marcus waved a dismissive hand. "I hope you understand that your expectations aren't my priority. My daughter is my priority."

Ken felt his lips purse. He hadn't considered that. It had escaped him. It shouldn't have. "Fair enough. But would you have asked me that question if I was the baby's father?"

"That's a moot point. You're not the father." Marcus tapped his upper lip with his fist. "The question is important, or else I would not have asked. In fact, this is a very important conversation. Nothing is easy about being the parents of a baby."

Ken waited for more clarification, but none came. Finally, he asked again, "Would you have asked me that question if I was the father?"

Marcus leaned his chair back and stared up at the ceiling for several moments, then said, "I think so. Yes."

Ken let out a breath. "Okay. I want to marry Daisy because I love her. But it's more than just that. I believe God made me just for her. I believe God designed her to be my wife. Before I knew she was pregnant, I bought the engagement ring, and I bought a house to build for her. The baby pushed up my timetable, a timetable that only existed for her sake, really. I would have married her after our first date."

Marcus sat straight in his chair with the squeak of springs and put his elbows on the desk. He leaned toward Ken as if about to convey some deep secret or vital piece of information. "And as you go into this marriage, when this little human being interferes with your new relationship, how will you feel? Will you grow to resent the child? Will you take exception to the way that her attention will be split?"

The men stared at each other for several moments. "Would you ask me that question if I was the father?"

Marcus let out a heavy sigh. "No. I don't think so."

"Fair enough." Ken leaned forward, too. He rested both elbows on his knees. "In my heart and in my mind, the baby's already mine. Don't much care what a paternity test would say. Doesn't matter. What I know is that I want to love Daisy as Christ loved the church, and I want to raise that child under an umbrella of love and wisdom that can only come from a household that puts God first. Much like Joseph raised Jesus as his son." He sat back. "So that is what I intend to do with your blessing. I am the father."

Suddenly, Marcus grinned and clapped his hands together once. "Ah, Ken, that makes my heart happy." He stood and walked around his desk. Ken stood with him, not surprised when this man he had loved so much as a teenager pulled him into his arms and tightly hugged him, then slapped his back hard. "You have my blessing!"

Immediately the nerves released. He felt them skate down his arms and through his fingertips. He smiled and barked a laugh. "Thank you! Now I just need to convince Daisy."

The soreness didn't set in until Daisy sat on her front porch Monday night. She'd worked—physically hard work—since seven Friday morning. As soon as she sat, the muscles finally gave in, and the thought of moving inside lost any appeal. She needed a shower, a snack, and her bed for the next twelve hours, in that order.

Instead, she lay her head back against the bench and used her toe to keep the swing gradually moving. Aloud, she said to herself, "Maybe you can just stay outside tonight. That would be fun, right? Like camping."

No matter how perky she made her voice sound, camping out on her porch did not appeal to her. The sound of Ken's truck had her sitting upright. She heard the slamming door, then he appeared in the glow of the porchlight. With a gentle smile, Ken said, "I wondered if you'd even still be upright."

"I sat and then my muscles said, 'Okay, we're

done.'" She toed the swing, and it slowly swayed. "I was just talking myself into sleeping out here tonight."

"Fun. Like camping out."

"Exactly."

He sat in a chair, and for a long moment, neither spoke. Every few seconds, she toed the ground, and the swing gently swayed beneath her. The slight squeak of the swing chains broke the silence around them. Ken just sat there. She didn't really know how to start, so she said nothing.

Finally, he cleared his throat. The sound startled her. She stopped the swing with the ball of her foot and looked at him. He said, "I handled that talk at Jon's wedding badly."

She snorted. "You're not the only one." She crossed her fingers in her lap and stared at them. "I'm so embarrassed about that day. I don't even know what to say."

"You have no reason to feel embarrassed." She lifted her head and looked at him. His mouth firmed. His eyes glowed with intensity. "I handled that talk badly. I should have apologized right away. Instead of staying put, I should have chased you down and let you vent."

Breaking eye contact, she looked back down at her hands. "I thought your family would turn away from me. I love them so much and didn't want to lose them, didn't want you to be placed in the middle."

Ken moved quicker than she expected. Before she could react, he sat next to her on the swing, covering both of her hands with his hand. His skin felt warm, the callouses rough. "Daisy, my family knows about the baby."

"Yeah, now. I had lunch with Valerie."

He squeezed her hands, and she looked up. He shook his head. "Before the wedding, before you had dinner at their house that first night, both my parents already knew."

Emotion flooded her throat. They had treated her with such kindness, had welcomed her like someone special and treasured. "Do they think the baby is yours, like Jon and Alex?"

"No. I don't hide anything from my folks." He reached out and cupped her cheek. "They know this. I love you, and, as far as I'm concerned, the baby's already mine. Or, I want it to be."

Even though she opened her mouth to speak, nothing came out. She slapped her hand over her mouth and tried to choke back a sob. Before she could think, he had his arms around her, the exact thing that she needed all along. She breathed in the smell of him, listened to the pounding of his heart, felt the warmth of his skin.

"I'm sorry I left like that," she said, remembering storming out of that pool house in the middle of the wedding festivities.

"Me too." He pressed his lips to her hair. "I missed you."

She raised her face to look at him. "I was in such a bad place mentally and emotionally. I don't know how to explain where my head was. It was almost like I was looking for an opportunity to walk out. It was so strange."

He nodded. "Your stress level would probably fell most humans." He leaned back and cupped her cheeks with his hands. "If I've contributed to your stress at all, you need to tell me. I want to help you, not burden you."

"You don't add to my stress. Like I said, my head was in a very strange place, and I'm out of that now. People are starting to find out. It's not been the horrible thing I thought it would be." She shrugged and thought about her lunch Thursday with her grandparents. "Well, almost not horrible. My grandparents had a problem. My grandfather even cried."

Ken's eyes roamed down her body. "Soon, it'll be hard to hide. I can see it."

She felt a flush of heat and ran her hands over her slightly rounded stomach. "Sixteen weeks. That's crazy."

He shook his head slowly from side to side. "Not crazy. Wonderful."

He leaned forward and pressed his lips against hers. That very instant, everything in her world set back to right. It all fell into place, and she knew everything would turn out okay. She wrapped her arms around his neck and leaned into his kiss, trying to let her lips convey her feelings in a way that her voice never could.

His lips spoke to her in return. Clouds swirled around her at this mountaintop altitude. The air felt thin, and the wind felt cool against her skin. Her pulse rushed in her ears, sounding like a roaring surf.

Ken ripped his mouth away and pressed his forehead against hers, his eyes closed, his breathing ragged. He had a hand gripping her hair and slowly relaxed, eventually running his fingers through the strands.

He raised his head enough to look into her eyes. "Marry me. Marry me, Daisy."

She smiled and said, "I thought you'd never ask."

"I'm not asking anymore." He pulled the ring box out of his pocket. "I've had this in my pocket since the middle of July, in case you think the baby is motivating me in any way."

She held her hand out and noticed the faint tremor. "Ken, I can tell you in all honesty that I believe the baby is not what's motivating you. I can't believe it's taken you seventeen years to finally ask me to marry you."

They laughed together as he slipped the ring onto her finger.

Daisy slipped the file folder into her bag as she and Ken walked out of the courthouse doors. Inside the manilla pages lay their birth certificates and now their wedding license. She couldn't stop the grin that covered her face.

He had just asked her to marry him thirteen and a half hours ago, and now they already had their license. Both of them agreed that they didn't want to wait much longer. Sitting on her porch swing, she had said, "We either do it now, or we wait until the baby comes. I don't want to be waddling on my wedding day."

Ken had kissed her with passion and promise and said, "Not waiting is good for me."

She thought about that conversation as she chuckled and blushed at the same time. When he got into the truck cab with her, he asked, "Penny?"

Heat flooded her face, and she fanned herself with her hand. She couldn't possibly share those thoughts with him, not even for a penny, so she said, "When you say move fast, you move fast."

"There's things I don't want to rush, but we aren't there yet." He started the truck while Daisy felt her entire body tingle. Immediately, cool air conditioning broke the heat. He half-grinned and said, "As long as you're not waddling."

About twenty minutes later, he pulled into the parking lot of her office. She stared at the words Gálatas Seis on the glass door. Ken started to turn the engine off, but she put her hand on his to stop him.

"Wait."

He took his hand off of the key and looked at her. "Okay."

Her mind whirled with all the plans they had made last night and today. They had talked and planned and talked, and now that the time had come, she suddenly didn't want to do it anymore. "Could we wait?"

He raised both eyebrows. "Wait? What for? 'Weight' is what broke the bridge down."

She chuckled at the pun. "It was a good idea to have Bev marry us using her notary. But I really want to wear my grandmother's veil and have my father perform the ceremony."

He stared at her for several long seconds and finally said, "Okay. Just tell me what to do."

She put her hands on either side of his cheeks and leaned in and kissed him. "I'll call my mom. You call your mom. We'll get married Thursday. That gives us enough time."

He smiled and ran a finger along her jaw. "How about we give it till Friday. That way, my mom won't completely lose her mind."

She smiled. "Deal. Can you take me to the house now? I want to see it."

He put the truck in reverse and backed out. She watched the scenery go by as they left the shopping center and headed to the new neighborhood. It didn't take long to drive the seven short miles there. As he turned onto the street, he gestured at a street sign and said, "Jon's new house is down that road." Barely a quarter of a mile later, he put on his blinker to turn into a drive and pointed at another street sign. "Brad's house is down that street."

He turned onto the drive, and she watched as the Tudor style house came into view. Angled roofs and arched windows with gray and tan brick mixed with dark shutters made her feel like she had completely come home. A large porch wrapped around the entire house. She could barely wait for him to walk around the front of the truck and open her door.

She stepped onto the porch and looked up, seeing rings already in the ceiling, waiting for her porch swing. The grin that covered her face grew wider as he unlocked the front door.

In a graceful move, much like a choreographed dance step, Ken picked Daisy up beneath her arms and set her feet across the threshold inside the house. She remembered that Ken held several black belts in the martial arts. Even so, the casual naked display of raw strength and perfect control surprised her.

Then, it occurred to her that he had carried her across the threshold. This wasn't his house. This was her house. This was their house. His strong, calloused hands built this house for a future that included her. Daisy scanned Ken's face for any trace of emotion but found nothing except the usual silent half-grin.

Before Daisy could even speak, he said, "Furniture comes next week, but you can get a good idea. Still have to finish the back room. Been living in there while I finished the rest of the house."

They walked into a foyer area, and she smelled fresh paint, clean wood, and varnish. She looked up at the skylight that lit up the room. The main room had a fireplace with a mantle that just waited for family pictures. The dining room cabinetry looked so beautiful, and she couldn't wait to choose a china pattern that would complete this room. The kitchen opened into a large breakfast area with a glass wall that looked out onto the backyard. Brushed nickel appliances gleamed in the recessed lighting. An island separated the kitchen from the dining area, and its black granite countertop added a richness to the room. She walked to the pantry that could easily measure almost as big as her current bedroom.

Through the kitchen, she found the unfinished

room. It had bare drywall walls and plywood floors. A single bed sat against the wall, and two folding chairs pulled up to a card table.

Ken said, "I haven't quite decided what this room needs to be yet. Maybe a family room or a game room."

The room had enough square footage to turn it into anything they wanted. She pushed open the back door and stepped out onto the back porch. Ken pointed at the trees tied with red tape. "Those are coming down. Pool goes there." He gestured at the stakes in the ground. "Not sure about the pool. Was gonna leave that up to you, what with a little one on the way. But we have it staked out, so it's ready just in case."

He took her upstairs, and her feet sank in the plush carpet in the master bedroom. She exclaimed over the sunken bathtub and the walk-in closet. She ran her fingers over the fireplace's mantle and opened the doors that took her out onto a balcony terrace.

He showed her three more bedrooms. "Didn't know which one you would want as the nursery. This one has its own bathroom. The other two share the main bathroom."

She ran her hands over her slightly rounded belly and said, "I don't know that it's important to decide right now. Let's get moved in and see how the house feels first."

His smile made her heart skip a beat. "Reckon the baby will sleep in our room for a while anyway. Plenty of time."

She held her arms out and spun, laughing as the joy inside of her just burst out. "I cannot wait to live here with you."

He went to her and said, "You're the one putting it off. I'm good for it to start today."

She laughed and said, "That's true. Speaking of which, I better start calling some family if we want to have this wedding by Friday."

Chapter 22

Ken stood next to the fireplace and looked out at the chairs set up in his future living room. He fingered the knot of his tie to make sure it lay straight. His gaze roamed over the cathedral ceiling with the wood beams and the light fixture that helped him design this room. His mother had hung tulle bunting on the second floor's balcony and placed a green wreath with white flowers in the center of the swooping material.

He crossed the room and went into the dining room. Against one wall, the two-tiered cake sat on a square table. Valerie had utilized the built-in sideboard to set out the finger foods Calla brought over a couple of hours ago. He crossed into the kitchen. Through the open pantry door, he could see Jon filling a silver tub with ice. He knew sodas and beer would go into that.

His mom rinsed strawberries at the sink. She

looked over her shoulder when he stepped onto the tile floor. She smiled at him and said, "The next time we have a wedding, a completely unfurnished house is the place to throw it."

He smiled. "I'll remember that." Furniture would arrive Monday morning. They'd scheduled movers to pack Daisy's house Tuesday so they could see what she wanted to keep from her home to bring into their home.

Jon carried the tub in and set it on the marble top of the island. "Is Alex coming?" his mom asked.

His eyes darkened, but he smiled at her. "No. Too much going on this weekend. She'll be home next month."

"Oh. That's a shame. I'm sorry she won't be here."

"Me, too."

Ken stepped forward. "Hey, mom. Did Daisy get settled upstairs?"

Focusing on Daisy instead of Alex, his mom smiled and wiped her hands on a dishtowel. "She did. Her mom and her cousin and sister-in-law are up there with her now."

He'd anticipated marrying Daisy Tuesday morning. When she asked to change plans, he hadn't missed a beat. But he'd had to push aside the romantic wedding night plans he'd already started formulating. The last few days had crawled by.

They had filled the days, though, with plans and details. She had worked out travel arrangements for her brother and family, food with Calla, and flowers with Camila. Daisy had gone shopping three times for dresses and shoes. A whirlwind of organization all came together, culminating in this moment.

Calla came through the back door carrying a silver hotel pan. "Last of it. This will just need to go into the warm oven," she said.

Ken took it from her, using the two cloths she used as potholders, and carried it over to the oven. Once he slipped it in, he turned to her and said, "That smells good."

"Stuffed mushrooms will be filling. Nice to have something hot along with the cold." Calla shifted her glasses on her nose and said, "I'm going to run upstairs. I have a dress to change into up there. Ian's parking and should be right in."

Brad and Valerie came through the back door. Ken had instructed his brothers to park in the adjacent lot, leaving the driveway and street available for Daisy's family members. "It smells so good in here," Valerie said, walking up to his mom and giving her a hug.

"Calla's been at it, even though I told her to keep it simple," Rosaline said.

"She probably did keep it simple; we just don't have the same definition of that word." She turned her attention to Ken. "How's the groom doing?"

He smiled and brushed his lips over her cheek. "Really, really ready."

"I bet you are."

He and Brad shook hands. Brad asked, "Anything left that needs doing?"

Jon came out of the pantry carrying a wooden box filled with soda bottles. "Nope. Your timing is impeccable as usual, Mister CEO."

Brad chuckled. "I try really hard, you know?"

Ken left them in the kitchen and wandered back into the living room. Marcus and Diego stood talking near the fireplace. They both looked at him as he entered the room. Marcus asked, "Ken, can we talk for a moment?"

"Yes, sir," he said, extending his hand. Marcus shook it, his grip strong. "Diego, glad you made it."

"It's good to see you, brother," his high-school buddy said, grinning. The two men hugged.

"What's up?" Ken asked Marcus.

"I think we need to go over the order of ceremony again." He gestured at a box laid across two chairs. "Camila made the lasso. Do you understand how that works?" Ken thought about the flowered garland fastened into a loop that Marcus and Diego would put around him and Daisy as a symbol of becoming one in marriage. He nodded. "Great."

Ken checked his watch. Impatience clawed at him from the inside like a beast trapped behind his rib cage. Twenty minutes to go. He glanced up at the balcony and waited.

Daisy ran her hands across her stomach and rested her hands on the waist of her dress. She could tell, but Camila assured her no one else could. Well, not really. Her dress had spaghetti straps, a heart-shaped bodice, and a skirt that fell straight down from the waist to the floor. She'd gone with simple. She didn't have a huge wedding party in a church, so she had no need for a long train.

Her cousin had pulled the sides of her hair back and twisted them into an elaborate bun, leaving the rest of her hair to fall in curled waves.

"Eyes," Camila said, holding up the can of hair spray. Daisy grinned and shielded her eyes while Camila doused her hair. She stepped back and examined her masterpiece.

"Perfect," her mom said, lifting the lace veil out of the box. Daisy's grandmother had worn it when she married her grandfather in Puebla, Mexico, before immigrating to the United States and taking a position with a Bible college. Daisy stayed seated in the chair, and her mom fastened the veil to the bun while Camila took a dozen photos. Daisy held up the mirror and checked. The veil cascaded down the back of her head to the tops of her shoulders. It took her breath away to think that her grandmother had worn it, along with her aunt and one cousin as well.

Diego's wife, Amy, unboxed the white satin heels and knelt to help Daisy slip her feet into them. Amy had gone to school with the Dixon brothers and had been friends with them and Diego all of her adult life.

"Perfect fit," Amy said, grinning up at her sister-in-law. Daisy wiggled her toes. She wondered if she should have gone for a slightly lower heel. Before she could mention it, a tap on the door brought Rosaline.

"Oh, Daisy," she said, walking around the chair, "how beautiful you look."

Her mom ran her finger over the lace. "My husband's family has had this veil for three generations now."

"Such a treasure," Rosaline breathed. She pulled a long jewel case out of her pocket. "I wore these pearls at my wedding. They were the first real piece of jewelry I ever owned. Valerie and Alex both wore them at their weddings. I would be so honored if you would wear them today."

She'd been present when Rosaline offered them to Alex. Daisy teared up but didn't want to mess up her makeup, so she waved at her eyes. "I was hoping you'd offer," she said. "I would be honored to wear them."

Rosaline secured them around her neck, then stood back, and Daisy got to her feet. The mothers held hands and admired her while Camila handed her the bouquet of white roses, white daisies, and rich green seeded eucalyptus greens.

"Ready?" Camila asked. She wore a dark blue dress with bright embroidered yellow, red, and white flowers along the bodice and the skirt. She'd put her black hair up in a loose bun, and tendrils fell in curls around her face, framing it. Daisy thought she'd never looked so beautiful.

Amy wore a bright red dress with blue and white flowers embroidered in the same pattern. Camila had pulled her blonde hair into a similar style.

Daisy nodded and took a deep breath. Even though the reality had almost nothing in common with her dreams of what her wedding day might entail, she could hardly believe this day had finally come. "Ready."

Her mom came up and put her hands on her shoulders. "Thank you for waiting so we could all celebrate with you." Rosaline echoed the sentiment.

She kissed both of their cheeks, still amazed at the way Ken's family had simply accepted her as one of their own. She ran her finger over the heavy pearls, a little shocked at their weight, feeling like that sealed the deal and made her one of Rosaline's children.

Camila picked up the bouquets of yellow and white daisies and handed one to Amy. "It's time."

Rosaline looked at her mother. "Ready, Rita?"

"Very much so."

She opened the door, and her grandfather stood outside it. Daisy took his arm and walked down the hall. As they passed the balcony, she glanced down and spotted Ken standing next to his brothers in front of the fireplace. He looked up at her, and her heart raced in reaction to his handsome face. She hoped he always invoked that kind of response in her.

As she walked down the staircase and ran her hand along the rail and felt the smooth surface, she thought about how he'd built this house for her, about how much she loved him and how proud she was of him. Getting married here, in this structure that he had fashioned for them with his own strong hands, made all the sense in the world.

Her grandfather handed her off to Ken. Her father spoke the traditional wedding words, talking about love in a Biblical sense, holy matrimony as God intended in the beginning. Brad and Jon stood near Ken, and Camila and Amy stood near her. While he spoke, she looked into Ken's gray eyes and felt solid, steady, not at all nervous or afraid.

Looking into his steady gaze, she realized that

they'd build a life together in this home. They'd raise a family. They could walk to either Brad's house or Jon's house in minutes. Their children would all grow up in the same community, with the same schools and the same peer groups. It filled her with wonder how God had worked everything out with an obvious plan and purpose.

They repeated their vows and exchanged rings. Daisy stared at the gold band set with the line of diamonds and realized her dream had come true. After she slipped the thick gold band onto Ken's finger, they still faced each other and gripped hands while Diego stood and carried the big gold box to her father. He opened the lid and pulled out the long loop of flowers made from white daisies, white roses, and greenery similar to the bouquet she carried.

Diego helped her father loop the strand over Ken's head, twist it, then loop it over her head, forming an eternity symbol. The gathered family and friends murmured. Daisy glanced at the audience and saw smiles and tears.

"The wedding lasso represents the coming together as one," her father announced. "Let us pray. God bless this union. We pray that Ken and Daisy continue to grow in faith and love as one for the rest of their lives. Amen."

Daisy smiled up at Ken as her father said, "You may now kiss the bride."

Ken smiled, flashing white teeth. "Finally. I've wanted to kiss you all day."

Ken kissed Daisy with warm, soft lips full of

promise, passion, and love. She heard the clapping and cheers, but even though they had an audience, she wanted this particular kiss, this special kiss, this one-of-a-kind kiss, to just go on and on. One of his hands rested on her hip, the other rested on her neck, and he gently pulled her closer, deeper into the kiss. Suddenly, she wanted to be much closer to him, much closer to her husband. She wanted every barrier between them to vanish. Nothing existed except for this moment.

He raised his head and smiled down at her as if he could read her thoughts.

Long after the last slice of lemon cheesecake disappeared from the rose-bordered platter, the family sat around the table and talked. Rosaline had offered to move into another room, but Valerie insisted that the dining room chair was more comfortable for her hip than anything else. The guests of honor, Wade Snyder and his wife Kristen, along with Wade's campaign manager, Evan Strickland, had come in town today and readily accepted the dinner invitation.

A week ago, neo-Nazis had attacked Wade in his hotel room, shooting and killing a staff member and wounding five, including Alex. Jon had been on the phone with Alex when it happened, so he immediately responded. He and his brothers made a scary and harrowing trip to Indianapolis to reach her side in the wake of the shooting.

Daisy's gaze roamed over Alex's face. She'd refused pain medicine in the wake of her surgery because of the baby. Daisy knew she had some rough nights in the hospital but already looked so much better. Jon brought her home this weekend. She and Valerie had taken turns with Rosaline, keeping her company in between their work schedules.

She returned her attention to Wade and found her place in the story he told about starting as a freshman when he was twenty-one.

"How did you get a scholarship?" Valerie asked. "You weren't exactly playing high school ball then."

"I was playing on a community team. A scout happened to be going by the court and saw me. Took him months to convince me to go to his college. I was working part-time at a grocery store and had just registered for online classes."

Kristin put her hand on his shoulder and squeezed, then ran her hand across his back. "Good thing, too," she said, her teeth bright white against her chocolate-colored skin. "We met at Freshmen orientation. He grabbed my coffee shop order instead of his. You ever see someone's face when they take a sip of caramel macchiato when they expected green tea?" She put a hand on her chest and laughed. "It still cracks me up."

"I'm glad I could be such a continual source of amusement," he replied dryly.

She turned her gaze to her husband. "And then you invited me to Bible study. You had my heart right then, Senator."

He wound one of her frosted curls around his finger. "Good thing, too, or I'd never have made Senator."

"Well," Evan interrupted, "you did have me. I mean, I'm not as good a kisser or anything."

Wade shook his head, "Not nearly as good looking, either."

Everyone at the table laughed. Ken slipped his arm over her shoulder and leaned in. "You good?" he asked low.

She turned her head close to his. "Yeah. You?"

He brushed a kiss over her temple and nodded.

Kristen stood abruptly and held up her phone. "My new assistant." For a moment, she paused. Daisy knew her assistant had died in the attack in Wade's hotel room. "She has the kids. Excuse me."

As she left the room, Alex asked, "How's she doing?"

"She's scared." Wade sat back and ran his hand over his head. "We knew there would be racial issues when we started our run. We had a few issues during my senatorial campaign in Alabama. It was something we specifically prayed about before I accepted the nomination. I just don't think either one of us expected the violence to actually enter our midst. I think we were arrogant in thinking that humanity was above that these days."

Even the tips of Evan's ears turned red. Daisy could feel the rage vibrating off of him. "Sometimes, I wish the shooters hadn't died in the attack so they could face justice."

Phillip cleared his throat. "I'm sure they've been receiving their due for a little over a week now."

Daisy gasped, realizing what he meant. Ken shrugged and squeezed her thigh, conveying understanding. Kristen walked back into the room then and said to

Wade, "Kennedy wanted help with her speech."

Wade interjected. "Kennedy will be speaking at tomorrow's fundraising dinner."

Alex grinned. "Oh, she's so funny." She looked around the table. "She's nine, but I've never met a more precocious child. She'll be a hoot."

Kristen returned to her seat. "She asked about you."

"That makes me happy." She picked up her teacup. "I miss those two."

Wade narrowed his eyes at her. "You're still planning to come back?"

"Just as soon as I can walk unaided. I pray that's before election day."

"We join you in that prayer."

Evan looked at his watch. "I'm afraid I need to be a bad guy and break us up. We're just under four weeks before election day. Wade has a lot more work to do tonight before I let him clock out."

Rosaline stood and said, "I know carving out these two hours was a hardship on your schedule, but it was so good to see you again."

"It was worth every minute. And dinner was amazing. I've heard rumors about your cooking," Kristen said. She bent and hugged Alex. "You stay right there. Get that leg better."

Brad spoke up. "Before you all leave, I'd like to pray over Wade and Kristen." He held out his hands. Valerie took one, his father took the other, and soon everyone held hands in a circle. "Father God, we love You, and we love the chance to spend fellowship time with

Wade, Kristen, and Evan. God, lay Your hand over this campaign. Guide Wade's thoughts and actions. Instill in him pure wisdom beyond his years, and give him the power of Your Holy Spirit as he maneuvers through the quagmire of racism and intolerance. Protect Kristen and the kids the way You have protected Wade, and instill in their team a strength to get through even the roughest times. Amen."

Daisy appreciated the power behind Brad's words. When she raised her head, she looked around the circle and thanked God silently for bringing her into this fold. She remembered the way Brad and Ken had immediately taken Jon to the airport when Jon called them. She prayed that if she ever had to lean on them, she would remember their strength of character and know that they would follow through with anything in their power to help.

Chapter 23

Stuffed as full as she had ever felt, Daisy stretched her arms up and twisted her body. She ran her hands along the sides of her stomach and said, "I shouldn't have had that second slice of pie."

Alex chuckled. "If Rosaline didn't make such good pie, we wouldn't have this problem."

"I've been eating Auntie Rose's pies my entire life. The problem is not the pie." Valerie rubbed the swell of her stomach. "The problem is having to share some space with the pie."

Daisy looked around at the women in this room who had taken her in as their family. Alex had come home permanently about three weeks ago. She spent the last two weeks of Wade's campaign with him and finished her contract by capturing the incumbent's concession speech.

The door opened, and Rosaline wheeled in a cart

with a teapot and several cups and saucers. "Tea, ladies?"

Daisy groaned. "You can't possibly expect me to fit anything else in this stomach."

Rosaline's eyes crinkled in the corners when she smiled. "You should've seen what it was like to have three little guys making themselves at home in there."

"Pshaw," Valerie said, waving her hand in her mother-in-law's direction. "All of your pregnancy stories feel like the old, 'When I was a kid, we had to walk uphill both ways barefoot in the snow.'"

Everyone laughed. "That's probably fair." Rosaline shook her head. "I don't mean to be that way."

"Of course, you don't," Alex said. "I can't imagine having three babies in here right now. You, woman, have every bit of my respect."

Rosaline's cheeks turned red. "By twenty-six weeks, I was in bed. I couldn't have eaten a Thanksgiving meal if I had tried." She poured herself a cup of tea and very gracefully perched on the edge of the cushion of the wingback chair. She wore cream-colored pants and a soft brown sweater. "I had to just snack and graze, like eat little meals all day long. But I was starving. All the time. And I have never been so thirsty, ever."

Daisy snorted. "Me, too." They all laughed. "Did you decide to keep working for Wade after he's sworn in?"

Alex rubbed at her thigh almost absently. Daisy wondered if she could feel the scar from the shooting through her skirt. "I told him I was going to stay home for a couple months, but to keep me in mind for the inauguration. After that, I think I need to wait and see how I feel. He and I talked about after the baby. I think that would be a fun job, don't you?"

Valerie raised an eyebrow. "You mean, being an official photographer for the President of the United States? I think it would be a hardship, but, you know, someone has to do it."

Alex laughed. "I really enjoyed working with him and his wife. But right now, I need to focus on Jon and me, and on our family. It was hard to leave just a couple weeks after we got married. We're just now getting into a rhythm with life."

Daisy ran her gaze over Valerie's face. She knew Valerie struggled physically with the way her body changed with pregnancy. After her fall from the second-floor balcony, she had required a hip replacement. She shifted in her chair and rubbed her hip. Daisy wondered what labor would look like for her. "Is the doctor going to let you go natural?"

Valerie nodded. "She says no problem. She said there might be some residual pain afterward that would require an adjustment to the prosthetic. But otherwise, we're good." She shifted again. "My hip aches almost all the time, though. I was told to expect that, but I didn't realize how distracting it would be. I wouldn't complain if this baby decided to come a little early."

Daisy wondered when they would all have their babies with just two weeks between all three of their due dates. "Did the boys come early?" She asked Rosaline.

Rosaline set her empty teacup on the table next to her. "Pretty early. I was thirty-three weeks when they were born. They just finally got to the point where they were too big for me."

"You should see the pictures," Valerie said. "Her stomach was gigantic."

With a nod, Rosaline said, "It was. Very uncomfortable. So, I went to a doctor's appointment, and he sent me straight to the hospital, and they checked me in. None of the boys were a full four pounds, but Jon came close."

Daisy tried to imagine having three infants but couldn't picture it in her mind. "You must've been exhausted."

Rosaline shrugged. "We had been trying for a long time. I had lost a couple of babies. Every single exhausted moment was precious to me. They were in the NICU for three weeks. My mom came and stayed a month after the boys came home from the hospital. So, by the time I had my groove, I'd had enough help to not feel completely exhausted."

Alex grinned a sheepish smile. "Who was the best baby?"

With a chuckle, Rosaline said, "Oh, let's see. Jon was the one who always needed me to touch him. He was fine as long as he was being touched, which wasn't as much as he wanted since there were three of them. Brad did everything harder and hated failure. Ken was the one who was completely fine just to be left alone. It was a beautiful experience."

Daisy gestured at Valerie. "Then you added another."

"Yeah, same age, too." She put a hand to her chest and sighed. "She was just three. I was so ready to take her on because her mom was my best friend. It made it easier, losing her, to have Valerie, to look into her eyes and see her mom in them."

Valerie stood and walked over to Rosaline's chair. Daisy felt a warm flood of emotions when Valerie leaned down and hugged her. Then Valerie stretched her arms above her head and shifted her weight from one foot to another. "I don't ever remember not being in that pack."

"You were a pack," Rosaline laughed. "Oh, what days." She gestured with her hand at Daisy, then Alex. "You girls, knowing I'm about to have three more babies to play with, I can't explain how that fills me."

"You've certainly waited long enough," Valerie said.

The door opened, and Ken strolled into the room. "Dishes are done," he announced. "Brad's putting the last platter away, and Jon took out the garbage."

"And your father?" Rosaline inquired.

"Oh, he and Buddy supervised like I can't explain." He glanced toward Daisy. "Ready to go?"

"I am." She pushed herself to her feet. Rosaline got up, too, and hugged her. "I enjoyed cooking with you today."

"Likewise," Daisy said, breathing in the floral scent of Rosaline's lotion. "With all of you."

After hugging Valerie and Alex, she preceded Ken from the room. Out in the foyer, she gathered her jacket and purse. Brad and Jon came and said goodbye. "We still have to do Thanksgiving again," Ken said.

"Hardship, having extended family in the same town," Brad said on a laugh.

Daisy nudged Ken. "Not until tomorrow."

"True. Give my stomach time to reset."

They left the house on a wave of cheer, confirming plans and bidding farewell. On the drive home, she leaned her head on her husband's shoulder. Another mountaintop day. "I think that was the best Thanksgiving ever."

At a red traffic light, he kissed the top of her head. "I agree. I think they're only going to get better from now on."

Ken sat back and watched as Daisy looked in the mirror, turning sideways. The ball gown's red lace top fell off her shoulders, tying just under her breasts in a red satin bow, then falling in loose waves to the ground. She'd thrown the red heels across the room in frustration and now wore a pair of nude ballet slippers.

She turned from the other direction and looked that way, finally slapping her hands over her eyes, a sound of frustration escaping from her mouth.

"What's wrong?" he finally asked, coming up behind her and slipping his arms around her. The faint floral scent of her perfume wafted up and filled his senses. He didn't think he'd ever get tired of the way she smelled.

"I'm a fat cow."

He spun her around and pulled her hands off of her face. She had tears in her eyes, but none fell down. "You," he said, kissing each temple, "are not," he added, in between kissing her eyelids and nose, "a cow."

For a moment, she paused, then she gasped and looked at him. Mirth filled her eyes instead of sadness. "But I'm fat."

"No." He put his hands on either side of her stomach and leaned down, pressing kisses along the top of it. The baby moved and shifted under his hands. "But you are very round." He straightened and looked down at her upturned face, overwhelmed with love and desire for her. "And incredibly sexy and beautiful."

She pouted out her bottom lip. "I don't feel beautiful. Or sexy."

"That's okay."

He straightened and stepped back. She ran a hand down the front of his tuxedo shirt. "Speaking of sexy," she said with a coy grin.

He picked up her hand and pressed a kiss to her wrist. "We need to get downstairs. You're not going to distract me."

"Fine," she snorted.

They left the bathroom and went into the bedroom of their hotel suite. The red wrap that went with her dress lay across the bed. "Since we're staying in the hotel, I don't think I'll need that," she said, picking up the end of it and letting it fall back to the bed. "No reason to have to keep up with it."

"Smart." He went into the main room, scooped the tickets for tonight's Presidential Inauguration Ball off the table, and slipped them into his jacket pocket. "Do you want me to hold your phone?"

She looked at it, plugged in on the desk, and shook

her head. "Nah. No reason. You have yours and a pocket."

"True."

As they headed toward the door, she said, "You know, you and your brothers turn heads enough looking so much alike, being so tall and handsome. Now you all three have very pregnant wives on your arms. People are going to think we're some weird cult or something."

He thought about the stares they received in the lobby yesterday. "Daisy, people always think something." He put his hand on the doorknob but turned to look at her. "I think you look incredible. You're healthy, glowing, and that color looks amazing on you. Quit worrying about what people think."

She let out a deep breath. "You're right. I'm sorry. I've never been good with attention. And lately, I've gotten a lot of it."

He opened the door, and she slipped her arm into his. Together, they strolled down the long hallway to the elevators. When they turned the corner, they nearly ran into Brad and Valerie. The men shook hands.

Valerie wore a silver gown that fit tight across her large stomach, and had a slit up the leg to mid-thigh. She accented the gown with a chunky necklace made from clear glass beads and a pair of clear acrylic shoes with silver soles. Her dark skin shone against the silver material.

"Oh, I wish I had the courage to dress like that. You look amazing, and I look like I'm wearing a tent," Daisy said, brushing her cheek against Valerie's.

"You do not look like you're wearing a tent," Valerie said. She put Daisy at arm's length. "I love it. Beautiful. And the color."

Brad asked Ken, "Is Jon already downstairs?"

"Yeah. Alex has worked the inauguration all day. I think she came up about two hours ago, changed, and went back down. Jon's been with her in case she needs him."

They stepped into the empty elevator. "You know," Daisy said, looking up at Ken, "a year ago, if you told me I'd be married, pregnant, and going to a presidential inauguration ball tonight, I'd have laughed in your face."

"Imagine how different life would be if I hadn't come to your office looking for a way to spend my money."

She giggled and squeezed closer to him.

Chapter 24

In the dream, Daisy leaned forward, gripping Ken's hand, and bore down and pushed. It was strange that she felt no pain. The room was green with green tile floors and green tile walls. The nurses wore green scrubs and green surgical masks on their faces.

"That's it, Daisy, keep pushing," Dr. Reynolds said from behind the green mask.

A cry filled the room. Daisy sniffed and leaned back, turning her head to look at Ken and tell him it was all okay, but he wasn't next to her anymore. He stood off to the side, holding the baby, but he didn't look at the baby. He stared at her with a look of sheer terror on his face.

"What's wrong? Ken, what's wrong?" she asked. The world shifted and turned. Somehow, she stood off to the side. A bright light shone down on the operating table where red blood covered the green sheets. All the red and all the green and the bright lights reminded her of Christmas.

"I can't stop the bleeding."

"Someone needs to go talk to the husband."

Daisy turned her head and saw a male doctor in green scrubs put a hand on Ken's back. Ken cradled the baby next to his chest like a football with one arm. He covered his face with his other hand, and his entire body shook with a silent sob.

Suddenly, her mother appeared next to him. "I'll take the baby now."

He looked up at her. "It's not your baby," he said in Spanish.

"No." Her mother shook her head. "It's not your baby. Give it here. Time for you to go now." She insistently held out her arms.

Daisy opened her eyes. She lay in her own bed. She rolled to a sitting position and put her hands over the swell of her stomach. Her heart beat a rapid rhythm, and her head pounded. She tried to shake off the cobwebs of the dream. Parts of it made no sense, while parts of it felt very real.

Before she could stop them, tears fell out of her eyes. She looked over her shoulder. Ken lay on the pillow, soundly sleeping, a look of peace and contentment on his face.

She quietly left the room and walked to the baby's room. They hadn't really done any work in here yet. The crib, dresser, and changing table sat in the middle of the room. They were waiting to find out what they had before they put the nursery together.

Daisy's Decision

She sat on the soft glider chair, her arms wrapped around her belly. "God," she whispered, "what did that mean? What do I need to do?"

She was due in two weeks. She felt good and had great energy. Was the dream an omen, a warning from God, or the result of cheese ravioli for dinner?

Rubbing the small of her back, Daisy paced in front of Ken's desk. He sat back and said, "Please sit down. You're making me dizzy."

Ken went back to writing numbers into a column on the pad in front of him as if that settled the matter. He had a big annual meeting in two weeks and hadn't fully prepared for it yet. Every day brought them closer to Daisy's due date, and he really wanted to have this work finished so he could focus on her.

She stopped and turned, putting her hands flat on his desk. "This is important, Ken, and I don't understand why you're reluctant to go over this paperwork with me."

He set the columnar pad aside and picked up the manila envelope she'd brought in with her. "I'm not reluctant. I just don't understand what the big deal is."

"It isn't a big deal right now, but if something happens to me, it might become a big deal," Daisy said.

She angled her body and slowly sat in the chair across from him. He pulled out the stack of papers. The first one was titled "Last Will and Testament." He also saw a notarized statement, a living will, and sealed envelopes addressed to both her parents and his.

"Why are you making such a fuss about this?" he

asked. She'd used a purple sticky note to flag a page on the will, so he turned to it. He frowned as he read the words.

> In the event of my death before all of the adoption paperwork can be finalized, I leave my first-born child to my husband, Kenneth Dixon. He is listed as the father on the birth certificate and is going through the adoption proceedings at the earliest available time. In attachment C, you will find the signed and sealed Voluntary Surrender of Parental Rights received from the child's natural father.

"Honey, do you really think all this is necessary?" He stood and walked around the desk, sitting in the chair next to hers. When her eyes filled with tears, he wanted to soothe her and make all of her fear go away, but he didn't know how to.

"Ken, I just feel like this is important," she said, breathing hard, "Like, I don't want to wish we had."

"What do you think is gonna happen?"

She waved his words away like batting at a fly. "If something happens to me, you need to be legally covered to take custody. Too many people know you aren't the biological father. I don't want anyone to take advantage of that and take the baby from you." Her voice ended on a high-pitched hiccup.

His jaw clenched at her words. Despite both of them knowing that he considered this baby completely his, he understood what she meant. "Nothing is going to happen."

"Will you please just initial and sign, then keep the letters here?"

"Of course." He took one of her hands in both of his. "What are these letters to our parents?"

She looked at their joined hands and then met his gaze. "The one to my parents is to ensure they understand how I feel about you taking the baby and to appeal to them not to fight it. The one to your parents is to ask them to support you in raising the baby and not try to convince you to give it up."

He closed his eyes, begging God to keep him from snapping in impatience at his very pregnant, very hormonal, and nearly hysterical wife. She'd had the same dream three nights in a row and hadn't been the same since the first one.

Finally, he said, "I'll sign the legal forms. You take them and file them. I'll keep the envelopes with me. But I won't need them because nothing is going to happen."

"One more thing," she stated. "I also signed a living will, but I want you to hear me. If it comes down to the baby or me, you save that baby. Do you understand?"

He knew a lot could go wrong during childbirth. He also knew that it almost never came down to an even choice between which person survived. Either the child or the mother would have a better chance. If it came down to it, he would make the logical choice. He also didn't want to lie to his wife. But informing her that he understood her wishes was not really lying. It took him several heartbeats to say, "I understand."

Immediately, she relaxed, and a smile lit her up as the tears faded away. "It's such a relief to finish it. Maybe now that I've taken care of this, the dream will go away."

"Yes, now your mind can rest. And so can you."

She cupped his cheek with her hand. He leaned into her touch, savoring it. "I know you're tolerating this. I appreciate it, though. I'm an attorney. It's just that I understand the legalities of what can happen. Now I know what can't happen." She stood and handed him a pen. "Sign where I've marked, and I'll go file everything."

Daisy followed Ken into Brad and Valerie's house. She felt immensely pregnant today, more than ever. Maybe because today marked her due date, and nothing at all gave any indication that she'd go into labor anytime soon.

At least she'd slept for the last week. The second she had all the paperwork filed and legal, her dreams faded, and sleep returned.

She walked into the living room and found Valerie lying in a recliner with her feet up. She had passed her due date almost a full week ago. Her doctor had told her they would consider inducing her if she didn't deliver today or tomorrow.

"Hi, you." Daisy perched on the edge of the couch. "How are you?"

Valerie screwed her face up and rubbed her hip. "I will be much better by this time next week. I feel confident about that."

As they talked, Alex strolled into the room. Daisy had never seen anyone so graceful and poised while pregnant. Alexandra had barely gained any weight, and if she didn't have such a large stomach, no one could have told she was due in a week. She rubbed the sides of her belly and said, "Brad laid out some breakfast makings for us in the kitchen."

Brad, Ken, and Jon all prepared to leave. They planned to be in their conference room by seven-thirty. Ken bent and kissed her and said, "This will be the fastest annual meeting in recorded history. I promise."

"Especially since I'm running it," Brad said, scrolling through his phone.

From the kitchen, Alex's cousin Jeremy came into the room. He carried a thick leather book and sat on the corner of the couch. "I got this. You guys go on."

Daisy looked at Ken and said, "Ken, we all have phones. We don't actually need a babysitter."

Ken shook his head. "The three of us feel better knowing someone's here who isn't pregnant."

Alex threw her head back and laughed. "You better go."

They walked out of the house, and Valerie put down the footrest of the recliner. "I think I do want to eat. Will someone please help me up?"

As Alex took one hand and Daisy took the other, Jeremy stood and said, "Ladies, please. I enjoy living, so I don't want to explain to your husbands why you all went into labor while helping Valerie get to her feet while I sat there like a bump on a pickle and watched."

He walked forward and took Valerie's hands in his, taking her weight and helping her stand. She rubbed her hip and shifted her body, then thanked him.

In the kitchen, Daisy grabbed a plate and selected a slice of rye bread and a scoop of egg salad. As she slathered mayonnaise on the bread, Alex said, "I can't believe the guys actually went to this meeting. Jon has been hovering like a helicopter for a month now. I can barely get him to spend the entire morning at work."

Valerie shook her head. "Big annual meeting with all the department heads. It's always the last Thursday in February. I imagine Brad could have changed the date this year, but they have consultants that come in from out of town."

Daisy shrugged. "I don't really care that they left us. I just think it's kind of funny."

Alex chuckled. "I think the only person who doesn't actually find it funny is Jeremy."

"Just hold your water, and all will be well," he said with a wink.

Alex walked over to the refrigerator and pulled out a pitcher of orange juice. At the sound of liquid hitting the ground, she gasped and inspected the pitcher as if it were the source of the noise. Daisy realized what happened and rushed toward her. Alex looked down and saw the puddle forming at her feet. "No. I'm not first!"

Jeremy immediately took her elbow and said, "What did I just say? Okay, cousin, you're with me."

Alex shook her head. "No. It's not me first. Valerie

goes first, then Daisy, then me. I'm not even due for another week."

"Sorry, sweetheart. We don't make these decisions."

"Do you have a change of clothes with you, maybe in your car?" Valerie asked. Alex pressed her lips together and shook her head. Valerie patted her on the shoulder and said, "It's okay. I can go get you something."

As Valerie started from the room, she froze and bent at the waist. Daisy rushed to her side. "Are you okay?"

Valerie looked up at her. She had sweat beading on her brow. She panted, "Contraction. Hard one."

Daisy met Jeremy's eyes. "Do you want to call them, or shall I?"

"You send text messages. I'll drive."

"We'll take my SUV," Valerie said. "Brad made sure it was accessible before he left."

Outside, Alex put her hand on the hood of the vehicle and leaned against it, moaning out loud. Daisy rubbed between her shoulders. "Can you get into the car?"

"I have to, don't I?"

Jeremy helped her into the back seat, then rushed around the hood to help Valerie. Daisy climbed into the passenger's seat and pulled her phone out of her pocket. She sent a text to Ken.

Alex's water broke. Valerie is having contractions. Jeremy is driving us to the hospital. I love you.

As soon as she got confirmation that it sent, she texted Rosaline.

> **Alex's water broke. Valerie is having contractions. Headed to the hospital.**

About a mile into the drive, Daisy had to close her eyes. Jeremy's darting in and out of traffic, ignoring speed limits, running lights, it all started to overwhelm her. Her heart skittered, and a sour taste in her mouth perpetuated some nausea. She trusted his driving because she didn't believe he'd intentionally put them in danger, but the tension mounted with every broken traffic law.

It took them twenty minutes to get to the hospital. In that time, Valerie had two more contractions, and Alex panted and moaned the entire time. Jeremy pulled to a stop outside of labor and delivery and left the vehicle at the curb. He ran in. Daisy could see him talking to someone at the desk.

"Oh no," Alex moaned, throwing her seatbelt off. "He needs to do something." Before Daisy could respond, Alex had the door open and stumbled out of the vehicle. Daisy opened her door and carefully scooted out of the seat. "Are you okay?"

"I think it's almost time," she panted, gripping her stomach. "I need to push."

Just then, Jeremy rushed out, followed by two nurses with wheelchairs. As Daisy helped Valerie out of the car, a pain doubled her over. She cried out and clutched her stomach.

Wide-eyed, Jeremy said, "You've got to be kidding. Not you, too!"

A pickup truck pulled up behind them, and three identical looking men jumped out of it. Daisy leaned against the door of the SUV, just as their husbands all ran up to them.

"Oh, thank You Lord above," Jeremy prayed.

Ken arrived at her side just as the pain subsided. A frown brought his eyebrows together. "You, too?"

"Apparently. That was the first one, though, so it might be a false alarm. Alex is in active labor, Valerie's is escalating."

"Do you need a chair?"

She shook her head. "I can walk." She pulled her phone out of her coat pocket. "I should probably let my mom know."

"Good call."

Daisy and Ken slowly followed his brothers and their wives into the building. The nurses took them to different rooms. Daisy stopped at the desk. "Hi. Daisy Dixon. I'm due today and just had a pretty strong contraction."

The woman behind the desk raised both eyebrows. "You all three went in labor on the same day? That has to be some kind of a record." She gestured at Ken. "Your brothers look just like you."

He smiled a tight-lipped smile. "You don't say."

"Just hang tight. We'll get you checked in. You preregistered?"

"We did," she said, then shot a text message to her mom and Camila.

An hour later, Daisy stood next to the window, wearing a hospital gown and a robe, looking out at the parking lot. She'd had two more contractions on the heels of the first one and could feel the changes happening in her body as labor progressed. It hurt, but so far, she'd hadn't had trouble working through the pain.

Little fingers of excitement kept dancing up and down her spine. It looked like today she would hold her new baby. She looked over her shoulder at Ken. He leaned against the wall with his hands in his pockets and a distant look on his face. *He will make such an excellent father*, she thought, as love threatened to beat her heart right out of her body.

Rosaline tapped on the door and walked in, her face glowing with a smile. "Alex and Jon have a baby girl."

"Oh, a girl, they wanted a girl."

Ken asked, "How's Alex?"

"Fine. It was fast. She barely had time to think about it before she was born."

"I can't wait to see her." As Daisy spoke, she put her hands on the bed and bent forward. It felt like something inside of her spread her stomach open and squeezed it together at the same time. "Ahhh," she said, leaning forward on her forearms and rocking her hips back and forth.

Ken rubbed her lower back, quietly supporting until the pain subsided. She chuckled as she straightened. "Well, that was stronger."

Rosaline gestured behind her. "I'm going to go check on Valerie, then head back to Alex. Ken, Dad has his phone in his pocket."

"Yes, ma'am." He stood close to Daisy. "Do you want to walk down the hall?"

"Maybe." Did she want to get so far away from the bed? "Yes. I think so. Can we go see Valerie?"

He smiled and brushed a lock of hair off of her forehead. "Sure."

She felt fine now. Rubbing the side of her belly, she and Ken slowly walked out of the room. Her parents sat in her private waiting room. Her father read his Bible and her mom watched a show on her tablet. They looked up as soon as her door opened. "I'm going down to see Valerie."

Her mom smiled. "We're right here."

Daisy nodded and walked next to Ken. Her mom had talked to her a few weeks ago about the birth. She remembered her mother's words as she waddled down the hall. "I just want it to be your time with Ken. I think the rest of us, and his family, can wait until the baby's born," she'd said. "It's a very special, intimate time between husband and wife. He isn't going to want to chat with people, and you're going to be busy."

She'd hugged her mom and thanked her for her insight and wisdom.

Now, they walked down the hall three doors, through the empty waiting room connected to her room, and into Valerie's room. She lay in her bed, monitors strapped to her belly and an IV in her arm. Brad stood next to the window, his hands in his pockets. "Hey, guys," she said with a smile. "I'm happy to see you. You just missed Auntie Rose and Uncle Phillip. They went to check on Alex. Did you hear she had a girl?"

"Mom told us." Ken gestured toward her.

"Everything okay? What's with all the monitors?"

"Oh, this? I had an epidural. I don't want to feel a thing." She patted her stomach. "I know I'm having a contraction because the machine tells me so."

Daisy walked over and looked at the printout that showed lines on graph paper. While she watched, the lines got larger and more frantic. "Is this a contraction?"

Valerie glanced over. "Yep. Looks like a good one, too."

Her sister-in-law hadn't even broken a sweat. Her hair was beautifully brushed, and her lip gloss gleamed. For the briefest moment, Daisy considered whether she should have asked for an epidural, but then she remembered the birth plan she and Ken had worked out. She'd made him promise to remind her she didn't want one.

"Valerie's had enough pain to last a lifetime," Brad said.

Daisy knew he alluded to an abusive relationship that ended with Valerie thrown from a second-story window. "Right. I don't blame her." She felt the tightening of her muscles and looked at Ken. "We better go... oh!"

She gripped the footboard of the bed and breathed in through her nose and out through her mouth. Ken immediately came to her side and put his hands on her hips. Somehow, his touch actually made things better, helped her cope.

As soon as the contraction eased, she straightened and said, "I think we better go back to our room."

"Can't wait to get together with all of us tonight," Valerie said with a grin. "Three babies on the same day. I wonder what those odds are?"

Brad walked over to the side of her bed and picked up her hand, pressing a kiss to the back of it. "God is not limited by odds," he said gruffly.

Chapter 25

Ken didn't know how much more he could take. Every time Daisy cried out, he wanted to make it stop. He wanted to make the person hurting her regret doing so, but he had no one to blame. He had to passively accept her pain, and he did not like that.

She stayed out of bed as long as she could. She felt better standing and bending and then walking off the contraction after it ended. At one point, hours after they arrived, her water broke. That's when the nurse put her in bed.

Doctor Reynolds came in and confirmed that she was close. "I've just left Valerie. I'm sure you'll hear her news soon," she said, stripping off her gloves and going to the door. "I'm going to grab a coffee, but I will be right back. It won't be long now."

As the doctor left and the door shut behind her, his mother came in. "Valerie had a girl. She's doing great.

Both of them are."

"Another girl!" Daisy exclaimed.

Ken stood and slipped his hands in his pockets. "Valerie's okay? No hip issues?"

Rosaline shook her head. "No. I think they'll know more once she gets up and moves around."

Ken checked his watch and paced to the window, staring out onto the parking lot. Daisy had started labor six hours ago. "Can't believe you all went into labor on the same day."

Daisy turned her head and smiled at him. "Kind of speaks more to God's hand, doesn't it?" She spoke in a rough, exhausted voice.

The emotion that filled him at that thought took his breath away. He nodded but did not speak. Instead, he looked from his wife to his mother and then back out the window and thought about thirty-three years ago and his mom giving birth to three baby boys in one day. He wondered if they would have a girl, making it three girls today.

A nurse came in, very chipper and loud. Ken hadn't seen her yet. She had a singsong voice that made the muscles in his neck tense. "How are we doing?"

Daisy smiled at her, always gracious. "They said I'm close."

The nurse nodded. "I know your birth plan says no epidural, but you're getting close to the point where it will be too late to have one if you don't get one now. Is that still your wish?"

Ken turned and avoided saying anything. He had promised to help talk her out of getting one if she claimed to want one, but he didn't realize how much pain she would actually experience. He also had not anticipated how he would react to seeing her in pain. Why not? Why had he not taken that into account ahead of time? He waited to see what she would say.

"Maybe," Daisy looked at Ken with pleading eyes. "No. No, I don't think so. I don't want one."

The nurse patted her pocket and said, "Then I guess you don't need this IV. I'm going to leave it in here just case we need to get to a vein." She set it on a silver tray that already had some medical implements laid out.

The way Daisy cried and moaned during the contractions, he knew they had grown in intensity and, with that, pain. Ken didn't understand her desire to experience the pain, but he had to respect it. The helplessness and impotence he experienced with each contraction frustrated him like nothing he had ever known.

After the nurse left, Ken walked over to Daisy's bed and pressed his lips to her forehead. She looked up at him. Her face had tired lines, but her brown eyes glowed with anticipation. "I admit it. I was tempted."

He smiled and didn't reply because any words that came to him would have encouraged her to get one. She had grown accustomed to his silences. His mom rubbed Daisy's shins through the blanket. "Do you need anything?"

She shook her head. "I need to dilate one more centimeter. I don't think you can help with that."

She chuckled. "I'm going to go find your parents."

Daisy smiled. "Thank you. They're down in the

cafeteria."

As the door shut behind his mom, Daisy held her hand up, and he grasped it, sandwiching it with both of his. "Ken!" She started to squeeze his hand almost painfully. "Oh!"

He brushed her hair away from her forehead and pressed the back of her hand against his cheek. She breathed through the contraction but yelled out at the end. "Okay! We're moving now!"

She barely finished the words when another contraction had her. For several minutes, Ken breathed with her, touched her, stroked her, and prayed for her. When she said, "I need to push!" he pressed the call button.

"Can I help you?"

Before Ken could speak, Daisy yelled out, "I need to push!"

Seconds later, a nurse came in the room pulling a glove on. She checked Daisy and then hit a button on the wall. Another nurse arrived.

Ken stayed near Daisy's head while they arranged her on the bed. By the time they had her set up, Doctor Reynolds had arrived.

"I hear we're ready! Let's welcome baby Dixon number three into this world." Doctor Reynolds murmured something to a nurse, and then she pushed a stool to the foot of the bed. "I'm just going to check." She glanced under the sheet the nurses had arranged, then peered over it and smiled at Daisy. "I see a head!"

She nodded to the nurses in the room. They moved to flank the bed, each one taking Daisy under her knee to hold her legs. The doctor said, "On your next good contraction, I want you to push."

Ken could tell when the contractions started because Daisy squeezed his hand and bared down. He slipped his arm behind her shoulders. "That's it," he said softly. "You got this."

Daisy bared her gritted teeth and groaned through them, sweat pouring off of her forehead and down her face. After several seconds, she lay back, panting.

"Almost there," Doctor Reynolds said. "Push again on the next contraction."

Ken's stomach tied itself in knots. He anticipated seeing the baby but didn't like watching Daisy go through this. He needed it to end so the pain would go away. He tried not to watch the activity with the doctor and the nurses. Instead, he focused on his wife, on the expressions as they crossed her face, on the sounds she made.

She relaxed again and rolled her head toward him. "I'm tired."

"I know. But you got this," he said.

"Okay, Daisy, one more time. Ready?"

Even though she whimpered, he watched her summon the strength, then lean forward and push. He hugged her to him and willed her to get a reserve of strength from him. Suddenly, the activity at her feet picked up. The doctor moved, and Daisy collapsed back as a sharp cry filled the room.

Doctor Reynolds stood and leaned over the sheet in one move and lay the baby on Daisy's chest. "It's a girl!" The baby had jet black hair and pink skin. A sob clogged his throat, and he kissed Daisy's temple.

Daisy cried and pressed her lips to the top of her head. "A girl," she said, tears filling her eyes. She looked at him and smiled. "Little Rosita."

They'd found a name that combined both of their mothers' names. He touched his finger to the little wet curl on Rosita's head. The joy Ken Dixon felt in that moment of completeness rocked him. Logic abandoned him, and pure joy poured into him and filled him until he felt it overflow. He felt like he soared above the clouds with Daisy and Rosita by his side. He felt like he flew high above the earth.

He had a home. He had a wife. He had a child. He was a husband and a father. Together, they were a family. Their family would grow closer and deeper in love from this day forward. Nothing could ever take away the complete bliss he felt in this moment.

Daisy laid her fingers lightly over his wrist as he stroked his daughter's hair. Ken uttered the only word that seemed to fit. "Perfection," he whispered.

"Ken?" Daisy whispered. Something about her quiet voice set off blaring alarms. Her grip on his wrist tightened to a bruising grip. "Ken? Something's wrong," she said with a gasp.

His eyes darted to hers. He studied her face. Something was wrong. Something was very, very wrong. She gasped, "I... can't... breathe."

As he watched, Daisy's eyes rolled up, and her head lolled back. "Daisy?" He straightened and shook her shoulder. "Daisy!"

She didn't respond. Her hands fell from the baby

Daisy's Decision

and his wrist and dangled lifelessly on either side of the bed. "Doctor Reynolds! Something's wrong!"

"Daisy?" The doctor stood up from between Daisy's legs. "Hey, Daisy? You with me?"

One nurse scooped the baby up, and the other cut the umbilical cord with precise, efficient movements. The nurse with the baby carried her to the waiting infant bed, and the other nurse straightened Daisy's legs and checked her pulse as she reclined the head of the bed so that Daisy lay flat. "Doctor!"

The doctor rushed to Daisy's side, lifted her eyelids, and then used her stethoscope to listen to her chest. Doctor Reynolds made a fist and jammed her knuckles into Daisy's breastbone, roughly rubbing up and down. Daisy didn't move at all. In two steps, Doctor Reynolds hit a button on the wall and yelled, "We need a crash cart in here!"

From lofty, mountainous heights, Ken slammed back to earth. Every part of his body went numb with the impact. Stunned, he watched everything happen as if somehow removed from his body. Completely out of his element, he didn't know what to think, how to react. One minute, everything was exactly perfect. The next, they guided him out of the way to put an IV in Daisy's arm and place electrodes on her chest. He stood next to Rosita's bed, helpless, numb, and mute.

While he observed, people ran into the room pushing a large cart with machines and equipment on it. A newly arrived male doctor shouted orders. Doctor Reynolds started CPR on Daisy as they tried to discover what happened. He heard "Clear!" and the top of

Daisy's body jerked.

For the first time in decades, Ken's mouth filled with the sharp copper taste of fear. He scooped Rosita into his arms and stepped further into the corner, out of the way of the action. The male doctor climbed onto the bed with Daisy, straddling her, and continued to administer CPR as two nurses lifted the bed's railings and kicked off the brakes. With efficiency, they smoothly pushed the bed out of the room. Dr. Reynolds gestured in his direction as she ran after the bed. The remaining nurse walked toward him.

"She suffered a cardiac arrest, and she's bleeding internally. We don't know what happened yet or why. They're going to take her into surgery. They need to assess her condition. As soon as they figure out what happened, someone will come out to speak with you."

She rushed out, leaving Ken standing there holding Rosita, who had been born just seven short minutes earlier. Silence descended on the room, replacing the chaos that had filled it just seconds before. Another nurse, one he hadn't seen before, came in. "Mr. Dixon?" she asked softly.

He stared at her but didn't respond. What was he supposed to say? Or do?

"Mr. Dixon, I need to take the baby to get her cleaned up and warm. You can come along with me if you want."

He blinked, and then her words clicked. "I have to talk to our parents."

He lay the baby in the tiny little bed with the plexiglass sides, and she wheeled it out of the room. In the doorway, she turned and looked at him. "You can come find me any time. We'll be in the nursery. There's a waiting room near the operating room. Someone can take you there when you're ready."

Ken exited via a different door and out into the waiting room just off their room. Daisy's mom looked up immediately. "What did we have?"

Opening and closing his mouth, he just stared at her, unable to form words. His dad came to his side. "What's wrong?"

"Daisy...," his throat froze, and his dad gripped both of his shoulders with his hands. Ken's voice sounded scratchy, hoarse. "Something was wrong."

"What?" Rita asked, standing and putting a hand on his arm. "What happened? Is the baby okay?"

"The baby?" He blinked and looked at her, a look of incomprehension. "She's okay." His breath hitched, and he blinked again.

Rita's eyes widened in panic. "Daisy?" She shook his arm and looked at the door of the waiting room as if it held all the answers. "What happened?"

His thoughts tumbled and avalanched and cycloned. What had happened? "I don't know. They took her. I have to..." He stepped away and put his hands on the top of his head. "We have to go."

His mom appeared at his side. "Come on, son. I know where to go." She wrapped her arms around Ken's arm and guided him to the doorway that led out into the hospital corridor. Over her shoulder, she said, "Phillip, call the boys."

Chapter 26

The time crawled by with glacial slowness. Ken felt like he was trapped under water, trying to move weighted limbs, struggling to breathe. His chest felt heavy, and every exhalation hurt. He'd sat for a long time in the waiting room, sandwiched between his mom and Daisy's mother. No one said anything, as if everyone knew if they spoke even one single word, the air around them would shatter like glass hit with a stone.

Eventually, he couldn't take the waiting anymore. He surged to his feet and rushed from the room. But once out in the hall, he had nowhere to go. Panting, desperate, he stopped in the corridor next to the double doors that led to the operating rooms and leaned against the wall. He wanted to build something—or demolish something. Either would do. He pressed the heels of his hands against his eyes and bent over double, his elbows against his knees.

Suddenly out of energy, he slid down the wall until he sat against it, his legs drawn up. He leaned his head back and closed his eyes as tears wet his temples. When Brad and Jon sat on either side of him, he didn't move.

Finally, he said, "I can't lose her. I was created to be her man."

Jon put a hand on his knee, but he didn't reply. Brad slipped his arm over his shoulders and squeezed, releasing the dam of emotion Ken held so precariously in check. His entire body shook with silent sobs as he replayed the last few minutes with Daisy in his mind. The image of them doing CPR on her took all the breath out of his body. When the flood of emotion dissipated, leaving him weak, he realized both brothers had their arms around him, shielding him with their love. As he returned to himself, he could hear Brad praying over him, praying for Daisy, and praying for Rosita.

"Mr. Dixon?"

Ken looked up and saw the nurse who took Rosita from him. "Yes?" he asked in a hoarse voice.

"You can come sit with the baby any time." He looked toward the double doors leading to the surgery area as Brad and Jon moved away from him and stood. She spoke as if she knew what he worried about. "We'll know where you are. We'll come find you immediately. I have a room for her. You can come sit and be alone." She looked at the men on either side of him. "Or you don't have to be."

Brad held out a hand, and Ken gripped it, letting

his brother haul him to his feet. He followed the nurse past the waiting room where their families assembled, expectant for news, down the corridor. She used her badge to grant them entrance through two different doorways. Finally, she opened a door and stepped back, gesturing into a room equipped with a rocking chair and a small sofa. "If you'll wait in here, I'll bring her to you."

He walked into the room, his hands in his pockets. Did he sit or stand? Did specific rules apply?

"Do you want us to stay?"

As he turned to answer, the nurse returned, wheeling Rosita in her bed into the room. Brad and Jon stepped aside as she parked the bed against the wall. "I need to check your wrist band," she explained.

He looked down at his wrist. When they admitted Daisy, they both were given wrist bands with the same number on them. The nurse looked at his, then compared it to the one on Rosita's ankle. "If you need anything, press that intercom button on the wall," she said softly, then left.

Ken walked over to the bed. The name tag on the bed read, "Baby Girl Dixon." Someone had wrapped her tightly in a white cotton blanket with blue and pink pinstripes. She had a little pink cap on her head. He carefully scooped her up. His hands looked enormous as they lifted her tiny form. Maybe, she just looked unbelievably tiny. When he brought her to his shoulder and inhaled her new baby smell, she made a little cooing sound that broke his heart all over again.

He turned and faced his brothers, the two men

who knew him best in this world. "This is the room they save for fathers. I bet your babies are in with their mamas right now. They have this room because we don't have a room anywhere else. It's like our manger."

Brad nodded. "It's good they have a room like this."

Ken pressed his lips against Rosita's little head then walked over to the rocking chair. "You two don't have to stay. Your wives are probably going out of their minds. Go be with them."

Jon came fully into the room. "Alex is busy with Anne. I'm here. Unless you don't want me here. Then I'm gone."

Brad sat on the sofa. "Same." He gestured toward Ken. "How could she possibly look so much like you?"

Ken cradled her in his arms and looked down at Rosita's face. He ran a fingertip over her black hair and down her cheek. "Because God intended me to be her daddy."

They sat in silence for two hours. At one point, Jon fielded a text and left, bringing back Rita and Rosaline.

"Ken," his mom said, laying a gentle hand on his shoulder. Still rocking the baby, he looked up at her, then back down at the infant. His mom said, "Go with Brad and get something to eat."

He stared down at Rosita's face. She had her eyes open, big black pools of amazement with ridiculously long curling eyelashes. His heart broke in new ways. "No," he said, his voice still sounded hoarse. "I'm okay to miss a meal. I'll stay."

Brad walked over to the window, and Rita took his

Daisy's Decision

place, perching on the edge of the couch. "May I hold her?" she asked with tears in her eyes.

He focused on her face and could read the worry etched into every line. Then his brain unjumbled her words, and he stopped rocking. "Of course, Rita. Sure. Of course."

She smiled down at Rosita and murmured to her. Ken took the opportunity to stand and stretch. His mom said, "Go, Ken. Rita and I are right here, and I have my phone."

He gave a pained look at Brad, expecting his brothers to come to his defense. Instead, Brad stepped forward and said, "That's a good idea. Let's all go get some food. It's been a long day."

Ken slipped his hands into his pockets and followed his brothers into the hall. "I'll stay here," he said.

Jon turned. "Ken, they're going to be a while, yet. I checked just a few minutes ago."

With a shrug, he said, "I know. I just don't want to leave Rosita."

"She's in the safest hands she could possibly be in," Brad said. "Let us take care of you for a little while."

As they walked down the long hallway, he paused at the doorway to the waiting room. He could see a sea of bodies on their knees and his father, their pastor Danny Brown, and Marcus standing next to each other, heads bowed.

"What's this?" he asked.

"Prayer vigil. They've been at it for about two hours now," Jon said. "Mom said she and Rita both stood up at the same time with the desire to come pray over the baby. That's when mom texted me."

In the cafeteria, they found a quiet table. In the lull after the dinner rush, very few people occupied the space. Some came for coffee and left. Others clearly grabbed a meal while they could. Ken stared down at his sandwich and wondered how he could possibly ever feel hungry again.

He rubbed his finger and thumb over his eyes, then pinched his nose. "Daisy knew something bad was going to happen," he said.

Brad set his fork down and leaned closer. "How so?"

"She had a dream. Well, same dream a few times. Couple of weeks ago. Sent her into a frenzy. I thought it was in some pregnancy-induced hysteria. I completely patronized her." Tears filled his eyes. "Stupid."

"Frenzy, how?"

"She filed all kinds of legal paperwork so Rosita would be fully mine if something happened to her, regardless of whether my adoption of the baby was finalized." He sighed. "She knew."

A doctor rushed into the cafeteria and looked around, then headed straight for them. Ken sat up straighter. He looked between the three men and finally asked, "Ken Dixon?"

"Yes?"

"Do you happen to know your blood type?"

"O-negative. Why?"

He sat in the fourth chair at their table. "Your wife

has received fifteen units of blood so far, and she's going to need at least that much more. She's also O-negative, which means she can only take O-neg blood type. Mr. Dixon, we're running out."

Ken stood, a thousand questions swirling in his mind. He didn't know what to ask first. But he knew how to act. "Take mine."

His brothers stood, and Jon said, "We're all O-neg. So's Dad."

The doctor nodded. "Come with me."

He took them back up to the surgical floor. While there, his father must have received his text because several of the parishioners from the waiting room lined the hallway outside of the blood donor room. Everyone who had O-negative blood stepped up to donate.

While the phlebotomist hooked him up for the blood donation, the doctor explained, "Your wife had what we call an amniotic fluid embolism. With AFE, often the first symptom is respiratory distress, followed by cardiac arrest. Then, bleeding from the birth starts, and the blood won't clot. What happened is some amniotic fluid got into Mrs. Dixon's circulatory system. That's not terribly uncommon, but in her case, she had a severe reaction to it."

Ken processed the information, categorized it, analyzed it. Then, he asked, "What next?"

"When I left, they were performing a hysterectomy."

A hysterectomy? He felt like the bottom of his world opened up and sent him spiraling down. How would he ever explain to Daisy?

The doctor was still talking. "It's our only option if we have a prayer of getting the bleeding under control. They'll keep up with the transfusions and check her arteries, make repairs as needed."

The doctor crossed his arms over his chest and leaned against the counter. "I can't tell you any more because, at this point, all we can do is react. It's like plugging a dam. She's survived this long. That's a good sign."

He gestured with his thumb. "Those people praying in the waiting room, that's definitely a good sign. And the hall is lined up with people giving blood. That might just save her life. She's going to need every drop. The more, the better."

After about fifteen minutes, the doctor gathered the blood donated from Ken and his brothers. They each took two bottles of juice and let three more people take their chairs. Ken looked at Jon. "I can't walk down that hall. I can't talk anymore. I just can't."

His brother nodded, knowing what Ken needed. He asked the phlebotomist for the alternate route out, and she swiped them through a doorway and into a different hall. Soon, they returned to the nursery.

He looked at Rita, who hovered over Rosaline holding the baby, and explained what the doctor told him. "Why don't you go see if you can give blood, Rita?"

Rosaline handed the baby to Ken and stood. "Yes. I'll go with you."

On her way out of the room, Rita paused at Ken's

shoulder and said, "You will come find me if you know something?"

"I'll call. Mama has her phone."

"Okay." Rosaline put her arm over Rita's shoulder on their way out of the room.

Brad gestured at the door. "Jon and I are going to go update the ladies; give you some alone time."

He nodded and lowered himself into the rocking chair, snuggling Rosita against his chest.

Through the fog of sleep, Ken heard the cries. He opened his eyes and got his bearings.

His home. His room. His empty bed.

His hungry baby.

He pushed himself out of bed and walked over to the bassinet. Red-faced Rosita kicked her legs, fisted her hands, and screamed to the world that she would like to eat now. Right now.

"Hey, hey," he said, scooping her up. "Until Mama comes home, this is not an instant thing."

He'd put his dorm fridge in the spare bathroom and stored the milk in there. Talking to her the whole time, he grabbed a bag of milk and put it in the warmer. Somehow, he found it easy to talk to Rosita. He never found himself at a loss for words.

"Five minutes, pretty girl," he cooed. "Enough time to get you out of this wet diaper."

In the emotional and mental whirlwind of hours and days following Rosita's birth, his mom and Rita had helped him figure out what he needed from moment to moment. He knew how much Daisy wanted to breastfeed, so he worked with the nurses, and his mom made inquiries to find donated milk.

Daisy had a cousin who brought a three-day supply over the day of Rosita's birth. Valerie and Alex had gotten their milk supply going enough to donate milk after the first few days. He knew as soon as they shifted Daisy's medications, Rosita could have her milk.

In Rosita's room, he lay her on the changing table and tried to tease her out of the angry, hungry cry. "You know, they say patience is a virtue. You're not being very virtuous right now. But you're beautiful and perfect. Yes, you are. And you're wet. Let's fix that."

She paused and looked up at him with big, brown eyes, then screwed her face up and screamed even louder. Ken chuckled. "I know. It's so hard being seven days old. You're unemployed, no bank account, no schooling to speak of, no references. How are you going to get your life together?"

He slipped the mint green gown back down over her legs then scooped her back up. She cried and nuzzled against his neck, seeking solace from the hunger. He walked back to the bathroom and checked the bottle, finding the milk at the perfect temperature. He collected it and gently rocked her as he headed back to his room.

"Don't worry, sweet girl. You've got time. You'll figure things out. You'll be up and around and on your feet before you know it."

In his room, he settled against the corner of the couch and held her the way the occupational therapist had taught him, the same way Daisy would hold her when she could finally nurse her. As he slipped the nipple into her mouth and she greedily latched onto it, he smiled down at her perfect face.

"You don't know your mom very well yet, but you're going to love her. And, oh my stars, she is going to love you, sweet girl. They'll move your Mama into a new room as soon as she wakes up. We get to stay with her there sometimes. Isn't that cool?"

But what if Daisy never woke up?

Tears filled his eyes before he could stop them. He had set aside emotions for a solid week because the need to make decisions, answer questions, and field phone calls took priority. Suddenly, the questions he had pushed to the back and the emotions he had ignored all overwhelmed him until he had a hard time catching his breath.

What if she dies in that hospital and we never get to speak to her again in this life?

He had always tried to live his life as an example of Christ. He stayed faithful, serving God with his heart and his hands. He avoided temptation and treated his neighbors with kindness.

Unlike eldest triplet Jon, who had always struggled with carnal temptations, Ken had stayed pure and sober, never wanting to treat his body as anything other than the medium through which he could physically work for God's kingdom. Unlike middle triplet Brad, who had always known he loved Valerie, Ken would have been content to stay single until the day he died. He could have gladly just poured his days and his energy into mission-oriented work.

Then Daisy came into his life, and for the first time ever, he thought maybe God wanted him to have someone beside him. He thought God had made her just for him. He felt certain God had made him for Daisy. Ken and Daisy made a whole unit, helpers to each other, faithful lovers, and much stronger together than when they lived their solitary lives.

Thinking of Daisy's dreams and how God had tried to prepare them for Rosita's birth made him realize that, maybe, God never intended for Daisy to come home.

What would that mean? Did she come in to his life only so that Rosita would have a father, not so that Ken would have a wife? Could Ken accept that?

Daisy can never have your children now.

Ken closed his eyes and shook his head like an angry wet dog as if he could shake these thoughts right out of his mind. He needed to pray. He needed to pray right now.

"God, please, I beg you," he said as Rosita's head lolled back, a dribble of milk sliding down her cheek. Love flowed through him with such force that it caused a painful squeeze of his heart. A more perfect baby did not exist on this planet. He shifted her to his shoulder and gently patted her back as he looked up at the ceiling. "Please don't let that be Your plan. Please heal Daisy's body and bring her home to me."

The loud burp brought a smile to his face even though his tears. He carried the baby back to the bassinet and gently laid her in it. In the dim light, he stared down at Rosita, noticing how much of Daisy he saw in the infant's features. "I know it's selfish to even ask, God. But I have to ask. I have to."

Right there next to the baby's bed, he fell on his knees and covered his face with his hands. "Please," he whispered, "bring Daisy home to Rosita. God, please, please bring her home to me. Don't leave me a fractured whole now that I finally found the rest of me."

After several minutes of pouring his appeals out to God, he pushed himself to his feet and glanced at the clock. Four-twenty-two. Mentally, he knew he should do his Bible study and get some exercise, but emotionally, he needed some restorative sleep. Without any guilt, he collapsed onto the bed and closed his eyes.

Chapter 27

Daisy floated in a sea of fog. The light varied. Sometimes the fog looked gray and misty, sometimes pitch black. Occasionally, she could hear sounds, someone speaking her name, cold wet applied to her mouth, her arms moving. Most of the time, though, she didn't hear anything, didn't know anything, didn't feel anything. Then, the black gave way to gray, which turned into a mist, which became a bright light, and she ripped her eyes open.

Hospital room. No window. What did that mean? Intensive care?

Turning her head took so much effort. It felt like she had weights strapped to her forehead. The room was small—definitely ICU. Through a glass wall, she could see a circular nurse's desk. A black-haired woman typed at a computer, and a blond man counted little cups on a tray.

Why a hospital? Had she been involved in an accident? Why couldn't she remember?

She made the effort to turn her head straight again and stared at the whiteboard on her wall.

Doctor: Mitchell
AM Nurse: Riley

Doctor Mitchell? She didn't recognize that name.

A whooshing sound made her turn her head again, and she identified the sound as the door sliding open. Ken walked in staring at his phone. When he raised his head and saw her staring at him, he froze. Then he slipped his phone into his pocket and rushed to the bed.

"Hi there," he said softly, smiling. He had haggard lines on his face, big dark circles under his eyes, and at least a week's beard growth. "I can't tell you how happy I am to see your eyes."

"What...?" Her voice came out in a hoarse whisper.

He stepped close and brushed her hair off her forehead. "It's okay now."

"I don't..." Exhausted, she closed her eyes and licked her lips. "Thirsty."

"I'm not sure you can drink yet. I'll find out."

She didn't turn her head again but listened to the whooshing sound of the door. A few seconds later, the door opened again, and the blond man she'd seen came into her vision. "Mrs. Dixon, I'm Nurse Riley. Just Riley works. It's great to see you awake." He checked her IV bag and her arm. "Do you have any pain?"

Pain? Trying to focus, it occurred to her that

everything felt like ticklish pins and needles. "No."

"Good. That means the good drugs are doing their job."

"Thirsty." She closed her eyes, unable to take his movement. It made her head swim.

"Doctor Mitchell said you can have ice chips. Let's start there. It's been a few days since you had anything on your stomach. I'll be right back."

Days? What had happened? She made the effort to turn her head again and saw Ken standing by the bed. She tried to lift her hand, but she could only manage to raise it slightly off the bed before it collapsed back. He must have perceived what she needed because he immediately scooped up her hand.

She licked her dry lips with her impossibly dry tongue and croaked, "What happened? I don't remember."

Ken pressed his lips against her wrist and said, "It's okay. We'll talk once you have some ice in you. You're super foggy from the pain medication, too."

Riley returned with a Styrofoam cup and a plastic spoon. He scooped a piece of ice onto the spoon and held it up to her lips. "Open."

The cold ice hitting her tongue felt like the most wonderful sensation she'd ever experienced. She closed her eyes and let the water melt and drip down her tongue to the back of her mouth.

The next time she opened her eyes, Ken was gone. The whiteboard had a new name for her nurse. This time it read:

Doctor: Mitchell
PM Nurse: Carla

The door whooshed. This time, her head turned with more ease. Ken walked in, his gaze searching her face as if trying to read her current state of being. "Hey," he said, walking up to the bed and kissing her forehead. "How are you?"

She lifted her hand, and this time could keep it up. He took it. "Less medicine head," she croaked. "Can I have more ice chips?"

"Don't know," he said with a smile. "Last one knocked you out for about four hours."

He picked up the cup on the table near her bed and lifted ice with the spoon. It felt so refreshing when it went into her mouth. She sucked and swallowed and tried to let the ice touch every part of her mouth. "Thank you," she said when she swallowed the last drop. "I am so thirsty. My throat hurts."

"That's from the breathing tube, I'm sure. Doctor Mitchell thought you'd be sore."

She searched his face, looking for anything that would hint as to what happened. "I don't remember."

He sat down and leaned his elbows on her bed. "Do you remember Rosita?"

As if unbidden, her free hand moved over the blankets covering her stomach. Flat. "Rosita?"

The smile lit his eyes up. "Yeah. A week old now. I've been working on getting her days and nights in the right place."

A week? She closed her eyes and tried to think of the last thing she remembered. "I remember the

Presidential ball," she said. "When was that?"

His eyes grew serious again. "Six weeks ago."

"Six weeks?" She gasped, and the sudden inhalation of breath sent pain through her ribs, which made her gasp, and the cycle began.

"Daisy?" He surged to his feet and rushed out of the room. Seconds later, a nurse with jet black hair wearing light green scrubs came running in.

She put a hand on Daisy's shoulder and read the monitors above her. "Okay, Mrs. Dixon. Is it hurting you to breathe?" Daisy nodded because she couldn't speak. "I'm going to give you some more pain medicine. It's about time for your dose anyway."

A syringe and an alcohol pad swam out of her scrubs pocket. She shifted the blankets on Daisy's bed, and seconds later, Daisy felt a sharp prick in the back of her hip. The warm rush of numbing medicine rushed up to her chest almost immediately, then over her shoulder and down her body. Everything started tingling but also turning numb at the same time. The pain subsided.

Carla deposited the syringe into the red box hanging on the wall and looked over her shoulder. "I'm going to call Doctor Mitchell and see if he wants to talk to you."

Ken picked her hand back up. She asked, "What happened?"

"You had that natural birth you wanted. Right after Rosita was born, you had a heart attack. Then you started bleeding. They called it amniotic fluid embolism. You took thirty-two pints of blood, and they repaired an artery with some procedure." He pressed the back of her hand against his cheek. His whiskers tickled her skin. "You had to have a hysterectomy. It was the only way they could stop the bleeding and save your life."

Her mind swirled. "Hysterectomy?" She grew more and more dizzy and finally closed her eyes, feeling like the bed spun and wobbled like a top.

When Daisy opened her eyes again, sunlight from a window lit up her room. New room. They must have moved her out of the ICU. She should take that as a good sign, right? This room was bigger, with calmer colors and a television perched in the corner. Her arms felt lighter. Her head felt less encumbered. A gentle cooing sound came from her right. She rolled her head on the pillow and her gaze encountered Ken reclined back in a leather chair, a baby sleeping on his chest.

The image invoked such emotion that it twisted her heart almost painfully. Tears filled her eyes. Her baby was a week old? She thought back, desperately trying to break through the dark patch in her memory. The men having to go to that big meeting, Alex's water breaking, Valerie's contractions. Jeremy's harrowing drive through Atlanta's streets. Little by little, lights started breaking up the blackness.

"Hey," she croaked softly.

Immediately, Ken opened his eyes. His face softened in a smile when he looked at her. "Hey, sleepyhead."

She lifted a finger. "New digs."

"Yeah. They let you out of ICU so I could bring the

baby to you."

Tears fell down her cheeks. He held Rosita close. He had tightly bundled her up in a blanket covered in pink foxes and put a little pink and green cap on her head. Long lashes rested on her cheeks as she slept. "Oh Ken," she whispered, brushing her finger over her cheek, causing her lips to pucker and make sucking motions. "She's incredible."

He found the buttons for the bed and raised her upper body so he could rest Rosita on her chest. "Is that painful?" he asked. "You have broken ribs from the CPR."

"No." She closed her eyes and rested her nose against Rosita's head, inhaling the smell of her with a slow, deep breath. Then she looked at Ken. "How are you doing with her?"

He lifted one shoulder in a small shrug. "She was here for three days. I was able to sit with you and leave her in the nursery. I slept in the little room they had for fathers. When they released her, it was a relief to take her home. My mom and your mom have been taking turns watching her in the waiting room here or sitting with you. I didn't want to be away from her all day long, so I've just kept her with me. We go home at night."

"How is she eating?"

She and Ken had very long talks about their expectations and desires. Both of them agreed wholeheartedly on Daisy breastfeeding. It never became an issue. If she'd been here a week, was it even possible anymore? Did a milk supply even exist? Ken's answer took her breath away. It occurred to her just how much he had taken care of the details.

"In the ICU, the nurses taught me how to pump your breast milk every few hours, to keep up some production. We couldn't use it because of the medications they've had you on. Alex and Valerie and your cousin Maria have been able to donate for now."

"Alex and Valerie? Are they okay?"

"Perfectly fine. They're home with their babies. Brad and Jon are sailing over the moon with me. We're all in love with our girls."

She longed for this to be a distant memory. "When can I go home?"

He shook his head. "Doctor Mitchell has no good idea about that. It might be weeks."

"Weeks?"

"You're not out of the woods all the way. They have to monitor your liver and kidneys. And they have to make sure your blood clots properly with the medication they're giving you." He rubbed his face. "We don't know what kind of neurological damage was done."

She shook her head. "I wish I could remember." Something he said earlier came back to her. "A hysterectomy? That means no more babies."

He reached out and cupped her cheek. "Good thing we did it so well on the first try, eh?"

"But, Ken, you won't have..."

He leaned forward and covered her lips with his. Then he said, "I'm sure you're not about to say what you're about to say." He kissed Rosita's head then sat back down. "Any pain?"

"I feel like if I move wrong, I know there's going to be pain. It's an odd sensation. But, mainly, I'm just super thirsty."

He nodded and pressed a button. A staticky sound came from the speaker before a woman's voice asked, "May I help you?"

"Can my wife have some water?"

After a pause, she said, "Yes. Slow sips."

He poured from a little pink pitcher into a little brown cup and unwrapped a plastic straw, bending the top. She took a tiny sip, afraid to make herself cough. As soon as she swallowed, she asked for a little more. After three sips, Ken pulled the straw away. "I think that's enough. Don't want to make you sick."

The weight of Rosita on her chest felt absolutely right. She rested her hand on her back and closed her eyes, relishing in the feel of the perfect little cheek against her collar bone. Her mind started to wander, and without effort, she remembered her dream and how she prepared all of that paperwork and letters for everyone. Silently thanking God for the dream that allowed her to prepare, she asked, "Everything okay legally with you and the baby?"

He sighed and rubbed his face with his hands. "Your mom thought she was doing the right thing by offering to take her with her. But I was able to talk her out of it without using your letter. My mom helped convince her I was capable of taking care of her." He put a hand on her shoulder. "I'm sorry I didn't take your dreams seriously."

Shaking her head, she kissed Rosita on her cap. "You finally listened, even if you didn't think you needed to. At least everything was ready."

"Well, we won't need it." He squeezed her shoulder with his strong hand.

Chapter 28

Daisy took slow, careful steps. She had quit using the walker two days ago. It had taken her months to regain good control and stability.

"Look at them," Valerie said, pointing at the girls on the blanket on the floor. Brad and Valerie's daughter, Alison, had dark brown skin and curly black hair. She sat on the blanket and chewed on a purple plastic oversized key. Valerie had named her after her mom, who died when she was three.

Jon and Alex's daughter, Anne, had blonde hair and creamy white skin. She lay on her back, banging a large red ring on the ground and kicking her feet. Rosita had tan skin with wavy brown hair. She had crawled over to the little piano and stared at it, occasionally touching an electronic key and squealing when it made a tone in reply.

Alex handed Valerie a glass of water and settled

into the corner of the couch. "I promised Jon I wouldn't take a thousand pictures today," she said, but she picked up her camera anyway. "Maybe he won't object to nine hundred."

Daisy settled into the leather chair. Rosita looked up and started furiously crawling in her direction. She reached Daisy and clawed her way up her leg until she stood and slapped her hands on Daisy's thighs. "Ba ba ba," she said.

Daisy giggled and picked her up. "Ba ba, huh? Why not, mama? Ma ma?"

Despite the time in the hospital, the doctor cleared her to start feeding Rosita right around her two-week birthday. They let her room with her, and Ken slept most nights there as well, his long body overflowing the hospital reclining chair in uncomfortable looking ways. Daisy settled Rosita against her breast and lifted the leg rest of the recliner so she could get into a comfortable position.

She'd come home on Rosita's six-week birthday. Her kidneys had started working again, and she had the upper body strength to use the walker for short distances. It surprised her how winded she got just walking to the bathroom. Ken had carried her upstairs and hired a full-time nurse to help for the first couple of months. Once she could traverse the stairs, the nurse shifted to part-time and eventually didn't need to come in anymore.

Alex snapped her photo then put her camera down. "It's cool to see you walking without the walker. You'll be back to normal in no time."

Daisy smiled. "You know, I felt so lousy at the beginning and didn't believe I could ever recover. Now the doctor is thinking I might be close to back to normal as possible by their first birthday. Incredible!"

About ten minutes later, the chime announcing the front door opening sounded. A few seconds later, Ken and Brad came in. Daisy smiled up at Ken, and he bent to kiss her. "How was the game?" she asked.

"You didn't watch it?"

She gestured at the babies all around. "We've been a little occupied."

"It was a phenomenal game." He held up a bag and pulled out a little baby-sized Atlanta Braves cap. "Next time, I'm taking Rosita here. I think she's ready to root, root, root for the home team. What do you say, baby girl?"

Rosita ignored him, more focused on her afternoon meal.

Brad sat on the arm of the couch near Valerie. When Alison saw him, she squealed and rolled over onto her stomach, maneuvered herself to her hands and knees, and crawled with enthusiasm in his direction. Brad laughed and scooped her up, lifting her high then bringing her back down to blow tickles on her neck. She squealed and clutched at his hair. Valerie grinned at them and absently rubbed her hip.

"They going to have to replace your hip?" Daisy asked as Rosita disengaged. She adjusted her shirt, then lifted her up against her shoulder and started patting her back.

"Maybe. Doctor said I'm on the cusp. I just haven't

decided if I'm willing to go through the pain."

Jon walked into the room. "I put the meat in the fridge." He scooped Anne up off the floor and tossed her into the air. She giggled with delight. When he brought her close to him, she grabbed his face with both hands and tried to bite his nose.

Ken clapped his hands once then rubbed them together. "Perfect. I'll get the grill going."

Alex stood. "I got some salads from that restaurant you guys like near your office."

Daisy pointed at Alex. "When you're ready to learn, I can show you how to do potato salad and coleslaw."

Alex batted her eyelashes. "I don't need to learn. I have a restaurant and caterer list. That's all I need to get by." The women laughed. "Besides, Jon can cook. His mom taught him. If he wants a home-cooked meal, he can get busy or head over to the castle."

Jon nodded. "She's not exaggerating. But I have no complaints." He set Anne back on the floor. "I'm going to help Ken with the grill. Did you bring the kiddie pool?"

Valerie spoke up. "It's set up in the back yard."

Daisy shifted to stand, and Ken scooped Rosita off of her lap. Once she gained her feet, she said, "I brought down her little swimsuit and a swim diaper. I think I set them on the kitchen table."

"I'll get her changed."

He slipped an arm over her shoulder and pulled her close. Rosita leaned toward her and grabbed at her cheek. She smiled and reached a finger out. Rosita gripped it and babbled.

Ken sat back in the canvas chair and hooked his shoe on his knee. Brad had a fire going in the fire pit. Jon stabbed at the coals with a metal poker.

The girls had gone inside, taking the babies away from the mosquitoes. Ken enjoyed watching the flames dance against the night. He thought over the last year and the roller coaster ride they'd experienced.

"You two doing anything for your anniversary?" Brad asked. "It's tomorrow, right?"

Ken nodded. "Mom's taking Rosita overnight. We're going to Savannah. That's about as far away as Daisy was willing to go."

"Fair enough. We haven't left Anne yet," Jon said. "But Alex has a friend in New York who's getting married in November. We're talking about possibly leaving her then and doing an overnight."

"I was surprised when she agreed. But, we've never had just the two of us." He grinned. "Rosita has always been there in some way."

"She'll still be there in some way," Brad said. "I find it fascinating as I think about the time before Alison was in our lives, and I have a really hard time remembering."

"Same," Jon said. "We don't have the history of time you and Valerie do, but I know what you mean. It's like I was always Anne's dad."

Ken smiled. "You always were. God is not restricted to our linear understanding of time, brothers. This has already been written. He prepared us long ago."

It overwhelmed him, left him in awe, the way God moved through his life and Daisy's life to bring them to the moment that they became husband and wife, one in His eyes. He loved the lasso ceremony performed at their wedding because it gave a visual representation of that idea.

Living life with Daisy had filled a hole he didn't know existed. Everything had led to the moment he walked into her office that fateful day in late June. When he saw her, he knew, and nothing over time changed it. Coming so close to losing her had made him see it as if a spotlight shone down on it.

Most women didn't survive an amniotic fluid embolism and many who did suffered strokes and permanent neurological damage. Daisy had full control of her mind, even though she still couldn't remember Rosita's birth. Her body would eventually heal all the way. The physical therapist had remarked on her amazement at Daisy's progress. Ken knew the prayers going up on Daisy's behalf during the traumatic days following her experience had much to do with how well she did now.

The door behind them opened. "Little Miss needs to get home and ready for bed," Valerie said. She walked out onto the patio. "Do you want me to take her?"

Brad stood. "No. I'll go with you." He slipped his arm over her shoulders and pulled her close. "It's good to see Daisy moving so well. Last time we were over here, she was still really weak."

"The improvements are starting to snowball." He

got to his feet. Jon stood with him. Ken put the lid on the fire.

As he turned, Jon slapped him on the back. "Have fun in Savannah. Try to talk about something other than the baby."

Ken chuckled. "Don't think that will be a problem."

They walked inside. Daisy sat on the floor with Rosita sitting between her legs. They had a cloth book in front of them, and Daisy said the letter B while she traced it with her finger. Then she said it in Spanish.

Alex asked, "You ready?"

Jon nodded. "I didn't see your car. Did you walk over?"

"Yeah. The stroller's on the front porch." She scooped Anne up and held her out to Jon. "I need to pack up my camera, and I'll be ready."

Ken helped his brothers gather bags, toys, and leftover food. After seeing them out the front door, he went back through the house and upstairs to Rosita's room. Daisy had her on the changing table, stripping her out of her outfit. She glanced over her shoulder. "Can you get a bath ready?"

He kissed her on the temple and went into Rosita's bathroom. Daisy had decorated it in ducks and frogs. He sat on the edge of the tub and ran the water until the temperature felt right, then filled it just enough to cover Rosita's lap. By the time he turned the water off, Daisy had her ready.

She handed the baby over to him, then sat against the counter while he bathed their daughter. As he dribbled water over her black hair, he talked quietly to her. "And tomorrow you get to go spend the night in the castle like a real princess. Won't that be amazing? You've never done that before."

Daisy chuckled. "Will your mom even know what to do with just one baby?"

He glanced at her over his shoulder. "It won't be long before she convinces all of us to leave all three with her. Then she'll be in her good grandma groove."

When he finished the bath, he lifted her out of the water, and Daisy wrapped her in a warm, yellow towel. Once she dried her off and put her in white pajamas with little pink roses all over them, they went into their bedroom.

Near the fireplace, they'd set two wing-backed chairs and a small love seat. Ken sat on the love seat, and Daisy snuggled into his side to nurse Rosita. As he did every night at bedtime, he pulled out his Bible and read the day's passage out loud. As he read, he ran his fingers through Daisy's hair and listened to the sounds of his daughter nursing herself to sleep. Contentment filled his heart, encouraged his soul, relaxed his mind.

"One year tomorrow," he murmured as he finished the Bible passage.

"It's certainly been a year." She grinned up at him. "Here's to a very boring second year of marriage."

He chuckled and squeezed her close as Rosita's eyes closed and her head lolled back, fast asleep.

Rare moments in life, we stand at the very top of the mountain. Looking all around in every direction from that lofty height, glorious beauty fills our eyes. The clouds look like a white ocean at our feet. Our hearts race. A light-headed feeling overtakes our senses from the thin air, the chill, the silence. We barely notice our shadows as pure golden sunlight, unfiltered by the clouds below, bathes our bodies like a halo. Even so, our skin turns to gooseflesh. Though exceptionally uncommon, these mountaintop moments do happen and—if we allow them to—overshadow the bulk of the time we exist down in the terrestrial valleys.

This was definitely a mountaintop moment.

The End

Acknowledgments

My sincere thanks to Dr. Doug Gates. He very patiently helped me brainstorm Daisy's pregnancy. I told him how I imagined a scene, and within minutes, he had given me everything I ever needed to know. It helps that his wife Brenda is also a Christian author (https://gatesgalwrites.blog/), and he knew how to help. I really appreciate his time and energy.

A special thank you to Natalie Harris, Executive Director of the Coalition for the Homeless in Louisville, Kentucky. I met Natalie through a fundraiser for the Coalition for the Homeless. Even amid the chaos around the fundraiser, she willingly agreed to an interview with me so that I could build Daisy's world in a way that would ring true. Natalie told me stories, gave me insight, and answered all of my questions with much grace. I appreciate her help, and I am thrilled to have been part of an event that raised so much money for the Coalition.

I would love to know your thoughts as my reader and acknowledge you, as well. I really would.

Writing is often a solitary profession, but it doesn't have to be. I personally read every single book review, positive or otherwise. I'm not exaggerating.

It would mean the world to me if you shared your thoughts with me. Hearing from my readers helps me prayerfully craft the next story. An honest review also helps other readers make informed decisions when they seek an exciting, clean, romantic Christian book for themselves.

Please use the link, or even your smartphone and the QR code on this page, to share your thoughts. Leave a review and tell me what you liked or didn't like about the story. I would so love to hear from you.

Share your thoughts about this book.
www.halleebridgeman.com/ThoughtsDaisy

A Change of A Dress

Please enjoy this special excerpt from book 4 in the Red Blood and Blue Grass Series, *A Change of A Dress*.

Anabelle "Belle" Merchant never looked good in black. Her flaming red hair and her light complexion made her look almost ghostly pale whenever she wore it. She didn't even own the proverbial "little black dress." In fact, the only black dress she owned she reserved for funerals. Today, her black-gloved hands clutched a snow-white lily and a triangular folded flag as she tried, and failed, to ignore the words the pastor spoke.

"Few people know this, and I am sure that the honor guard present today from Fort Jackson surprised some of you. Many years ago, Catherine's late husband, Dylan, served in the Army in Europe, and newlywed Catherine Merchant joined the Women's Army Corps. She was just sixteen years old at the time. I believe I got that right. Today, we honor her for her life and her service."

The pastor had a nice voice, a strong voice. Belle had always thought so. It was the kind of voice one expected to hear on the airwaves, perhaps announcing local sporting events in measured baritone expressions and phrases that always seemed on the very edge of masculine laughter. His voice had soothed her so many times in the past. Today it grated on her ears, each word sounding more like the rending metal of a train wreck than a soothing syllable.

"In the book of John, Jesus said, 'I am the resurrection and the life. He who believes in me will live, even though he dies; and whoever lives and believes in me will never die.' Like all believers, Catherine Merchant believed these words spoken by our Savior so many years ago."

Belle stared at the rather plain bronze coffin. She had liked the casket better when the flag had covered it. Now she could see the distorted reflection of her ivory skin and black dress in the sheen of the burnished metal. She had to stare at her funhouse reflection and keep her chin from quivering.

But it was just a box. It didn't really matter. What lay inside mattered. Belle had not quite accepted the fact that the lifeless body of her grandmother lay inside. Perhaps this gathering, this ceremony, this often-repeated ritual was designed to bring her to a place of acceptance.

She had spent the last three years of her life beside Grandma Cathy, nursing her, feeding her, cleaning up after her, driving her to appointments, picking up her medications, reading to her, and even singing with her. Each and every day had centered around Grandma Cathy. Belle could barely imagine a different way of living her life. When she left here today, she would not so much return home to her residence as she would start her new life as a full-time docent in the empty museum and relic room where she now lived. Belle had nothing of her own and no one to call her own. She was no longer really a part of anyone.

"Brothers and sisters, Catherine Merchant lived ninety-two years in this fallen world. She lived a life that I could hold up as a standard to which we all should strive. She acted with a kindness that is so rare in our culture. She spoke with an implicit gentleness born of love. Even so, she never shied away from fearlessly speaking her mind."

The last time Belle stood beside a grave, she had laid her father to rest. That day, Grandma Cathy had held her hand, and Belle had taken strength from that touch, knowing that she would have a home, that she would not continue on orphaned and alone, that someone in this world loved her. Now she had no one.

That day not so long ago, it had rained on and off in angry, interrupted fits, as if the very sky mourned her father's passing and would not suffer a single dry face. Today, the sun shone joyously down on the manicured emerald green grass of the cemetery grounds and turned the little pond down the slope to Belle's left into a lake of shimmering gold. Belle wondered if she might get a little sunburned.

"In the light of these promises God has given us in His Word, and in as much as it has pleased the Lord in His sovereign wisdom and purpose to take from our midst one whom we have loved, we now commit her body to the earth. Ashes to ashes and dust to dust, for from the dust of the earth we were made, and to dust we shall return."

Belle hadn't cried yet. She had wept inconsolably for days after her father died, so she knew it would happen, probably when she least expected it and felt least equipped to handle it. For now, Belle realized that most of her thoughts selfishly turned to her own personal loss. It didn't seem right that she could grieve selfishly. Her grief should be for her departed Grandma, her dear friend, her loved one. Her grief should express the loss that the world had suffered when her grandmother left it.

The military honor guard consisted of a man with a bugle and seven men with rifles. Even knowing what would happen, the sound of seven simultaneous rifle bursts made Belle gasp and jump. She nearly dropped the folded flag she clutched in her gloved hands. Then they fired again, and then again, twenty-one shots in all. Before the echo of the last volley faded, the mournful sound of the bugle playing Taps resonated all around them.

Belle barely heard it. She had closed her eyes, and the sound of her heartbeat drumming in her own ears sounded much louder. When the last note began to fade, the casket lowered into the grave, and the pastor said a brief prayer. Belle obediently closed her eyes again as he prayed.

"Heavenly Father, we thank You for the glorious hope and great consolation concerning those who sleep in Jesus as believers in Christ; that our Lord Jesus Christ has prepared a place for those who have placed their faith in Him, and that the gift of God is eternal life through Jesus Christ our Lord. We lay Catherine to rest here until the day comes when, very soon, we hear the final trumpet sound. Amen."

The wetness on her cheeks surprised her. When had she started to cry? She hoped she could maintain a calm demeanor until she made her way home. She had a lot to do, so much to do. She could barely wait to change out of this awful black dress.

The pastor's gentle touch to her elbow surprised her. He stood beside his wife, Donna, and Belle suddenly realized that others had lined up behind the couple. "Anabelle, you have our deepest sympathies."

Donna added, "If there's anything you need, you call me. I'm gonna bring you a casserole tonight, so don't even worry about supper. Okay?"

Belle had no idea what to say. She had known this couple for nearly five years—since he had come in as senior pastor—but she just could not think of words to say that would fit. She didn't think Donna would appreciate Belle telling her she had no desire to eat anything, much less a casserole. Nothing felt right, so she just said, "Thank you. Thank you both. It was a wonderful service. I'm sure Grandma would have loved it."

Donna dug around in her little purse until she excavated a clean tissue, and she swiped the tears from Belle's cheeks. She handed Belle the tissue then patted her cheeks with her fingertips as if she were a very small, young child.

Others made the obligatory march past the bereaved; Catherine's neighbors, nurses, physicians, pharmacists, fellow congregants, and friends. It seemed like a lot of people, most of whom Belle knew casually and some she knew not at all. The only people who didn't offer some words of comfort or consolation were relatives.

There were no relatives. No family. No one.

Belle was the last, and she felt very alone.

For a limited time, this book is one of twelve great stories available as part of *Save the Date: A Christian Romance Anthology of Faith-Filled Weddings*. Each story takes on a different month of the year. Get your copy today wherever books are sold.

www.halleebridgeman.com/sd

Readers Guide Questions

Suggested discussion questions for *Daisy's Decision* by Hallee Bridgeman.

When asking ourselves how important the truth is to our Creator, we can look to the reason our Savoir said He was born. In the book of John chapter 18 and verse 37, Christ explains that He was born for this reason, and for this reason He came into the world. The reason? To testify to the truth.

Our Lord often used fiction in the form of parables to illustrate very real truths. In the same way, we can minister to one another by the use of fictional characters and situations to help us reach logical, valid, cogent, and very sound conclusions about our real lives here on earth.

While the characters and situations in The Dixon

Brothers Series are fictional, I pray that these extended parables can help readers come to a better understanding of truth. Please prayerfully consider the questions that follow, consult scripture, and pray upon your conclusions. May the Lord of the universe richly bless you.

At the beginning of the book, it's apparent Daisy has recently made some sinful decisions. One of the things holding her back from accepting God's grace and forgiveness is the shame she'll feel when people find out what she did. She didn't feel this way about her sin until it was going to be found out.

1. Do you think this is a normal reaction for people, to feel the weight and burden only when it's known?

2. If so, shouldn't we always feel that way, knowing the Holy Spirit is privy to all of our thoughts and actions all the time?

Daisy tells her cousin that she doesn't want to tell Jason's wife about her affair or the baby because she doesn't want to risk Jason coming after the baby.

3. Do you think she should have given Jason more of an opportunity to accept his child?

4. Do you think she should have told Jason's wife about her affair with Jason?

Daisy asks God to forgive her; however, the burden of shame still weighs heavily on her shoulders and overwhelms her emotionally.

5. Do you think her thoughts in the emergency room were a normal, human reaction? Or do you think they perpetuated the sin she'd already committed?

Jon counseled Ken that men could never understand the desperation women can feel as they face the public judgment stemming from an unwed pregnancy.

6. Do you think this is a valid assessment?

Ken reacts with strong emotion at the news that Daisy could have wished harm to her baby for even a moment.

7. Do you think that was fair of him?

8. How do you think you would feel or act or react in Daisy's or Ken's place?

Ken claims he loves Daisy and the baby she's carrying. He believes he was made for Daisy and always meant to be Rosita's father.

9. Do you think it's possible for Ken to love Rosita with the same depth of emotion that Brad and Jon feel toward their natural daughters?

10. Is it possible to think that God always intended for Daisy to be pregnant when she and Ken met?

Daisy dreams she is going to die in childbirth. Ken patronizes her about her dreams, attributing them to the unpredictable hormones often associated with pregnancy.

11. Could this dream have been God preparing her for the complications she experienced?

12. Even though she survived, do you think all the preparations she made in advance of her labor and delivery were still necessary?

13. Do you think Ken should have taken her dream more seriously when she told him about it?

All three wives can identify their husbands at a glance, even in the company of their identical brothers.

14. Do you think this is just a flight of fancy typical of a fiction novel? Or do you think there is such a thing as a heart prepared for the spouse God intended for you?

Readers Guide Menu

Suggested luncheon menu for a group discussion about *Daisy's Decision*.

Those who followed my Hallee the Homemaker website years ago know that one thing I am passionate about in life is selecting, cooking, and savoring good, whole, real food. A special luncheon just goes hand in hand with hospitality and ministry.

In case you're planning a discussion group luncheon surrounding this book, I offer some humble suggestions to help your special luncheon talk come off as a success. Quick as you like, you can whip up an unforgettable meal from the book that is sure to please and certain to enhance the discussion and your special time of friendship and fellowship.

Roasted Bass with Anchovy Tomato Sauce

Daisy is amazed at Ken's deftness in the kitchen and is surprised that his special ingredient in his sauce is anchovies. He explains how the fish enhances the flavors of the garlic and tomatoes.

1 1/2 to 2 lbs bass filets
2 TBS extra virgin olive oil
2 TBS unsalted butter
Salt to taste (Kosher or sea salt is best)
Pepper to taste (Fresh ground is always best)
1/4 cup diced onion
1 TBS minced garlic
1 TBS tablespoon drained capers
4 anchovy fillets to taste
1 15-ounce can crushed tomatoes
1 lemon (sliced for garnish and 1 tsp juice for sauce)
Chopped fresh parsley for garnish

Clean and prepare the fish fillets, if needed.
Heat oven to 400° degrees F (200° degrees C).
Dice the onion.
Chop the parsley.
Slice half the lemon. Squeeze the other half for at least a teaspoon of juice.

Directions

Heat the oil and butter over medium-high heat in a large skillet. Add fish.

Season lightly with salt and pepper. Brown fish, then turn and brown other side.

Remove the fish from the pan and place on an oven-safe plate or baking dish. Place in oven.

Leave in oven until cooked through (about 5-10 minutes depending on thickness of filets.)

Reduce heat on stove to medium. Add the onion. Cook until onion is soft. Add garlic and anchovies.

Cook, stirring regularly, until the anchovies break up—about five minutes. Add tomatoes and 1 tsp lemon juice (to taste). Turn heat to high.

Bring pan to boiling, stirring regularly. Cook until tomato sauce thickens.

Return the fish to the pan. Turn to coat with sauce. Garnish with fresh parsley and lemon slices.

Herbed Couscous

Couscous is one of those dishes that takes very little effort in exchange for great reward. It is the perfect accompaniment to the flaky white fish and anchovy sauce because it will help sop up some of the sauce, and you won't miss a bite of it.

1 cup vegetable broth
1 tsp extra virgin olive oil
Pinch of salt (Kosher or sea salt is best)
1 cup couscous
1 clove garlic, minced
2 green onions, chopped
2 TBS fresh parsley

Mince the garlic.
Chop the onions.
Chop the parsley.

In a saucepan, heat the olive oil over medium-high heat. Add the garlic. Cook, stirring constantly, for about 2 minutes.

Stir in the vegetable broth and a pinch of salt. Bring to a boil.

Stir in the couscous, onions, and parsley. Remove from heat. Cover. Let stand for 10 minutes.

Fluff with a fork before serving.

Garden Salad with Homemade French Dressing

Homemade dressings are easy to make and come with a freshness of flavor that you cannot get from a bottle. This is one of my favorite dressings to serve. The sharp garlic pairs perfectly with the vinegar, and the smoky paprika brings out the vegetables' flavor in the salad in beautiful harmony.

The French Dressing
1 clove garlic, crushed
1 TBS honey
1 tsp salt (Kosher or sea salt is best)
1 tsp paprika
1 tsp dry mustard
1/4 tsp fresh ground black pepper
1/4 cup white vinegar
3/4 cup organic canola oil, or safflower oil, or sunflower oil (your taste preference). You can use olive oil, but the dressing won't keep as long. It does taste amazing, though.

The Salad

Make a salad using your favorite fresh vegetables like lettuce, cucumbers, onions, radishes, broccoli, cauliflower, carrots, cabbage – whatever you like in your salad.

Preparation

Crush the garlic using a garlic press.
Chop the veggies for the salad to your preference.

Directions

The French Dressing
In a jar, mix all ingredients. Put on a tight lid. Shake well. Serve with your fresh salad.

The Salad
Make a salad using your favorite fresh vegetables like lettuce, cucumbers, onions, radishes, broccoli, cauliflower, carrots, cabbage – whatever you like in your salad.

More Great Reads

by Hallee Bridgeman

Find the latest information and connect with Hallee on her website: www.halleebridgeman.com

FICTION BOOKS BY HALLEE

Red Blood and Bluegrass series:
Book 1: Black Belt, White Dress
Book 2: Blizzard in the Bluegrass
Book 3: The Seven Year Glitch
Book 4: A Change of A Dress

The Song of Suspense Series:
Book 1: A Melody for James
Book 2: An Aria for Nick
Book 3: A Carol for Kent
Book 4: A Harmony for Steve

The Jewel Series:

Book 1: Sapphire Ice
Book 2: Greater Than Rubies
Book 3: Emerald Fire
Book 4: Topaz Heat
Book 5: Christmas Diamond
Book 6: Christmas Star Sapphire
Book 7: Jade's Match
Book 8: Chasing Pearl

Virtues and Valor series:

Book 1: Temperance's Trial
Book 2: Homeland's Hope
Book 3: Charity's Code
Book 4: A Parcel for Prudence
Book 5: Grace's Ground War
Book 6: Mission of Mercy
Book 7: Flight of Faith
Book 8: Valor's Vigil

PARODY COOKBOOKS BY HALLEE

Vol 1: Fifty Shades of Gravy, a Christian Gets Saucy!
Vol 2: The Walking Bread, the Bread Will Rise
Vol 3: Iron Skillet Man, the Stark Truth about Pepper & Pots
Vol 4: Hallee Crockpotter & the Chamber of Sacred Ingredients

The Dixon Brothers

Courting Calla
Dixon Brothers book 1

Ian knows God has chosen Calla as the woman for him, but Calla is hiding something big. Can Calla trust Ian with her secret, or will she let it destroy any possible hope for a future they may have?

Valerie's Verdict
Dixon Brothers book 2

Since boyhood days, Brad has always carried a flame for Valerie. Her engagement to another man shattered

his dreams. When she comes home, battered and bruised, recovering from a nearly fatal relationship, he prays God will use him to help her heal.

Alexandra's Appeal
Dixon Brothers book 3

Jon falls very quickly in love with Alex's zest for life and her perspective of the world around her. He steps off of his path to be with her. When forces move against them and rip them apart, he wants to believe God will bring them back together, but it might take a miracle.

Daisy's Decision
Dixon Brothers book 4

Daisy has had a crush on Ken since high school, so going on just one date with him can't possibly hurt,

can it? Even if she's just been painfully dumped by the man she planned to spend the rest of her life with, and whose unborn baby she carries? Just one date?

About the Author

www.halleebridgeman.com

With nearly a million sales and more than 30 books in print, Hallee is a best-selling Christian author who writes romance and action-packed romantic suspense focusing on realistic characters who face real-world problems.

An Army brat turned Floridian, Hallee finally settled in central Kentucky with her family so she could enjoy the beautiful changing of the seasons. She enjoys the roller-coaster ride thrills that life with a National Guard husband, a daughter away at college, and two middle-school-aged sons delivers.

A prolific writer, when she's not penning novels, you will find her in the kitchen, which she considers the "heart of the home." Her passion for cooking spurred her to launch a whole food, real food "Parody" cookbook series. Besides nutritious, biblically grounded recipes, readers will find that each cookbook also confronts some controversial aspect of secular pop culture.

She is a former Director for the Kentucky Christian Writers Conference (KCWC) and currently serves on the executive board. She is a Gold member of the American Christian Fiction Writers (ACFW), a past American Christian Writers (ACW) member, and Secretary of the board for Novelists, Inc. (NINC). A long-time member of the Published Author Network (PAN) and past president of the Faith, Hope, & Love chapter of Romance Writers of America (RWA), she discontinued her RWA membership in 2019.

Hallee loves coffee, campy action movies, and regular date nights with her husband. Above all else, she loves God with all of her heart, soul, mind, and strength; has been redeemed by the blood of Christ, and relies on the presence of the Holy Spirit to guide her. She prays her work here on earth is a blessing to you and would love to hear from you.

Sign up for Hallee's monthly newsletter! You will receive a link to download Hallee's romantic suspense novella, *On The Ropes*. Every newsletter recipient is automatically entered into a monthly giveaway! The real prize is never missing updates about upcoming releases, book signings, appearances, or other events.

Find Hallee Online

Newsletter Sign Up:
halleebridgeman.com/newsletter

Author Site:
halleebridgeman.com/

Facebook:
facebook.com/authorhalleebridgeman

Twitter:
twitter.com/halleeb

Goodreads:
goodreads.com/author/show/5815249.Hallee_Bridgeman

Homemaking Blog:
halleethehomemaker.com

Newsletter

Sign up for Hallee's monthly newsletter! When you sign up, you will get a link to download Hallee's romantic suspense novella, *On The Ropes*. In addition, every newsletter recipient is automatically entered into a monthly giveaway! The real prize is never missing updates about upcoming releases, book signings, appearances, or other events.

Hallee's Newsletter: Hallee's Happenings
http://www.halleebridgeman.com/newsletter/

Made in the USA
Middletown, DE
12 March 2021